D1497980

Under the Deodars
The Phantom 'Rickshaw
Wee Willie Winkie

Rudyard Kipling

Under the Deodars
The Phantom 'Rickshaw
Wee Willie Winkie

By Rudyard Kipling

PUBLISHED BY
DOUBLEDAY, PAGE & COMPANY
FOR
REVIEW OF REVIEWS CO.
1914

Copyright, 1895,
By MACMILLAN AND CO.

Copyright, 1899,
By RUDYARD KIPLING

CONTENTS

THE EDUCATION OF OTIS YEERE

I

In the pleasant orchard-closes
 'God bless all our gains,' say we;
But 'May God bless all our losses,'
 Better suits with our degree.
The Lost Bower.

THIS is the history of a failure; but the woman who failed said that it might be an instructive tale to put into print for the benefit of the younger generation. The younger generation does not want instruction, being perfectly willing to instruct if any one will listen to it. None the less, here begins the story where every right-minded story should begin, that is to say at Simla, where all things begin and many come to an evil end.

The mistake was due to a very clever woman making a blunder and not retrieving it. Men are licensed to stumble, but a clever woman's mistake is outside the regular course of Nature and Providence; since all good people know that a woman is the only infallible thing in this world, except Government Paper of the '79 issue, bearing interest at four and a half per cent. Yet, we have to remember that six consecutive days of rehearsing the leading part of *The Fallen Angel*, at the New Gaiety Theatre where the plaster is not yet properly dry, might have brought about an unhinge-

ment of spirits which, again, might have led to eccen-
tricities.

Mrs. Hauksbee came to 'The Foundry' to tiffin with
Mrs. Mallowe, her one bosom friend, for she was in no
sense 'a woman's woman.' And it was a woman's tiffin,
the door shut to all the world; and they both talked
chiffons, which is French for Mysteries.

'I've enjoyed an interval of sanity,' Mrs. Hauksbee
announced, after tiffin was over and the two were comfortably settled in the little writing-room that opened
out of Mrs. Mallowe's bedroom.

'My dear girl, what has *he* done?' said Mrs. Mallowe
sweetly. It is noticeable that ladies of a certain age
call each other 'dear girl,' just as commissioners of
twenty-eight years' standing address their equals in the
Civil List as 'my boy.'

'There's no *he* in the case. Who am I that an imaginary man should be always credited to me? Am I an
Apache?'

'No, dear, but somebody's scalp is generally drying
at your wigwam-door. Soaking, rather.'

This was an allusion to the Hawley Boy, who was in
the habit of riding all across Simla in the Rains, to call
on Mrs. Hauksbee. That lady laughed.

'For my sins, the Aide at Tyrconnel last night told
me off to The Mussuck. Hsh! Don't laugh. One of
my most devoted admirers. When the duff came—
some one really ought to teach them to make puddings
at Tyrconnel—The Mussuck was at liberty to attend
to me.'

'Sweet soul! I know his appetite,' said Mrs. Mallowe. 'Did he, oh *did* he, begin his wooing?'

'By a special mercy of Providence, *no*. He explained

his importance as a Pillar of the Empire. I didn't laugh.'

'Lucy, I don't believe you.'

'Ask Captain Sangar; he was on the other side. Well, as I was saying, The Mussuck dilated.'

'I think I can see him doing it,' said Mrs. Mallowe pensively, scratching her fox-terrier's ears.

'I was properly impressed. Most properly. I yawned openly. "Strict supervision, and play them off one against the other," said The Mussuck, shovelling down his ice by *tureenfuls*, I assure you. "*That*, Mrs. Hauksbee, is the secret of our Government."'

Mrs. Mallowe laughed long and merrily. 'And what did you say?'

'Did you ever know me at loss for an answer yet? I said: "So I have observed in my dealings with you." The Mussuck swelled with pride. He is coming to call on me to-morrow. The Hawley Boy is coming too.'

'"Strict supervision and play them off one against the other. *That*, Mrs. Hauksbee, is the secret of *our* Government." And I daresay if we could get to The Mussuck's heart, we should find that he considers himself a man of the world.'

'As he is of the other two things. I like The Mussuck, and I won't have you call him names. He amuses me.'

'He has reformed you, too, by what appears. Explain the interval of sanity, and hit *Tim* on the nose with the paper-cutter, please. That dog is too fond of sugar. Do you take milk in yours?'

'No, thanks. Polly, I'm wearied of this life. It's hollow.'

'Turn religious, then. I always said that Rome would be your fate.'

'Only exchanging half a dozen *attachés* in red for one in black, and if I fasted, the wrinkles would come, and never, *never* go. Has it ever struck you, dear, that I'm getting old?'

'Thanks for your courtesy. I'll return it. Ye-es, we are both not exactly — how shall I put it?'

'What we have been. "I feel it in my bones," as Mrs. Crossley says. Polly, I've wasted my life.'

'As how?'

'Never mind how. I feel it. I want to be a Power before I die.'

'Be a Power then. You've wits enough for anything — and beauty?'

Mrs. Hauksbee pointed a teaspoon straight at her hostess. 'Polly, if you heap compliments on me like this, I shall cease to believe that you're a woman. Tell me how I am to be a Power.'

'Inform The Mussuck that he is the most fascinating and slimmest man in Asia, and he'll tell you anything and everything you please.'

'Bother The Mussuck! I mean an intellectual Power — not a gas-power. Polly, I'm going to start a *salon*.'

Mrs. Mallowe turned lazily on the sofa and rested her head on her hand. 'Hear the words of the Preacher, the son of Baruch,' she said.

'*Will* you talk sensibly?'

'I will, dear, for I see that you are going to make a mistake.'

'I never made a mistake in my life — at least, never one that I couldn't explain away afterwards.'

'Going to make a mistake,' went on Mrs. Mallowe

composodly. 'It is impossible to start a *salon* in Simla. A bar would be much more to the point.'

'Perhaps, but why? It seems so easy.'

'Just what makes it so difficult How many clever women are there in Simla?'

'Myself and yourself,' said Mrs. Hauksbee, without a moment's hesitation.

'Modest woman! Mrs. Feardon would thank you for that. And how many clever men?'

'Oh — er — hundreds,' said Mrs. Hauksbee vaguely.

'What a fatal blunder! Not one. They are all bespoke by the Government. Take my husband, for instance. Jack *was* a clever man, though I say so who shouldn't. Government has eaten him up. All his ideas and powers of conversation — he really used to be a good talker, even to his wife, in the old days — are taken from him by this — this kitchen-sink of a Government. That's the case with every man up here who is at work. I don't suppose a Russian convict under the knout is able to amuse the rest of his gang; and all our men-folk here are gilded convicts.'

'But there are scores ——'

'I know what you're going to say. Scores of idle men up on leave. I admit it, but they are all of two objectionable sets. The Civilian who'd be delightful if he had the military man's knowledge of the world and style, and the military man who'd be adorable if he had the Civilian's culture.'

'Detestable word! *Have* Civilians culchaw? I never studied the breed deeply.'

'Don't make fun of Jack's service. Yes. They're like the teapoys in the Lakka Bazar — good material but not polished. They can't help themselves, poor dears. A Civilian only begins to be tolerable after he has knocked about the world for fifteen years.'

'And a military man?'

'When he has had the same amount of service. The young of both species are horrible. You would have scores of them in your *salon*.'

'I would *not!*' said Mrs. Hauksbee fiercely. 'I would tell the bearer to *darwaza band* them. I'd put their own colonels and commissioners at the door to turn them away. I'd give them to the Topsham girl to play with.'

'The Topsham girl would be grateful for the gift. But to go back to the *salon*. Allowing that you had gathered all your men and women together, what would you do with them? Make them talk? They would all with one accord begin to flirt. Your *salon* would become a glorified Peliti's — a "Scandal Point" by lamplight.'

'There's a certain amount of wisdom in that view.'

'There's all the wisdom in the world in it. Surely, twelve Simla seasons ought to have taught you that you can't focus anything in India ; and a *salon*, to be any good at all, must be permanent. In two seasons your roomful would be scattered all over Asia. We are only little bits of dirt on the hillsides — here one day and blown down the *khud* the next. We have lost the art of talking — at least our men have. We have no cohesion ——'

'George Eliot in the flesh,' interpolated Mrs. Hauksbee wickedly.

'And collectively, my dear scoffer, we, men and women alike, have *no* influence. Come into the veranda and look at the Mall!'

The two looked down on the now rapidly filling road, for all Simla was abroad to steal a stroll between a shower and a fog.

'How do you propose to fix that river? Look! There's The Mussuck — head of goodness knows what. He is a power in the land, though he *does* eat like a costermonger. There's Colonel Blone, and General Grucher, and Sir Dugald Delane, and Sir Henry Haughton, and Mr. Jellalatty. All Heads of Departments, and all powerful.'

'And all my fervent admirers,' said Mrs. Hauksbee piously. 'Sir Henry Haughton raves about me. But go on.'

'One by one, these men are worth something. Collectively, they're just a mob of Anglo-Indians. Who cares for what Anglo-Indians say? Your *salon* won't weld the Departments together and make you mistress of India, dear. And these creatures won't talk administrative "shop" in a crowd — your *salon* — because they are so afraid of the men in the lower ranks overhearing it. They have forgotten what of Literature and Art they ever knew, and the women ——'

'Can't talk about anything except the last Gymkhana, or the sins of their last nurse. I was calling on Mrs. Derwills this morning.'

'You admit that? They can talk to the subalterns though, and the subalterns can talk to them. Your *salon* would suit their views admirably, if you respected the religious prejudices of the country and provided plenty of *kala juggahs*.'

'Plenty of *kala juggahs*. Oh my poor little idea! *Kala juggahs* in a *salon*! But who made you so awfully clever?'

'Perhaps I've tried myself; or perhaps I know a woman who has. I have preached and expounded the whole matter and the conclusion thereof——'

'You needn't go on. "Is Vanity." Polly, I thank you. These vermin'—— Mrs. Hauksbee waved her hand from the veranda to two men in the crowd below who had raised their hats to her—— 'these vermin shall not rejoice in a new Scandal Point or an extra Peliti's. I will abandon the notion of a *salon*. It did seem so tempting, though. But what shall I do? I must do something.'

'Why? Are not Abana and Pharphar——'

'Jack has made you nearly as bad as himself! I want to, of course. I'm tired of everything and everybody, from a moonlight picnic at Seepee to the blandishments of The Mussuck.'

'Yes—— that comes, too, sooner or later. Have you nerve enough to make your bow yet?'

Mrs. Hauksbee's mouth shut grimly. Then she laughed. 'I think I see myself doing it. Big pink placards on the Mall: "Mrs. Hauksbee! Positively her last appearance on *any* stage! This is to give notice!" No more dances; no more rides; no more luncheons; no more theatricals with supper to follow; no more sparring with one's dearest, dearest friend; no more fencing with an inconvenient man who hasn't wit enough to clothe what he's pleased to call his sentiments in passable speech; no more parading of The Mussuck while Mrs. Tarkass calls all round Simla, spreading horrible stories about me! No more of anything that is thoroughly wearying, abominable and detestable, but, all the same, makes life worth the having. Yes! I see it all! Don't interrupt, Polly,

I'm inspired. A mauve and white striped "cloud" round my excellent shoulders, a seat in the fifth row of the Gaiety, and *both* horses sold. Delightful vision! A comfortable arm-chair, situated in three different draughts, at every ballroom; and nice, large, sensible shoes for all the couples to stumble over as they go into the veranda! Then at supper. Can't you imagine the scene? The greedy mob gone away. Reluctant subaltern, pink all over like a newly-powdered baby, — they really ought to *tan* subalterns before they are exported, Polly — sent back by the hostess to do his duty. Slouches up to me across the room, tugging at a glove two sizes too large for him — I *hate* a man who wears gloves like overcoats — and trying to look as if he'd thought of it from the first. "May I ah-have the pleasure 'f takin' you 'nt' supper?" Then I get up with a hungry smile. Just like this.'

'Lucy, how *can* you be so absurd?'

'And sweep out on his arm. So! After supper I shall go away early, you know, because I shall be afraid of catching cold. No one will look for my '*rickshaw*. *Mine*, so please you! I shall stand, always with that mauve and white "cloud" over my head, while the wet soaks into my dear, old, venerable feet and Tom swears and shouts for the *mem-sahib's gharri*. Then home to bed at half-past eleven! Truly excellent life — helped out by the visits of the *Padri*, just fresh from burying somebody down below there.' She pointed through the pines, toward the Cemetery, and continued with vigorous dramatic gesture —

'Listen! I see it all — down, down even to the stays! *Such* stays! Six-eight a pair, Polly, with red flannel — or list is it? — that they put into the tops of those fearful things. I can draw you a picture of them.'

'Lucy, for Heaven's sake, don't go waving your arms about in that idiotic manner! Recollect, every one can see you from the Mall.'

'Let them see! They'll think I am rehearsing for *The Fallen Angel*. Look! There's The Mussuck. How badly he rides. There!'

She blew a kiss to the venerable Indian administrator with infinite grace.

'Now,' she continued, 'he'll be chaffed about that at the Club in the delicate manner those brutes of men affect, and the Hawley Boy will tell me all about it — softening the details for fear of shocking me. That boy is too good to live, Polly. I've serious thoughts of recommending him to throw up his Commission and go into the Church. In his present frame of mind he would obey me. Happy, happy child!'

'Never again,' said Mrs. Mallowe, with an affectation of indignation, 'shall you tiffin here! "Lucindy, your behaviour is scand'lus."'

'All your fault,' retorted Mrs. Hauksbee, 'for suggesting such a thing as my abdication. No! *Jamais-nevaire*! I will act, dance, ride, frivol, talk scandal, dine out, and appropriate the legitimate captives of any woman I choose, until I d-r-r-rop, or a better woman than I puts me to shame before all Simla, — and it's dust and ashes in my mouth while I'm doing it!'

She swept into the drawing-room. Mrs. Mallowe followed and put an arm round her waist.

'I'm *not*!' said Mrs. Hauksbee defiantly, rummaging for her handkerchief. 'I've been dining out the last ten nights, and rehearsing in the afternoon.   You'd be tired yourself.   It's only because I'm tired.'

Mrs. Mallowe did not offer Mrs. Hauksbee any pity or ask her to lie down, but gave her another cup of tea, and went on with the talk.

' I've been through that too, dear,' she said.

' I remember,' said Mrs. Hauksbee, a gleam of fun on her face.   ' In '84, wasn't it?   You went out a great deal less next season.'

Mrs. Mallowe smiled in a superior and Sphinx-like fashion.

' I became an Influence,' said she.

' Good gracious, child, you didn't join the Theosophists and kiss Buddha's big toe, did you?   I tried to get into their set once, but they cast me out for a sceptic — without a chance of improving my poor little mind, too.'

' No, I didn't Theosophilander.   Jack says —— '

' Never mind Jack.   What a husband says is known before.   What did you do? '

' I made a lasting impression.'

' So have I — for four months.   But that didn't console me in the least.   I hated the man.   *Will* you stop smiling in that inscrutable way and tell me what you mean? '

Mrs. Mallowe told.

*   *   *   *   *   *   *   *   *

' And — you — mean — to — say that it is absolutely Platonic on both sides? '

' Absolutely, or I should never have taken it up.'

' And his last promotion was due to you? '

Mrs. Mallowe nodded.

' And you warned him against the Topsham girl? '

Another nod.

'And told him of Sir Dugald Delane's private memo about him?'

A third nod.

' *Why?* '

'What a question to ask a woman! Because it amused me at first. I am proud of my property now. If I live, he shall continue to be successful. Yes, I will put him upon the straight road to Knighthood, and everything else that a man values. The rest depends upon himself.'

'Polly, you are a most extraordinary woman.'

'Not in the least. I'm concentrated, that's all. You diffuse yourself, dear; and though all Simla knows your skill in managing a team——'

'Can't you choose a prettier word?'

' *Team*, of half a dozen, from The Mussuck to the Hawley Boy, you gain nothing by it. Not even amusement.'

'And you?'

'Try my recipe. Take a man, not a boy, mind, but an almost mature, unattached man, and be his guide, philosopher, and friend. You'll find it *the* most interesting occupation that you ever embarked on. It can be done—you needn't look like that—because I've done it.'

'There's an element of risk about it that makes the notion attractive. I'll get such a man and say to him, "Now, understand that there must be no flirtation. Do exactly what I tell you, profit by my instruction and counsels, and all will yet be well." Is that the idea?'

'More or less,' said Mrs. Mallowe, with an unfathomable smile. 'But be sure he understands.'

II

Dribble-dribble — trickle-trickle —
What a lot of raw dust!
My dollie's had an accident
And out came all the sawdust!

Nursery Rhyme.

So Mrs. Hauksbee, in 'The Foundry' which over-
looks Simla Mall, sat at the feet of Mrs. Mallowe and
gathered wisdom. The end of the Conference was
the Great Idea upon which Mrs. Hauksbee so plumed
herself.

'I warn you,' said Mrs. Mallowe, beginning to repent
of her suggestion, 'that the matter is not half so easy
as it looks. Any woman — even the Topsham girl —
can catch a man, but very, *very* few know how to
manage him when caught.'

'My child,' was the answer, 'I've been a female St.
Simon Stylites looking down upon men for these —
these years past. Ask The Mussuck whether I can
manage them.'

Mrs. Hauksbee departed humming, '*I'll go to him
and say to him in manner most ironical.*' Mrs. Mallowe
laughed to herself. Then she grew suddenly sober.
'I wonder whether I've done well in advising that
amusement? Lucy's a clever woman, but a thought
too careless.'

A week later, the two met at a Monday Pop.
'Well?' said Mrs. Mallowe.

13

'I've caught him!' said Mrs. Hauksbee; her eyes were dancing with merriment.

'Who is it, mad woman? I'm sorry I ever spoke to you about it.'

'Look between the pillars. In the third row; fourth from the end. You can see his face now. Look!'

'Otis Yeere! Of *all* the improbable and impossible people! I don't believe you.'

'Hsh! Wait till Mrs. Tarkass begins murdering Milton Wellings; and I'll tell you all about it. *S-s-ss!* That woman's voice always reminds me of an Underground train coming into Earl's Court with the brakes on. Now listen. It is *really* Otis Yeere.'

'So I see, but does it follow that he is your property!'

'He *is!* By right of trove. I found him, lonely and unbefriended, the very next night after our talk, at the Dugald Delane's *burra-khana*. I liked his eyes, and I talked to him. Next day he called. Next day we went for a ride together, and to-day he's tied to my *'rickshaw*-wheels hand and foot. You'll see when the concert's over. He doesn't know I'm here yet.'

'Thank goodness you haven't chosen a boy. What are you going to do with him, assuming that you've got him?'

'Assuming, indeed! Does a woman — do *I* — ever make a mistake in that sort of thing? First' — Mrs. Hauksbee ticked off the items ostentatiously on her little gloved fingers — 'First, my dear, I shall dress him properly. At present his raiment is a disgrace, and he wears a dress-shirt like a crumpled sheet of the *Pioneer*. Secondly, after I have made him presentable, I shall form his manners — his morals are above reproach.'

'You seem to have discovered a great deal about him considering the shortness of your acquaintance.'

'Surely *you* ought to know that the first proof a man gives of his interest in a woman is by talking to her about his own sweet self. If the woman listens without yawning, he begins to like her. If she flatters the animal's vanity, he ends by adoring her.'

'In some cases.'

'Never mind the exceptions. I know which one you are thinking of. Thirdly, and lastly, after he is polished and made pretty, I shall, as you said, be his guide, philosopher, and friend, and he shall become a success — as great a success as your friend. I always wondered how that man got on. *Did* The Mussuck come to you with the Civil List and, dropping on one knee — no, two knees, *à la Gibbon* — hand it to you and say, " Adorable angel, choose your friend's appointment "?'

'Lucy, your long experiences of the Military Department have demoralised you. One doesn't do that sort of thing on the Civil Side.'

'No disrespect meant to Jack's Service, my dear. I only asked for information. Give me three months, and see what changes I shall work in my prey.'

'Go your own way since you must. But I'm sorry that I was weak enough to suggest the amusement.'

' "I am all discretion, and may be trusted to an infin-ite extent," ' quoted Mrs. Hauksbee from *The Fallen Angel;* and the conversation ceased with Mrs. Tarkass's last, long-drawn war-whoop.

Her bitterest enemies — and she had many — could hardly accuse Mrs. Hauksbee of wasting her time. Otis Yeere was one of those wandering 'dumb' characters, foredoomed through life to be nobody's property. Ten years in Her Majesty's Bengal Civil Service, spent, for the most part, in undesirable Districts, had given him little to be proud of, and nothing to bring confidence. Old enough to have lost the first fine careless rapture that showers on the immature 'Stunt imaginary Commissionerships and Stars, and sends him into the collar with coltish earnestness and abandon; too young to be yet able to look back upon the progress he had made, and thank Providence that under the conditions of the day he had come even so far, he stood upon the dead-centre of his career. And when a man stands still, he feels the slightest impulse from without. Fortune had ruled that Otis Yeere should be, for the first part of his service, one of the rank and file who are ground up in the wheels of the Administration; losing heart and soul, and mind and strength, in the process. Until steam replaces manual power in the working of the Empire, there must always be this percentage — must always be the men who are used up, expended, in the mere mechanical routine. For these promotion is far off and the mill-grind of every day very instant. The Secretariats know them only by name; they are not the picked men of the Districts with Divisions and Collectorates awaiting them. They are simply the rank and file — the food for fever — sharing with the *ryot* and the plough-bullock the honour of being the plinth on which the State rests. The older ones have lost their aspirations; the younger are putting theirs aside with a sigh. Both learn to endure patiently until the end of the day. Twelve years in the rank and file, men say, will sap the hearts of the bravest and dull the wits of the most keen.

Out of this life Otis Yeere had fled for a few months; drifting, in the hope of a little masculine society, into Simla. When his leave was over he would return to his swampy, sour-green, under-manned Bengal district; to the native Assistant, the native Doctor, the native Magistrate, the steaming, sweltering Station, the ill-kempt City, and the undisguised insolence of the Municipality that babbled away the lives of men. Life was cheap, however. The soil spawned humanity, as it bred frogs in the Rains, and the gap of the sickness of one season was filled to overflowing by the fecundity of the next. Otis was unfeignedly thankful to lay down his work for a little while and escape from the seething, whining, weakly hive, impotent to help itself, but strong in its power to cripple, thwart, and annoy the sunken-eyed man who, by official irony, was said to be 'in charge' of it.

*   *   *   *   *   *   *   *   *

'I knew there were women-dowdies in Bengal. They come up here sometimes. But I didn't know that there were men-dowds, too.'

Then, for the first time, it occurred to Otis Yeere that his clothes wore the mark of the ages. It will be seen that his friendship with Mrs. Hauksbee had made great strides.

As that lady truthfully says, a man is never so happy as when he is talking about himself. From Otis Yeere's lips Mrs. Hauksbee, before long, learned everything that she wished to know about the subject of her experiment: learned what manner of life he had led in what she vaguely called 'those awful cholera districts'; learned, too, but this knowledge came later, what manner of life he had purposed to lead and what dreams he had dreamed in the year of grace '77, before the reality had knocked the heart out of him.   Very pleasant are the shady bridle-paths round Prospect Hill for the telling of such confidences.

'Not yet,' said Mrs. Hauksbee to Mrs. Mallowe. 'Not yet.   I must wait until the man is properly dressed, at least.   Great Heavens, is it possible that he doesn't know what an honour it is to be taken up by *Me!*'

Mrs. Hauksbee did not reckon false modesty as one of her failings.

'Always with Mrs. Hauksbee!' murmured Mrs. Mallowe, with her sweetest smile, to Otis.   'Oh you men, you men!   Here are our Punjabis growling because you've monopolised the nicest woman in Simla. They'll tear you to pieces on the Mall, some day, Mr. Yeere.'

Mrs. Mallowe rattled down-hill, having satisfied herself, by a glance through the fringe of her sunshade, of the effect of her words.

The shot went home.   Of a surety Otis Yeere was somebody in this bewildering whirl of Simla — had monopolised the nicest woman in it and the Punjabis were growling.   The notion justified a mild glow of vanity.   He had never looked upon his acquaintance with Mrs. Hauksbee as a matter for general interest.

The knowledge of envy was a pleasant feeling to the man of no account.   It was intensified later in the day when a luncher at the Club said spitefully, 'Well, for a debilitated Ditcher, Yeere, you *are* going it.   Hasn't any kind friend told you that she's the most dangerous woman in Simla?'

Yeere chuckled and passed out.   When, oh when,

would his new clothes be ready? He descended into the Mall to inquire; and Mrs. Hauksbee, coming over the Church Ridge in her *'rickshaw*, looked down upon him approvingly. 'He's learning to carry himself as if he were a man, instead of a piece of furniture,—and,' she screwed up her eyes to see the better through the sunlight—'he *is* a man when he holds himself iike that. Oh blessed Conceit, what should we be without you?'

With the new clothes came a new stock of self-confidence. Otis Yeere discovered that he could enter a room without breaking into a gentle perspiration—could cross one, even to talk to Mrs. Hauksbee, as though rooms were meant to be crossed. He was for the first time in nine years proud of himself, and contented with his life, satisfied with his new clothes, and rejoicing in the friendship of Mrs. Hauksbee.

'Conceit is what the poor fellow wants,' she said in confidence to Mrs. Mallowe. 'I believe they must use Civilians to plough the fields with in Lower Bengal. You see I have to begin from the very beginning—haven't I? But you'll admit, won't you, dear, that he is immensely improved since I took him in hand. Only give me a little more time and he won't know himself.'

Indeed, Yeere was rapidly beginning to forget what he had been. One of his own rank and file put the matter brutally when he asked Yeere, in reference to nothing, 'And who has been making *you* a Member of Council, lately? You carry the side of half a dozen of 'em.'

'I—I'm awf'ly sorry. I didn't mean it, you know,' said Yeere apologetically.

'There'll be no holding you,' continued the old stager grimly. 'Climb down, Otis—climb down, and get all

that beastly affectation knocked out of you with fever!
Three thousand a month wouldn't support it.'

Yeere repeated the incident to Mrs. Hauksbee. He
had come to look upon her as his Mother Confessor.

'And you apologised!' she said. 'Oh, shame! I
hate a man who apologises. Never apologise for what
your friend called "side." *Never!* It's a man's business to be insolent and overbearing until he meets with
a stronger. Now, you bad boy, listen to me.'

Simply and straightforwardly, as the '*rickshaw* loitered
round Jakko, Mrs. Hauksbee preached to Otis Yeere
the Great Gospel of Conceit, illustrating it with living
pictures encountered during their Sunday afternoon
stroll.

'Good gracious!' she ended with the personal argu-
ment, 'you'll apologise next for being my *attaché?*'

'Never!' said Otis Yeere. 'That's another thing
altogether. I shall always be——'

'What's coming?' thought Mrs. Hauksbee.

'Proud of that,' said Otis.

'Safe for the present,' she said to herself.

'But I'm afraid I have grown conceited. Like Jeshu-
run, you know. When he waxed fat, then he kicked.
It's the having no worry on one's mind and the Hill
air, I suppose.'

'Hill air, indeed!' said Mrs. Hauksbee to herself.
'He'd have been hiding in the Club till the last day of
his leave, if I hadn't discovered him.' And aloud —

'Why shouldn't you be? You have every right to.'

'I! Why?'

'Oh, hundreds of things. I'm not going to waste
this lovely afternoon by explaining; but I know you
have. What was that heap of manuscript you showed

me about the grammar of the aboriginal — what's their names?'

'*Gullals.* A piece of nonsense. I've far too much work to do to bother over *Gullals* now. You should see my District. Come down with your husband some day and I'll show you round. Such a lovely place in the Rains! A sheet of water with the railway-embankment and the snakes sticking out, and, in the summer, green flies and green squash. The people would die of fear if you shook a dogwhip at 'em. But they know you're forbidden to do that, so they conspire to make your life a burden to you. My District's worked by some man at Darjiling, on the strength of a native pleader's false reports. Oh, it's a heavenly place!'

Otis Yeere laughed bitterly.

'There's not the least necessity that you should stay in it. Why do you?'

'Because I must. How'm I to get out of it?'

'How! In a hundred and fifty ways. If there weren't so many people on the road, I'd like to box your ears. Ask, my dear boy, *ask!* Look! There is young Hexarly with six years' service and half your talents. He asked for what he wanted, and he got it. See, down by the Convent! There's McArthurson who has come to his present position by asking — sheer, downright asking — after he had pushed himself out of the rank and file. One man is as good as another in your service — believe me. I've seen Simla for more seasons than I care to think about. Do you suppose men are chosen for appointments because of their special fitness *beforehand?* You have all passed a high test — what do you call it? — in the beginning, and, except for the few who have gone altogether to the

bad, you can all work hard. Asking does the rest.
Call it cheek, call it insolence, call it anything you
like, but *ask!* Men argue — yes, I know what men
say — that a man, by the mere audacity of his request,
must have some good in him. A weak man doesn't
say : " Give me this and that." He whines : " Why
haven't I been given this and that?" If you were in
the Army, I should say learn to spin plates or play a
tambourine with your toes. As it is — *ask!* You
belong to a Service that ought to be able to command
the Channel Fleet, or set a leg at twenty minutes'
notice, and *yet* you hesitate over asking to escape from
a squashy green district where you *admit* you are
not master. Drop the Bengal Government altogether.
Even Darjiling is a little out-of-the-way hole. I was
there once, and the rents were extortionate. Assert
yourself. Get the Government of India to take you
over. Try to get on the Frontier, where *every* man
has a grand chance if he can trust himself. *Go* somewhere ! *Do* something ! You have twice the wits and
three times the presence of the men up here, and, and '
— Mrs. Hauksbee paused for breath ; then continued
— 'and in *any* way you look at it, you *ought* to. *You*
who could go so far ! '

'I don't know,' said Yeere, rather taken aback by
the unexpected eloquence. 'I haven't such a good
opinion of myself.'

It was not strictly Platonic, but it was Policy.
Mrs. Hauksbee laid her hand lightly upon the un-
gloved paw that rested on the turned-backed '*rickshaw*
hood, and, looking the man full in the face, said tenderly, almost too tenderly, '*I* believe in you if you
mistrust yourself. Is that enough, my friend?'

'It is enough,' answered Otis very solemnly.

He was silent for a long time, redreaming the dreams that he had dreamed eight years ago, but through them all ran, as sheet-lightning through golden cloud, the light of Mrs. Hauksbee's violet eyes.

Curious and impenetrable are the mazes of Simla life — the only existence in this desolate land worth the living. Gradually it went abroad among men and women, in the pauses between dance, play, and Gymkhana, that Otis Yeere, the man with the newly-lit light of self-confidence in his eyes, had 'done something decent' in the wilds whence he came. He had brought an erring Municipality to reason, appropriated the funds on his own responsibility, and saved the lives of hundreds. He knew more about the *Gullals* than any living man. Had a vast knowledge of the aboriginal tribes; was, in spite of his juniority, the greatest authority on the aboriginal *Gullals*. No one quite knew who or what the *Gullals* were till The Mussuck, who had been calling on Mrs. Hauksbee, and prided himself upon picking people's brains, explained they were a tribe of ferocious hillmen, somewhere near Sikkim, whose friendship even the Great Indian Empire would find it worth her while to secure. Now we know that Otis Yeere had showed Mrs. Hauksbee his MS. notes of six years' standing on these same *Gullals*. He had told her, too, how, sick and shaken with the fever their negligence had bred, crippled by the loss of his pet clerk, and savagely angry at the desolation in his charge, he had once damned the collective eyes of his 'intelligent local board' for a set of *haramzadas*. Which act of 'brutal and tyrannous oppression' won him a Reprimand Royal from the Bengal Government;

but in the anecdote as amended for Northern consumption we find no record of this. Hence we are forced to conclude that Mrs. Hauksbee edited his reminiscences before sowing them in idle ears, ready, as she well knew, to exaggerate good or evil. And Otis Yeere bore himself as befitted the hero of many tales.

'You can talk to *me* when you don't fall into a brown study. Talk now, and talk your brightest and best,' said Mrs. Hauksbee.

Otis needed no spur. Look to a man who has the counsel of a woman of or above the world to back him. So long as he keeps his head, he can meet both sexes on equal ground — an advantage never intended by Providence, who fashioned Man on one day and Woman on another, in sign that neither should know more than a very little of the other's life. Such a man goes far, or, the counsel being withdrawn, collapses suddenly while his world seeks the reason.

Generalled by Mrs. Hauksbee, who, again, had all Mrs. Mallowe's wisdom at her disposal, proud of himself and, in the end, believing in himself because he was believed in, Otis Yeere stood ready for any fortune that might befall, certain that it would be good. He would fight for his own hand, and intended that this second struggle should lead to better issue than the first helpless surrender of the bewildered 'Stunt.

What might have happened, it is impossible to say. This lamentable thing befell, bred directly by a statement of Mrs. Hauksbee that she would spend the next season in Darjiling.

'Are you certain of that?' said Otis Yeere.

'Quite. We're writing about a house now.'

Otis Yeere 'stopped dead,' as Mrs. Hauksbee put it in discussing the relapse with Mrs. Mallowe.

'He has behaved,' she said angrily, 'just like Captain Kerrington's pony — only Otis is a donkey — at the last Gymkhana. Planted his forefeet and refused to go on another step. Polly, my man's going to disappoint me. What shall I do?'

As a rule, Mrs. Mallowe does not approve of staring, but on this occasion she opened her eyes to the utmost.

'You have managed cleverly so far,' she said. 'Speak to him, and ask him what he means.'

'I will — at to-night's dance.'

'No—o, not at a dance,' said Mrs. Mallowe cautiously. 'Men are never themselves quite at dances. Better wait till to-morrow morning.'

'Nonsense. If he's going to 'vert in this insane way, there isn't a day to lose. Are you going? No? Then sit up for me, there's a dear. I shan't stay longer than supper under any circumstances.'

Mrs. Mallowe waited through the evening, looking long and earnestly into the fire, and sometimes smiling to herself.

*   *   *   *   *   *   *   *   *

'Oh! oh! oh! The man's an idiot! A raving, positive idiot! I'm sorry I ever saw him!'

Mrs. Hauksbee burst into Mrs. Mallowe's house, at midnight, almost in tears.

'What in the world has happened?' said Mrs. Mallowe, but her eyes showed that she had guessed an answer.

'Happened! Everything has happened! He was there. I went to him and said, "Now, what does this nonsense mean?" Don't laugh, dear, I can't bear it.

But you know what I mean I said. Then it was a
square, and I sat it out with him and wanted an ex-
pianation, and *he* said — Oh! I haven't patience with
such idiots! You know what I said about going to
Darjiling next year? It doesn't matter to me *where* I
go. I'd have changed the Station and lost the rent to
have saved this. He said, in so many words, that he
wasn't going to try to work up any more, because —
because he would be shifted into a province away from
Darjiling, and his own District, where these creatures
are, is within a day's journey——'

'Ah—hh!' said Mrs. Mallowe, in a tone of one who
has successfully tracked an obscure word through a
large dictionary.

'Did you ever *hear* of anything so mad — so absurd?
And he had the ball at his feet. He had only to kick
it! I would have made him *anything!* Anything in
the wide world. He could have gone to the world's
end. I would have helped him. I made him, didn't
I, Polly? Didn't I *create* that man? Doesn't he owe
everything to me? And to reward me, just when
everything was nicely arranged, by this lunacy that
spoilt everything!'

'Very few men understand your devotion thoroughly.'

'Oh, Polly, *don't* laugh at me! I give men up from
this hour. I could have killed him then and there.
What *right* had this man — this *Thing* I had picked out
of his filthy paddy-fields — to make love to me?'

'He did that, did he?'

'He did. I don't remember half he said, I was so
angry. Oh, but such a funny thing happened! I
can't help laughing at it now, though I felt nearly

ready to cry with rage. He raved and I stormed —
I'm afraid we must have made an awful noise in our
kala juggah. Protect my character, dear, if it's all
over Simla by to-morrow — and then he bobbed forward
in the middle of this insanity — I *firmly* believe the
man's demented — and kissed me ! '

' Morals above reproach,' purred Mrs. Mallowe.

'So they were — so they are ! It was the most
absurd kiss. I don't believe he'd ever kissed a woman
in his life before. I threw my head back, and it was
a sort of slidy, pecking dab, just on the end of the
chin — here.' Mrs. Hauksbee tapped her masculine
little chin with her fan. ' Then, of course, I was *furiously* angry, and told him that he was no gentleman,
and I was sorry I'd ever met him, and so on. He was
crushed so easily that I couldn't be *very* angry. Then
I came away straight to you.'

' Was this before or after supper ? '

' Oh ! before — oceans before. Isn't it perfectly dis-
gusting ? '

' Let me think. I withhold judgment till to-morrow.
Morning brings counsel.'

But morning brought only a servant with a dainty
bouquet of Annandale roses for Mrs. Hauksbee to
wear at the dance at Viceregal Lodge that night.

'He doesn't seem to be very penitent,' said Mrs.
Mallowe. ' What's the *billet-doux* in the centre ? '

Mrs. Hauksbee opened the neatly-folded note, —
another accomplishment that she had taught Otis, —
read it, and groaned tragically.

' Last wreck of a feeble intellect ! Poetry ! Is it
his own, do you think ? Oh, that I ever built my
hopes on such a maudlin idiot ! '

'No. It's a quotation from Mrs. Browning, and, in view of the facts of the case, as Jack says, uncommonly well chosen.   Listen —

> Sweet thou hast trod on a heart,
>   Pass! There's a world full of men;
> And women as fair as thou art,
>   Must do such things now and then.
>
> Thou only hast stepped unaware —
>   Malice not one can impute;
> And why should a heart have been there,
>   In the way of a fair woman's foot?'

'I didn't — I didn't — I didn't!' — said Mrs. Hauksbee angrily, her eyes filling with tears; 'there was no malice at all.   Oh, it's *too* vexatious!'

'You've misunderstood the compliment,' said Mrs Mallowe.   'He clears you completely and — ahem — I should think by this, that *he* has cleared completely too.   My experience of men is that when they begin to quote poetry, they are going to flit.   Like swans singing before they die, you know.'

'Polly, you take my sorrows in a most unfeeling way.'

'Do I?   Is it so terrible?   If he's hurt your vanity, I should say that you've done a certain amount of damage to his heart.'

'Oh, you never can tell about a man!' said Mrs. Hauksbee.

AT THE PIT'S MOUTH

Men say it was a stolen tide —
  The Lord that sent it he knows all,
But in mine ear will aye abide
  The message that the bells let fall,
And awesome bells they were to me,
That in the dark rang, 'Enderby.'

Jean Ingelow.

ONCE upon a time there was a Man and his Wife and a Tertium Quid.

All three were unwise, but the Wife was the unwisest. The Man should have looked after his Wife, who should have avoided the Tertium Quid, who, again, should have married a wife of his own, after clean and open flirtations, to which nobody can possibly object, round Jakko or Observatory Hill. When you see a young man with his pony in a white lather, and his hat on the back of his head flying down-hill at fifteen miles an hour to meet a girl who will be properly surprised to meet him, you naturally approve of that young man, and wish him Staff appointments, and take an interest in his welfare, and, as the proper time comes, give them sugar-tongs or side-saddles according to your means and generosity.

The Tertium Quid flew down-hill on horseback, but it was to meet the Man's Wife; and when he flew up-hill it was for the same end. The Man was in the Plains, earning money for his Wife to spend on dresses and four-hundred-rupee bracelets, and inexpensive lux-

uries of that kind. He worked very hard, and sent
her a letter or a post-card daily. She also wrote to
him daily, and said that she was longing for him to
come up to Simla. The Tertium Quid used to lean
over her shoulder and laugh as she wrote the notes.
Then the two would ride to the Post-office together.

Now, Simla is a strange place and its customs are
peculiar; nor is any man who has not spent at least
ten seasons there qualified to pass judgment on circum-
stantial evidence, which is the most untrustworthy in
the Courts. For these reasons, and for others which
need not appear, I decline to state positively whether
there was anything irretrievably wrong in the relations between the Man's Wife and the Tertium Quid.
If there was, and hereon you must form your own
opinion, it was the Man's Wife's fault. She was kit-
tenish in her manners, wearing generally an air of soft
and fluffy innocence. But she was deadlily learned
and evil-instructed; and, now and again, when the
mask dropped, men saw this, shuddered and — almost
drew back. Men are occasionally particular, and the
least particular men are always the most exacting.

Simla is eccentric in its fashion of treating friendships. Certain attachments which have set and crys-
tallised through half a dozen seasons acquire almost
the sanctity of the marriage bond, and are revered as
such. Again, certain attachments equally old, and,
to all appearance, equally venerable, never seem to win
any recognised official status; while a chance-sprung
acquaintance, not two months born, steps into the place
which by right belongs to the senior. There is no law
reducible to print which regulates these affairs.

Some people have a gift which secures them in-

finite toleration, and others have not. The Man's
Wife had not. If she looked over the garden wall,
for instance, women taxed her with stealing their hus-
bands. She complained pathetically that she was not
allowed to choose her own friends. When she put up
her big white muff to her lips, and gazed over it and
under her eyebrows at you as she said this thing, you
felt that she had been infamously misjudged, and that
all the other women's instincts were all wrong ; which
was absurd. She was not allowed to own the Tertium
Quid in peace; and was so strangely constructed that
she would not have enjoyed peace has she been so permitted. She preferred some semblance of intrigue to
cloak even her most commonplace actions.

After two months of riding, first round Jakko, then
Elysium, then Summer Hill, then Observatory Hill,
then under Jutogh, and lastly up and down the Cart
Road as far as the Tara Devi gap in the dusk, she said
to the Tertium Quid, 'Frank, people say we are too
much together, and people are so horrid.'

The Tertium Quid pulled his moustache, and replied
that horrid people were unworthy of the consideration
of nice people.

'But they have done more than talk — they have
written — written to my hubby — I'm sure of it,' said
the Man's Wife, and she pulled a letter from her husband out of her saddle-pocket and gave it to the
Tertium Quid.

It was an honest letter, written by an honest man,
then stewing in the Plains on two hundred rupees a
month (for he allowed his wife eight hundred and fifty),
and in a silk banian and cotton trousers. It is said
that, perhaps, she had not thought of the unwisdom of

allowing her name to be so generally coupled with the Tertium Quid's ; that she was too much of a child to understand the dangers of that sort of thing; that he, her husband, was the last man in the world to interfere jealously with her little amusements and interests, but that it would be better were she to drop the Tertium Quid quietly and for her husband's sake. The letter was sweetened with many pretty little pet names, and it amused the Tertium Quid considerably. He and She laughed over it, so that you, fifty yards away, could see their shoulders shaking while the horses slouched along side by side.

Their conversation was not worth reporting. The upshot of it was that, next day, no one saw the Man's Wife and the Tertium Quid together. They had both gone down to the Cemetery, which, as a rule, is only visited officially by the inhabitants of Simla.

A Simla funeral with the clergyman riding, the mourners riding, and the coffin creaking as it swings between the bearers, is one of the most depressing things on this earth, particularly when the procession passes under the wet, dank dip beneath the Rockcliffe Hotel, where the sun is shut out, and all the hill streams are wailing and weeping together as they go down the valleys.

Occasionally, folk tend the graves, but we in India shift and are transferred so often that, at the end of the second year, the Dead have no friends — only acquaintances who are far too busy amusing themselves up the hill to attend to old partners. The idea of using a Cemetery as a rendezvous is distinctly a feminine one. A man would have said simply, 'Let people talk. We'll go down the Mall.' A woman is made differently, especially if she be such a woman as the Man's Wife. She and the Tertium Quid enjoyed each other's society among the graves of men and women whom they had known and danced with aforetime.

They used to take a big horse-blanket and sit on the grass a little to the left of the lower end, where there is a dip in the ground, and where the occupied graves stop short and the ready-made ones are not ready. Each well-regulated Indian Cemetery keeps half a dozen graves permanently open for contingencies and incidental wear and tear. In the Hills these are more usually baby's size, because children who come up weakened and sick from the Plains often succumb to the effects of the Rains in the Hills or get pneumonia from their *ayahs* taking them through damp pine-woods after the sun has set. In Cantonments, of course, the man's size is more in request ; these arrangements vary-ing with the climate and population.

One day when the Man's Wife and the Tertium Quid had just arrived in the Cemetery, they saw some coolies breaking ground. They had marked out a full-size grave, and the Tertium Quid asked them whether any *Sahib* was sick. They said that they did not know ; but it was an order that they should dig a *Sahib's* grave.

'Work away,' said the Tertium Quid, 'and let's see how it's done.'

The coolies worked away, and the Man's Wife and the Tertium Quid watched and talked for a couple of hours while the grave was being deepened. Then a coolie, taking the earth in baskets as it was thrown up, jumped over the grave.

'That's queer,' said the Tertium Quid. 'Where's my ulster ?'

D

'What's queer?' said the Man's Wife.

'I have got a chill down my back—just as if a goose had walked over my grave.'

'Why do you look at the thing, then?' said the Man's Wife. 'Let us go.'

The Tertium Quid stood at the head of the grave, and stared without answering for a space. Then he said, dropping a pebble down, 'It is nasty — and cold: horribly cold. I don't think I shall come to the Cemetery any more. I don't think grave-digging is cheerful.'

The two talked and agreed that the Cemetery was depressing. They also arranged for a ride next day out from the Cemetery through the Mashobra Tunnel up to Fagoo and back, because all the world was going to a garden-party at Viceregal Lodge, and all the people of Mashobra would go too.

Coming up the Cemetery road, the Tertium Quid's horse tried to bolt up-hill, being tired with standing so long, and managed to strain a back sinew.

'I shall have to take the mare to-morrow,' said the Tertium Quid, 'and she will stand nothing heavier than a snaffle.'

They made their arrangements to meet in the Cemetery, after allowing all the Mashobra people time to pass into Simla. That night it rained heavily, and, next day, when the Tertium Quid came to the trysting-place, he saw that the new grave had a foot of water in it, the ground being a tough and sour clay.

''Jove! That looks beastly,' said the Tertium Quid. 'Fancy being boarded up and dropped into that well!'

They then started off to Fagoo, the mare playing with the snaffle and picking her way as though she were shod with satin, and the sun shining divinely.

The road below Mashobra to Fagoo is officially styled the Himalayan-Thibet Road; but in spite of its name it is not much more than six feet wide in most places, and the drop into the valley below may be anything between one and two thousand feet.

'Now we're going to Thibet,' said the Man's Wife merrily, as the horses drew near to Fagoo. She was riding on the cliff-side.

'Into Thibet,' said the Tertium Quid, 'ever so far from people who say horrid things, and hubbies who write stupid letters. With you — to the end of the world!'

A coolie carrying a log of wood came round a corner, and the mare went wide to avoid him — forefeet in and haunches out, as a sensible mare should go.

'To the world's end,' said the Man's Wife, and looked unspeakable things over her near shoulder at the Tertium Quid.

He was smiling, but, while she looked, the smile froze stiff as it were on his face, and changed to a nervous grin — the sort of grin men wear when they are not quite easy in their saddles. The mare seemed to be sinking by the stern, and her nostrils cracked while she was trying to realise what was happening. The rain of the night before had rotted the drop-side of the Himalayan-Thibet Road, and it was giving way under her. 'What are you doing?' said the Man's Wife. The Tertium Quid gave no answer. He grinned nervously and set his spurs into the mare, who rapped with her forefeet on the road, and the struggle began The Man's Wife screamed, 'Oh, Frank, get off!'

But the Tertium Quid was glued to the saddle — his face blue and white — and he looked into the Man's

Wife's eyes. Then the Man's Wife clutched at the mare's head and caught her by the nose instead of the bridle. The brute threw up her head and went down with a scream, the Tertium Quid upon her, and the nervous grin still set on his face.

The Man's Wife heard the tinkle-tinkle of little stones and loose earth falling off the roadway, and the sliding roar of the man and horse going down. Then everything was quiet, and she called on Frank to leave his mare and walk up. But Frank did not answer. He was underneath the mare, nine hundred feet below, spoiling a patch of Indian corn.

As the revellers came back from Viceregal Lodge in the mists of the evening, they met a temporarily insane woman, on a temporarily mad horse, swinging round the corners, with her eyes and her mouth open, and her head like the head of a Medusa. She was stopped by a man at the risk of his life, and taken out of the saddle, a limp heap, and put on the bank to explain herself. This wasted twenty minutes, and then she was sent home in a lady's *'rickshaw*, still with her mouth open and her hands picking at her riding-gloves.

She was in bed through the following three days, which were rainy; so she missed attending the funeral of the Tertium Quid, who was lowered into eighteen inches of water, instead of the twelve to which he had first objected.

A WAYSIDE COMEDY

Because to every purpose there is time and judgment, therefore the
misery of man is great upon him. — *Eccles*. viii. 6.

FATE and the Government of India have turned the
Station of Kashima into a prison; and, because there is
no help for the poor souls who are now lying there in
torment, I write this story, praying that the Government of India may be moved to scatter the European
population to the four winds.

Kashima is bounded on all sides by the rock-tipped
circle of the Dosehri hills. In Spring, it is ablaze with
roses; in Summer, the roses die and the hot winds blow
from the hills; in Autumn, the white mists from the
jhils cover the place as with water, and in Winter the
frosts nip everything young and tender to earth-level.
There is but one view in Kashima — a stretch of perfectly flat pasture and plough-land, running up to the
gray-blue scrub of the Dosehri hills.

There are no amusements, except snipe and tiger
shooting; but the tigers have been long since hunted
from their lairs in the rock-caves, and the snipe only
come once a year. Narkarra — one hundred and forty-
three miles by road — is the nearest station to Kashima.
But Kashima never goes to Narkarra, where there are
at least twelve English people. It stays within the
circle of the Dosehri hills.

All Kashima acquits Mrs. Vansuythen of any intention to do harm ; but all Kashima knows that she, and she alone, brought about their pain.

Boulte, the Engineer, Mrs. Boulte, and Captain Kurrell know this. They are the English population of Kashima, if we except Major Vansuythen, who is of no importance whatever, and Mrs. Vansuythen, who is the most important of all.

You must remember, though you will not understand, that all laws weaken in a small and hidden community where there is no public opinion. When a man is absolutely alone in a Station he runs a certain risk of falling into evil ways. This risk is multiplied by every addition to the population up to twelve — the Jury-number. After that, fear and consequent restraint begin, and human action becomes less grotesquely jerky.

There was deep peace in Kashima till Mrs. Vansuythen arrived. She was a charming woman, every one said so everywhere ; and she charmed every one. In spite of this, or, perhaps, because of this, since Fate is so perverse, she cared only for one man, and he was Major Vansuythen. Had she been plain or stupid, this matter would have been intelligible to Kashima. But she was a fair woman, with very still gray eyes, the colour of a lake just before the light of the sun touches it. No man who had seen those eyes could, later on, explain what fashion of woman she was to look upon. The eyes dazzled him. Her own sex said that she was 'not bad looking, but spoilt by pretending to be so grave.' And yet her gravity was natural. It was not her habit to smile. She merely went through life, looking at those who passed ; and the women objected while the men fell down and worshipped.

She knows and is deeply sorry for the evil she has done to Kashima; but Major Vansuythen cannot understand why Mrs. Boulte does not drop in to afternoon tea at least three times a week. 'When there are only two women in one Station, they ought to see a great deal of each other,' says Major Vansuythen.

Long and long before ever Mrs. Vansuythen came out of those far-away places where there is society and amusement, Kurrell had discovered that Mrs. Boulte was the one woman in the world for him and — you dare not blame them. Kashima was as out of the world as Heaven or the Other Place, and the Dosehri hills kept their secret well. Boulte had no concern in the matter. He was in camp for a fortnight at a time. He was a hard, heavy man, and neither Mrs. Boulte nor Kurrell pitied him. They had all Kashima and each other for their very, very own; and Kashima was the Garden of Eden in those days. When Boulte returned from his wanderings he would slap Kurrell between the shoulders and call him 'old fellow,' and the three would dine together. Kashima was happy then when the judgment of God seemed almost as distant as Narkarra or the railway that ran down to the sea. But the Government sent Major Vansuythen to Kashima, and with him came his wife.

The etiquette of Kashima is much the same as that of a desert island. When a stranger is cast away there, all hands go down to the shore to make him welcome. Kashima assembled at the masonry platform close to the Narkarra Road, and spread tea for the Vansuythens. That ceremony was reckoned a formal call, and made them free of the Station, its rights and privileges. When the Vansuythens were settled down,

they gave a tiny house-warming to all Kashima; and
that made Kashima free of their house, according to
the immemorial usage of the Station.

Then the Rains came, when no one could go into
camp, and the Narkarra Road was washed away by the
Kasun River, and in the cup-like pastures of Kashima
the cattle waded knee-deep. The clouds dropped down
from the Dosehri hills and covered everything.

At the end of the Rains, Boulte's manner towards
his wife changed and became demonstratively affec-
tionate. They had been married twelve years, and the
change startled Mrs. Boulte, who hated her husband
with the hate of a woman who has met with nothing
but kindness from her mate, and, in the teeth of this
kindness, has done him a great wrong. Moreover, she
had her own trouble to fight with — her watch to keep
over her own property, Kurrell. For two months the
Rains had hidden the Dosehri hills and many other
things besides; but, when they lifted, they showed
Mrs. Boulte that her man among men, her Ted — for
she called him Ted in the old days when Boulte was
out of earshot — was slipping the links of the allegiance.

'The Vansuythen Woman has taken him,' Mrs.
Boulte said to herself; and when Boulte was away,
wept over her belief, in the face of the over-vehement
blandishments of Ted. Sorrow in Kashima is as fortunate as Love, because there is nothing to weaken it
save the flight of Time. Mrs. Boulte had never breathed
her suspicion to Kurrell because she was not certain;
and her nature led her to be very certain before she
took steps in any direction. That is why she behaved
as she did.

Boulte came into the house one evening, and leaned against the door-posts of the drawing-room, chewing his moustache. Mrs. Boulte was putting some flowers into a vase. There is a pretence of civilisation even in Kashima.

'Little woman,' said Boulte quietly, 'do you care for me?'

'Immensely,' said she, with a laugh. 'Can you ask it?'

'But I'm serious,' said Boulte. '*Do* you care for me?'

Mrs. Boulte dropped the flowers, and turned round quickly. 'Do you want an honest answer?'

'Ye-es, I've asked for it.'

Mrs. Boulte spoke in a low, even voice for five minutes, very distinctly, that there might be no misunderstanding her meaning. When Samson broke the pillars of Gaza, he did a little thing, and one not to be compared to the deliberate pulling down of a woman's homestead about her own ears. There was no wise female friend to advise Mrs. Boulte, the singularly cautious wife, to hold her hand. She struck at Boulte's heart, because her own was sick with suspicion of Kurrell, and worn out with the long strain of watching alone through the Rains. There was no plan or purpose in her speaking. The sentences made themselves; and Boulte listened, leaning against the door-post with his hands in his pockets. When all was over, and Mrs. Boulte began to breathe through her nose before breaking out into tears, he laughed and stared straight in front of him at the Dosehri hills.

'Is that all?' he said. 'Thanks, I only wanted to know, you know.'

'What are you going to do?' said the woman, between her sobs.

'Do! Nothing. What should I do? Kill Kurrell or send you Home, or apply for leave to get a divorce? It's two days' *dâk* into Narkarra.' He laughed again and went on: 'I'll tell you what *you* can do. You can ask Kurrell to dinner to-morrow — no, on Thursday, that will allow you time to pack — and you can bolt with him. I give you my word I won't follow.'

He took up his helmet and went out of the room, and Mrs. Boulte sat till the moonlight streaked the floor, thinking and thinking and thinking. She had done her best upon the spur of the moment to pull the house down; but it would not fall. Moreover, she could not understand her husband, and she was afraid. Then the folly of her useless truthfulness struck her, and she was ashamed to write to Kurrell, saying: 'I have gone mad and told everything. My husband says that I am free to elope with you. Get a *dâk* for Thursday, and we will fly after dinner.' There was a cold-bloodedness about that procedure which did not appeal to her. So she sat still in her own house and thought.

At dinner-time Boulte came back from his walk, white and worn and haggard, and the woman was touched at his distress. As the evening wore on, she muttered some expression of sorrow, something approaching to contrition. Boulte came out of a brown study and said, 'Oh, *that!* I wasn't thinking about that. By the way, what does Kurrell say to the elopement?'

'I haven't seen him,' said Mrs. Boulte. 'Good God! is that all?'

But Boulte was not listening, and her sentence ended in a gulp.

The next day brought no comfort to Mrs. Boulte, for Kurrell did not appear, and the new life that she, in the five minutes' madness of the previous evening, had hoped to build out of the ruins of the old, seemed to be no nearer.

Boulte ate his breakfast, advised her to see her Arab pony fed in the veranda, and went out. The morning wore through, and at midday the tension became unendurable. Mrs. Boulte could not cry. She had finished her crying in the night, and now she did not want to be left alone. Perhaps the Vansuythen Woman would talk to her; and, since talking opens the heart, perhaps there might be some comfort to be found in her company. She was the only other woman in the Station.

In Kashima there are no regular calling-hours. Every one can drop in upon every one else at pleasure. Mrs. Boulte put on a big *terai* hat, and walked across to the Vansuythen's house to borrow last week's *Queen*. The two compounds touched, and instead of going up the drive, she crossed through the gap in the cactus-hedge, entering the house from the back. As she passed through the dining-room, she heard, behind the *purdah* that cloaked the drawing-room door, her husband's voice, saying —

'But on my Honour! On my Soul and Honour, I tell you she doesn't care for me. She told me so last night. I would have told you then if Vansuythen hadn't been with you. If it is for *her* sake that you'll have nothing to say to me, you can make your mind easy. It's Kurrell——'

'What?' said Mrs. Vansuythen, with an hysterical

little laugh. 'Kurrell! Oh, it can't be! You two must have made some horrible mistake. Perhaps you —you lost your temper, or misunderstood, or something. Things *can't* be as wrong as you say.'

Mrs. Vansuythen had shifted her defence to avoid the man's pleading, and was desperately trying to keep him to a side-issue.

'There must be some mistake,' she insisted, 'and it can be all put right again.'

Boulte laughed grimly.

'It can't be Captain Kurrell! He told me that he had never taken the least—the least interest in your wife, Mr. Boulte. Oh, *do* listen! He said he had not. He swore he had not,' said Mrs. Vansuythen.

The *purdah* rustled, and the speech was cut short by the entry of a little, thin woman, with big rings round her eyes. Mrs. Vansuythen stood up with a gasp.

'What was that you said?' asked Mrs. Boulte. 'Never mind that man. What did Ted say to you? What did he say to you? What did he say to you?'

Mrs. Vansuythen sat down helplessly on the sofa overborne by the trouble of her questioner.

'He said—I can't remember exactly what he said— but I understood him to say—that is—— But, really, Mrs. Boulte, isn't it rather a strange question?'

'*Will* you tell me what he said?' repeated Mrs. Boulte. Even a tiger will fly before a bear robbed of her whelps, and Mrs. Vansuythen was only an ordinarily good woman. She began in a sort of desperation: 'Well, he said that he never cared for you at all, and, of course, there was not the least reason why he should have, and—and—that was all.'

'You said he *swore* he had not cared for me. Was that true?'

'Yes,' said Mrs. Vansuythen very softly.

Mrs. Boulte wavered for an instant where she stood, and then fell forward fainting.

'What did I tell you?' said Boulte, as though the conversation had been unbroken. 'You can see for yourself. She cares for *him*.' The light began to break into his dull mind, and he went on — 'And he — what was *he* saying to you?'

But Mrs. Vansuythen, with no heart for explanations or impassioned protestations, was kneeling over Mrs. Boulte.

'Oh, you brute!' she cried. 'Are *all* men like this? Help me to get her into my room — and her face is cut against the table. Oh, *will* you be quiet, and help me to carry her? I hate you, and I hate Captain Kurrell. Lift her up carefully and now — go! Go away!'

Boulte carried his wife into Mrs. Vansuythen's bedroom and departed before the storm of that lady's wrath and disgust, impenitent and burning with jealousy. Kurrell had been making love to Mrs. Vansuythen — would do Vansuythen as great a wrong as he had done Boulte, who caught himself considering whether Mrs. Vansuythen would faint if she discovered that the man she loved had foresworn her.

In the middle of these meditations, Kurrell came cantering along the road and pulled up with a cheery, 'Good-mornin'. 'Been mashing Mrs. Vansuythen as usual, eh? Bad thing for a sober, married man, that. What will Mrs. Boulte say?'

Boulte raised his head and said slowly, 'Oh, you

liar!' Kurrell's face changed. 'What's that?' he asked quickly.

'Nothing much,' said Boulte. 'Has my wife told you that you two are free to go off whenever you please? She has been good enough to explain the situation to me. You've been a true friend to me, Kurrell — old man — haven't you?'

Kurrell groaned, and tried to frame some sort of idiotic sentence about being willing to give 'satisfaction.' But his interest in the woman was dead, had died out in the Rains, and, mentally, he was abusing her for her amazing indiscretion. It would have been so easy to have broken off the thing gently and by degrees, and now he was saddled with —— Boulte's voice recalled him.

'I don't think I should get any satisfaction from killing you, and I'm pretty sure you'd get none from killing me.'

Then in a querulous tone, ludicrously disproportioned to his wrongs, Boulte added —

''Seems rather a pity that you haven't the decency to keep to the woman, now you've got her. You've been a true friend to *her* too, haven't you?'

Kurrell stared long and gravely. The situation was getting beyond him.

'What do you mean?' he said.

Boulte answered, more to himself than the questioner: 'My wife came over to Mrs. Vansuythen's just now; and it seems you'd been telling Mrs. Vansuythen that you'd never cared for Emma. I suppose you lied, as usual. What had Mrs. Vansuythen to do with you, or you with her? Try to speak the truth for once in a way.'

Kurrell took the double insult without wincing, and replied by another question: 'Go on. What happened?'

'Emma fainted,' said Boulte simply. 'But, look here, what had you been saying to Mrs. Vansuythen?'

Kurrell laughed. Mrs. Boulte had, with unbridled tongue, made havoc of his plans; and he could at least retaliate by hurting the man in whose eyes he was humiliated and shown dishonourable.

'Said to her? What *does* a man tell a lie like that for? I suppose I said pretty much what you've said, unless I'm a good deal mistaken.'

'I spoke the truth,' said Boulte, again more to himself than Kurrell. 'Emma told me she hated me. She has no right in me.'

'No! I suppose not. You're only her husband, y'know. And what did Mrs. Vansuythen say after you had laid your disengaged heart at her feet?'

Kurrell felt almost virtuous as he put the question.

'I don't think that matters,' Boulte replied; 'and it doesn't concern you.'

'But it does! I tell you it does'—began Kurrell shamelessly.

The sentence was cut by a roar of laughter from Boulte's lips. Kurrell was silent for an instant, and then he, too, laughed—laughed long and loudly, rocking in his saddle. It was an unpleasant sound—the mirthless mirth of these men on the long, white line of the Narkarra Road. There were no strangers in Kashima, or they might have thought that captivity within the Dosehri hills had driven half the European population mad. The laughter ended abruptly, and Kurrell was the first to speak.

'Well, what are you going to do?'

Boulte looked up the road, and at the hills. 'Nothing,' said he quietly; 'what's the use? It's too ghastly for anything. We must let the old life go on. I can only call you a hound and a liar, and I can't go on calling you names for ever. Besides which, I don't feel that I'm much better. We can't get out of this place. What *is* there to do?'

Kurrell looked round the rat-pit of Kashima and made no reply. The injured husband took up the wondrous tale.

'Ride on, and speak to Emma if you want to. God knows *I* don't care what you do.'

He walked forward, and left Kurrell gazing blankly after him. Kurrell did not ride on either to see Mrs. Boulte or Mrs. Vansuythen. He sat in his saddle and thought, while his pony grazed by the roadside.

The whir of approaching wheels roused him. Mrs. Vansuythen was driving home Mrs. Boulte, white and wan, with a cut on her forehead.

'Stop, please,' said Mrs. Boulte, 'I want to speak to Ted.'

Mrs. Vansuythen obeyed, but as Mrs. Boulte leaned forward, putting her hand upon the splash-board of the dog-cart, Kurrell spoke.

'I've seen your husband, Mrs. Boulte.'

There was no necessity for any further explanation. The man's eyes were fixed, not upon Mrs. Boulte, but her companion. Mrs. Boulte saw the look.

'Speak to him!' she pleaded, turning to the woman at her side. 'Oh, speak to him! Tell him what you told me just now. Tell him you hate him. Tell him you hate him!'

She bent forward and wept bitterly, while the *sais*, impassive, went forward to hold the horse.   Mrs. Vansuythen turned scarlet and dropped the reins.   She wished to be no party to such unholy explanations.

'I've nothing to do with it,' she began coldly; but Mrs. Boulte's sobs overcame her, and she addressed herself to the man.   'I don't know what I am to say, Captain Kurrell.   I don't know what I can call you. I think you've — you've behaved abominably, and she has cut her forehead terribly against the table.'

'It doesn't hurt.   It isn't anything,' said Mrs. Boulte feebly.   '*That* doesn't matter.   Tell him what you told me.   Say you don't care for him.   Oh, Ted, *won't* you believe her?'

'Mrs. Boulte has made me understand that you were — that you were fond of her once upon a time,' went on Mrs. Vansuythen.

'Well!' said Kurrell brutally.   'It seems to me that Mrs. Boulte had better be fond of her own husband first.'

'Stop!' said Mrs. Vansuythen.   'Hear me first.   I don't care — I don't want to know anything about you and Mrs. Boulte; but I want *you* to know that I hate you, that I think you are a cur, and that I'll never, *never* speak to you again.   Oh, I don't dare to say what I think of you, you —— man!'

'I want to speak to Ted,' moaned Mrs. Boulte, but the dog-cart rattled on, and Kurrell was left on the road, shamed, and boiling with wrath against Mrs. Boulte.

He waited till Mrs. Vansuythen was driving back to her own house, and, she being freed from the embarrassment of Mrs. Boulte's presence, learned for the second time her opinion of himself and his actions.

E

In the evenings, it was the wont of all Kashima to meet at the platform on the Narkarra Road, to drink tea, and discuss the trivialities of the day. Major Vansuythen and his wife found themselves alone at the gathering-place for almost the first time in their remembrance; and the cheery Major, in the teeth of his wife's remarkably reasonable suggestion that the rest of the Station might be sick, insisted upon driving round to the two bungalows and unearthing the population.

'Sitting in the twilight!' said he, with great indignation, to the Boultes. 'That'll never do! Hang it all, we're one family here! You *must* come out, and so must Kurrell. I'll make him bring his banjo.'

So great is the power of honest simplicity and a good digestion over guilty consciences that all Kashima did turn out, even down to the banjo; and the Major embraced the company in one expansive grin. As he grinned, Mrs. Vansuythen raised her eyes for an instant and looked at all Kashima. Her meaning was clear. Major Vansuythen would never know anything. He was to be the outsider in that happy family whose cage was the Dosehri hills.

'You're singing villainously out of tune, Kurrell,' said the Major truthfully. 'Pass me that banjo.'

And he sang in excruciating-wise till the stars came out and all Kashima went to dinner.

*   *   *   *   *   *   *   *   *

That was the beginning of the New Life of Kashima —the life that Mrs. Boulte made when her tongue was loosened in the twilight.

Mrs. Vansuythen has never told the Major; and since he insists upon keeping up a burdensome geniality, she has been compelled to break her vow of not speaking to Kurrell. This speech, which must of necessity preserve the semblance of politeness and interest, serves admirably to keep alight the flame of jealousy and dull hatred in Boulte's bosom, as it awakens the same passions in his wife's heart. Mrs. Boulte hates Mrs. Vansuythen because she has taken Ted from her, and, in some curious fashion, hates her because Mrs. Vansuythen — and here the wife's eyes see far more clearly than the husband's — detests Ted. And Ted — that gallant captain and honourable man — knows now that it is possible to hate a woman once loved, to the verge of wishing to silence her for ever with blows. Above all, is he shocked that Mrs. Boulte cannot see the error of her ways.

Boulte and he go out tiger-shooting together in all friendship. Boulte has put their relationship on a most satisfactory footing.

'You're a blackguard,' he says to Kurrell, 'and I've lost any self-respect I may ever have had ; but when you're with me, I can feel certain that you are not with Mrs. Vansuythen, or making Emma miserable.'

Kurrell endures anything that Boulte may say to him. Sometimes they are away for three days together, and then the Major insists upon his wife going over to sit with Mrs. Boulte ; although Mrs. Vansuythen has repeatedly declared that she prefers her husband's company to any in the world. From the way in which she clings to him, she would certainly seem to be speaking the truth.

But of course, as the Major says, 'in a little Station we must all be friendly.'

THE PIT THAT THEY DIGGED [1]

MR. HAWKINS MUMRATH, of Her Majesty's Bengal Civil Service, lay down to die of enteric fever; and, being a thorough-minded man, so nearly accomplished his purpose that all his friends, two doctors, and the Government he served gave him up for lost. Indeed, upon a false rumour the night before he rallied, several journals published very pleasant obituary notices, which, three weeks later, Mr. Mumrath sat up in bed and studied with interest. It is strange to read about yourself in the past tense, and soothing to discover that for all your faults, your world 'might have spared a better man.' When a Bengal civilian is tepid and harmless, newspapers always conclude their notices with this reflection. It entirely failed to amuse Mr. Mumrath.

The loving-kindness of the Government provides for the use of its servants in the East luxuries undreamed of by other civilizations. A State-paid doctor closed Mumrath's eyes, — till Mumrath insisted upon opening them again; a subventionized undertaker bought Government timber for a Government coffin, and the great cemetery of St. Golgotha-in-Partibus prepared, according to regulation, a brick-lined grave, headed and edged, with masonry rests for the coffin. The cost of that grave was 175 rupees 14 annas, including the lease

[1] Copyright, 1895, by MACMILLAN & CO.

of the land in perpetuity. Very minute are the instructions of the Government for the disposal, wharfage, and demurrage of its dead; but the actual arrangements are not published in any appendix to pay and pension rules, for the same reason that led a Prussian officer not to leave his dead and wounded too long in the sight of a battery under fire.

Mr. Mumrath recovered and went about his work, to the disgust of his juniors who had hoped promotion from his decease. The undertaker sold the coffin, at a profit, to a fat Armenian merchant in Calcutta, and the State-paid doctor profited in practice by Mumrath's resurrection from the dead. The Cemetery of St. Golgotha-in-Partibus sat down by the head of the new-made grave with the beautiful brick lining, and waited for the corpse then signing despatches in an office three miles away. The yearly accounts were made up; and there remained over, unpaid for, one grave, cost 175 rupees 14 annas. The vouchers for all the other graves carried the name of a deceased servant of the Government. Only one space was blank in the column.

Then Ahutosh Lal Deb, Sub-deputy Assistant in the Accounts Department, being full of zeal for the State and but newly appointed to his important post, wrote officially to the Cemetery, desiring to know the inwardness of that grave, and 'having the honour to be,' etc. The Cemetery wrote officially that there was no inwardness at all, but a complete emptiness; said grave having been ordered for Mr. Hawkins Mumrath, and 'had the honour to remain.' Ahutosh Lal Deb had the honour to point out that, the grave being unused, the Government could by no means pay for it. The Cemetery wished to know if the account could be carried over to the next year, 'pending anticipated taking-up of grave.'

Ahutosh Lal Deb said that he was not going to have the accounts confused. Discrepancy was the soul of badinage and defalcations. The Cemetery would be good enough to adjust on the financial basis of that year.

The Cemetery wished they might be buried if they saw their way to doing it, and there really had been more than two thousand burned bricks put into the lining of the grave. Meantime, they complained, the Government Brickfield Audit was waiting until all material should have been paid for.

Ahutosh Lal Deb wrote: 'Refer to Mr. Mumrath.' The Cemetery referred semi-officially. It struck them as being rather a delicate matter, but orders are orders.

Hawkins Mumrath wrote back, saying that he had the honour to be quite well, and not in the least in need of a grave, brick-lined or otherwise. He recommended the head of the Cemetery to get into that grave and stay there. The Cemetery forwarded the letter to Ahutosh Lal Deb, for reference and order.

Ahutosh Lal Deb forwarded it to the Provincial Government, who filed it behind a mass of other files and forgot all about it.

A fat she-cobra crawled into the neglected grave, and laid her eggs among the bricks. The Rains fell, and a little sprinkling of grass jewelled the brick floor.

The Cemetery wrote to Ahutosh Lal Deb, advising him that Mr. Mumrath had not paid for the grave, and requesting that the sum might be stopped from his monthly pay. Ahutosh Lal Deb sent the letter to Hawkins Mumrath as a reminder.

Hawkins Mumrath swore ; but when he had sworn, he began to feel frightened. The enteric fever had destroyed his nerve. He wrote to the Accounts Department, protesting against the injustice of paying for a grave beforehand. Deductions for pension or widow's annuity were quite right, but this sort of deduction was an imposition besides being sarcastic.

Ahutosh Lal Deb wrote that Mr. Mumrath's style was not one usually employed in official correspondence, and requested him to modulate it and pay for the grave. Hawkins Mumrath tossed the letter into the fire, and wrote to the Provincial Government.

The Provincial Government had the honour to point out that the matter rested entirely between Mr. Hawkins Mumrath and the Accounts Department. They saw no reason to interfere till the money was actually deducted from the pay. In that eventuality, if Mr. Hawkins Mumrath appealed through the proper channels, he might, if the matter were properly reported upon, get a refund, less the cost of his last letter, which was under-stamped. The Cemetery wrote to Ahutosh Lal Deb, enclosing triplicate of grave-bill and demanding some sort of settlement.

Ahutosh Lal Deb deducted 175 rupees 14 annas from Mumrath's monthly pay. Mumrath appealed through the proper channels. The Provincial Government wrote that the expenses of all Government graves solely concerned the Supreme Government, to whom his letter had been forwarded.

Mumrath wrote to the Supreme Government. The Supreme Government had the honour to explain that the management of St. Golgotha-in-Partibus was under direct control of the Provincial Government, to whom

they had had the honour of forwarding his communication. Mumrath telegraphed to the Cemetery to this
effect.

The Cemetery telegraphed: 'Fiscal and finance,
Supreme; management of internal affairs, Provincial
Government. Refer Revenue and Agricultural De-
partment for grave details.'

Mumrath referred to the Revenue and Agricultural
Department. That Department had the honour to
make clear that it was only concerned in the planta-
tion of trees round the Cemetery. The Forest Department controlled the reboisement of the edges of the
paths.

Mumrath forwarded all the letters to Ahutosh Lal
Deb, with a request for an immediate refund under
'Rule 431 A, Supplementary Addenda, Bengal.' He
invented rule and reference *pro re nata*, having some
knowledge of the workings of the Babu mind.

The crest of the Revenue and Agricultural Department frightened Ahutosh Lal Deb more than the
reference. He bewilderedly granted the refund, and
recouped the Government from the Cemetery Establishment allowance.

The Cemetery Establishment Executive Head wanted
to know what Ahutosh Lal Deb meant.

The Accountant-General wanted to know what Ahutosh Lal Deb meant.

The Provincial Government wanted to know what
Ahutosh Lal Deb meant.

The Revenue and Agriculture, the Forest Department, and the Government Harness Depot, which supplies the leather slings for the biers, all wanted to
know what the deuce Ahutosh Lal Deb meant.

Ahutosh Lal Deb referred them severally to Mr. Hawkins Mumrath, who had driven out to chuckle over his victory all alone at the head of the brick-lined grave with the masonry foot rests.

The she-cobra was sunning herself by the edge of the grave with her little ones about her, for the eggs had hatched out beautifully. Hawkins Mumrath stepped absently on the old lady's tail, and she bit him in the ankle.

Hawkins Mumrath drove home very quickly, and died in five hours and three-quarters.

Then Ahutosh Lal Deb passed the entry to 'regular account,' and there was peace in India.

THE HILL OF ILLUSION

What rendered vain their deep desire?
A God, a God their severance ruled,
And bade between their shores to be
The unplumbed, salt, estranging sea.

Matthew Arnold.

HE. Tell your *jhampanis* not to hurry so, dear. They forget I'm fresh from the Plains.

SHE. Sure proof that *I* have not been going out with any one. Yes, they *are* an untrained crew. Where do we go?

HE. As usual — to the world's end. No, Jakko.

SHE. Have your pony led after you, then. It's a long round.

HE. And for the last time, thank Heaven!"

SHE. Do you mean *that* still? I didn't dare to write to you about it — all these months.

HE. Mean it! I've been shaping my affairs to that end since Autumn. What makes you speak as though it had occurred to you for the first time?

SHE. I? Oh! I don't know. I've had long enough to think, too.

HE. And you've changed your mind?

SHE. No. You ought to know that I am a miracle of constancy. What are your — arrangements?

HE. *Ours*, Sweetheart, please.

SHE. Ours, be it then. My poor boy, how the prickly heat has marked your forehead! Have you ever tried sulphate of copper in water?

HE. It'll go away in a day or two up here. The arrangements are simple enough. Tonga in the early morning — reach Kalka at twelve — Umballa at seven — down, straight by night train, to Bombay, and then the steamer of the 21st for Rome. That's my idea. The Continent and Sweden — a ten-week honeymoon.

SHE. Ssh! Don't talk of it in that way. It makes me afraid. Guy, how long have we two been insane?

HE. Seven months and fourteen days, I forget the odd hours exactly, but I'll think.

SHE. I only wanted to see if you remembered. Who are those two on the Blessington Road?

HE. Eabrey and the Penner woman. What do they matter to *us?* Tell me everything that you've been doing and saying and thinking.

SHE. Doing little, saying less, and thinking a great deal. I've hardly been out at all.

HE. That was wrong of you. You haven't been moping?

SHE. Not very much. Can you wonder that I'm disinclined for amusement?

HE. Frankly, I do. Where was the difficulty?

SHE. In this only. The more people I know and the more I'm known here, the wider spread will be the news of the crash when it comes. I don't like that.

HE. Nonsense. We shall be out of it.

SHE. You think so?

HE. I'm sure of it, if there is any power in steam or horse-flesh to carry us away. Ha! ha!

SHE. And the *fun* of the situation comes in — where, my Lancelot?

HE. Nowhere, Guinevere. I was only thinking of something.

SHE.   They say men have a keener sense of humour than women.   Now *I* was thinking of the scandal.

HE.   Don't think of anything so ugly.   We shall be beyond it.

SHE.   It will be there all the same — in the mouths of Simla — telegraphed over India, and talked of at the dinners — and when He goes out they will stare at Him to see how He takes it.   And we shall be dead, Guy dear — dead and cast into the outer darkness where there is ——

HE.   Love at least.   Isn't that enough?

SHE.   I have said so.

HE.   And you think so still?

SHE.   What do *you* think?

HE.   What have I *done?*   It means equal ruin to me, as the world reckons it — outcasting, the loss of my appointment, the breaking off my life's work.   I pay my price.

SHE.   And are you so much above the world that you can afford to pay it?   Am I?

HE.   My Divinity — what else?

SHE.   A very ordinary woman I'm afraid, but, so far, respectable.   How d'you do, Mrs. Middleditch?   Your husband?   I think he's riding down to Annandale with Colonel Statters.   Yes, isn't it divine after the rain? —— Guy, how long am I to be allowed to bow to Mrs. Middleditch?   Till the 17th?

HE.   Frowsy Scotchwoman!   What is the use of bringing her into the discussion?   You were saying?

SHE.   Nothing.   Have you ever seen a man hanged?

HE.   Yes.   Once.

SHE.   What was it for?

HE.   Murder, of course.

SHE.   Murder.   Is *that* so great a sin after all?   I wonder how he felt before the drop fell.

HE.   I don't think he felt much.   What a gruesome little woman it is this evening!   You're shivering.   Put on your cape, dear.

SHE.   I think I will.   Oh!   Look at the mist coming over Sanjaoli; and I thought we should have sunshine on the Ladies' Mile!   Let's turn back.

HE.   What's the good?   There's a cloud on Elysium Hill, and that means it's foggy all down the Mall.   We'll go on.   It'll blow away before we get to the Convent, perhaps.   'Jove!   It *is* chilly.

SHE.   You feel it, fresh from below.   Put on your ulster.   What do you think of my cape?

HE.   Never ask a man his opinion of a woman's dress when he is desperately and abjectly in love with the wearer.   Let me look.   Like everything else of yours it's perfect.   Where did you get it from?

SHE.   He gave it me, on Wednesday — our wedding-day, you know.

HE.   The Deuce He did!   He's growing generous in his old age.   D'you like all that frilly, bunchy stuff at the throat?   I don't.

SHE.   Don't you?

> Kind Sir, o' your courtesy,
>   As you go by the town, Sir,
> 'Pray you o' your love for me,
>   Buy me a russet gown, Sir.

HE.   I won't say: 'Keek into the draw-well, Janet, Janet.'   Only wait a little, darling, and you shall be stocked with russet gowns and everything else.

SHE.   And when the frocks wear out, you'll get me new ones — and everything else?

HE. Assuredly.

SHE. I wonder!

HE. Look here, Sweetheart, I didn't spend two days and two nights in the train to hear you wonder. I thought we'd settled all that at Shaifazehat.

SHE (*dreamily*). At Shaifazehat? Does the Station go on still? That was ages and *ages* ago. It must be crumbling to pieces. All except the Amirtollah *kutcha* road. I don't believe *that* could crumble till the Day of Judgment.

HE. You think so? What *is* the mood now?

SHE. I can't tell. How cold it is! Let us get on quickly.

HE. 'Better walk a little. Stop your *jhampanis* and get out. What's the matter with you this evening, dear?

SHE. Nothing. You must grow accustomed to my ways. If I'm boring you I can go home. Here's Captain Congleton coming, I daresay he'll be willing to escort me.

HE. Goose! Between *us*, too! *Damn* Captain Congleton!

SHE. Chivalrous Knight. Is it your habit to swear much in talking? It jars a little, and you might swear at me.

HE. My angel! I didn't know what I was saying; and you changed so quickly that I couldn't follow. I'll apologise in dust and ashes.

SHE. There'll be enough of those later on —— Good-night, Captain Congleton. Going to the singing-quadrilles already? What dances am I giving you next week? No! You must have written them down wrong. Five and Seven, *I* said. If you've made a mistake, I certainly don't intend to suffer for it. You must alter your programme.

HE. I thought you told me that you had not been going out much this season?

SHE. Quite true, but when I do I dance with Captain Congleton. He dances very nicely.

HE. And sit out with him I suppose?

SHE. Yes. Have you any objection? Shall I stand under the chandelier in future?

HE. What does he talk to you about?

SHE. What do men talk about when they sit out?

HE. Ugh! Don't! Well now I'm up, you must dispense with the fascinating Congleton for a while. I don't like him.

SHE (*after a pause*). Do you know what you have said?

HE. 'Can't say that I do exactly. I'm not in the best of tempers.

SHE. So I see, — and feel. My true and faithful lover, where is your 'eternal constancy,' 'unalterable trust,' and 'reverent devotion'? I remember those phrases; you seem to have forgotten them. I mention a man's name ——

HE. A good deal more than that.

SHE. Well, speak to him about a dance — perhaps the last dance that I shall ever dance in my life before I, — before I go away; and you at once distrust and insult me.

HE. I never said a word.

SHE. How much did you imply? Guy, is *this* amount of confidence to be our stock to start the new life on?

HE. No, of course not. I didn't mean that. On

my word and honour, I didn't. Let it pass, dear.
Please let it pass.

SHE. This once — yes — and a second time, and
again and again, all through the years when I shall be
unable to resent it. You want too much, my Lancelot, and, — you know too much.

HE. How do you mean?

SHE. That is a part of the punishment. There
cannot be perfect trust between us.

HE. In Heaven's name, why not?

SHE. Hush! The Other Place is quite enough.
Ask yourself.

HE. I don't follow.

SHE. You trust me so implicitly that when I look
at another man —— Never mind. Guy. Have you
ever made love to a girl — a *good* girl?

HE. Something of the sort. Centuries ago — in
the Dark Ages, before I ever met you, dear.

SHE. Tell me what you said to her.

HE. What does a man say to a girl? I've forgotten.

SHE. *I* remember. He tells her that he trusts her
and worships the ground she walks on, and that he'll
love and honour and protect her till her dying day;
and so she marries in that belief. At least, I speak of
one girl who was *not* protected.

HE. Well, and then?

SHE. And then, Guy, and then, that girl needs *ten*
times the love and trust and honour — yes, *honour* —
that was enough when she was only a mere wife if —
if — the other life she chooses to lead is to be made
even bearable. Do you understand?

HE. Even bearable! It'll be Paradise.

SHE. Ah! Can you give me all I've asked for—
not now, nor a few months later, but when you begin
to think of what you might have done if you had kept
your own appointment and your caste here—when
you begin to look upon me as a drag and a burden?   I
shall want it most, then, Guy, for there will be no one
in the wide world but you.

HE. You're a little over-tired to-night, Sweetheart,
and you're taking a stage view of the situation.   After
the necessary business in the Courts, the road is clear
to——

SHE. 'The holy state of matrimony!' Ha! ha!
ha!

HE. Ssh! Don't laugh in that horrible way!

SHE. I—I c-c-c-can't help it! Isn't it too absurd!
Ah! Ha! ha! ha! Guy, stop me quick or I shall—
l-l-laugh till we get to the Church.

HE. For goodness' sake, stop! Don't make an exhibition of yourself.   What *is* the matter with you?

SHE. N-nothing.   I'm better now.

HE. That's all right.   One moment, dear.   There's
a little wisp of hair got loose from behind your right
ear and it's straggling over your cheek.   So!

SHE. Thank'oo. I'm 'fraid my hat's on one side,
too.

HE. What do you wear these huge dagger bonnet-
skewers for? They're big enough to kill a man with.

SHE. Oh! Don't kill *me*, though.   You're sticking it into my head! Let *me* do it.   You men are so
clumsy.

HE. Have you had many opportunities of compar-
ing us—in this sort of work?

SHE. Guy, what is my name?

F

HE.   Eh!   I don't follow.

SHE.   Here's my card-case.   Can you read?

HE.   Yes.   Well?

SHE.   Well, that answers your question.   You know the other man's name.   Am I sufficiently humbled, or would you like to ask me if there is any one else?

HE.   I see now.   My darling, I never meant that for an instant. I was only joking. There! Lucky there's no one on the road. They'd be scandalised.

SHE.   They'll be more scandalised before the end.

HE.   Do-on't! I don't like you to talk in that way.

SHE.   Unreasonable man! Who asked me to face the situation and accept it? — Tell me, do I look like Mrs. Penner? *Do* I look like a naughty woman! *Swear* I don't! Give me your word of honour, my *honourable* friend, that I'm not like Mrs. Buzgago. That's the way she stands, with her hands clasped at the back of her head. D'you like that?

HE.   Don't be affected.

SHE.   I'm not. I'm Mrs. Buzgago. Listen!

> Pendant une anne' toute entière
> Le régiment n'a pas r'paru.
> Au Ministère de la Guerre
> On le r'porta comme perdu.
>
> On se r'noncait à r'trouver sa trace,
> Quand un matin subitement,
> On le vit r'paraître sur la place,
> L'Colonel toujours en avant.

That's the way she rolls her r's. *Am* I like her?

HE.   No, but I object when you go on like an actress and sing stuff of that kind. Where in the world did you pick up the *Chanson du Colonel*? It isn't a drawing-room song. It isn't proper.

SHE. Mrs. Buzgago taught it me. She is both drawing-room and proper, and in another month she'll shut her drawing-room to me, and thank God she isn't as improper as I am. Oh, Guy, Guy! I wish I was like some women and had no scruples about — what is it Keene says? — 'Wearing a corpse's hair and being false to the bread they eat.'

HE. I am only a man of limited intelligence, and, just now, very bewildered. When you have *quite* finished flashing through all your moods tell me, and I'll try to understand the last one.

SHE. Moods, Guy! I haven't any. I'm sixteen years old and you're just twenty, and you've been waiting for two hours outside the school in the cold. And now I've met you, and now we're walking home together. Does *that* suit you, My Imperial Majesty?

HE. No. We aren't children. Why can't you be rational?

SHE. He asks me that when I'm going to commit suicide for his sake, and, and — I don't want to be French and rave about my mother, but have I ever told you that I have a mother, and a brother who was my pet before I married? He's married now. Can't you imagine the pleasure that the news of the elopement will give him? Have *you* any people at Home, Guy, to be pleased with your performances?

HE. One or two. One can't make omelets without breaking eggs.

SHE (*slowly*). I don't see the necessity——

HE. Hah! What do you mean?

SHE. Shall I speak the truth?

He.   Under the circumstances, perhaps it *would* be as well.

She.   Guy, I'm afraid.

He.   I thought we'd settled all that.   What of?

She.   Of you.

He.   Oh, damn it all!   The old business!   This is *too* bad!

She.   Of *you*.

He.   And what now?

She.   What do you think of me?

He.   Beside the question altogether.   What do you intend to do?

She.   I daren't risk it.   I'm afraid.   If I could only cheat ——

He.   *A la Buzgago?*   No, *thanks*.   That's the one point on which I have any notion of Honour.   I won't eat his salt and steal too.   I'll loot openly or not at all.

She.   I never meant anything else.

He.   Then, why in the world do you pretend not to be willing to come?

She.   It's *not* pretence, Guy.   I *am* afraid.

He.   Please explain.

She.   It can't last, Guy.   It can't last.   You'll get angry, and then you'll swear, and then you'll get jealous, and then you'll mistrust me — you do *now* — and you yourself will be the best reason for doubting.   And I — what shall *I* do?   I shall be no better than Mrs. Buzgago found out — no better than any one.   And you'll *know* that.   Oh, Guy, can't you *see?*

He.   I see that you are desperately unreasonable, little woman.

She.   There!   The moment I begin to object, you get angry.   What will you do when I am only your property — stolen property? It can't be, Guy. It can't be! I thought it could, but it *can't*. You'll get tired of me.

HE. I tell you I shall *not*. Won't anything make you understand that?

SHE. There, can't you see? If you speak to me like that now, you'll call me horrible names later, if I don't do everything as you like. And if you were cruel to me, Guy, where should I go — where should I go? I can't trust you. Oh! I *can't* trust you!

HE. I suppose I ought to say that I *can* trust you. I've ample reason.

SHE. *Please* don't, dear. It hurts as much as if you hit me.

HE. It isn't exactly pleasant for *me*.

SHE. I can't help it. I wish I were dead! I can't trust you, and I don't trust myself. Oh, Guy, let it die away and be forgotten!

HE. Too late now. I don't understand you — I won't — and I can't trust myself to talk this evening. May I call to-morrow?

SHE. Yes. *No!* Oh, give me time! The day after. I get into my *'rickshaw* here and meet Him at Peliti's. You ride.

HE. I'll go on to Peliti's too. I think I want a drink. My world's knocked about my ears and the stars are falling. Who are those brutes howling in the Old Library?

SHE. They're rehearsing the singing-quadrilles for the Fancy Ball. Can't you hear Mrs. Buzgago's voice? She has a solo. It's quite a new idea. Listen.

MRS. BUZGAGO (*in the Old Library, con. molt. exp.*).

> See saw! Margery Daw!
> Sold her bed to lie upon straw.
> Wasn't she a silly slut
> To sell her bed and lie upon dirt?

Captain Congleton, I'm going to alter that to 'flirt.' It sounds better.

HE. No, I've changed my mind about the drink. Good-night, little lady. I shall see you to-morrow?

SHE. Ye—es. Good-night, Guy. *Don't* be angry with me.

HE. Angry! You *know* I trust you absolutely. Good-night and — God bless you!

(*Three seconds later. Alone.*) Hmm! I'd give something to discover whether there's another man at the back of all this.

A SECOND-RATE WOMAN

Est fuga, volvitur rota,
  On we drift: where looms the dim port?
One Two Three Four Five contribute their quota:
  Something is gained if one caught but the import,
Show it us, Hugues of Saxe-Gotha.

Master Hugues of Saxe-Gotha.

'DRESSED! Don't tell me that woman ever dressed in her life. She stood in the middle of the room while her *ayah* — no, her husband — it *must* have been a man — threw her clothes at her. She then did her hair with her fingers, and rubbed her bonnet in the flue under the bed. I *know* she did, as well as if I had assisted at the orgie. Who is she?' said Mrs. Hauksbee.

'Don't!' said Mrs. Mallowe feebly. 'You make my head ache. I'm miserable to-day. Stay me with *fondants*, comfort me with chocolates, for I am —— Did you bring anything from Peliti's?'

'Questions to begin with. You shall have the sweets when you have answered them. Who and what is the creature? There were at least half a dozen men round her, and she appeared to be going to sleep in their midst.'

'Delville,' said Mrs. Mallowe, '"Shady" Delville, to distinguish her from Mrs. Jim of that ilk. She dances as untidily as she dresses, I believe, and her husband is somewhere in Madras. Go and call, if you are so interested.'

'What have I to do with Shigramitish women? She

71

merely caught my attention for a minute, and I wondered at the attraction that a dowd has for a certain
type of man. I expected to see her walk out of her
clothes — until I looked at her eyes.'

'Hooks and eyes, surely,' drawled Mrs. Mallowe.

'Don't be clever, Polly. You make my head ache.
And round this hayrick stood a crowd of men — a
positive crowd!'

'Perhaps *they* also expected ——'

'Polly, don't be Rabelaisian!'

Mrs. Mallowe curled herself up comfortably on the
sofa, and turned her attention to the sweets. She and
Mrs. Hauksbee shared the same house at Simla; and
these things befell two seasons after the matter of Otis
Yeere, which has been already recorded.

Mrs. Hauksbee stepped into the veranda and looked
down upon the Mall, her forehead puckered with
thought.

'Hah!' said Mrs. Hauksbee shortly. 'Indeed!'

'What is it?' said Mrs. Mallowe sleepily.

'That dowd and The Dancing Master — to whom I
object.'

'Why to The Dancing Master? He is a middle-aged
gentleman, of reprobate and romantic tendencies, and
tries to be a friend of mine.'

'Then make up your mind to lose him. Dowds cling
by nature, and I should imagine that this animal — how
terrible her bonnet looks from above! — is specially
clingsome.'

'She is welcome to The Dancing Master so far as I
am concerned. I never could take an interest in a
monotonous liar. The frustrated aim of his life is to
persuade people that he is a bachelor.'

'O-oh! I think I've met that sort of man before. And isn't he?'

'No. He confided that to me a few days ago. Ugh! Some men ought to be killed.'

'What happened then?'

'He posed as the horror of horrors—a misunderstood man. Heaven knows the *femme incomprise* is sad enough and bad enough—but the other thing!'

'And so fat too! *I* should have laughed in his face. Men seldom confide in me. How is it they come to you?'

'For the sake of impressing me with their careers in the past. Protect me from men with confidences!'

'And yet you encourage them?'

'What can I do? They talk, I listen, and they vow that I am sympathetic. I know I always profess astonishment even when the plot is—of the most old possible.'

'Yes. Men are so unblushingly explicit if they are once allowed to talk, whereas women's confidences are full of reservations and fibs, except——'

'When they go mad and babble of the Unutterabilities after a week's acquaintance. Really, if you come to consider, we know a great deal more of men than of our own sex.'

'And the extraordinary thing is that men will never believe it. They say we are trying to hide something.'

'They are generally doing that on their own account. Alas! These chocolates pall upon me, and I haven't eaten more than a dozen. I think I shall go to sleep.'

'Then you'll get fat, dear. If you took more exercise and a more intelligent interest in your neighbours you would——'

'Be as much loved as Mrs. Hauksbee. You're a darling in many ways and I like you — you are not a woman's woman — but *why* do you trouble yourself about mere human beings?'

'Because in the absence of angels, who I am sure would be horribly dull, men and women are the most fascinating things in the whole wide world, lazy one. I am interested in The Dowd — I am interested in The Dancing Master — I am interested in the Hawley Boy — and I am interested in *you.*'

'Why couple me with the Hawley Boy? He is your property.'

'Yes, and in his own guileless speech, I'm making a good thing out of him. When he is slightly more reformed, and has passed his Higher Standard, or whatever the authorities think fit to exact from him, I shall select a pretty little girl, the Holt girl, I think, and ' — here she waved her hands airily — ' "whom Mrs. Hauksbee hath joined together let no man put asunder." That's all.'

'And when you have yoked May Holt with the most notorious detrimental in Simla, and earned the undying hatred of Mamma Holt, what will you do with me, Dispenser of the Destinies of the Universe?'

Mrs. Hauksbee dropped into a low chair in front of the fire, and, chin in hand, gazed long and steadfastly at Mrs. Mallowe.

'I do not know,' she said, shaking her head, '*what* I shall do with you, dear. It's obviously impossible to marry you to some one else — your husband would object and the experiment might not be successful after all. I think I shall begin by preventing you from — what is it? — "sleeping on ale-house benches and snoring in the sun." '

'Don't! I don't like your quotations. They are so rude. Go to the Library and bring me new books.'

'While you sleep? *No!* If you don't come with me, I shall spread your newest frock on my *'rickshaw*-bow, and when any one asks me what I am doing, I shall say that I am going to Phelps's to get it let out. I shall take care that Mrs. MacNamara sees me. Put your things on, there's a good girl.'

Mrs. Mallowe groaned and obeyed, and the two went off to the Library, where they found Mrs. Delville and the man who went by the nickname of The Dancing Master. By that time Mrs. Mallowe was awake and eloquent.

'That is the Creature!' said Mrs. Hauksbee, with the air of one pointing out a slug in the road.

'No,' said Mrs. Mallowe. 'The man is the Creature. Ugh! Good-evening, Mr. Bent. I thought you were coming to tea this evening.'

'Surely it was for to-morrow, was it not?' answered The Dancing Master. 'I understood . . . I fancied . . . I'm so sorry . . . How very unfortunate!' . . .

But Mrs. Mallowe had passed on.

'For the practised equivocator you said he was,' murmured Mrs. Hauksbee, 'he strikes *me* as a failure. Now wherefore should he have preferred a walk with The Dowd to tea with us? Elective affinities, I sup-pose — both grubby. Polly, I'd never forgive that woman as long as the world rolls.'

'I forgive every woman everything,' said Mrs. Mallowe. 'He will be a sufficient punishment for her. What a common voice she has!'

Mrs. Delville's voice was not pretty, her carriage was even less lovely, and her raiment was strikingly neglected.   All these things Mrs. Mallowe noticed over the top of a magazine.

'Now *what* is there in her?' saib Mrs. Hauksdee. 'Do you see what I meant about the clothes falling off?   If I were a man I would perish sooner than be seen with that rag-bag.   And yet, she has good eyes, but — Oh!'

'What is it?'

'She doesn't know how to use them!   On my Honour, she does not.   Look!   Oh look!   Untidiness I can endure, but ignorance never!   The woman's a fool.'

'Hsh!   She'll hear you.'

'All the women in Simla are fools.   She'll think I mean some one else.   Now she's going out.   What a thoroughly objectionable couple she and The Dancing Master make!   Which reminds me.   Do you suppose they'll ever dance together?'

'Wait and see.   I don't envy her the conversation of The Dancing Master — loathly man!   His wife ought to be up here before long.'

'Do you know anything about him?'

'Only what he told me.   It may be all a fiction. He married a girl bred in the country, I think, and, being an honourable, chivalrous soul, told me that he repented his bargain and sent her to her mother as often as possible — a person who has lived in the Doon since the memory of man and goes to Mussoorie when other people go Home.   The wife is with her at present.   So he says.'

'Babies?'

'One only, but he talks of his wife in a revolting way.   I hated him for it.   *He* thought he was being epigrammatic and brilliant.'

'That is a vice peculiar to men. I dislike him because he is generally in the wake of some girl, disappointing the Eligibles. He will persecute May Holt no more, unless I am much mistaken.'

'No. I think Mrs. Delville may occupy his attention for a while.'

'Do you suppose she knows that he is the head of a family?'

'Not from his lips. He swore me to eternal secrecy. Wherefore I tell you. Don't you know that type of man?'

'Not intimately, thank goodness! As a general rule, when a man begins to abuse his wife to me, I find that the Lord gives me wherewith to answer him according to his folly; and we part with a coolness between us. I laugh.'

'I'm different. I've no sense of humour.'

'Cultivate it, then. It has been my mainstay for more years than I care to think about. A well-educated sense of Humour will save a woman when Religion, Training, and Home influences fail; and we may all need salvation sometimes.'

'Do you suppose that the Delville woman has humour?'

'Her dress bewrays her. How can a Thing who wears her *supplément* under her left arm have any notion of the fitness of things — much less their folly? If she discards The Dancing Master after having once seen him dance, I may respect her. Otherwise——'

'But are we not both assuming a great deal too much, dear? You saw the woman at Peliti's — half an hour later you saw her walking with The Dancing Master — an hour later you met her here at the Library.'

'Still with The Dancing Master, remember.'

'Still with The Dancing Master, I admit, but why on the strength of that should you imagine ——'

'I imagine nothing. I have no imagination. I am only convinced that The Dancing Master is attracted to The Dowd because he is objectionable in every way and she in every other. If I know the man as you have described him, he holds his wife in slavery at present.'

'She is twenty years younger than he.'

'Poor wretch! And, in the end, after he has posed and swaggered and lied — he has a mouth under that ragged moustache simply made for lies — he will be rewarded according to his merits.'

'I wonder what those really are,' said Mrs. Mallowe.

But Mrs. Hauksbee, her face close to the shelf of the new books, was humming softly: '*What shall he have who killed the Deer!*' She was a lady of unfettered speech.

One month later, she announced her intention of calling upon Mrs. Delville. Both Mrs. Hauksbee and Mrs. Mallowe were in morning wrappers, and there was a great peace in the land.

'I should go as I was,' said Mrs. Mallowe. 'It would be a delicate compliment to her style.'

Mrs. Hauksbee studied herself in the glass.

'Assuming for a moment that she ever darkened these doors, I should put on this robe, after all the others, to show her what a morning wrapper ought to be. It might enliven her. As it is, I shall go in the dove-coloured — sweet emblem of youth and innocence — and shall put on my new gloves.'

'If you really are going, dirty tan would be too

good; and you know that dove-colour spots with the rain.'

'I care not. I may make her envious. At least I shall try, though one cannot expect very much from a woman who puts a lace tucker into her habit.'

'Just Heavens! When did she do that?'

'Yesterday — riding with The Dancing Master. I met them at the back of Jakko, and the rain had made the lace lie down. To complete the effect, she was wearing an unclean *terai* with the elastic under her chin. I felt almost too well content to take the trouble to despise her.'

'The Hawley Boy was riding with you. What did he think?'

'Does a boy ever notice these things? Should I like him if he did? He stared in the rudest way, and just when I thought he had seen the elastic, he said, "There's something very taking about that face." I rebuked him on the spot. I don't approve of boys being taken by faces.'

'Other than your own. I shouldn't be in the least surprised if the Hawley Boy immediately went to call.'

'I forbade him. Let her be satisfied with The Dancing Master, and his wife when she comes up. I'm rather curious to see Mrs. Bent and the Delville woman together.'

Mrs. Hauksbee departed and, at the end of an hour, returned slightly flushed.

'There is no limit to the treachery of youth! I *ordered* the Hawley Boy, as he valued my patronage, not to call. The first person I stumble over — literally stumble over — in her poky, dark, little drawing-room is, of course, the Hawley Boy. She kept us waiting ten minutes, and then emerged as though she had been tipped out of the dirty-clothes basket. You know my way, dear, when I am at all put out. I was Superior, *crrrrushingly* Superior! 'Lifted my eyes to Heaven, and had heard of nothing — 'dropped my eyes on the carpet and "really didn't know" — 'played with my card-case and "supposed so." The Hawley Boy giggled like a girl, and I had to freeze him with scowls between the sentences.'

'And she?'

'She sat in a heap on the edge of a couch, and managed to convey the impression that she was suffering from stomach-ache, at the very least. It was all I could do not to ask after her symptoms. When I rose, she grunted just like a buffalo in the water — too lazy to move.'

'Are you certain? —— '

'Am I blind, Polly? Laziness, sheer laziness, nothing else — or her garments were only constructed for sitting down in. I stayed for a quarter of an hour trying to penetrate the gloom, to guess what her surroundings were like, while she stuck out her tongue.'

'Lu—*cy!*'

'Well — I'll withdraw the tongue, though I'm sure if she didn't do it when I was in the room, she did the minute I was outside. At any rate, she lay in a lump and grunted. Ask the Hawley Boy, dear. I believe the grunts were meant for sentences, but she spoke so indistinctly that I can't swear to it.'

'You are incorrigible, simply.'

'I am *not!* Treat me civilly, give me peace with honour, don't put the only available seat facing the window, and a child may eat jam in my lap before

Church. But I resent being grunted at. Wouldn't you? Do you suppose that she communicates her views on life and love to The Dancing Master in a set of modulated "Grmphs?"'

'You attach too much importance to The Dancing Master.'

'He came as we went, and The Dowd grew almost cordial at the sight of him. He smiled greasily, and moved about that darkened dog-kennel in a suspiciously familiar way.'

'Don't be uncharitable. Any sin but that I'll forgive.'

'Listen to the voice of History. I am only describing what I saw. He entered, the heap on the sofa revived slightly, and the Hawley Boy and I came away together. *He* is disillusioned, but I felt it my duty to lecture him severely for going there. And that's all.'

'Now for Pity's sake leave the wretched creature and The Dancing Master alone. They never did you any harm.'

'No harm? To dress as an example and a stumbling-block for half Simla, and then to find this Person who is dressed by the hand of God—not that I wish to disparage *Him* for a moment, but you know the *tikka dhurzie* way He attires those lilies of the field—this Person draws the eyes of men—and some of them nice men? It's almost enough to make one discard clothing. I told the Hawley Boy so.'

'And what did that sweet youth do?'

'Turned shell-pink and looked across the far blue hills like a distressed cherub. *Am* I talking wildly, Polly? Let me say my say, and I shall be calm. Other-

G

wise I may go abroad and disturb Simla with a few
original reflections.   Excepting always your own sweet
self, there isn't a single woman in the land who understands me when I am — what's the word ? '

' *Tête-fêlée*,' suggested Mrs. Mallowe.

'Exactly !   And now let us have tiffin.   The demands of Society are exhausting, and as Mrs. Delville
says——'   Here Mrs. Hauksbee, to the horror of the
khitmatgars, lapsed into a series of grunts, while Mrs.
Mallowe stared in lazy surprise.

' "God gie us a gude conceit of oorselves," ' said Mrs.
Hauksbee piously, returning to her natural speech.
'Now, in any other woman that would have been vul-
gar.   I am consumed with curiosity to see Mrs. Bent.
I expect complications.'

'Woman of one idea,' said Mrs. Mallowe shortly;
'all complications are as old as the hills !   I have lived
through or near all — *all* — ALL ! '

'And yet do not understand that men and women
never behave twice alike.   I am old who was young —
if ever I put my head in your lap, you dear, big sceptic,
you will learn that my parting is gauze — but never,
no never, have I lost my interest in men and women.
Polly, I shall see this business out to the bitter end.'

'I am going to sleep,' said Mrs. Mallowe calmly.
'I never interfere with men or women unless I am
compelled,' and she retired with dignity to her own
room.

Mrs. Hauksbee's curiosity was not long left ungrati-
fied, for Mrs. Bent came up to Simla a few days after
the conversation faithfully reported above, and pervaded
the Mall by her husband's side.

'Behold !' said Mrs. Hauksbee, thoughtfully rubbing

her nose. 'That is the last link of the chain, if we omit the husband of the Delville, whoever he may be. Let me consider. The Bents and the Delvilles inhabit the same hotel; and the Delville is detested by the Waddy — do you know the Waddy? — who is almost as big a dowd. The Waddy also abominates the male Bent, for which, if her other sins do not weigh too heavily, she will eventually go to Heaven.'

'Don't be irreverent,' said Mrs. Mallowe, 'I like Mrs. Bent's face.'

'I am discussing the Waddy,' returned Mrs. Hauksbee loftily. 'The Waddy will take the female Bent apart, after having borrowed — yes! — everything that she can, from hairpins to babies' bottles. Such, my dear, is life in a hotel. The Waddy will tell the female Bent facts and fictions about The Dancing Master and The Dowd.'

'Lucy, I should like you better if you were not always looking into people's back-bedrooms.'

'Anybody can look into their front drawing-rooms; and remember whatever I do, and whatever I look, I never talk — as the Waddy will. Let us hope that The Dancing Master's greasy smile and manner of the pedagogue will soften the heart of that cow, his wife. If mouths speak truth, I should think that little Mrs. Bent could get very angry on occasion.'

'But what reason has she for being angry?'

'What reason! The Dancing Master in himself is a reason. How does it go? "If in his life some trivial errors fall, Look in his face and you'll believe them all." I am prepared to credit *any* evil of The Dancing Master, because I hate him so. And The Dowd is so disgustingly badly dressed —— '

'That she, too, is capable of every iniquity? I always prefer to believe the best of everybody. It saves so much trouble.'

'Very good. I prefer to believe the worst. It saves useless expenditure of sympathy. And you may be quite certain that the Waddy believes with me.'

Mrs. Mallowe sighed and made no answer.

The conversation was holden after dinner while Mrs. Hauksbee was dressing for a dance.

'I am too tired to go,' pleaded Mrs. Mallowe, and Mrs. Hauksbee left her in peace till two in the morning, when she was aware of emphatic knocking at her door.

'Don't be *very* angry, dear,' said Mrs. Hauksbee. 'My idiot of an *ayah* has gone home, and, as I hope to sleep to-night, there isn't a soul in the place to unlace me.'

'Oh, this is too bad!' said Mrs. Mallowe sulkily.

''Can't help it. I'm a lone, lorn grass-widow, dear, but I will *not* sleep in my stays. And such news too! Oh, *do* unlace me, there's a darling! The Dowd — The Dancing Master — I and the Hawley Boy — You know the North veranda?'

'How can I do anything if you spin round like this?' protested Mrs. Mallowe, fumbling with the knot of the laces.

'Oh, I forget. I must tell my tale without the aid of your eyes. Do you know you've lovely eyes, dear? Well, to begin with, I took the Hawley Boy to a *kala juggah.*'

'Did he want much taking?'

'Lots! There was an arrangement of loose-boxes in *kanats*, and *she* was in the next one talking to *him.*'

'Which? How? Explain.'

'You know what I mean — The Dowd and The
Dancing Master. We could hear every word, and
we listened shamelessly — 'specially the Hawley Boy.
Polly, I quite love that woman!'

'This is interesting. There! Now turn round.
What happened?'

'One moment. Ah—h! Blessed relief. I've been
looking forward to taking them off for the last half-
hour — which is ominous at my time of life. But, as
I was saying, we listened and heard The Dowd drawl
worse than ever. She drops her final g's like a barmaid
or a blue-blooded Aide-de-Camp. "Look he-ere, you're
gettin' too fond o' me," she said, and The Dancing
Master owned it was so in language that nearly made
me ill. The Dowd reflected for a while. Then we
heard her say, "Look he-ere, Mister Bent, why are
you such an aw-ful liar?" I nearly exploded while
The Dancing Master denied the charge. It seems that
he never told her he was a married man.'

'I said he wouldn't.'

'And she had taken this to heart, on personal
grounds, I suppose. She drawled along for five minutes, reproaching him with his perfidy and grew quite
motherly. "Now you've got a nice little wife of your
own — you have," she said. " She's ten times too good
for a fat old man like you, and, look he-ere, you never
told me a word about her, and I've been thinkin' about
it a good deal, and I think you're a liar." Wasn't that
delicious? The Dancing Master maundered and raved
till the Hawley Boy suggested that he should burst in
and beat him. His voice runs up into an impassioned
squeak when he is afraid. The Dowd must be an ex-

traordinary woman. She explained that had he been a
bachelor she might not have objected to his devotion;
but since he was a married man and the father of a very
nice baby, she considered him a hypocrite, and this she
repeated twice. She wound up her drawl with: " An'
I'm tellin' you this because your wife is angry with me,
an' I hate quarrellin' with any other woman, an' I like
your wife. You know how you have behaved for the
last six weeks. You shouldn't have done it, indeed you
shouldn't. You're too old an' too fat." Can't you
imagine how The Dancing Master would wince at that!
" Now go away," she said. " I don't want to tell you
what I think of you, because I think you are not nice.
I'll stay he-ere till the next dance begins." Did you
think that the creature had so much in her?'

'I never studied her as closely as you did. It sounds
unnatural. What happened?'

'The Dancing Master attempted blandishment, reproof, jocularity, and the style of the Lord High Warden, and I had almost to pinch the Hawley Boy to make
him keep quiet. She grunted at the end of each sentence and, in the end, *he* went away swearing to himself,
quite like a man in a novel. He looked more objectionable than ever. I laughed. I love that woman —
in spite of her clothes. And now I'm going to bed.
What do you think of it?'

'I shan't begin to think till the morning,' said Mrs.
Mallowe yawning. 'Perhaps she spoke the truth. They
do fly into it by accident sometimes.'

Mrs. Hauksbee's account of her eavesdropping was
an ornate one but truthful in the main. For reasons
best known to herself, Mrs. 'Shady' Delville had turned
upon Mr. Bent and rent him limb from limb, casting him

away limp and disconcerted ere she withdrew the light of her eyes from him permanently. Being a man of resource, and anything but pleased in that he had been called both old and fat, he gave Mrs. Bent to understand that he had, during her absence in the Doon, been the victim of unceasing persecution at the hands of Mrs. Delville, and he told the tale so often and with such eloquence that he ended in believing it, while his wife marvelled at the manners and customs of 'some women.' When the situation showed signs of languishing, Mrs. Waddy was always on hand to wake the smouldering fires of suspicion in Mrs. Bent's bosom and to contribute generally to the peace and comfort of the hotel. Mr. Bent's life was not a happy one, for if Mrs. Waddy's story were true, he was, argued his wife, untrustworthy to the last degree. If his own statement was true, his charms of manner and conversation were so great that he needed constant surveillance. And he received it, till he repented genuinely of his marriage and neglected his personal appearance. Mrs. Delville alone in the hotel was unchanged. She removed her chair some six paces towards the head of the table, and occasionally in the twilight ventured on timid overtures of friendship to Mrs. Bent, which were repulsed.

'She does it for my sake,' hinted the virtuous Bent.

'A dangerous and designing woman,' purred Mrs. Waddy.

Worst of all, every other hotel in Simla was full!

* * * * * * * * *

'Polly, are you afraid of diphtheria?'

'Of nothing in the world except smallpox. Diphtheria kills, but it doesn't disfigure. Why do you ask?'

'Because the Bent baby has got it, and the whole

hotel is upside down in consequence. The Waddy has "set her five young on the rail" and fled. The Dancing Master fears for his precious throat, and that miserable little woman, his wife, has no notion of what ought to be done. She wanted to put it into a mustard bath —for croup!'

'Where did you learn all this?'

'Just now, on the Mall. Dr. Howlen told me. The Manager of the hotel is abusing the Bents, and the Bents are abusing the manager. They *are* a feckless couple.'

'Well. What's on your mind?'

'This; and I know it's a grave thing to ask. Would you seriously object to my bringing the child over here, with its mother?'

'On the most strict understanding that we see nothing of The Dancing Master.'

'He will be only too glad to stay away. Polly, you're an angel. The woman really is at her wits' end.'

'And you know nothing about her, careless, and would hold her up to public scorn if it gave you a minute's amusement. Therefore you risk your life for the sake of her brat. No, Loo, *I'm* not the angel. I shall keep to my rooms and avoid her. But do as you please — only tell me why you do it.'

Mrs. Hauksbee's eyes softened; she looked out of the window and back into Mrs. Mallowe's face.

'I don't know,' said Mrs. Hauksbee simply.

'You dear!'

'Polly! — and for aught you knew you might have taken my fringe off. Never do that again without warning. Now we'll get the rooms ready. I don't suppose I shall be allowed to circulate in society for a month.'

'And I also. Thank goodness I shall at last get all the sleep I want.'

Much to Mrs. Bent's surprise she and the baby were brought over to the house almost before she knew where she was. Bent was devoutly and undisguisedly thankful, for he was afraid of the infection, and also hoped that a few weeks in the hotel alone with Mrs. Delville might lead to explanations. Mrs. Bent had thrown her jealousy to the winds in her fear for her child's life.

'We can give you good milk,' said Mrs. Hauksbee to her, 'and our house is much nearer to the Doctor's than the hotel, and you won't feel as though you were living in a hostile camp. Where is the dear Mrs. Waddy? She seemed to be a particular friend of yours.'

'They've all left me,' said Mrs. Bent bitterly. 'Mrs. Waddy went first. She said I ought to be ashamed of myself for introducing diseases there, and I am *sure* it wasn't my fault that little Dora——'

'How nice!' cooed Mrs. Hauksbee. 'The Waddy is an infectious disease herself — "more quickly caught than the plague and the taker runs presently mad." I lived next door to her at the Elysium, three years ago. Now see, you won't give us the *least* trouble, and I've ornamented all the house with sheets soaked in carbolic. It smells comforting, doesn't it? Remember I'm always in call, and my *ayah's* at your service when yours goes to her meals and — and — if you cry I'll *never* forgive you.'

Dora Bent occupied her mother's unprofitable attention through the day and the night. The Doctor called thrice in the twenty-four hours, and the house reeked with the smell of the Condy's Fluid, chlorine-water, and carbolic acid washes. Mrs. Mallowe kept to her own rooms — she considered that she had made sufficient concessions in the cause of humanity — and Mrs. Hauksbee was more esteemed by the Doctor as a help in the sick-room than the half-distraught mother.

'I know nothing of illness,' said Mrs. Hauksbee to the Doctor. 'Only tell me what to do, and I'll do it.'

'Keep that crazy woman from kissing the child, and let her have as little to do with the nursing as you possibly can,' said the Doctor; 'I'd turn her out of the sick-room, but that I honestly believe she'd die of anxiety. She is less than no good, and I depend on you and the *ayahs*, remember.'

Mrs. Hauksbee accepted the responsibility, though it painted olive hollows under her eyes and forced her to her oldest dresses. Mrs. Bent clung to her with more than childlike faith.

'I *know* you'll make Dora well, won't you?' she said at least twenty times a day; and twenty times a day Mrs. Hauksbee answered valiantly, 'Of course I will.'

But Dora did not improve, and the Doctor seemed to be always in the house.

'There's some danger of the thing taking a bad turn,' he said; 'I'll come over between three and four in the morning to-morrow.'

'Good gracious!' said Mrs. Hauksbee. 'He never told me what the turn would be! My education has been horribly neglected; and I have only this foolish mother-woman to fall back upon.'

The night wore through slowly, and Mrs. Hauksbee

dozed in a chair by the fire. There was a dance at the Viceregal Lodge, and she dreamed of it till she was aware of Mrs. Bent's anxious eyes staring into her own.

'Wake up! Wake up! Do something!' cried Mrs. Bent piteously. 'Dora's choking to death! Do you mean to let her die?'

Mrs. Hauksbee jumped to her feet and bent over the bed. The child was fighting for breath, while the mother wrung her hands despairing.

'Oh, what can I do? What can you do? She won't stay still! I can't hold her. Why didn't the Doctor say this was coming?' screamed Mrs. Bent. '*Won't* you help me? She's dying!'

'I — I've never seen a child die before!' stammered Mrs. Hauksbee feebly, and then — let none blame her weakness after the strain of long watching — she broke down, and covered her face with her hands. The *ayahs* on the threshold snored peacefully.

There was a rattle of *'rickshaw* wheels below, the clash of an opening door, a heavy step on the stairs, and Mrs. Delville entered to find Mrs. Bent screaming for the Doctor as she ran round the room. Mrs. Hauksbee, her hands to her ears, and her face buried in the chintz of a chair, was quivering with pain at each cry from the bed, and murmuring, 'Thank God, I never bore a child! Oh! thank God, I never bore a child!'

Mrs. Delville looked at the bed for an instant, took Mrs. Bent by the shoulders, and said quietly, 'Get me some caustic. Be quick.'

The mother obeyed mechanically. Mrs. Delville had thrown herself down by the side of the child and was opening its mouth.

'Oh, you're killing her!' cried Mrs. Bent. 'Where's the Doctor? Leave her alone!'

Mrs. Delville made no reply for a minute, but busied herself with the child.

'Now the caustic, and hold a lamp behind my shoulder. *Will* you do as you are told? The acid-bottle, if you don't know what I mean,' she said.

A second time Mrs. Delville bent over the child. Mrs. Hauksbee, her face still hidden, sobbed and shivered. One of the *ayahs* staggered sleepily into the room, yawning: '*Doctor Sahib* come.'

Mrs. Delville turned her head.

'You're only just in time,' she said. 'It was chokin' her when I came an' I've burnt it.'

'There was no sign of the membrane getting to the air-passages after the last steaming. It was the general weakness, I feared,' said the Doctor half to himself, and he whispered as he looked, 'You've done what I should have been afraid to do without consultation.'

'She was dyin',' said Mrs. Delville, under her breath. 'Can you do anythin'? What a mercy it was I went to the dance!'

Mrs. Hauksbee raised her head.

'Is it all over?' she gasped. 'I'm useless — I'm worse than useless! What are *you* doing here?'

She stared at Mrs. Delville, and Mrs. Bent, realising for the first time who was the Goddess from the Machine, stared also.

Then Mrs. Delville made explanation, putting on a dirty long glove and smoothing a crumpled and ill-fitting ball-dress.

'I was at the dance, an' the Doctor was tellin' me about your baby bein' so ill. So I came away early, an' your door was open, an' I — I — lost my boy this way six months ago, an' I've been tryin' to forget it ever since, an' I — I — I am very sorry for intrudin' an' anythin' that has happened.'

Mrs. Bent was putting out the Doctor's eye with a lamp as he stooped over Dora.

'Take it away,' said the Doctor. 'I think the child will do, thanks to you, Mrs. Delville. *I* should have come too late, but, I assure you' — he was addressing himself to Mrs. Delville — 'I had not the faintest reason to expect *this*. The membrane must have grown like a mushroom. Will one of you help me, please ?'

He had reason for the last sentence. Mrs. Hauksbee had thrown herself into Mrs. Delville's arms, where she was weeping bitterly, and Mrs. Bent was unpicturesquely mixed up with · both, while from the tangle came the sound of many sobs and much promiscuous kissing.

'Good gracious! I've spoilt all your beautiful roses!' said Mrs. Hauksbee, lifting her head from the lump of crushed gum and calico atrocities on Mrs. Delville's shoulder and hurrying to the Doctor.

Mrs. Delville picked up her shawl, and slouched out of the room, mopping her eyes with the glove that she had not put on.

'I always said she was more than a woman,' sobbed Mrs. Hauksbee hysterically, 'and *that* proves it!'

*　*　*　*　*　*　*　*　*

Six weeks later, Mrs. Bent and Dora had returned to the hotel. Mrs. Hauksbee had come out of the Valley of Humiliation, had ceased to reproach herself for her collapse in an hour of need, and was even beginning to direct the affairs of the world as before.

'So nobody died, and everything went off as it should, and I kissed The Dowd, Polly. I feel so old. Does it show in my face ?'

'Kisses don't as a rule, do they? Of course you know what the result of The Dowd's providential arrival has been.'

'They ought to build her a statue—only no sculptor dare copy those skirts.'

'Ah!' said Mrs. Mallowe quietly. 'She has found another reward. The Dancing Master has been smirking through Simla, giving every one to understand that she came because of her undying love for him—for him—to save *his* child, and all Simla naturally believes this.'

'But Mrs. Bent——'

'Mrs. Bent believes it more than any one else. She won't speak to The Dowd now. *Isn't* The Dancing Master an angel?'

Mrs. Hauksbee lifted up her voice and raged till bedtime. The doors of the two rooms stood open.

'Polly,' said a voice from the darkness, 'what did that American-heiress-globe-trotter girl say last season when she was tipped out of her *'rickshaw* turning a corner? Some absurd adjective that made the man who picked her up explode.'

'"Paltry,"' said Mrs. Mallowe. 'Through her nose—like this—"Ha-ow pahltry!"'

'Exactly,' said the voice. 'Ha-ow pahltry it all is!'

'Which?'

'Everything. Babies, Diphtheria, Mrs. Bent and The Dancing Master, I whooping in a chair, and The Dowd dropping in from the clouds. I wonder what the motive was—*all* the motives.'

'Um!'

'What do *you* think?'

'Don't ask me. Go to sleep.'

ONLY A SUBALTERN

. . . Not only to enforce by command but to encourage by example the energetic discharge of duty and the steady endurance of the difficulties and privations inseparable from Military Service. — *Bengal Army Regulations.*

THEY made Bobby Wick pass an examination at Sandhurst. He was a gentleman before he was gazetted, so, when the Empress announced that 'Gentleman-Cadet Robert Hanna Wick' was posted as Second Lieutenant to the Tyneside Tail Twisters at Krab Bokhar, he became an officer *and* a gentleman, which is an enviable thing ; and there was joy in the house of Wick where Mamma Wick and all the little Wicks fell upon their knees and offered incense to Bobby by virtue of his achievements.

Papa Wick had been a Commissioner in his day, holding authority over three millions of men in the Chota-Buldana Division, building great works for the good of the land, and doing his best to make two blades of grass grow where there was but one before. Of course, nobody knew anything about this in the little English village where he was just 'old Mr. Wick' and had forgotten that he was a Companion of the Order of the Star of India.

He patted Bobby on the shoulder and said: 'Well done, my boy ! '

There followed, while the uniform was being prepared, an interval of pure delight, during which Bobby took brevet-rank as a 'man' at the women-swamped tennis-parties and tea-fights of the village, and, I daresay, had his joining-time been extended, would have fallen in love with several girls at once. Little country villages at Home are very full of nice girls, because all the young men come out to India to make their fortunes.

'India,' said Papa Wick, 'is the place. I've had thirty years of it and, begad, I'd like to go back again. When you join the Tail Twisters you'll be among friends, if every one hasn't forgotten Wick of Chota-Buldana, and a lot of people will be kind to you for our sakes. The mother will tell you more about outfit than I can, but remember this. Stick to your Regiment, Bobby—stick to your Regiment. You'll see men all round you going into the Staff Corps, and doing every possible sort of duty but regimental, and you may be tempted to follow suit. Now so long as you keep within your allowance, and I haven't stinted you there, stick to the Line, the whole Line and nothing but the Line. Be careful how you back another young fool's bill, and if you fall in love with a woman twenty years older than yourself, don't tell *me* about it, that's all.'

With these counsels, and many others equally valuable, did Papa Wick fortify Bobby ere that last awful night at Portsmouth when the Officers' Quarters held more inmates than were provided for by the Regulations, and the liberty-men of the ships fell foul of the drafts for India, and the battle raged from the Dockyard Gates even to the slums of Longport, while the drabs of Fratton came down and scratched the faces of the Queen's Officers.

Bobby Wick, with an ugly bruise on his freckled nose, a sick and shaky detachment to manœuvre inship and the comfort of fifty scornful females to attend to, had no time to feel homesick till the *Malabar* reached mid-Channel, when he doubled his emotions with a little guard-visiting and a great many other matters.

The Tail Twisters were a most particular Regiment. Those who knew them least said that they were eaten up with 'side.' But their reserve and their internal arrangements generally were merely protective diplomacy. Some five years before, the Colonel commanding had looked into the fourteen fearless eyes of seven plump and juicy subalterns who had all applied to enter the Staff Corps, and had asked them why the three stars should he, a colonel of the Line, command a dashed nursery for double-dashed bottle-suckers who put on condemned tin spurs and rode qualified mokes at the hiatused heads of forsaken Black Regiments. He was a rude man and a terrible. Wherefore the remnant took measures [with the half-butt as an engine of public opinion] till the rumour went abroad that young men who used the Tail Twisters as a crutch to the Staff Corps, had many and varied trials to endure. However, a regiment had just as much right to its own secrets as a woman.

When Bobby came up from Deolali and took his place among the Tail Twisters, it was gently but firmly borne in upon him that the Regiment was his father and his mother and his indissolubly wedded wife, and that there was no crime under the canopy of heaven blacker than that of bringing shame on the Regiment, which was the best-shooting, best-drilled, best set-up, bravest, most illustrious, and in all respects most desirable Regiment within the compass of the Seven Seas. He was taught the legends of the Mess Plate, from the great

H

grinning Golden Gods that had come out of the Summer Palace in Pekin to the silver-mounted markhor-horn snuff-mull presented by the last C. O. [he who spake to the seven subalterns]. And every one of those legends told him of battles fought at long odds, without fear as without support; of hospitality catholic as an Arab's; of friendships deep as the sea and steady as the fighting-line; of honour won by hard roads for honour's sake; and of instant and unquestioning devotion to the Regiment — the Regiment that claims the lives of all and lives for ever.

More than once, too, he came officially into contact with the Regimental colours, which looked like the lining of a bricklayer's hat on the end of a chewed stick. Bobby did not kneel and worship them, because British subalterns are not constructed in that manner. Indeed, he condemned them for their weight at the very moment that they were filling with awe and other more noble sentiments.

But best of all was the occasion when he moved with the Tail Twisters in review order at the breaking of a November day. Allowing for duty-men and sick, the Regiment was one thousand and eighty strong, and Bobby belonged to them; for was he not a Subaltern of the Line — the whole Line and nothing but the Line — as the tramp of two thousand one hundred and sixty sturdy ammunition boots attested? He would not have changed places with Deighton of the Horse Battery, whirling by in a pillar of cloud to a chorus of 'Strong right! Strong left!' or Hogan-Yale of the White Hussars, leading his squadron for all it was worth, with the price of horseshoes thrown in; or 'Tick' Boileau, trying to live up to his fierce blue and gold turban while the wasps of the Bengal Cavalry stretched to a gallop in the wake of the long, lollopping Walers of the White Hussars.

They fought through the clear cool day, and Bobby felt a little thrill run down his spine when he heard the *tinkle-tinkle-tinkle* of the empty cartridge-cases hopping from the breech-blocks after the roar of the volleys; for he knew that he should live to hear that sound in action. The review ended in a glorious chase across the plain — batteries thundering after cavalry to the huge disgust of the White Hussars, and the Tyneside Tail Twisters hunting a Sikh Regiment, till the lean lathy Singhs panted with exhaustion. Bobby was dusty and dripping long before noon, but his enthusiasm was merely focused — not diminished.

He returned to sit at the feet of Revere, his 'skipper,' that is to say, the Captain of his Company, and to be instructed in the dark art and mystery of managing men, which is a very large part of the Profession of Arms.

'If you haven't a taste that way,' said Revere between his puffs of his cheroot, 'you'll never be able to get the hang of it, but remember, Bobby, 'tisn't the best drill, though drill is nearly everything, that hauls a Regiment through Hell and out on the other side. It's the man who knows how to handle men — goat-men, swine-men, dog-men, and so on.'

'Dormer, for instance,' said Bobby, 'I think he comes under the head of fool-men. He mopes like a sick owl.'

'That's where you make your mistake, my son. Dormer isn't a fool *yet*, but he's a dashed dirty soldier, and his room corporal makes fun of his socks before

kit-inspection.   Dormer, being two-thirds pure brute,
goes into a corner and growls.'

'How do you know?' said Bobby admiringly.

'Because a Company commander has to know these
things — because, if he does *not* know, he may have
crime — ay, murder — brewing under his very nose
and yet not see that it's there.   Dormer is being badg-
ered out of his mind — big as he is — and he hasn't
intellect enough to resent it.   He's taken to quiet
boozing and, Bobby, when the butt of a room goes on
the drink, or takes to moping by himself, measures are
necessary to pull him out of himself.'

'What measures?   'Man can't run round coddling
his men for ever.'

'No.   The men would precious soon show him that
he was not wanted.   You've got to —— '

Here the Colour-sergeant entered with some papers ;
Bobby reflected for a while as Revere looked through
the Company forms.

'Does Dormer do anything, Sergeant?' Bobby
asked with the air of one continuing an interrupted
conversation.

'No, sir.   Does 'is dooty like a hortomato,' said the
Sergeant, who delighted in long words.   'A dirty soldier, and 'e's under full stoppages for new kit.   It's
covered with scales, sir.'

'Scales?   What scales?'

'Fish-scales, sir.   'E's always pokin' in the mud
by the river an' a-cleanin' them *muchly*-fish with 'is
thumbs.'   Revere was still absorbed in the Company
papers, and the Sergeant, who was sternly fond of
Bobby, continued, — ' 'E generally goes down there
when 'e's got 'is skinful, beggin' your pardon, sir, an'

they *do* say that the more lush — in-*he*-briated 'e is, the more fish 'e catches. They call 'im the Looney Fishmonger in the Comp'ny, sir.'

Revere signed the last paper and the Sergeant retreated.

'It's a filthy amusement,' sighed Bobby to himself. Then aloud to Revere : 'Are you really worried about Dormer ? '

'A little. You see he's never mad enough to send to hospital, or drunk enough to run in, but at any minute he may flare up, brooding and sulking as he does. He resents any interest being shown in him, and the only time I took him out shooting he all but shot *me* by accident.'

'I fish,' said Bobby with a wry face. 'I hire a country-boat and go down the river from Thursday to Sunday, and the amiable Dormer goes with me — if you can spare us both.'

'You blazing young fool ! ' said Revere, but his heart was full of much more pleasant words.

Bobby, the Captain of a *dhoni*, with Private Dormer for mate, dropped down the river on Thursday morning — the Private at the bow, the Subaltern at the helm. The Private glared uneasily at the Subaltern, who respected the reserve of the Private.

After six hours, Dormer paced to the stern, saluted, and said — 'Beg y' pardon, sir, but *was* you ever on the Durh'm Canal ? '

'No,' said Bobby Wick. 'Come and have some tiffin.'

They ate in silence. As the evening fell, Private Dormer broke forth, speaking to himself —

'Hi was on the Durh'm Canal, jes' such a night,

come next week twelve month, a-trailin' *of* my toes in the water.' He smoked and said no more till bedtime.

The witchery of the dawn turned the gray river-reaches to purple, gold, and opal; and it was as though the lumbering *dhoni* crept across the splendours of a new heaven.

Private Dormer popped his head out of his blanket and gazed at the glory below and around.

'Well — damn — my eyes!' said Private Dormer in an awed whisper. 'This 'ere is like a bloomin' gallantry-show!' For the rest of the day he was dumb, but achieved an ensanguined filthiness through the cleaning of big fish.

The boat returned on Saturday evening. Dormer had been struggling with speech since noon. As the lines and luggage were being disembarked, he found tongue.

'Beg y' pardon, sir,' he said, 'but would you — would you min' shakin' 'ands with me, sir?'

'Of course not,' said Bobby, and he shook accordingly. Dormer returned to barracks and Bobby to mess.

'He wanted a little quiet and some fishing, I think,' said Bobby. 'My aunt, but he's a filthy sort of animal! Have you ever seen him clean " them, *muchly-* fish with 'is thumbs"?'

'Anyhow,' said Revere three weeks later, 'he's doing his best to keep his things clean.'

When the spring died, Bobby joined in the general scramble for Hill leave, and to his surprise and delight secured three months.

'As good a boy as I want,' said Revere the admiring skipper.

'The best of the batch,' said the Adjutant to the Colonel. 'Keep back that young skrimshanker Porkiss, sir, and let Revere make him sit up.'

So Bobby departed joyously to Simla Pahar with a tin box of gorgeous raiment.

''Son of Wick — old Wick of Chota-Buldana? Ask him to dinner, dear,' said the aged men.

'What a nice boy!' said the matrons and the maids.

'First-class place, Simla. Oh, ri—ipping!' said Bobby Wick, and ordered new white cord breeches on the strength of it.

'We're in a bad way,' wrote Revere to Bobby at the end of two months. 'Since you left, the Regiment has taken to fever and is fairly rotten with it — two hundred in hospital, about a hundred in cells — drinking to keep off fever — and the Companies on parade fifteen file strong at the outside. There's rather more sickness in the out-villages than I care for, but then I'm so blistered with prickly-heat that I'm ready to hang myself. What's the yarn about your mashing a Miss Haverley up there? Not serious, I hope? You're over-young to hang millstones round your neck, and the Colonel will turf you out of that in double-quick time if you attempt it.'

It was not the Colonel that brought Bobby out of Simla, but a much more to be respected Commandant. The sickness in the out-villages spread, the Bazar was put out of bounds, and then came the news that the Tail Twisters must go into camp. The message flashed to the Hill stations. — 'Cholera — Leave stopped — Officers recalled.' Alas, for the white gloves in the neatly soldered boxes, the rides and the dances and picnics that were to be, the loves half spoken, and the debts unpaid! Without demur and without question, fast as tonga could fly or pony gallop, back to their Regiments and their Batteries, as though they were hastening to their weddings, fled the subalterns.

Bobby received his orders on returning from a dance at Viceregal Lodge where he had —— but only the Haverley girl knows what Bobby had said or how many waltzes he had claimed for the next ball. Six in the morning saw Bobby at the Tonga Office in the drenching rain, the whirl of the last waltz still in his ears, and an intoxication due neither to wine nor waltzing in his brain.

'Good man!' shouted Deighton of the Horse Battery through the mists. 'Whar you raise dat tonga? I'm coming with you. Ow! But I've a head and half. *I* didn't sit out all night. They say the Battery's awful bad, and he hummed dolorously —

> 'Leave the what at the what's-its-name,
> Leave the flock without shelter,
> Leave the corpse uninterred,
> Leave the bride at the altar!

'My faith! It'll be more bally corpse than bride, though, this journey. Jump in, Bobby. Get on, *Coachwan!*'

On the Umballa platform waited a detachment of officers discussing the latest news from the stricken cantonment, and it was here that Bobby learned the real condition of the Tail Twisters.

'They went into camp,' said an elderly Major recalled from the whist-tables at Mussoorie to a sickly Native Regiment, 'they went into camp with two hundred and ten sick in carts. Two hundred and ten fever cases only, and the balance looking like so many ghosts with sore eyes. A Madras Regiment could have walked through 'em.'

'But they were as fit as be-damned when I left them!' said Bobby.

'Then you'd better make them as fit as be-damned when you rejoin,' said the Major brutally.

Bobby pressed his forehead against the rain-splashed window pane as the train lumbered across the sodden Doab, and prayed for the health of the Tyneside Tail Twisters. Naini Tal had sent down her contingent with all speed; the lathering ponies of the Dalhousie Road staggered into Pathankot, taxed to the full stretch of their strength; while from cloudy Darjiling the Calcutta Mail whirled up the last straggler of the little army that was to fight a fight, in which was neither medal nor honour for the winning, against an enemy none other than 'the sickness that destroyeth in the noonday.'

And as each man reported himself, he said: 'This is a bad business,' and went about his own forthwith, for every Regiment and Battery in the cantonment was under canvas, the sickness bearing them company.

Bobby fought his way through the rain to the Tail Twisters' temporary mess, and Revere could have fallen on the boy's neck for the joy of seeing that ugly, wholesome phiz once more.

'Keep 'em amused and interested,' said Revere. 'They went on the drink, poor fools, after the first two cases, and there was no improvement. Oh, it's good to have you back, Bobby! Porkiss is a — never mind.'

Deighton came over from the Artillery camp to

attend a dreary mess dinner, and contributed to the
general gloom by nearly weeping over the condition of
his beloved Battery. Porkiss so far forgot himself as
to insinuate that the presence of the officers could do
no earthly good, and that the best thing would be to
send the entire Regiment into hospital and 'let the
doctors look after them.' Porkiss was demoralised
with fear, nor was his peace of mind restored when
Revere said coldly: 'Oh! The sooner *you* go out the
better, if that's your way of thinking. Any public
school could send us fifty *good* men in your place, but
it takes time, time, Porkiss, and money, and a certain
amount of trouble, to make a Regiment. 'S'pose *you're*
the person we go into camp for, eh?'

Whereupon Porkiss was overtaken with a great and
chilly fear which a drenching in the rain did not allay,
and, two days later, quitted this world for another
where, men do fondly hope, allowances are made for
the weaknesses of the flesh. The Regimental Sergeant-
Major looked wearily across the Sergeants' Mess tent
when the news was announced.

'There goes the worst of them,' he said. 'It'll take
the best, and then, please God, it'll stop.' The Sergeants were silent till one said: 'It couldn't be *him!*'
and all knew of whom Travis was thinking.

Bobby Wick stormed through the tents of his Company, rallying, rebuking, mildly, as is consistent with
the Regulations, chaffing the faint-hearted; haling the
sound into the watery sunlight when there was a break
in the weather, and bidding them be of good cheer for
their trouble was nearly at an end; scuttling on his
dun pony round the outskirts of the camp and heading
back men who, with the innate perversity of British

soldiers, were always wandering into infected villages, or drinking deeply from rain-flooded marshes; comforting the panic-stricken with rude speech, and more than once tending the dying who had no friends — the men without 'townies'; organising, with banjos and burnt cork, Sing-songs which should allow the talent of the Regiment full play; and generally, as he explained, 'playing the giddy garden-goat all round.'

' You're worth half a dozen of us, Bobby,' said Revere in a moment of enthusiasm. ' How the devil do you keep it up?'

Bobby made no answer, but had Revere looked into the breast-pocket of his coat he might have seen there a sheaf of badly-written letters which perhaps accounted for the power that possessed the boy. A letter came to Bobby every other day. The spelling was not above reproach, but the sentiments must have been most satisfactory, for on receipt Bobby's eyes softened marvellously, and he was wont to fall into a tender abstraction for a while ere, shaking his cropped head, he charged into his work.

By what power he drew after him the hearts of the roughest, and the Tail Twisters counted in their ranks some rough diamonds indeed, was a mystery to both skipper and C. O., who learned from the regimental chaplain that Bobby was considerably more in request in the hospital tents than the Reverend John Emery.

' The men seem fond of you. Are you in the hospitals much?' said the Colonel, who did his daily round and ordered the men to get well with a hardness that did not cover his bitter grief.

' A little, sir,' said Bobby.

' 'Shouldn't go there too often if I were you. They

say it's not contagious, but there's no use in running unnecessary risks. We can't afford to have you down, y' know.'

Six days later, it was with the utmost difficulty that the post-runner plashed his way out to the camp with the mail-bags, for the rain was falling in torrents. Bobby received a letter, bore it off to his tent, and, the programme for the next week's Sing-song being satisfactorily disposed of, sat down to answer it. For an hour the unhandy pen toiled over the paper, and where sentiment rose to more than normal tide-level, Bobby Wick stuck out his tongue and breathed heavily. He was not used to letter-writing.

'Beg y' pardon, sir,' said a voice at the tent door; 'but Dormer's 'orrid bad, sir, an' they've taken him orf, sir.'

'Damn Private Dormer and you too!' said Bobby Wick, running the blotter over the half-finished letter. 'Tell him I'll come in the morning.'

''E's awful bad, sir,' said the voice hesitatingly. There was an undecided squelching of heavy boots.

'Well?' said Bobby impatiently.

'Excusin' 'imself before'and for takin' the liberty, 'e says it would be a comfort for to assist 'im, sir, if——'

'*Tattoo lao!* Get my pony! Here, come in out of the rain till I'm ready. What blasted nuisances you are! That's brandy. Drink some; you want it. Hang on to my stirrup and tell me if I go too fast.

Strengthened by a four-finger 'nip' which he swallowed without a wink, the Hospital Orderly kept up with the slipping, mud-stained, and very disgusted pony as it shambled to the hospital tent.

Private Dormer was certainly ''orrid bad.' He

had all but reached the stage of collapse and was not pleasant to look upon.

'What's this, Dormer?' said Bobby, bending over the man. 'You're not going out this time. You've got to come fishing with me once or twice more yet.'

The blue lips parted and in the ghost of a whisper said, — 'Beg y' pardon, sir, disturbin' of you now, but would you min' 'oldin' my 'and, sir?'

Bobby sat on the side of the bed, and the icy cold hand closed on his own like a vice, forcing a lady's ring which was on the little finger deep into the flesh. Bobby set his lips and waited, the water dripping from the hem of his trousers. An hour passed and the grasp of the hand did not relax, nor did the expression of the drawn face change. Bobby with infinite craft lit himself a cheroot with the left hand, his right arm was numbed to the elbow, and resigned himself to a night of pain.

Dawn showed a very white-faced Subaltern sitting on the side of a sick man's cot, and a Doctor in the doorway using language unfit for publication.

'Have you been here all night, you young ass?' said the Doctor.

'There or thereabouts,' said Bobby ruefully. 'He's frozen on to me.'

Dormer's mouth shut with a click. He turned his head and sighed. The clinging hand opened, and Bobby's arm fell useless at his side.

'He'll do,' said the Doctor quietly. 'It must have been a toss-up all through the night. 'Think you're to be congratulated on this case.'

'Oh, bosh!' said Bobby. 'I thought the man had gone out long ago — only — only I didn't care to take

my hand away. Rub my arm down, there's a good
chap. What a grip the brute has ! I'm chilled to the
marrow ! ' He passed out of the tent shivering.

Private Dormer was allowed to celebrate his repulse
of Death by strong waters. Four days later, he sat on
the side of his cot and said to the patients mildly: ' I'd
'a' liken to 'a' spoken to 'im — so I should.'

But at that time Bobby was reading yet another letter — he had the most persistent correspondent of any
man in camp — and was even then about to write that
the sickness had abated, and in another week at the outside would be gone. He did not intend to say that the
chill of a sick man's hand seemed to have struck into
the heart whose capacities for affection he dwelt on at
such length. He did intend to enclose the illustrated
programme of the forthcoming Sing-song whereof he
was not a little proud. He also intended to write on
many other matters which do not concern us, and doubt-
less would have done so but for the slight feverish head-
ache which made him dull and unresponsive at mess.

'You are overdoing it, Bobby,' said his skipper.
' 'Might give the rest of us credit of doing a little
work. You go on as if you were the whole Mess
rolled into one. Take it easy.'

' I will,' said Bobby. ' I'm feeling done up, somehow.' Revere looked at him anxiously and said nothing.

There was a flickering of lanterns about the camp
that night, and a rumour that brought men out of
their cots to the tent doors, a paddling of the naked
feet of doolie-bearers and the rush of a galloping horse.

' Wot's up ? ' asked twenty tents ; and through
twenty tents ran the answer — ' Wick, 'e's down.'

They brought the news to Revere and he groaned.
'Any one but Bobby and I shouldn't have cared! The
Sergeant-Major was right.'

'Not going out this journey,' gasped Bobby, as he
was lifted from the doolie. 'Not going out this journey.' Then with an air of supreme conviction — 'I
can't, you see.'

'Not if I can do anything!' said the Surgeon-Major,
who had hastened over from the mess where he had
been dining.

He and the Regimental Surgeon fought together with
Death for the life of Bobby Wick. Their work was
interrupted by a hairy apparition in a blue-gray dress-
ing-gown who stared in horror at the bed and cried —
'Oh, my Gawd! It can't be *'im!*' until an indignant
Hospital Orderly whisked him away.

If care of man and desire to live could have done
aught, Bobby would have been saved. As it was, he
made a fight of three days, and the Surgeon-Major's
brow uncreased. 'We'll save him yet,' he said; and
the Surgeon, who, though he ranked with the Captain,
had a very youthful heart, went out upon the word and
pranced joyously in the mud.

'Not going out this journey,' whispered Bobby Wick
gallantly, at the end of the third day.

'Bravo!' said the Surgeon-Major. 'That's the way
to look at it, Bobby.'

As evening fell a gray shade gathered round Bobby's
mouth, and he turned his face to the tent wall wearily.
The Surgeon-Major frowned.

'I'm awfully tired,' said Bobby, very faintly. 'What's
the use of bothering me with medicine? I — don't —
want — it. Let me alone.'

The desire for life had departed, and Bobby was content to drift away on the easy tide of Death.

'It's no good,' said the Surgeon-Major. 'He doesn't want to live. He's meeting it, poor child.' And he blew his nose.

Half a mile away, the regimental band was playing the overture to the Sing-song, for the men had been told that Bobby was out of danger. The clash of the brass and the wail of the horns reached Bobby's ears.

> Is there a single joy or pain,
> That I should never kno—ow?
> You do not love me, 'tis in vain,
> Bid me good-bye and go!

An expression of hopeless irritation crossed the boy's face, and he tried to shake his head.

The Surgeon-Major bent down — 'What is it? Bobby?' — 'Not that waltz,' muttered Bobby. 'That's our own — our very ownest own. . . . Mummy dear.'

With this he sank into the stupor that gave place to death early next morning.

Revere, his eyes red at the rims and his nose very white, went into Bobby's tent to write a letter to Papa Wick which should bow the white head of the ex-Commissioner of Chota-Buldana in the keenest sorrow of his life. Bobby's little store of papers lay in confusion on the table, and among them a half-finished letter. The last sentence ran: 'So you see, darling, there is really no fear, because as long as I know you care for me and I care for you, nothing can touch me.'

Revere stayed in the tent for an hour. When he came out, his eyes were redder than ever.

* * * * * * * * *

Private Conklin sat on a turned-down bucket, and listened to a not unfamiliar tune. Private Conklin was a convalescent and should have been tenderly treated.

'Ho!' said Private Conklin. 'There's another bloomin' orf'cer da—ed.'

The bucket shot from under him, and his eyes filled with a smithyful of sparks. A tall man in a blue-gray bedgown was regarding him with deep disfavour.

'You ought to take shame for yourself, Conky! Orf'cer?—bloomin' orf'cer? I'll learn you to mis-name the likes of 'im. Hangel! *Bloomin*' Hangel! That's wot 'e is!'

And the Hospital Orderly was so satisfied with the justice of the punishment that he did not even order Private Dormer back to his cot.

THE PHANTOM 'RICKSHAW

May no ill dreams disturb my rest,
Nor Powers of Darkness me molest.

Evening Hymn.

ONE of the few advantages that India has over England is a great Knowability. After five years' service a
man is directly or indirectly acquainted with the two or
three hundred Civilians in his Province, all the Messes
of ten or twelve Regiments and Batteries, and some
fifteen hundred other people of the non-official caste.
In ten years his knowledge should be doubled, and at
the end of twenty he knows, or knows something about,
every Englishman in the Empire, and may travel anywhere and everywhere without paying hotel-bills.

Globe-trotters who expect entertainment as a right,
have, even within my memory, blunted this open-heart-
edness, but none the less to-day, if you belong to the
Inner Circle and are neither a Bear nor a Black Sheep,
all houses are open to you, and our small world is very,
very kind and helpful.

Rickett of Kamartha stayed with Polder of Kumaon
some fifteen years ago. He meant to stay two nights,
but was knocked down by rheumatic fever, and for
six weeks disorganised Polder's establishment, stopped
Polder's work, and nearly died in Polder's bedroom.
Polder behaves as though he had been placed under
eternal obligation by Rickett, and yearly sends the little
Ricketts a box of presents and toys. It is the same

everywhere. The men who do not take the trouble to conceal from you their opinion that you are an incompetent ass, and the women who blacken your character and misunderstand your wife's amusements, will work themselves to the bone in your behalf if you fall sick or into serious trouble.

Heatherlegh, the Doctor, kept, in addition to his regular practice, a hospital on his private account—an arrangement of loose boxes for Incurables, his friend called it—but it was really a sort of fitting-up shed for craft that had been damaged by stress of weather. The weather in India is often sultry, and since the tale of bricks is always a fixed quantity, and the only liberty allowed is permission to work overtime and get no thanks, men occasionally break down and become as mixed as the metaphors in this sentence.

Heatherlegh is the dearest doctor that ever was, and his invariable prescription to all his patients is, 'Lie low, go slow, and keep cool.' He says that more men are killed by overwork than the importance of this world justifies. He maintains that overwork slew Pansay, who died under his hands about three years ago. He has, of course, the right to speak authoritatively, and he laughs at my theory that there was a crack in Pansay's head and a little bit of the Dark World came through and pressed him to death. 'Pansay went off the handle,' says Heatherlegh, 'after the stimulus of long leave at Home. He may or he may not have behaved like a blackguard to Mrs. Keith-Wessington. My notion is that the work of the Kata-bundi Settlement ran him off his legs, and that he took to brooding and making much of an ordinary P. & O. flirtation. He certainly was engaged to Miss Mannering, and she certainly broke off the engagement. Then he took a feverish chill and all that nonsense about ghosts developed. Overwork started his illness, kept it alight, and killed him, poor devil. Write him off to the System that uses one man to do the work of two and a half men.'

I do not believe this. I used to sit up with Pansay sometimes when Heatherlegh was called out to patients and I happened to be within claim. The man would make me most unhappy by describing in a low, even voice, the procession that was always passing at the bottom of his bed. He had a sick man's command of language. When he recovered I suggested that he should write out the whole affair from beginning to end, knowing that ink might assist him to ease his mind.

He was in a high fever while he was writing, and the blood-and-thunder Magazine diction he adopted did not calm him. Two months afterwards he was reported fit for duty, but, in spite of the fact that he was urgently needed to help an undermanned Commission stagger through a deficit, he preferred to die; vowing at the last that he was hag-ridden. I got his manuscript before he died, and this is his version of the affair, dated 1885, exactly as he wrote it : —

My doctor tells me that I need rest and change of air. It is not improbable that I shall get both ere long — rest that neither the red-coated messenger nor the mid-day gun can break, and change of air far beyond that which any homeward-bound steamer can give me. In the meantime I am resolved to stay where I am ; and, in flat defiance of my doctor's orders, to take all the world into my confidence. You shall learn for yourselves the precise nature of my malady, and shall, too, judge for yourselves whether any man born of woman on this weary earth was ever so tormented as I.

Speaking now as a condemned criminal might speak ere the drop-bolts are drawn, my story, wild and hideously improbable as it may appear, demands at least attention. That it will ever receive credence I utterly disbelieve. Two months ago I should have scouted as mad or drunk the man who had dared tell me the like. Two months ago I was the happiest man in India. To-day, from Peshawar to the sea, there is no one more wretched. My doctor and I are the only two who know this. His explanation is, that my brain, digestion, and eyesight are all slightly affected; giving rise to my frequent and persistent 'delusions.' Delusions, indeed! I call him a fool; but he attends me still with the same unwearied smile, the same bland professional manner, the same neatly-trimmed red whiskers, till I begin to suspect that I am an ungrateful, evil-tempered invalid. But you shall judge for yourselves.

Three years ago it was my fortune — my great misfortune — to sail from Gravesend to Bombay, on return from long leave, with one Agnes Keith-Wessington, wife of an officer on the Bombay side. It does not in the least concern you to know what manner of woman she was. Be content with the knowledge that, ere the voyage had ended, both she and I were desperately and unreasoningly in love with one another. Heaven knows that I can make the admission now without one particle of vanity. In matters of this sort there is always one who gives and another who accepts. From the first day of our ill-omened attachment, I was conscious that Agnes's passion was a stronger, a more dominant, and — if I may use the expression — a purer sentiment than mine. Whether she recognised the fact then, I do not know. Afterwards it was bitterly plain to both of us.

Arrived at Bombay in the spring of the year, we went our respective ways, to meet no more for the next three or four months, when my leave and her love took us both to Simla. There we spent the season together; and there my fire of straw burnt itself out to a pitiful end with the closing year. I attempt no excuse. I make no apology. Mrs. Wessington had given up much for my sake, and was prepared to give up all. From my own lips, in August 1882, she learnt that I was sick of her presence, tired of her company, and weary of the sound of her voice. Ninety-nine women out of a hundred would wearied of me as I wearied of them; seventy-five of that number would have promptly avenged themselves by active and obtrusive flirtation with other men. Mrs. Wessington was the hundredth. On her neither my openly-expressed aversion nor the cutting brutalities with which I garnished our interviews had the least effect.

'Jack, darling!' was her one eternal cuckoo cry: 'I'm sure it's all a mistake — a hideous mistake ; and we'll be good friends again some day. *Please* forgive me, Jack, dear.'

I was the offender, and I knew it. That knowledge transformed my pity into passive endurance, and, eventually, into blind hate — the same instinct, I suppose, which prompts a man to savagely stamp on the spider he has but half killed. And with this

hate in my bosom the season of 1882 came to an
end.

Next year we met again at Simla — she with her
monotonous face and timid attempts at reconciliation,
and I with loathing of her in every fibre of my frame.
Several times I could not avoid meeting her alone ; and
on each occasion her words were identically the same.
Still the unreasoning wail that it was all a 'mistake';
and still the hope of eventually 'making friends.'   I
might have seen, had I cared to look, that that hope
only was keeping her alive.   She grew more wan and
thin month by month.   You will agree with me, at
least, that such conduct would have driven any one to
despair.   It was uncalled for ; childish ; unwomanly.
I maintain that she was much to blame.   And again,
sometimes, in the black, fever-stricken night-watches,
I have begun to think that I might have been a little
kinder to her.   But that really *is* a 'delusion.'   I could
not have continued pretending to love her when I didn't;
could I ?   It would have been unfair to us both.

Last year we met again — on the same terms as
before.   The same weary appeals, and the same curt
answers from my lips.   At least I would make her see
how wholly wrong and hopeless were her attempts at
resuming the old relationship.   As the season wore on,
we fell apart — that is to say, she found it difficult to
meet me, for I had other and more absorbing interests
to attend to.   When I think it over quietly in my sick-
room, the season of 1884 seems a confused nightmare
wherein light and shade were fantastically intermingled
— my courtship of little Kitty Mannering ; my hopes,
doubts, and fears ; our long rides together ; my trembling avowal of attachment ; her reply ; and now and

again a vision of a white face flitting by in the 'rickshaw with the black and white liveries I once watched for so earnestly; the wave of Mrs. Wessington's gloved hand; and, when she met me alone, which was but seldom, the irksome monotony of her appeal. I loved Kitty Mannering; honestly, heartily loved her, and with my love for her grew my hatred for Agnes. In August Kitty and I were engaged. The next day I met those accursed 'mag-pie' *jhampanies* at the back of Jakko, and, moved by some passing sentiment of pity, stopped to tell Mrs. Wessington everything. She knew it already.

'So I hear you're engaged, Jack dear.' Then, without a moment's pause: 'I'm sure it's all a mistake—a hideous mistake. We shall be as good friends some day, Jack, as we ever were.'

My answer might have made even a man wince. It cut the dying woman before me like the blow of a whip. 'Please forgive me, Jack; I didn't mean to make you angry; but it's true, it's true!'

And Mrs. Wessington broke down completely. I turned away and left her to finish her journey in peace, feeling, but only for a moment or two, that I had been an unutterably mean hound. I looked back, and saw that she had turned her 'rickshaw with the idea, I suppose, of overtaking me.

The scene and its surroundings were photographed on my memory. The rain-swept sky (we were at the end of the wet weather), the sodden, dingy pines, the muddy road, and the black powder-riven cliffs formed a gloomy background against which the black and white liveries of the *jhampanies*, the yellow-panelled 'rickshaw and Mrs. Wessington's down-bowed golden head stood out clearly. She was holding her handkerchief in her left hand and was leaning back exhausted against the 'rickshaw cushions. I turned my horse up a bypath near the Sanjowlie Reservoir and literally ran away. Once I fancied I heard a faint call of 'Jack!' This may have been imagination. I never stopped to verify it. Ten minutes later I came across Kitty on horse-back; and, in the delight of a long ride with her, forgot all about the interview.

A week later Mrs. Wessington died, and the inex-pressible burden of her existence was removed from my life. I went Plainsward perfectly happy. Before three months were over I had forgotten all about her, except that at times the discovery of some of her old letters reminded me unpleasantly of our bygone relationship. By January I had disinterred what was left of our correspondence from among my scattered belongings and had burnt it. At the beginning of April of this year, 1885, I was at Simla — semi-deserted Simla — once more, and was deep in lover's talks and walks with Kitty. It was decided that we should be married at the end of June. You will understand, therefore, that, loving Kitty as I did, I am not saying too much when I pronounce myself to have been, at that time, the happiest man in India.

Fourteen delightful days passed almost before I noticed their flight. Then, aroused to the sense of what was proper among mortals circumstanced as we were, I pointed out to Kitty that an engagement ring was the outward and visible sign of her dignity as an engaged girl; and that she must forthwith come to Hamilton's to be measured for one. Up to that moment, I give you my word, we had completely forgotten so

trivial a matter.   To Hamilton's we accordingly went
on the 15th of April 1885.   Remember that — whatever
my doctor may say to the contrary — I was then in perfect health, enjoying a well-balanced mind and an *absolutely* tranquil spirit.   Kitty and I entered Hamilton's
shop together, and there, regardless of the order of
affairs, I measured Kitty for the ring in the presence of
the amused assistant.   The ring was a sapphire with
two diamonds.   We then rode out down the slope that
leads to the Combermere Bridge and Peliti's shop.

While my Waler was cautiously feeling his way over
the loose shale, and Kitty was laughing and chattering
at my side — while all Simla, that is to say as much of
it as had then come from the Plains, was grouped round
the Reading-room and Peliti's veranda, — I was aware
that some one, apparently at a vast distance, was calling me by my Christian name.   It struck me that I
had heard the voice before, but when and where I could
not at once determine.   In the short space it took to
cover the road between the path from Hamilton's shop
and the first plank of the Combermere Bridge I had
thought over half a dozen people who might have committed such a solecism, and had eventually decided that
it must have been some singing in my ears.   Immediately opposite Peliti's shop my eye was arrested by the
sight of four *jhampanies* in ' mag-pie ' livery, pulling a
yellow-panelled, cheap, bazar 'rickshaw.   In a moment
my mind flew back to the previous season and Mrs.
Wessington with a sense of irritation and disgust.   Was
it not enough that the woman was dead and done with,
without her black and white servitors reappearing to
spoil the day's happiness?   Whoever employed them
now I thought I would call upon, and ask as a personal

favour to change her *jhampanies*' livery. I would hire
the men myself, and, if necessary, buy their coats from
off their backs. It is impossible to say here what a
flood of undesirable memories their presence evoked.

'Kitty,' I cried, 'there are poor Mrs. Wessington's
jhampanies turned up again! I wonder who has them
now?'

Kitty had known Mrs. Wessington slightly last
season, and had always been interested in the sickly
woman.

'What? Where?' she asked. 'I can't see them
anywhere.'

Even as she spoke, her horse, swerving from a laden
mule, threw himself directly in front of the advancing
'rickshaw. I had scarcely time to utter a word of
warning when to my unutterable horror, horse and
rider passed *through* men and carriage as if they had
been thin air.

'What's the matter?' cried Kitty; 'what made you
call out so foolishly, Jack? If I *am* engaged I don't
want all creation to know about it. There was lots of
space between the mule and the veranda; and, if you
think I can't ride —— There!'

Whereupon wilful Kitty set off, her dainty little
head in the air, at a hand-gallop in the direction of
the Band-stand; fully expecting, as she herself afterwards told me, that I should follow her. What was the
matter? Nothing indeed. Either that I was mad or
drunk, or that Simla was haunted with devils. I reined
in my impatient cob, and turned round. The 'rickshaw
had turned too, and now stood immediately facing me,
near the left railing of the Combermere Bridge.

'Jack! Jack, darling!' (There was no mistake

about the words this time : they rang through my brain as if they had been shouted in my ear.) 'It's some hideous mistake, I'm sure. *Please* forgive me, Jack, and let's be friends again.'

The 'rickshaw-hood had fallen back, and inside, as I hope and pray daily for the death I dread by night, sat Mrs. Keith-Wessington, handkerchief in hand, and golden head bowed on her breast.

How long I stared motionless I do not know. Finally, I was aroused by my syce taking the Waler's bridle and asking whether I was ill. From the horrible to the commonplace is but a step. I tumbled off my horse and dashed, half fainting, into Peliti's for a glass of cherry-brandy. There two or three couples were gathered round the coffee-tables discussing the gossip of the day. Their trivialities were more comforting to me just then than the consolations of religion could have been. I plunged into the midst of the conversation at once ; chatted, laughed, and jested with a face (when I caught a glimpse of it in a mirror) as white and drawn as that of a corpse. Three or four men noticed my condition ; and, evidently setting it down to the results of over-many pegs, charitably endeavoured to draw me apart from the rest of the loungers. But I refused to be led away. I wanted the company of my kind — as a child rushes into the midst of the dinner-party after a fright in the dark. I must have talked for about ten minutes or so, though it seemed an eternity to me, when I heard Kitty's clear voice outside enquiring for me. In another minute she had entered the shop, prepared to upbraid me for failing so signally in my duties. Something in my face stopped her.

'Why, Jack,' she cried, 'what *have* you been doing?
What *has* happened? Are you ill?' Thus driven into
a direct lie, I said that the sun had been a little too
much for me. It was close upon five o'clock of a
cloudy April afternoon, and the sun had been hidden
all day. I saw my mistake as soon as the words were
out of my mouth: attempted to recover it; blundered
hopelessly and followed Kitty, in a regal rage, out of
doors, amid the smiles of my acquaintances. I made
some excuse (I have forgotten what) on the score of
my feeling faint; and cantered away to my hotel, leaving Kitty to finish the ride by herself.

In my room I sat down and tried calmly to reason
out the matter. Here was I, Theobald Jack Pansay,
a well-educated Bengal Civilian in the year of grace
1885, presumably sane, certainly healthy, driven in
terror from my sweetheart's side by the apparition of
a woman who had been dead and buried eight months
ago. These were facts that I could not blink. Nothing was further from my thought than any memory
of Mrs. Wessington when Kitty and I left Hamilton's
shop. Nothing was more utterly commonplace than the
stretch of wall opposite Peliti's. It was broad daylight.
The road was full of people; and yet here, look you, in
defiance of every law of probability, in direct outrage of
Nature's ordinance, there had appeared to me a face
from the grave.

Kitty's Arab had gone *through* the 'rickshaw: so that
my first hope that some woman marvellously like Mrs.
Wessington had hired the carriage and the coolies with
their old livery was lost. Again and again I went round
this treadmill of thought; and again and again gave up
baffled and in despair. The voice was as inexplicable as

the apparition. I had originally some wild notion of confiding it all to Kitty; of begging her to marry me at once; and in her arms defying the ghostly occupant of the 'rickshaw. 'After all,' I argued, 'the presence of the 'rickshaw is in itself enough to prove the existence of a spectral illusion. One may see ghosts of men and women, but surely never coolies and carriages. The whole thing is absurd. Fancy the ghost of a hillman!'

Next morning I sent a penitent note to Kitty, imploring her to overlook my strange conduct of the previous afternoon. My Divinity was still very wroth, and a personal apology was necessary. I explained, with a fluency born of night-long pondering over a falsehood, that I had been attacked with a sudden palpitation of the heart — the result of indigestion. This eminently practical solution had its effect: and Kitty and I rode out that afternoon with the shadow of my first lie dividing us.

Nothing would please her save a canter round Jakko. With my nerves still unstrung from the previous night I feebly protested against the notion, suggesting Observatory Hill, Jutogh, the Boileaugunge road — anything rather than the Jakko round. Kitty was angry and a little hurt; so I yielded from fear of provoking further misunderstanding, and we set out together towards Chota Simla. We walked a greater part of the way, and, according to our custom, cantered from a mile or so below the Convent to the stretch of level road by the Sanjowlie Reservoir. The wretched horses appeared to fly, and my heart beat quicker and quicker as we neared the crest of the ascent. My mind had been full of Mrs. Wessington all the afternoon; and every inch of the Jakko road bore witness to our old-time walks and talks. The bowlders were full of it; the pines sang it aloud overhead; the rain-fed torrents giggled and chuckled unseen over the shameful story; and the wind in my ears chanted the iniquity aloud.

As a fitting climax, in the middle of the level men call the Ladies' Mile the Horror was awaiting me. No other 'rickshaw was in sight — only the four black and white *jhampanies*, the yellow-panelled carriage, and the golden head of the woman within — all apparently just as I had left them eight months and one fortnight ago! For an instant I fancied that Kitty *must* see what I saw — we were so marvellously sympathetic in all things. Her next words undeceived me — 'Not a soul in sight! Come along, Jack, and I'll race you to the Reservoir buildings!' Her wiry little Arab was off like a bird, my Waler following close behind, and in this order we dashed under the cliffs. Half a minute brought us within fifty yards of the 'rickshaw. I pulled my Waler and fell back a little. The 'rickshaw was directly in the middle of the road; and once more the Arab passed through it, my horse following. 'Jack! Jack dear! *Please* forgive me,' rang with a wail in my ears, and, after an interval: 'It's all a mistake, a hideous mistake!'

I spurred my horse like a man possessed. When I turned my head at the Reservoir works, the black and white liveries were still waiting — patiently waiting — under the gray hillside, and the wind brought me a mocking echo of the words I had just heard. Kitty bantered me a good deal on my silence throughout the remainder of the ride. I had been talking up till then wildly and at random. To save my life I could not speak afterwards naturally, and from Sanjowlie to the Church wisely held my tongue.

I was to dine with the Mannerings that night, and had barely time to canter home to dress. On the road to Elysium Hill I overheard two men talking together in the dusk.— 'It's a curious thing,' said one, 'how completely all trace of it disappeared. You know my wife was insanely fond of the woman (never could see anything in her myself), and wanted me to pick up her old 'rickshaw and coolies if they were to be got for love or money. Morbid sort of fancy I call it; but I've got to do what the *Memsahib* tells me. Would you believe that the man she hired it from tells me that all four of the men — they were brothers — died of cholera on the way to Hardwar, poor devils; and the 'rickshaw has been broken up by the man himself. 'Told me he never used a dead *Memsahib's* 'rickshaw. 'Spoilt his luck. Queer notion, wasn't it? Fancy poor little Mrs. Wessington spoiling any one's luck except her own!' I laughed aloud at this point; and my laugh jarred on me as I uttered it. So there *were* ghosts of 'rickshaws after all, and ghostly employments in the other world! How much did Mrs. Wessington give her men? What were their hours? Where did they go?

And for visible answer to my last question I saw the infernal Thing blocking my path in the twilight. The dead travel fast, and by short cuts unknown to ordinary coolies. I laughed aloud a second time and checked my laughter suddenly, for I was afraid I was going mad. Mad to a certain extent I must have been, for I recollect that I reined in my horse at the head of the 'rickshaw, and politely **wish**ed Mrs. Wessington 'Good-evening.' Her answer was one I knew only too well. I listened to the end; and replied that I had heard it all before, but should be delighted if she had anything further to say. Some malignant devil stronger than I must have entered into me that evening, for I have a dim recollection of talking the commonplaces of the day for five minutes to the Thing in front of me.

'Mad as a hatter, poor devil — or drunk. Max, try and get him to come home.'

Surely *that* was not Mrs. Wessington's voice! The two men had overheard me speaking to the empty air, and had returned to look after me. They were very kind and considerate, and from their words evidently gathered that I was extremely drunk. I thanked them confusedly and cantered away to my hotel, there changed, and arrived at the Mannerings' ten minutes late. I pleaded the darkness of the night as an excuse; was rebuked by Kitty for my unlover-like tardiness; and sat down.

The conversation had already become general; and under cover of it, I was addressing some tender small talk to my sweetheart when I was aware that at the further end of the table a short red-whiskered man was describing, with much broidery, his encounter with a mad unknown that evening.

A few sentences convinced me that he was repeating the incident of half an hour ago. In the middle of the story he looked round for applause, as professional story-tellers do, caught my eye, and straightway collapsed. There was a moment's awkward silence, and the red-whiskered man muttered something to the effect that he had 'forgotten the rest,' thereby sacrificing a reputation as a good story-teller which he had

K

built up for six seasons past. I blessed him from the bottom of my heart, and — went on with my fish.

In the fulness of time that dinner came to an end; and with genuine regret I tore myself away from Kitty — as certain as I was of my own existence that It would be waiting for me outside the door. The red-whiskered man, who had been introduced to me as Dr. Heatherlegh of Simla, volunteered to bear me company as far as our roads lay together. I accepted his offer with gratitude.

My instinct had not deceived me. It lay in readiness in the Mall, and, in what seemed devilish mockery of our ways, with a lighted head-lamp. The red-whiskered man went to the point at once, in a manner that showed he had been thinking over it all dinner-time.

' I say, Pansay, what the deuce was the matter with you this evening on the Elysium Road ? ' The suddenness of the question wrenched an answer from me before I was aware.

' That ! ' said I, pointing to It.

' *That* may be either D. T. or Eyes for aught I know. Now you don't liquor. I saw as much at dinner, so it can't be *D. T.* There's nothing whatever where you're pointing, though you're sweating and trembling with fright, like a scared pony. Therefore, I conclude that it's Eyes. And I ought to understand all about them. Come along home with me. I'm on the Blessington lower road.'

To my intense delight the 'rickshaw instead of waiting for us kept about twenty yards ahead — and this, too, whether we walked, trotted, or cantered. In the course of that long night ride I had told my companion almost as much as I have told you here.

'Well, you've spoilt one of the best tales I've ever laid tongue to,' said he, 'but I'll forgive you for the sake of what you've gone through. Now come home and do what I tell you; and when I've cured you, young man, let this be a lesson to you to steer clear of women and indigestible food till the day of your death.'

The 'rickshaw kept steady in front; and my red-whiskered friend seemed to derive great pleasure from my account of its exact whereabouts.

'Eyes, Pansay — all Eyes, Brain, and Stomach. And the greatest of these three is Stomach. You've too much conceited Brain, too little Stomach, and thoroughly unhealthy Eyes. Get your Stomach straight and the rest follows. And all that's French for a liver pill. I'll take sole medical charge of you from this hour! for you're too interesting a phenomenon to be passed over.'

By this time we were deep in the shadow of the Blessington lower road and the 'rickshaw came to a dead stop under a pine-clad, overhanging shale cliff. Instinctively I halted too, giving my reason. Heatherlegh rapped out an oath.

'Now, if you think I'm going to spend a cold night on the hillside for the sake of a Stomach-*cum*-Brain-*cum*-Eye illusion—— Lord, ha' mercy! What's that?'

There was a muffled report, a blinding smother of dust just in front of us, a crack, the noise of rent boughs, and about ten yards of the cliff-side — pines, undergrowth, and all — slid down into the road below, completely blocking it up. The uprooted trees swayed and tottered for a moment like drunken giants in the gloom, and then fell prone among their fellows with a thunderous crash. Our two horses stood motionless and sweating with fear. As soon as the rattle of falling earth and stone had subsided, my companion muttered: 'Man, if we'd gone forward we should have been ten feet deep in our graves by now. "There are more things in heaven and earth" . . . Come home, Pansay, and thank God. I want a peg badly.'

We retraced our way over the Church Ridge, and I arrived at Dr. Heatherlegh's house shortly after midnight.

His attempts towards my cure commenced almost immediately, and for a week I never left his sight. Many a time in the course of that week did I bless the good-fortune which had thrown me in contact with Simla's best and kindest doctor. Day by day my spirits grew lighter and more equable. Day by day, too, I became more and more inclined to fall in with Heatherlegh's 'spectral illusion' theory, implicating eyes, brain, and stomach. I wrote to Kitty, telling her that a slight sprain caused by a fall from my horse kept me indoors for a few days; and that I should be recovered before she had time to regret my absence.

Heatherlegh's treatment was simple to a degree. It consisted of liver pills, cold-water baths, and strong exercise, taken in the dusk or at early dawn — for, as he sagely observed: 'A man with a sprained ankle doesn't walk a dozen miles a day, and your young woman might be wondering if she saw you.'

At the end of the week, after much examination of pupil and pulse, and strict injunctions as to diet and pedestrianism, Heatherlegh dismissed me as brusquely as he had taken charge of me.   Here is his parting benediction : ' Man, I certify to your mental cure, and that's as much as to say I've cured most of your bodily ailments.   Now, get your traps out of this as soon as you can ; and be off to make love to Miss Kitty.'

I was endeavouring to express my thanks for his kindness.   He cut me short.

' Don't think I did this because I like you.   I gather that you've behaved like a blackguard all through. But, all the same, you're a phenomenon, and as queer a phenomenon as you are a blackguard.   No! ' — checking me a second time — ' not a rupee, please.   Go out and see if you can find the eyes-brain-and-stomach business again.   I'll give you a lakh for each time you see it.'

Half an hour later I was in the Mannerings' drawing-room with Kitty — drunk with the intoxication of present happiness and the foreknowledge that I should never more be troubled with Its hideous presence. Strong in the sense of my new-found security, I proposed a ride at once ; and, by preference, a canter round Jakko.

Never had I felt so well, so overladen with vitality and mere animal spirits, as I did on the afternoon of the 30th of April.   Kitty was delighted at the change in my appearance, and complimented me on it in her delightfully frank and outspoken manner.   We left the Mannerings' house together, laughing and talking, and cantered along the Chota Simla road as of old.

I was in haste to reach the Sanjowlie Reservoir and there make my assurance doubly sure.   The horses did their best, but seemed all too slow to my impatient mind.   Kitty was astonished at my boisterousness.

'Why, Jack!' she cried at last, 'you are behaving like a child. What are you doing?'

We were just below the Convent, and from sheer wantonness I was making my Waler plunge and curvet across the road as I tickled it with the loop of my riding-whip.

'Doing?' I answered; 'nothing, dear. That's just it. If you'd been doing nothing for a week except lie up, you'd be as riotous as I.

> 'Singing and murmuring in your feastful mirth,
>   Joying to feel yourself alive;
> Lord over Nature, Lord of the visible Earth,
>   Lord of the senses five.'

My quotation was hardly out of my lips before we had rounded the corner above the Convent; and a few yards further on could see across to Sanjowlie. In the centre of the level road stood the black and white liveries, the yellow-panelled 'rickshaw, and Mrs. Keith-Wessington. I pulled up, looked, rubbed my eyes, and, I believe, must have said something. The next thing I knew was that I was lying face downward on the road, with Kitty kneeling above me in tears.

'Has it gone, child!' I gasped. Kitty only wept more bitterly.

'Has what gone, Jack dear? what does it all mean? There must be a mistake somewhere, Jack. A hideous mistake.' Her last words brought me to my feet — mad — raving for the time being.

'Yes, there *is* a mistake somewhere,' I repeated, 'a hideous mistake. Come and look at It.'

I have an indistinct idea that I dragged Kitty by the wrist along the road up to where It stood, and im-

plored her for pity's sake to speak to It; to tell It
that we were betrothed; that neither Death nor Hell
could break the tie between us: and Kitty only knows
how much more to the same effect.   Now and again
I appealed passionately to the Terror in the 'rickshaw
to bear witness to all I had said, and to release me
from a torture that was killing me.   As I talked I
suppose I must have told Kitty of my old relations
with Mrs. Wessington, for I saw her listen intently
with white face and blazing eyes.

'Thank you, Mr. Pansay,' she said, 'that's *quite*
enough.   *Syce ghora láo.*'

The syces, impassive as Orientals always are, had
come up with the recaptured horses; and as Kitty
sprang into her saddle I caught hold of her bridle,
entreating her to hear me out and forgive.   My answer
was the cut of her riding-whip across my face from
mouth to eye, and a word or two of farewell that even
now I cannot write down.   So I judged and judged
rightly, that Kitty knew all; and I staggered back
to the side of the 'rickshaw.   My face was cut and
bleeding, and the blow of the riding-whip had raised
a livid blue wheal on it.   I had no self-respect.   Just
then, Heatherlegh, who must have been following Kitty
and me at a distance, cantered up.

'Doctor,' I said, pointing to my face, 'here's Miss
Mannering's signature to my order of dismissal and
—— I'll thank you for that lakh as soon as convenient.'

Heatherlegh's face, even in my abject misery, moved
me to laughter.

'I'll stake my professional reputation ——' he began.

'Don't be a fool,' I whispered.   'I've lost my life's
happiness and you'd better take me home.'

As I spoke the 'rickshaw was gone. Then I lost all knowledge of what was passing. The crest of Jakko seemed to heave and roll like the crest of a cloud and fall in upon me.

Seven days later (on the 7th of May, that is to say) I was aware that I was lying in Heatherlegh's room as weak as a little child. Heatherlegh was watching me intently from behind the papers on his writing-table. His first words were not encouraging; but I was too far spent to be much moved by them.

'Here's Miss Kitty has sent back your letters. You corresponded a good deal, you young people. Here's a packet that looks like a ring, and a cheerful sort of a note from Mannering Papa, which I've taken the liberty of reading and burning. The old gentleman's not pleased with you.'

'And Kitty?' I asked dully.

'Rather more drawn than her father from what she says. By the same token you must have been letting out any number of queer reminiscences just before I met you. 'Says that a man who would have behaved to a woman as you did to Mrs. Wessington ought to kill himself out of sheer pity for his kind. She's a hot-headed little virago, your mash. 'Will have it too that you were suffering from *D. T.* when that row on the Jakko road turned up. 'Says she'll die before she ever speaks to you again.'

I groaned and turned over on the other side.

'Now you've got your choice, my friend. This engagement has to be broken off; and the Mannerings don't want to be too hard on you. Was it broken through *D. T.* or epileptic fits? Sorry I can't offer you a better exchange unless you'd prefer hereditary insanity. Say the word and I'll tell 'em it's fits. All Simla knows about that scene on the Ladies' Mile. Come! I'll give you five minutes to think over it.'

During those five minutes I believe that I explored thoroughly the lowest circles of the Inferno which it is permitted man to tread on earth. And at the same time I myself was watching myself faltering through the dark labyrinths of doubt, misery, and utter despair. I wondered, as Heatherlegh in his chair might have wondered, which dreadful alternative I should adopt. Presently I heard myself answering in a voice that I hardly recognised —

'They're confoundedly particular about morality in these parts. Give 'em fits, Heatherlegh, and my love. Now let me sleep a bit longer.'

Then my two selves joined, and it was only I (half-crazed, devil-driven I) that tossed in my bed tracing step by step the history of the past month.

'But I am in Simla,' I kept repeating to myself. 'I, Jack Pansay, am in Simla, and there are no ghosts here. It's unreasonable of that woman to pretend there are. Why couldn't Agnes have left me alone? I never did her any harm. It might just as well have been me as Agnes. Only I'd never have come back on purpose to kill *her*. Why can't I be left alone — left alone and happy?'

It was high noon when I first awoke: and the sun was low in the sky before I slept — slept as the tortured criminal sleeps on his rack, too worn to feel further pain.

Next day I could not leave my bed. Heatherlegh told me in the morning that he had received an answer from Mr. Mannering, and that, thanks to his (Heatherlegh's) friendly offices, the story of my affliction had travelled through the length and breadth of Simla, where I was on all sides much pitied.

'And that's rather more than you deserve,' he concluded pleasantly, 'though the Lord knows you've been going through a pretty severe mill. Never mind; we'll cure you yet, you perverse phenomenon.'

I declined firmly to be cured. 'You've been much too good to me already, old man,' said I; 'but I don't think I need trouble you further.'

In my heart I knew that nothing Heatherlegh could do would lighten the burden that had been laid upon me.

With that knowledge came also a sense of hopeless, impotent rebellion against the unreasonableness of it all. There were scores of men no better than I whose punishments had at least been reserved for another world; and I felt that it was bitterly, cruelly unfair that I alone should have been singled out for so hideous a fate. This mood would in time give place to another where it seemed that the 'rickshaw and I were the only realities in a world of shadows; that Kitty was a ghost; that Mannering, Heatherlegh, and all the other men and women I knew were all ghosts; and the great, gray hills themselves but vain shadows devised to torture me. From mood to mood I tossed backwards and forwards for seven weary days; my body growing daily stronger and stronger, until the bedroom looking-glass told me that I had returned to every-day life, and was as other men once more. Curiously enough my face showed no signs of the struggle I had gone through. It was pale indeed, but as expressionless and commonplace as ever. I had expected some permanent alteration — visible evidence of the disease that was eating me away. I found nothing.

On the 15th of May I left Heatherlegh's house at eleven o'clock in the morning ; and the instinct of the bachelor drove me to the Club. There I found that every man knew my story as told by Heatherlegh, and was, in clumsy fashion, abnormally kind and attentive. Nevertheless I recognised that for the rest of my natural life I should be among but not of my fellows ; and I envied very bitterly indeed the laughing coolies on the Mall below. I lunched at the Club, and at four o'clock wandered aimlessly down the Mall in the vague hope of meeting Kitty. Close to the Band-stand the black and white liveries joined me ; and I heard Mrs. Wessington's old appeal at my side. I had been expecting this ever since I came out ; and was only surprised at her delay. The phantom 'rickshaw and I went side by side along the Chota Simla road in silence. Close to the bazar, Kitty and a man on horseback overtook and passed us. For any sign she gave I might have been a dog in the road. She did not even pay me the compliment of quickening her pace ; though the rainy afternoon had served for an excuse.

So Kitty and her companion, and I and my ghostly Light-o'-Love, crept round Jakko in couples. The road was streaming with water ; the pines dripped like roof-pipes on the rocks below, and the air was full of fine, driving rain. Two or three times I found myself saying to myself almost aloud : 'I'm Jack Pansay on leave at Simla—*at Simla!* Every-day, ordinary Simla. I mustn't forget that—I mustn't forget that.' Then I would try to recollect some of the gossip I had heard at the Club : the prices of So-and-So's horses—anything, in fact, that related to the work-a-day Anglo-Indian world I knew so well. I even repeated the multiplication-table rapidly to myself, to make quite sure that I was not taking leave of my senses. It gave me much comfort; and must have prevented my hearing Mrs. Wessington for a time.

Once more I wearily climbed the Convent slope and entered the level road. Here Kitty and the man started off at a canter, and I was left alone with Mrs. Wessington. 'Agnes,' said I, 'will you put back your hood and tell me what it all means?' The hood dropped noiselessly, and I was face to face with my dead and buried mistress. She was wearing the dress in which I had last seen her alive; carried the same tiny handkerchief in her right hand; and the same card-case in her left. (A woman eight months dead with a card-case!) I had to pin myself down to the multiplication-table, and to set both hands on the stone parapet of the road, to assure myself that that at least was real.

'Agnes,' I repeated, 'for pity's sake tell me what it all means.' Mrs. Wessington leaned forward, with that odd, quick turn of the head I used to know so well, and spoke.

If my story had not already so madly overleaped the bounds of all human belief I should apologise to you now. As I know that no one—no, not even Kitty, for whom it is written as some sort of justification of my conduct—will believe me, I will go on. Mrs. Wessington spoke and I walked with her from the Sanjowlie road to the turning below the Commander-in-Chief's house as I might walk by the side of any living woman's 'rickshaw, deep in conversation. The second and most tormenting of my moods of sickness had suddenly laid hold upon me, and like the Prince in Tennyson's poem,

'I seemed to move amid a world of ghosts.' There had been a garden-party at the Commander-in-Chief's, and we two joined the crowd of homeward-bound folk. As I saw them it seemed that *they* were the shadows — impalpable fantastic shadows — that divided for Mrs. Wessington's 'rickshaw to pass through. What we said during the course of that weird interview I cannot — indeed, I dare not — tell. Heatherlegh's comment would have been a short laugh and a remark that I had been 'mashing a brain-eye-and-stomach chimera.' It was a ghastly and yet in some indefinable way a marvellously dear experience. Could it be possible, I wondered, that I was in this life to woo a second time the woman I had killed by my own neglect and cruelty?

I met Kitty on the homeward road — a shadow among shadows.

If I were to describe all the incidents of the next fortnight in their order, my story would never come to an end; and your patience would be exhausted. Morning after morning and evening after evening the ghostly 'rickshaw and I used to wander through Simla together. Wherever I went there the four black and white liveries followed me and bore me company to and from my hotel. At the Theatre I found them amid the crowd of yelling *jhampanies;* outside the Club veranda, after a long evening of whist; at the Birthday Ball, waiting patiently for my reappearance; and in broad daylight when I went calling. Save that it cast no shadow, the 'rickshaw was in every respect as real to look upon as one of wood and iron. More than once, indeed, I have had to check myself from warning some hard-riding friend against cantering over it. More than once I have walked down the Mall deep in conversation with

Mrs. Wessington to the unspeakable amazement of the passers-by.

Before I had been out and about a week I learned that the 'fit' theory had been discarded in favour of insanity.   However, I made no change in my mode of life.   I called, rode, and dined out as freely as ever. I had a passion for the society of my kind which I had never felt before; I hungered to be among the realities of life; and at the same time I felt vaguely unhappy when I had been separated too long from my ghostly companion.   It would be almost impossible to describe my varying moods from the 15th of May up to to-day.

The presence of the 'rickshaw filled me by turns with horror, blind fear, a dim sort of pleasure, and utter despair.   I dared not leave Simla; and I knew that my stay there was killing me.   I knew, moreover, that it was my destiny to die slowly and a little every day. My only anxiety was to get the penance over as quietly as might be.   Alternately I hungered for a sight of Kitty and watched her outrageous flirtations with my successor—to speak more accurately, my successors— with amused interest.   She was as much out of my life as I was out of hers.   By day I wandered with Mrs. Wessington almost content.   By night I implored Heaven to let me return to the world as I used to know it.   Above all these varying moods lay the sensation of dull, numbing wonder that the seen and the Unseen should mingle so strangely on this earth to hound one poor soul to its grave.

*   *   *   *   *   *   *   *   *

August 27. — Heatherlegh has been indefatigable in his attendance on me; and only yesterday told me that I ought to send in an application for sick leave.   An application to escape the company of a phantom! A request that the Government would graciously permit me to get rid of five ghosts and an airy 'rickshaw by going to England! Heatherlegh's proposition moved me to almost hysterical laughter. I told him that I should await the end quietly at Simla; and I am sure that the end is not far off. Believe me that I dread its advent more than any word can say; and I torture myself nightly with a thousand speculations as to the manner of my death.

Shall I die in my bed decently and as an English gentleman should die; or, in one last walk on the Mall, will my soul be wrenched from me to take its place for ever and ever by the side of that ghastly phantasm? Shall I return to my old lost allegiance in the next world, or shall I meet Agnes loathing her and bound to her side through all eternity? Shall we two hover over the scene of our lives till the end of Time? As the day of my death draws nearer, the intense horror that all living flesh feels toward escaped spirits from beyond the grave grows more and more powerful. It is an awful thing to go down quick among the dead with scarcely one-half of your life completed. It is a thousand times more awful to wait as I do in your midst, for I know not what unimaginable terror. Pity me, at least on the score of my 'delusion,' for I know you will never believe what I have written here. Yet as surely as ever a man was done to death by the Powers of Darkness, I am that man.

In justice, too, pity her. For as surely as ever woman was killed by man, I killed Mrs. Wessington. And the last portion of my punishment is even now upon me.

MY OWN TRUE GHOST STORY

As I came through the Desert thus it was —
As I came through the Desert.
The City of Dreadful Night.

THIS story deals entirely with ghosts. There are,
in India, ghosts who take the form of fat, cold, pobby
corpses, and hide in trees near the roadside till a
traveller passes. Then they drop upon his neck and
remain. There are also terrible ghosts of women who
have died in childbed. These wander along the path-
ways at dusk, or hide in the crops near a village, and
call seductively. But to answer their call is death in
this world and the next. Their feet are turned backwards that all sober men may recognise them. There
are ghosts of little children who have been thrown into
wells. These haunt well-curbs and the fringes of
jungles, and wail under the stars, or catch women by
the wrist and beg to be taken up and carried. These
and the corpse-ghosts, however, are only vernacular
articles and do not attack Sahibs. No native ghost
has yet been authentically reported to have frightened
an Englishman; but many English ghosts have scared
the life out of both white and black.

Nearly every other Station owns a ghost. There are
said to be two at Simla, not counting the woman who
blows the bellows at Syree dâk-bungalow on the Old
Road; Mussoorie has a house haunted by a very lively

144

Thing; a White Lady is supposed to do night-watch-man round a house in Lahore; Dalhousie says that one of her houses 'repeats' on autumn evenings all the incidents of a horrible horse-and-precipice accident; Murree has a merry ghost, and, now that she has been swept by cholera, will have room for a sorrowful one; there are Officers' Quarters in Mian Mir whose doors open without reason, and whose furniture is guaranteed to creak, not with the heat of June but with the weight of Invisibles who come to lounge in the chairs; Peshawur possesses houses that none will willingly rent; and there is something — not fever — wrong with a big bungalow in Allahabad. The older Provinces simply bristle with haunted houses, and march phantom armies along their main thorough-fares.

Some of the dâk-bungalows on the Grand Trunk Road have handy little cemeteries in their compound — witnesses to the 'changes and chances of this mortal life' in the days when men drove from Calcutta to the Northwest. These bungalows are objectionable places to put up in. They are generally very old, always dirty, while the *khansamah* is as ancient as the bunga-low. He either chatters senilely, or falls into the long trances of age. In both moods he is useless. If you get angry with him, he refers to some Sahib dead and buried these thirty years, and says that when he was in that Sahib's service not a *khansamah* in the Province could touch him. Then he jabbers and mows and trembles and fidgets among the dishes, and you repent of your irritation.

Not long ago it was my business to live in dâk-bun-galows. I never inhabited the same house for three

L

nights running, and grew to be learned in the breed.
I lived in Government-built ones with red brick walls
and rail ceilings, an inventory of the furniture posted
in every room, and an excited cobra on the threshold
to give welcome. I lived in 'converted' ones — old
houses officiating as dâk-bungalows — where nothing
was in its proper place and there was not even a fowl
for dinner. I lived in second-hand palaces where the
wind blew through open-work marble tracery just as
uncomfortably as through a broken pane. I lived in
dâk-bungalows where the last entry in the visitors'
book was fifteen months old, and where they slashed
off the curry-kid's head with a sword. It was my good-
luck to meet all sorts of men, from sober travelling
missionaries and deserters flying from British Regiments, to drunken loafers who threw whiskey bottles
at all who passed; and my still greater good-fortune
just to escape a maternity case. Seeing that a fair pro-
portion of the tragedy of our lives in India acted itself
in dâk-bungalows, I wondered that I had met no ghosts.
A ghost that would voluntarily hang about a dâk-bungalow would be mad of course; but so many men have
died mad in dâk-bungalows that there must be a fair
percentage of lunatic ghosts.

In due time I found my ghost, or ghosts rather, for
there were two of them.

We will call the bungalow Katmal dâk-bungalow;
but *that* was the smallest part of the horror. A man
with a sensitive hide has no right to sleep in dâk-bungalows. He should marry. Katmal dâk-bungalow was
old and rotten and unrepaired. The floor was of worn
brick, the walls were filthy, and the windows were
nearly black with grime. It stood on a bypath largely

used by native Sub-Deputy Assistants of all kinds, from Finance to Forests ; but real Sahibs were rare. The *khansamah*, who was nearly bent double with old age, said so.

When I arrived, there was a fitful, undecided rain on the face of the land, accompanied by a restless wind, and every gust made a noise like the rattling of dry bones in the stiff toddy-palms outside. The *khansamah* completely lost his head on my arrival. He had served a Sahib once. Did I know that Sahib ? He gave me the name of a well-known man who has been buried for more than a quarter of a century, and showed me an ancient daguerreotype of that man in his prehistoric youth. I had seen a steel engraving of him at the head of a double volume of Memoirs a month before, and I felt ancient beyond telling.

The day shut in and the *khansamah* went to get me food. He did not go through the pretence of calling it '*khana*,'—man's victuals. He said '*ratub*,' and that means, among other things, 'grub'—dog's rations. There was no insult in his choice of the term. He had forgotten the other word, I suppose.

While he was cutting up the dead bodies of animals, I settled myself down, after exploring the dâk-bunga-low. There were three rooms, beside my own, which was a corner kennel, each giving into the other through dingy white doors fastened with long iron bars. The bungalow was a very solid one, but the partition-walls of the rooms were almost jerry-built in their flimsiness. Every step or bang of a trunk echoed from my room down the other three, and every footfall came back tremulously from the far walls. For this reason I shut the door. There were no lamps—only candles in long glass shades. An oil wick was set in the bathroom.

For bleak, unadulterated misery that dâk-bungalow was the worst of the many that I had ever set foot in. There was no fireplace, and the windows would not open; so a brazier of charcoal would have been useless. The rain and the wind splashed and gurgled and moaned round the house, and the toddy-palms rattled and roared. Half a dozen jackals went through the compound singing, and a hyena stood afar off and mocked them. A hyena would convince a Sadducee of the Resurrection of the Dead — the worst sort of Dead. Then came the *ratub* — a curious meal, half native and half English in composition — with the old *khansamah* babbling behind my chair about dead and gone English people, and the wind-blown candles playing shadow-bo-peep with the bed and the mosquito-curtains. It was just the sort of dinner and evening to make a man think of every single one of his past sins, and of all the others that he intended to commit if he lived.

Sleep, for several hundred reasons, was not easy. The lamp in the bathroom threw the most absurd shadows into the room, and the wind was beginning to talk nonsense.

Just when the reasons were drowsy with blood-sucking I heard the regular — 'Let-us-take-and-heave-him-over' grunt of doolie-bearers in the compound. First one doolie came in, then a second, and then a third. I heard the doolies dumped on the ground, and the shutter in front of my door shook.

'That's some one trying to come in,' I said. But no one spoke, and I persuaded myself that it was the gusty wind. The shutter of the room next to mine was attacked, flung back, and the inner door opened. 'That's some Sub-Deputy Assistant,' I said, 'and he has brought his friends with him. Now they'll talk and spit and smoke for an hour.'

But there were no voices and no footsteps. No one was putting his luggage into the next room. The door shut, and I thanked Providence that I was to be left in peace. But I was curious to know where the doolies had gone. I got out of bed and looked into the darkness. There was never a sign of a doolie. Just as I was getting into bed again, I heard, in the next room, the sound that no man in his senses can possibly mistake — the whir of a billiard ball down the length of the slate when the striker is stringing for break. No other sound is like it. A minute afterwards there was another whir, and I got into bed. I was not frightened — indeed I was not. I was very curious to know what had become of the doolies. I jumped into bed for that reason.

Next minute I heard the double click of a cannon, and my hair sat up. It is a mistake to say that hair stands up. The skin of the head tightens and you can feel a faint, prickly bristling all over the scalp. That is the hair sitting up.

There was a whir and a click, and both sounds could only have been made by one thing — a billiard ball. I argued the matter out at great length with myself; and the more I argued the less probable it seemed that one bed, one table, and two chairs — all the furniture of the room next to mine — could so exactly duplicate the sounds of a game of billiards. After another cannon, a three-cushion one to judge by the whir, I argued

no **more.** I had found my ghost and would have
given worlds to have escaped from that dâk-bungalow
I listened, and with each listen the game grew clearer.
There was whir on whir and click on click. Sometimes there was a double click and a whir and another
click. Beyond any sort of doubt, people were playing billiards in the next room. And the next room
was not big enough to hold a billiard table !

Between the pauses of the wind I heard the game
go forward — stroke after stroke. I tried to believe
that I could not hear voices ; but that attempt was
a failure.

Do you know what fear is ? Not ordinary fear of
insult, injury, or death, but abject, quivering dread of
something that you cannot see — fear that dries the inside
of the mouth and half of the throat — fear that makes
you sweat on the palms of the hands, and gulp in order
to keep the uvula at work ? This is a fine Fear — a
great cowardice, and must be felt to be appreciated.
The very improbability of billiards in a dâk-bungalow
proved the reality of the thing. No man — drunk or
sober — could imagine a game at billiards, or invent
the spitting crack of a ' screw cannon.'

A severe course of dâk-bungalows has this disadvan-
tage — it breeds infinite credulity. If a man said to a
confirmed dâk-bungalow-haunter : ' There is a corpse
in the next room, and there's a mad girl in the next
one, and the woman and man on that camel have just
eloped from a place sixty miles away,' the hearer would
not disbelieve because he would know that nothing is
too wild, grotesque, or horrible to happen in a dâk-
bungalow.

This credulity, unfortunately, extends to ghosts. A

rational person fresh from his own house would have
turned on his side and slept. I did not. So surely as
I was given up for a dry carcass by the scores of things
in the bed, because the bulk of my blood was in my
heart, so surely did I hear every stroke of a long game
at billiards played in the echoing room behind the iron-
barred door. My dominant fear was that the players
might want a marker. It was an absurd fear; because
creatures who could play in the dark would be above
such superfluities. I only know that that was my
terror; and it was real.

After a long, long while, the game stopped, and the
door banged. I slept because I was dead tired. Otherwise I should have preferred to have kept awake. Not
for everything in Asia would I have dropped the door-
bar and peered into the dark of the next room.

When the morning came, I considered that I had
done well and wisely, and enquired for the means of
departure.

'By the way, *khansamah*,' I said, 'what were those
three doolies doing in my compound in the night?'

' There were no doolies,' said the *khansamah*.

I went into the next room, and the daylight streamed
through the open door. I was immensely brave. I
would, at that hour, have played Black Pool with the
owner of the big Black Pool down below.

'Has this place always been a dâk-bungalow?' I
asked.

'No,' said the *khansamah*. 'Ten or twenty years
ago, I have forgotten how long, it was a billiard-room.'

' A what? '

' A billiard-room for the Sahibs who built the Railway. I was *khansamah* then in the big house where all

the Railway-Sahibs lived, and I used to come across
with brandy-*shrab*.   These three rooms were all one,
and they held a big table on which the Sahibs played
every evening.   But the Sahibs are all dead now, and
the Railway runs, you say, nearly to Kabul.'

'Do you remember anything about the Sahibs?'

'It is long ago, but I remember that one Sahib, a fat
man, and always angry, was playing here one night,
and he said to me: "Mangal Khan, brandy-*pani do*,"
and I filled the glass, and he bent over the table to
strike, and his head fell lower and lower till it hit the
table, and his spectacles came off, and when we — the
Sahibs and I myself — ran to lift him he was dead.   I
helped to carry him out.   Aha, he was a strong Sahib!
But he is dead, and I, old Mangal Khan, am still living,
by your favour.'

That was more than enough!   I had my ghost —
a first-hand, authenticated article.   I would write to
the Society for Psychical Research — I would paralyse
the Empire with the news!   But I would, first of all,
put eighty miles of assessed crop-land between myself
and that dâk-bungalow before nightfall.   The Society
might send their regular agent to investigate later on.

I went into my own room and prepared to pack, after
noting down the facts of the case.   As I smoked I
heard the game begin again, — with a miss in balk this
time, for the whir was a short one.

The door was open, and I could see into the room.
Click — click!   That was a cannon.   I entered the
room without fear, for there was sunlight within and
a fresh breeze without.   The unseen game was going
on at a tremendous rate.   And well it might, when
a restless little rat was running to and fro inside the

dingy ceiling-cloth, and a piece of loose window-sash was making fifty breaks off the window-bolt as it shook in the breeze!

Impossible to mistake the sound of billiard balls! Impossible to mistake the whir of a ball over the slate! But I was to be excused. Even when I shut my enlightened eyes the sound was marvellously like that of a fast game.

Entered angrily the faithful partner of my sorrows, Kadir Baksh.

'This bungalow is very bad and low-caste! No wonder the Presence was disturbed and is speckled. Three sets of doolie-bearers came to the bungalow late last night when I was sleeping outside, and said that it was their custom to rest in the rooms set apart for the English people! What honour has the *khansamah?* They tried to enter, but I told them to go. No wonder, if these *Oorias* have been here, that the Presence is sorely spotted. It is shame, and the work of a dirty man!'

Kadir Baksh did not say that he had taken from each gang two annas for rent in advance, and then, beyond my earshot, had beaten them with the big green umbrella whose use I could never before divine. But Kadir Baksh has no notions of morality.

There was an interview with the *khansamah,* but as he promptly lost his head, wrath gave place to pity, and pity led to a long conversation, in the course of which he put the fat Engineer-Sahib's tragic death in three separate stations—two of them fifty miles away. The third shift was to Calcutta, and there the Sahib died while driving a dog-cart.

I did not go away as soon as I intended. I stayed

for the night, while the wind and the rat and the sash and the window-bolt played a ding-dong 'hundred and fifty up.' Then the wind ran out and the billiards stopped, and I felt that I had ruined my one genuine ghost story.

Had I only ceased investigating at the proper time, I could have made *anything* out of it.

That was the bitterest thought of all!

THE TRACK OF A LIE [1]

'CONSEQUENCES of our acts eternal? Bosh!' said Blawkins, at the Club. 'That's what the Padres say. See, now!' The smoking room was empty, except for Blawkins and myself. 'I'll tell you an idiotic little superstition I picked up the other day,' said he. 'The natives say that Allah allows the tiger one rupee eight annas a day for his food; and if you total up the month's cattle bill of an average tiger, not a man-eater, you'll find that it's exactly forty-five rupees *per mensem*.'

'I know that,' said I. 'And it happens to be true.'

'Very good,' said Blawkins. 'Do you mean to say that anything is going to come of an idle sentence like that? I say it. You hear it. Well?' Blawkins swung out of the Club, leaving me vanquished.

But the statement rang in my head. There was something catching about the words, 'Allah allows the tiger one rupee eight annas a day for his food.' It was a quaint superstition, and one not generally known. Would the local paper care for it? It fitted a corner, empty for the moment; and one or two readers said, 'What a curious idea!'

That the tiny paragraph should have wandered to Southern India was not very strange, though there was

[1] Copyright, 1895, by MACMILLAN & Co.

no reason why it should not have trickled to the Bombay side, instead of dropping straight as a plummet to Madras. That it should have jumped Adam's Bridge, and been copied in a Ceylon journal, was strange; but Blawkins had been transferred to the other end of the Empire, just two days before the Ceylon papers told their cinchona planters that 'Allah allows the tiger one rupee eight annas a day,' etc.

Three weeks passed, and from the eastern side of the Bay of Bengal came in the Burma mail. Boh Ottima was dead, and the Field Force was hard worked; Mandalay was suffering from cholera, but at the bottom of the last page the rest of the world might read that 'Allah allows the tiger,' etc. Blawkins was on duty in the Bolan, very sick with fever. It was not worth while to follow him with a letter.

Week by week Europe grew to be a hornet-hive, throbbing and humming angrily, as the messages pulsed through the wires. Then Singapur reported that 'Allah allows the tiger,' etc. Here, assuredly, was the limit of my paragraph's wandering. It might struggle into the Malayan Archipelago, but beyond that scattered heap of islands it could not pass.

Germany called for more men; France answered the call with fresh battalions on her side; and the strangely scented, straw-hued journals of Shanghai and Yokohama made public to the Far East the news that 'Allah allows the tiger,' etc. Blawkins, now at Poona, was desperately in love with a Miss Blandyre. What were paragraphs to a passionate lover? I never sent him a line, though he bombarded me with a very auctioneer's catalogue of Miss Blandyre's charms. What would my paragraph do? It had reached the open Pacific now, and must surely drown in five thousand miles of black water. After all, it had lived long.

Yet, I had presentiments, and waited anxiously for what might come. The flying keel stayed at the Golden Gate, where the sea-lions romp and gurgle and bask : Europe shook with the tread of armed men, but — where was my paragraph? In America — for San Francisco wished to know, if 'Allah allowed the tiger,' etc., how much a Los Angeles hotel-keeper would be justified in charging a millionnaire with *delirium tremens?* Would Eastern America accept it? The paragraph touched Salt Lake City; and thenceforward, straight as a homeward-bound bee, headed New York-wards. They took it; they cut, chipped, chopped, laughed; were ribald, pious, profane, cynical, and frankly foolish over it; but, as though it were under a special and mysterious protection of Providence, it returned, always, to its original shape. It ran southward into New Orleans, northward to Toronto; and week after week the weather-beaten exchanges recorded its eastward progress. Boston appreciated it as something perfectly original; and at last, as a lone light dies on an extreme headland, Philadelphia sent back the news that the Emperor William was dead, and 'Allah allows the tiger,' etc. But Blawkins had, long ago, wedded Miss Blandyre. What was the use of writing to him? The main point of existence was, whether the paragraph could come over the Atlantic to the West Coast of England, where the country papers were lichened with the growth of local politics.

There was a long pause, and I feared that my paragraph was dead. But I did it an injustice. Over the foaming surf of the local Government Bill, through the rapids of compensation to publicans, in the teeth of the current of Mr. Gladstone's appeals to the free and enlightened electors of Wales, came my paragraph — for Birmingham found room for the announcement that 'Allah allows the tiger,' etc.   Blawkins sent an announcement also.   It cost him two rupees, was a purely local matter, and ended up with the words 'of a son.' But the paragraph was Imperial — nay, Universal.   I felt safe, for there was one journal in London whom nothing unusual, or alas, unclean, ever escaped.   I waited with confidence the arrival of the *Yellow Wrapper*.   When the mails came in, the Bombay papers had already quoted and commended to the notice of the Bombay Zoological Society the curious statement hailing from England in the *Yellow Wrapper* that 'Allah allows the tiger,' etc.!   The circuit was complete; and as the shears snipped out the announcement, before putting it afresh into the very cradle in which it had been born fifteen months and six days before, I felt that I had shaken hands with the whole round world.   My paragraph had come home indeed!

*   *   *   *   *   *   *   *   *

Tenderly as a mother shows the face of her sleeping child, I led Blawkins through the paper-cuttings, and step by step pointed out the path of the paragraph. His lower jaw dropped.   'By Jove!' said he, 'I was wrong — it should have been a rupee — one rupee only — not one eight.'

'Then, Blawkins,' said I, 'you have swindled the whole wide world of the sum of eight annas,' nominally one shilling.

THE STRANGE RIDE OF MORROWBIE JUKES

Alive or dead — there is no other way. — *Native Proverb.*

THERE is no invention about this tale. Jukes by accident stumbled upon a village that is well known to exist, though he is the only Englishman who has been there. A somewhat similar institution used to flourish on the outskirts of Calcutta, and there is a story that if you go into the heart of Bikanir, which is in the heart of the Great Indian Desert, you shall come across not a village but a town where the Dead who did not die but may not live have established their headquarters. And, since it is perfectly true that in the same Desert is a wonderful city where all the rich money-lenders retreat after they have made their fortunes (fortunes so vast that the owners cannot trust even the strong hand of the Government to protect them, but take refuge in the waterless sands), and drive sumptuous C-spring barouches, and buy beautiful girls and decorate their palaces with gold and ivory and Minton tiles and mother-o'-pearl, I do not see why Jukes's tale should not be true. He is a Civil Engineer, with a head for plans and distances and things of that kind, and he certainly would not take the trouble to invent imaginary traps. He could earn more by doing his legitimate work. He never varies the tale in the telling, and grows very hot and indignant when he thinks of the

159

disrespectful treatment he received.   He wrote this
quite straightforwardly at first, but he has touched
it up in places and introduced Moral Reflections :
thus : —

In the beginning it all arose from a slight attack of
fever.   My work necessitated my being in camp for
some months between Pakpattan and Mubarakpur — a
desolate sandy stretch of country as every one who has
had the misfortune to go there may know.   My coolies
were neither more nor less exasperating than other
gangs, and my work demanded sufficient attention to
keep me from moping, had I been inclined to so unmanly a weakness.

On the 23rd December 1884, I felt a little feverish.
There was a full moon at the time, and, in consequence,
every dog near my tent was baying it.   The brutes
assembled in twos and threes and drove me frantic.   A
few days previously I had shot one loud-mouthed singer
and suspended his carcass *in terrorem* about fifty yards
from my tent-door, but his friends fell upon, fought for,
and ultimately devoured the body : and, as it seemed
to me, sang their hymns of thanksgiving afterwards
with renewed energy.

The light-headedness which accompanies fever acts
differently on different men.   My irritation gave way,
after a short time, to a fixed determination to slaughter
one huge black and white beast who had been foremost
in song and first in flight throughout the evening.
Thanks to a shaking hand and a giddy head I had
already missed him twice with both barrels of my shot-
gun, when it struck me that my best plan would be to
ride him down in the open and finish him off with a
hog-spear.   This, of course, was merely the semi-delir-

ious notion of a fever-patient ; but I remember that it struck me at the time as being eminently practical and feasible.

I therefore ordered my groom to saddle Pornic and bring him round quietly to the rear of my tent. When the pony was ready, I stood at his head prepared to mount and dash out as soon as the dog should again lift up his voice. Pornic, by the way, had not been out of his pickets for a couple of days ; the night air was crisp and chilly ; and I was armed with a specially long and sharp pair of persuaders with which I had been rousing a sluggish cob that afternoon. You will easily believe, then, that when he was let go he went quickly. In one moment, for the brute bolted as straight as a die, the tent was left far behind, and we were flying over the smooth sandy soil at racing speed. In another we had passed the wretched dog, and I had almost forgotten why it was that I had taken horse and hog-spear.

The delirium of fever and the excitement of rapid motion through the air must have taken away the remnant of my senses. I have a faint recollection of standing upright in my stirrups, and of brandishing my hog-spear at the great white Moon that looked down so calmly on my mad gallop ; and of shouting challenges to the camelthorn bushes as they whizzed past. Once or twice, I believe, I swayed forward on Pornic's neck, and literally hung on by my spurs—as the marks next morning showed.

The wretched beast went forward like a thing possessed, over what seemed to be a limitless expanse of moonlit sand. Next, I remember, the ground rose suddenly in front of us, and as we topped the ascent I saw the waters of the Sutlej shining like a silver bar below.

Then Pornic blundered heavily on his nose, and we rolled together down some unseen slope.

I must have lost consciousness, for when I recovered I was lying on my stomach in a heap of soft white sand, and the dawn was beginning to break dimly over the edge of the slope down which I had fallen. As the light grew stronger I saw I was at the bottom of a horseshoe-shaped crater of sand, opening on one side directly on to the shoals of the Sutlej. My fever had altogether left me, and, with the exception of a slight dizziness in the head, I felt no bad effects from the fall over night.

Pornic, who was standing a few yards away, was naturally a good deal exhausted, but had not hurt himself in the least. His saddle, a favourite polo one, was much knocked about, and had been twisted under his belly. It took me some time to put him to rights, and in the meantime I had ample opportunities of observing the spot into which I had so foolishly dropped.

At the risk of being considered tedious, I must describe it at length; inasmuch as an accurate mental picture of its peculiarities will be of material assistance in enabling the reader to understand what follows.

Imagine then, as I have said before, a horseshoe-shaped crater of sand with steeply-graded sand walls about thirty-five feet high. (The slope, I fancy, must have been about 65°.) This crater enclosed a level piece of ground about fifty yards long by thirty at its broadest part, with a rude well in the centre. Round the bottom of the crater, about three feet from the level of the ground proper, ran a series of eighty-three semicircular, ovoid, square, and multilateral holes, all about three feet at the mouth. Each hole on inspection

showed that it was carefully shored internally with
drift-wood and bamboos, and over the mouth a wooden
drip-board projected, like the peak of a jockey's cap,
for two feet. No sign of life was visible in these
tunnels, but a most sickening stench pervaded the
entire amphitheatre — a stench fouler than any which
my wanderings in Indian villages have introduced
me to.

Having remounted Pornic, who was as anxious as
I to get back to camp, I rode round the base of the
horseshoe to find some place whence an exit would
be practicable. The inhabitants, whoever they might
be, had not thought fit to put in an appearance, so
I was left to my own devices. My first attempt to
'rush' Pornic up the steep sand-banks showed me that
I had fallen into a trap exactly on the same model as
that which the ant-lion sets for its prey. At each
step the shifting sand poured down from above in
tons, and rattled on the drip-boards of the holes like
small shot. A couple of ineffectual charges sent us
both rolling down to the bottom, half choked with the
torrents of sand ; and I was constrained to turn my
attention to the river-bank.

Here everything seemed easy enough. The sand
hills ran down to the river edge, it is true, but there
were plenty of shoals and shallows across which I
could gallop Pornic, and find my way back to *terra
firma* by turning sharply to the right or the left. As
I led Pornic over the sands I was startled by the faint
pop of a rifle across the river ; and at the same moment a bullet dropped with a sharp '*whit*' close to
Pornic's head.

There was no mistaking the nature of the missile

—a regulation Martini-Henry 'picket.' About five
hundred yards away a country-boat was anchored in
midstream ; and a jet of smoke drifting away from
its bows in the still morning air showed me whence
the delicate attention had come. Was ever a respectable gentlemen in such an *impasse?* The treacherous
sand slope allowed no escape from a spot which I had
visited most involuntarily, and a promenade on the
river frontage was the signal for a bombardment from
some insane native in a boat. I'm afraid that I lost my
temper very much indeed.

Another bullet reminded me that I had better save
my breath to cool my porridge ; and I retreated hastily
up the sands and back to the horseshoe, where I saw
that the noise of the rifle had drawn sixty-five human
beings from the badger-holes which I had up till that
point supposed to be untenanted. I found myself in
the midst of a crowd of spectators — about forty men,
twenty women, and one child who could not have been
more than five years old. They were all scantily
clothed in that salmon coloured cloth which one associates with Hindu mendicants, and, at first sight, gave
me the impression of a band of loathsome *fakirs*.
The filth and repulsiveness of the assembly were beyond all description, and I shuddered to think what
their life in the badger-holes must be.

Even in these days, when local self-government has
destroyed the greater part of a native's respect for
a Sahib, I have been accustomed to a certain amount
of civility from my inferiors, and on approaching the
crowd naturally expected that there would be some
recognition of my presence. As a matter of fact there
was; but it was by no means what I had looked for.

The ragged crew actually laughed at me — such laughter I hope I may never hear again. They cackled, yelled, whistled, and howled as I walked into their midst; some of them literally throwing themselves down on the ground in convulsions of unholy mirth. In a moment I had let go Pornic's head, and, irritated beyond expression at the morning's adventure, commenced cuffing those nearest to me with all the force I could. The wretches dropped under my blows like nine-pins, and the laughter gave place to wails for mercy; while those yet untouched clasped me round the knees, imploring me in all sorts of uncouth tongues to spare them.

In the tumult, and just when I was feeling very much ashamed of myself for having thus easily given way to my temper, a thin, high voice murmured in English from behind my shoulder: 'Sahib! Sahib! Do you not know me? Sahib, it is Gunga Dass, the telegraph-master.'

I spun round quickly and faced the speaker.

Gunga Dass (I have, of course, no hesitation in mentioning the man's real name) I had known four years before as a Deccanee Brahmin lent by the Punjab Government to one of the Khalsia States. He was in charge of a branch telegraph-office there, and when I had last met him was a jovial, full-stomached, portly Government servant with a marvellous capacity for making bad puns in English — a peculiarity which made me remember him long after I had forgotten his services to me in his official capacity. It is seldom that a Hindu makes English puns.

Now, however, the man was changed beyond all recognition. Caste-mark, stomach, slate-coloured continua-

tions, and unctuous speech were all gone. I looked at a
withered skeleton, turbanless and almost naked, with
long matted hair and deep-set codfish-eyes. But for a
crescent-shaped scar on the left cheek—the result of an
accident for which I was responsible—I should never
have known him. But it was indubitably Gunga Dass,
and—for this I was thankful—an English-speaking
native who might at least tell me the meaning of all
that I had gone through that day.

The crowd retreated to some distance as I turned
towards the miserable figure, and ordered him to show
me some method of escaping from the crater. He held
a freshly-plucked crow in his hand, and in reply to my
question climbed slowly on a platform of sand which
ran in front of the holes, and commenced lighting a fire
there in silence. Dried bents, sand-poppies, and drift-
wood burn quickly; and I derived much consolation
from the fact that he lit them with an ordinary sulphur
match. When they were in a bright glow, and the
crow was neatly spitted in front thereof, Gunga Dass
began without a word of preamble:—

'There are only two kinds of men, Sar. The alive
and the dead. When you are dead you are dead, but
when you are alive you live.' (Here the crow demanded his attention for an instant as it twirled before
the fire in danger of being burnt to a cinder.) 'If you
die at home and do not die when you come to the ghât
to be burnt you come here.'

The nature of the reeking village was made plain
now, and all that I had known or read of the grotesque
and the horrible paled before the fact just communi-
cated by the ex-Brahmin. Sixteen years ago, when I
first landed in Bombay, I had been told by a wandering

Armenian of the existence, somewhere in India, of a place to which such Hindus as had the misfortune to recover from trance or catalepsy were conveyed and kept, and I recollect laughing heartily at what I was then pleased to consider a traveller's tale. Sitting at the bottom of the sand-trap, the memory of Watson's Hotel, with its swinging punkahs, white-robed servants and the sallow-faced Armenian, rose up in my mind as vividly as a photograph, and I burst into a loud fit of laughter. The contrast was too absurd!

Gunga Dass, as he bent over the unclean bird, watched me curiously. Hindus seldom laugh, and his surroundings were not such as to move him that way. He removed the crow solemnly from the wooden spit and as solemnly devoured it. Then he continued his story, which I give in his own words:—

'In epidemics of the cholera you are carried to be burnt almost before you are dead. When you come to the riverside the cold air, perhaps, makes you alive, and then, if you are only little alive, mud is put on your nose and mouth and you die conclusively. If you are rather more alive, more mud is put; but if you are too lively they let you go and take you away. I was too lively, and made protestation with anger against the indignities that they endeavoured to press upon me. In those days I was Brahmin and proud man. Now I am dead man and eat'—here he eyed the well-gnawed breast bone with the first sign of emotion that I had seen in him since we met—'crows, and—other things. They took me from my sheets when they saw that I was too lively and gave me medicines for one week, and I survived successfully. Then they sent me by rail from my place to Okara Station, with a man to

take care of me; and at Okara Station we met two other
men, and they conducted we three on camels, in the
night, from Okara Station to this place, and they pro-
pelled me from the top to the bottom, and the other
two succeeded, and I have been here ever since two
and a half years.   Once I was Brahmin and proud
man, and now I eat crows.'

'There is no way of getting out?'

'None of what kind at all.   When I first came I
made experiments frequently and all the others also,
but we have always succumbed to the sand which is
precipitated upon our heads.'

'But surely,' I broke in at this point, 'the river-front
is open, and it is worth while dodging the bullets;
while at night ——'

I had already matured a rough plan of escape which
a natural instinct of selfishness forbade me sharing
with Gunga Dass.   He, however, divined my unspoken
thought almost as soon as it was formed; and, to my
intense astonishment, gave vent to a long low chuckle
of derision — the laughter, be it understood, of a superior or at least of an equal.

'You will not' — he had dropped the Sir after his
first sentence — 'make any escape that way.   But you
can try.   I have tried.   Once only.'

The sensation of nameless terror which I had in
vain attempted to strive against, overmastered me completely.   My long fast — it was now close upon ten
o'clock, and I had eaten nothing since tiffin on the previous day — combined with the violent agitation of the
ride had exhausted me, and I verily believe that, for a
few minutes, I acted as one mad.   I hurled myself
against the sand-slope.   I ran round the base of the

crater, blaspheming and praying by turns. I crawled out among the sedges of the river-front, only to be driven back each time in an agony of nervous dread by the rifle-bullets which cut up the sand round me — for I dared not face the death of a mad dog among that hideous crowd — and so fell, spent and raving, at the curb of the well. No one had taken the slightest notice of an exhibition which makes me blush hotly even when I think of it now.

Two or three men trod on my panting body as they drew water, but they were evidently used to this sort of thing, and had no time to waste upon me. Gunga Dass, indeed, when he had banked the embers of his fire with sand, was at some pains to throw half a cupful of fetid water over my head, an attention for which I could have fallen on my knees and thanked him, but he was laughing all the while in the same mirthless, wheezy key that greeted me on my first attempt to force the shoals. And so, in a half-fainting state, I lay till noon. Then, being only a man after all, I felt hungry, and said as much to Gunga Dass, whom I had begun to regard as my natural protector. Following the impulse of the outer world when dealing with natives, I put my hand into my pocket and drew out four annas. The absurdity of the gift struck me at once, and I was about to replace the money.

Gunga Dass, however, cried : ' Give me the money, all you have, or I will get help, and we will kill you ! '

A Briton's first impulse, I believe, is to guard the contents of his pockets ; but a moment's thought showed me of the folly of differing with the one man who had it in his power to make me comfortable ; and with whose help it was possible that I might eventually escape from the crater. I gave him all the money in my possession, Rs. 9-8-5 — nine rupees, eight annas, and five pie — for I always keep small change as *bakshish* when I am in camp. Gunga Dass clutched the coins, and hid them at once in his ragged loin-cloth, looking round to assure himself that no one had observed us.

'*Now* I will give you something to eat,' said he.

What pleasure my money could have given him I am unable to say ; but inasmuch as it did please him I was not sorry that I had parted with it so readily, for I had no doubt that he would have had me killed if I had refused. One does not protest against the doings of a den of wild beasts ; and my companions were lower than any beasts. While I eat what Gunga Dass had provided, a coarse *chapatti* and a cupful of the foul well-water, the people showed not the faintest sign of curiosity — that curiosity which is so rampant, as a rule, in an Indian village.

I could even fancy that they despised me. At all events they treated me with the most chilling indiffer-ence, and Gunga Dass was nearly as bad. I plied him with questions about the terrible village, and received ex-tremely unsatisfactory answers. So far as I could gather, it had been in existence from time immemorial — whence I concluded that it was at least a century old — and during that time no one had ever been known to escape from it. [I had to control myself here with both hands, lest the blind terror should lay hold of me a second time and drive me raving round the crater.] Gunga Dass took a malicious pleasure in emphasising this point and in watching me wince. Nothing that I could do would induce him to tell me who the mysterious 'They' were.

'It is so ordered,' he would reply, 'and I do not yet know any one who has disobeyed the orders.'

'Only wait till my servant finds that I am missing,' I retorted, 'and I promise you that this place shall be cleared off the face of the earth, and I'll give you a lesson in civility, too, my friend.'

'Your servants would be torn in pieces before they came near this place; and, besides, you are dead, my dear friend. It is not your fault, of course, but none the less you are dead *and* buried.'

At irregular intervals supplies of food, I was told, were dropped down from the land side into the amphitheatre, and the inhabitants fought for them like wild beasts. When a man felt his death coming on he retreated to his lair and died there. The body was sometimes dragged out of the hole and thrown on to the sand, or allowed to rot where it lay.

The phrase 'thrown on to the sand' caught my attention, and I asked Gunga Dass whether this sort of thing was not likely to breed a pestilence.

'That,' said he, with another of his wheezy chuckles, 'you may see for yourself subsequently. You will have much time to make observations.'

Whereat, to his great delight, I winced once more and hastily continued the conversation: 'And how do you live here from day to day? What do you do?' The question elicited exactly the same answer as before — coupled with the information that 'this place is like your European heaven; there is neither marrying nor giving in marriage.'

Gunga Dass had been educated at a Mission School, and, as he himself admitted, had he only changed his religion 'like a wise man,' might have avoided the living grave which was now his portion.   But as long as I was with him I fancy he was happy.

Here was a Sahib, a representative of the dominant race, helpless as a child and completely at the mercy of his native neighbours.   In a deliberate lazy way he set himself to torture me as a schoolboy would devote a rapturous half-hour to watching the agonies of an impaled beetle, or as a ferret in a blind burrow might glue himself comfortably to the neck of a rabbit.   The burden of his conversation was that there was no escape 'of no kind whatever,' and that I should stay here till I died and was 'thrown on to the sand.'   If it were possible to forejudge the conversation of the Damned on the advent of a new soul in their abode, I should say that they would speak as Gunga Dass did to me throughout that long afternoon.   I was powerless to protest or answer ; all my energies being devoted to a struggle against the inexplicable terror that threatened to overwhelm me again and again.   I can compare the feeling to nothing except the struggles of a man against the overpowering nausea of the Channel passage — only my agony was of the spirit and infinitely more terrible.

As the day wore on, the inhabitants began to appear in full strength to catch the rays of the afternoon sun, which were now sloping in at the mouth of the crater. They assembled by little knots, and talked among themselves without even throwing a glance in my direction. About four o'clock, so far as I could judge, Gunga Dass rose and dived into his lair for a moment, emerging with a live crow in his hands.   The wretched bird was in a most draggled and deplorable condition, but seemed to be in no way afraid of its master.   Advancing cautiously to the river-front, Gunga Dass stepped from tussock to tussock until he had reached a smooth patch of sand directly in the line of the boat's fire. The occupants of the boat took no notice. Here he stopped, and, with a couple of dexterous turns of the wrist, pegged the bird on its back with outstretched wings. As was only natural, the crow began to shriek at once and beat the air with its claws. In a few seconds the clamour had attracted the attention of a bevy of wild crows on a shoal a few hundred yards away, where they were discussing something that looked like a corpse. Half a dozen crows flew over at once to see what was going on, and also, as it proved, to attack the pinioned bird. Gunga Dass, who had lain down on a tussock, motioned to me to be quiet, though I fancy this was a needless precaution. In a moment, and before I could see how it happened, a wild crow, who had grappled with the shrieking and helpless bird, was entangled in the latter's claws, swiftly disengaged by Gunga Dass, and pegged down beside its companion in adversity. Curiosity, it seemed, overpowered the rest of the flock, and almost before Gunga Dass and I had time to withdraw to the tussock, two more captives were struggling in the upturned claws of the decoys. So the chase — if I can give it so dignified a name — continued until Gunga Dass had captured seven crows. Five of them he throttled at once, reserving two for further operations another day. I was a good deal impressed by this, to me, novel method of securing food, and complimented Gunga Dass on his skill.

'It is nothing to do,' said he. 'To-morrow you must do it for me. You are stronger than I am.'

This calm assumption of superiority upset me not a

little, and I answered peremptorily: 'Indeed, you old
ruffian? What do you think I have given you money
for?'

'Very well,' was the unmoved reply. 'Perhaps not
to-morrow, nor the day after, nor subsequently; but in
the end, and for many years, you will catch crows and
eat crows, and you will thank your European God that
you have crows to catch and eat.'

I could have cheerfully strangled him for this; but
judged it best under the circumstances to smother my
resentment. An hour later I was eating one of the
crows; and, as Gunga Dass had said, thanking my
God that I had a crow to eat. Never as long as I live
shall I forget that evening meal. The whole population
were squatting on the hard sand platform opposite their
dens, huddled over tiny fires of refuse and dried rushes.
Death, having once laid his hand upon these men and
forborne to strike, seemed to stand aloof from them
now; for most of our company were old men, bent
and worn and twisted with years, and women aged
to all appearance as the Fates themselves. They sat
together in knots and talked — God only knows what
they found to discuss — in low equable tones, curiously in contrast to the strident babble with which
natives are accustomed to make day hideous. Now
and then an access of that sudden fury which had possessed me in the morning would lay hold on a man or
woman; and with yells and imprecations the sufferer
would attack the steep slope until, baffled and bleeding,
he fell back on the platform incapable of moving a
limb. The others would never even raise their eyes
when this happened, as men too well aware of the
futility of their fellows' attempts and wearied with

their useless repetition. I saw four such outbursts in the course of that evening.

Gunga Dass took an eminently business-like view of my situation, and while we were dining — I can afford to laugh at the recollection now, but it was painful enough at the time — propounded the terms of which he would consent to 'do' for me. My nine rupees eight annas, he argued, at the rate of three annas a day, would provide me with food for fifty-one days, or about seven weeks; that is to say, he would be willing to cater for me for that length of time. At the end of it I was to look after myself. For a further consideration — *videlicet* my boots — he would be willing to allow me to occupy the den next to his own, and would supply me with as much dried grass for bedding as he could spare.

'Very well, Gunga Dass,' I replied; 'to the first terms I cheerfully agree, but, as there is nothing on earth to prevent my killing you as you sit here and taking everything that you have' (I thought of the two invaluable crows at the time), 'I flatly refuse to give you my boots and shall take whichever den I please.'

The stroke was a bold one, and I was glad when I saw that it had succeeded. Gunga Dass changed his tone immediately, and disavowed all intention of asking for my boots. At the time it did not strike me as at all strange that I, a Civil Engineer, a man of thirteen years' standing in the Service, and, I trust, an average Englishman, should thus calmly threaten murder and violence against the man who had, for a consideration it is true, taken me under his wing. I had left the world, it seemed, for centuries. I was as certain then as I am now of my own existence, that in the accursed settlement there was no law save that of the strongest; that the living dead men had thrown behind them every canon of the world which had cast them out; and that I had to depend for my own life on my strength and vigilance alone. The crew of the ill-fated *Mignonette* are the only men who would understand my frame of mind. 'At present,' I argued to myself, 'I am strong and a match for six of these wretches. It is imperatively necessary that I should, for my own sake, keep both health and strength until the hour of my release comes — if it ever does.'

Fortified with these resolutions, I ate and drank as much as I could, and made Gunga Dass understand that I intended to be his master, and that the least sign of insubordination on his part would be visited with the only punishment I had it in my power to inflict — sudden and violent death. Shortly after this I went to bed. That is to say, Gunga Dass gave me a double armful of dried bents which I thrust down the mouth of the lair to the right of his, and followed myself, feet foremost; the hole running about nine feet into the sand with a slight downward inclination, and being neatly shored with timbers. From my den, which faced the river-front, I was able to watch the waters of the Sutlej flowing past under the light of a young moon and compose myself to sleep as best I might.

The horrors of that night I shall never forget. My den was nearly as narrow as a coffin, and the sides had been worn smooth and greasy by the contact of innumerable naked bodies, added to which it smelt abominably. Sleep was altogether out of the question to one in my excited frame of mind. As the night wore on, it seemed that the entire amphitheatre was filled with legions of unclean devils that, trooping up from the shoals below, mocked the unfortunates in their lairs.

Personally I am not of an imaginative temperament — very few Engineers are — but on that occasion I was as completely prostrated with nervous terror as any woman. After half an hour or so, however, I was able once more to calmly review my chances of escape. Any exit by the steep sand walls was, of course, impracticable. I had been thoroughly convinced of this some time before. It was possible, just possible, that I might, in the uncertain moonlight, safely run the gauntlet of the rifle shots. The place was so full of terror for me that I was prepared to undergo any risk in leaving it. Imagine my delight, then, when after creeping stealthily to the river-front I found that the infernal boat was not there. My freedom lay before me in the next few steps!

By walking out to the first shallow pool that lay at the foot of the projecting left horn of the horseshoe, I could wade across, turn the flank of the crater, and make my way inland. Without a moment's hesitation I marched briskly past the tussocks where Gunga Dass had snared the crows, and out in the direction of the smooth white sand beyond. My first step from the tufts of dried grass showed me how utterly futile was any hope of escape; for, as I put my foot down, I felt an indescribable drawing, sucking motion of the sand below. Another moment and my leg was swallowed up nearly to the knee. In the moonlight the whole surface of the sand seemed to be shaken with devilish delight at my disappointment. I struggled clear, sweating with terror and exertion, back to the tussocks behind me and fell on my face.

N

My only means of escape from the semicircle was protected with a quicksand!

How long I lay I have not the faintest idea; but I was roused at the last by the malevolent chuckle of Gunga Dass at my ear. 'I would advise you, Protector of the Poor' (the ruffian was speaking English) 'to return to your house. It is unhealthy to lie down here. Moreover, when the boat returns, you will most certainly be rifled at.' He stood over me in the dim light of the dawn, chuckling and laughing to himself. Suppressing my first impulse to catch the man by the neck and throw him on to the quicksand, I rose sullenly and followed him to the platform below the burrows.

Suddenly, and futilely as I thought while I spoke, I asked: 'Gunga Dass, what is the good of the boat if I can't get out *anyhow?*' I recollect that even in my deepest trouble I had been speculating vaguely on the waste of ammunition in guarding an already well protected foreshore.

Gunga Dass laughed again and made answer: 'They have the boat only in daytime. It is for the reason that *there is a way*. I hope we shall have the pleasure of your company for much longer time. It is a pleasant spot when you have been here some years and eaten roast crow long enough.'

I staggered, numbed and helpless, towards the fetid burrow allotted to me, and fell asleep. An hour or so later I was awakened by a piercing scream — the shrill, high-pitched scream of a horse in pain. Those who have once heard that will never forget the sound. I found some little difficulty in scrambling out of the burrow. When I was in the open, I saw Pornic, my poor old Pornic, lying dead on the sandy soil. How they had killed him I cannot guess. Gunga Dass explained that horse was better than crow, and 'greatest good of greatest number is political maxim. We are now Republic, Mister Jukes, and you are entitled to a fair share of the beast. If you like, we will pass a vote of thanks. Shall I propose?'

Yes, we were a Republic indeed! A Republic of wild beasts penned at the bottom of a pit, to eat and fight and sleep till we died. I attempted no protest of any kind, but sat down and stared at the hideous sight in front of me. In less time almost than it takes me to write this, Pornic's body was divided, in some unclean way or other; the men and women had dragged the fragments on to the platform and were preparing their morning meal. Gunga Dass cooked mine. The almost irresistible impulse to fly at the sand walls until I was wearied laid hold of me afresh, and I had to struggle against it with all my might. Gunga Dass was offensively jocular till I told him that if he addressed another remark of any kind whatever to me I should strangle him where he sat. This silenced him till silence became insupportable, and I bade him say something.

'You will live here till you die like the other Feringhi,' he said coolly, watching me over the fragment of gristle that he was gnawing.

'What other Sahib, you swine? Speak at once, and don't stop to tell me a lie.'

'He is over there,' answered Gunga Dass, pointing to a burrow-mouth about four doors to the left of my own. 'You can see for yourself. He died in the burrow as you will die, and I will die, and as all these men and women and the one child will also die.'

'For pity's sake tell me all you know about him.

Who was he? When did he come, and when did he die?'

This appeal was a weak step on my part. Gunga Dass only leered and replied : ' I will not — unless you give me something first.'

Then I recollected where I was, and struck the man between the eyes, partially stunning him. He stepped down from the platform at once, and, cringing and fawning and weeping and attempting to embrace my feet, led me round to the burrow which he had indicated.

'I know nothing whatever about the gentleman. Your God be my witness that I do not. He was as anxious to escape as you were, and he was shot from the boat, though we all did all things to prevent him from attempting. He was shot here.' Gunga Dass laid his hand on his lean stomach and bowed to the earth.

'Well, and what then? Go on ! '

'And then — and then, Your Honour, we carried him into his house and gave him water, and put wet cloths on the wound, and he laid down in his house and gave up the ghost.'

'In how long? In how long?'

'About half an hour, after he received his wound. I call Vishn to witness,' yelled the wretched man, 'that I did everything for him. Everything which was possible, that I did ! '

He threw himself down on the ground and clasped my ankles. But I had my doubts about Gunga Dass's benevolence, and kicked him off as he lay protesting.

'I believe you robbed him of everything he had.

But I can find out in a minute or two. How long was the Sahib here?'

'Nearly a year and a half. I think he must have gone mad. But hear me swear, Protector of the Poor! Won't Your Honour hear me swear that I never touched an article that belonged to him? What is Your Worship going to do?'

I had taken Gunga Dass by the waist and had hauled him on to the platform opposite the deserted burrow. As I did so I thought of my wretched fellow-prisoner's unspeakable misery among all these horrors for eighteen months, and the final agony of dying like a rat in a hole, with a bullet wound in the stomach. Gunga Dass fancied I was going to kill him and howled pitifully. The rest of the population, in the plethora that follows a full flesh meal, watched us without stirring.

'Go inside, Gunga Dass,' said I, 'and fetch it out.'

I was feeling sick and faint with horror now. Gunga Dass nearly rolled off the platform and howled aloud.

'But I am Brahmin, Sahib — a high-caste Brahmin. By your soul, by your father's soul, do not make me do this thing!'

'Brahmin or no Brahmin, by my soul and my father's soul, in you go!' I said, and, seizing him by the shoulders, I crammed his head into the mouth of the burrow, kicked the rest of him in, and, sitting down, covered my face with my hands.

At the end of a few minutes I heard a rustle and a creak; then Gunga Dass in a sobbing, choking whisper speaking to himself; then a soft thud — and I uncovered my eyes.

The dry sand had turned the corpse entrusted to its keeping into a yellow-brown mummy. I told Gunga Dass to stand off while I examined it. The body — clad in an olive-green hunting-suit much stained and worn, with leather pads on the shoulders — was that of a man between thirty and forty, above middle height, with light, sandy hair, long moustache, and a rough unkempt beard. The left canine of the upper jaw was missing, and a portion of the lobe of the right ear was gone. On the second finger of the left hand was a ring — a shield-shaped blood-stone set in gold, with a monogram that might have been either 'B. K.' or 'B. L.' On the third finger of the right hand was a silver ring in the shape of a coiled cobra, much worn and tarnished. Gunga Dass deposited a handful of trifles he had picked out of the burrow at my feet, and, covering the face of the body with my handkerchief, I turned to examine these. I give the full list in the hope that it may lead to the identification of the unfortunate man : —

1. Bowl of a briarwood pipe, serrated at the edge ; much worn and blackened ; bound with string at the screw.

2. Two patent-lever keys ; wards of both broken.

3. Tortoise-shell-handled penknife, silver or nickel, name-plate, marked with monogram 'B. K.'

4. Envelope, postmark undecipherable, bearing a Victorian stamp, addressed to 'Miss Mon——' (rest illegible) — 'ham' — 'nt.'

5. Imitation crocodile-skin notebook with pencil. First forty-five pages blank ; four and a half illegible ; fifteen others filled with private memoranda relating chiefly to three persons — a Mrs. L. Singleton, abbrevi-

ated several times to 'Lot Single,' 'Mrs. S. May,' and 'Garmison,' referred to in places as 'Jerry' or 'Jack.'

6. Handle of small-sized hunting-knife.   Blade snapped short.   Buck's horn, diamond-cut, with swivel and ring on the butt; fragment of cotton cord attached.

It must not be supposed that I inventoried all these things on the spot as fully as I have here written them down.   The notebook first attracted my attention, and I put it in my pocket with a view to studying it later on.   The rest of the articles I conveyed to my burrow for safety's sake, and there, being a methodical man, I inventoried them.   I then returned to the corpse and ordered Gunga Dass to help me to carry it out to the river-front. While we were engaged in this, the exploded shell of an old brown cartridge dropped out of one of the pockets and rolled at my feet.   Gunga Dass had not seen it ; and I fell to thinking that a man does not carry exploded cartridge-cases, especially 'browns,' which will not bear loading twice, about with him when shooting.   In other words, that cartridge-case had been fired inside the crater.   Consequently there must be a gun somewhere.   I was on the verge of asking Gunga Dass, but checked myself, knowing that he would lie.   We laid the body down on the edge of the quicksand by the tussocks.   It was my intention to push it out and let it be swallowed up -- the only possible mode of burial that I could think of.   I ordered Gunga Dass to go away.

Then I gingerly put the corpse out on the quicksand. In doing so, it was lying face downward, I tore the frail and rotten khaki shooting-coat open, disclosing a hideous cavity in the back.   I have already told you that the dry sand had, as it were, mummified the body.   A moment's glance showed that the gaping hole had been caused by a gunshot wound; the gun must have been fired with the muzzle almost touching the back. The shooting-coat, being intact, had been drawn over the body after death, which must have been instantaneous. The secret of the poor wretch's death was plain to me in a flash. Some one of the crater, presumably Gunga Dass, must have shot him with his own gun — the gun that fitted the brown cartridges. He had never attempted to escape in the face of the rifle-fire from the boat.

I pushed the corpse out hastily, and saw it sink from sight literally in a few seconds. I shuddered as I watched. In a dazed, half-conscious way I turned to peruse the notebook. A stained and discoloured slip of paper had been inserted between the binding and the back, and dropped out as I opened the pages. This is what it contained : '*Four out from crow-clump; three left; nine out; two right; three back; two left; fourteen out; two left; seven out; one left; nine back; two right; six back; four right; seven back.*' The paper had been burnt and charred at the edges. What it meant I could not understand. I sat down on the dried bents turning it over and over between my fingers, until I was aware of Gunga Dass standing immediately behind me with glowing eyes and outstretched hands.

'Have you got it?' he panted. 'Will you not let me look at it also? I swear that I will return it.'

'Got what? Return what?' I asked.

'That which you have in your hands. It will help us both.' He stretched out his long, bird-like talons, trembling with eagerness.

'I could never find it,' he continued. 'He had se-

creted it about his person.   Therefore I shot him, but
nevertheless I was unable to obtain it.'

Gunga Dass had quite forgotten his little fiction about
the rifle-bullet. I heard him calmly. Morality is blunted
by consorting with the Dead who are alive.

'What on earth are you raving about?   What is it
you want me to give you?'

'The piece of paper in the notebook. It will help us
both. Oh, you fool! You fool! Can you not see what
it will do for us?   We shall escape!'

His voice rose almost to a scream, and he danced
with excitement before me.   I own I was moved at
the chance of getting away.

'Do you mean to say that this slip of paper will help
us?   What does it mean?'

'Read it aloud!   Read it aloud!   I beg and I pray
to you to read it aloud.'

I did so. Gunga Dass listened delightedly, and drew
an irregular line in the sand with his fingers.

'See now!   It was the length of his gun-barrels without the stock. I have those barrels. Four gun-barrels
out from the place where I caught crows. Straight out;
do you mind me?   Then three left.   Ah!   Now well I
remember how that man worked it out night after
night.   Then nine out, and so on.   Out is always
straight before you across the quicksand to the North.
He told me so before I killed him.'

'But if you knew all this why didn't you get out
before?'

'I did *not* know it.   He told me that he was working
it out a year and a half ago, and how he was working
it out night after night when the boat had gone away,
and he could get out near the quicksand safely.   Then

he said that we would get away together. But I was afraid that he would leave me behind one night when he had worked it all out, and so I shot him. Besides, it is not advisable that the men who once get in here should escape. Only I, and *I* am a Brahmin.'

The hope of escape had brought Gunga Dass's caste back to him. He stood up, walked about and gesticulated violently. Eventually I managed to make him talk soberly, and he told me how this Englishman had spent six months night after night in exploring, inch by inch, the passage across the quicksand; how he had declared it to be simplicity itself up to within about twenty yards of the river bank after turning the flank of the left horn of the horseshoe. This much he had evidently not completed when Gunga Dass shot him with his own gun.

In my frenzy of delight at the possibilities of escape I recollect shaking hands wildly with Gunga Dass, after we had decided that we were to make an attempt to get away that very night. It was weary work waiting throughout the afternoon.

About ten o'clock, as far as I could judge, when the Moon had just risen above the lip of the crater, Gunga Dass made a move for his burrow to bring out the gun-barrels whereby to measure our path. All the other wretched inhabitants had retired to their lairs long ago. The guardian boat drifted down-stream some hours before, and we were utterly alone by the crow-clump. Gunga Dass, while carrying the gun-barrels, let slip the piece of paper which was to be our guide. I stooped down hastily to recover it, and, as I did so, I was aware that the creature was aiming a violent blow at the back of my head with the gun-barrels. It was too late to turn round. I must have received the blow somewhere on the nape of my neck, for I fell senseless at the edge of the quicksand.

When I recovered consciousness, the Moon was going down, and I was sensible of intolerable pain in the back of my head. Gunga Dass had disappeared and my mouth was full of blood. I lay down again and prayed that I might die without more ado. Then the unreasoning fury which I have before mentioned laid hold upon me, and I staggered inland towards the walls of the crater. It seemed that some one was calling to me in a whisper — 'Sahib! Sahib! Sahib!' exactly as my bearer used to call me in the mornings. I fancied that I was delirious until a handful of sand fell at my feet. Then I looked up and saw a head peering down into the amphitheatre — the head of Dunnoo, my dog-boy, who attended to my collies. As soon as he had attracted my attention, he held up his hand and showed a rope. I motioned, staggering to and fro the while, that he should throw it down. It was a couple of leather punkah-ropes knotted together, with a loop at one end. I slipped the loop over my head and under my arms; heard Dunnoo urge something forward; was conscious that I was being dragged, face downward, up the steep sand-slope, and the next instant found myself choked and half-fainting on the sand hills overlooking the crater. Dunnoo, with his face ashy gray in the moonlight, implored me not to stay but to get back to my tent at once.

It seems that he had tracked Pornic's footprints fourteen miles across the sands to the crater; had returned

and told my servants, who flatly refused to meddle with
any one, white or black, once fallen into the hideous
Village of the Dead ; whereupon Dunnoo had taken
one of my ponies and a couple of punkah ropes, returned to the crater, and hauled me out as I have
described.

THE MAN WHO WOULD BE KING

Brother to a Prince and fellow to a beggar if he be found worthy.

THE Law, as quoted, lays down a fair conduct of life, and one not easy to follow. I have been fellow to a beggar again and again under circumstances which prevented either of us finding out whether the other was worthy. I have still to be brother to a Prince, though I once came near to kinship with what might have been a veritable King and was promised the reversion of a Kingdom — army, law-courts, revenue and policy all complete. But, to-day, I greatly fear that my King is dead, and if I want a crown I must go hunt it for myself.

The beginning of everything was in a railway train upon the road to Mhow from Ajmir. There had been a Deficit in the Budget, which necessitated travelling, not Second-class, which is only half as dear as First-class, but by Intermediate, which is very awful indeed. There are no cushions in the Intermediate class, and the population are either Intermediate, which is Eurasian, or native, which for a long night journey is nasty, or Loafer, which is amusing though intoxicated. Intermediates do not buy from refreshment-rooms. They carry their food in bundles and pots, and buy sweets from the native sweetmeat-sellers, and drink the roadside water. That is why in hot weather Intermediates

189

are taken out of the carriages dead, and in all weathers are most properly looked down upon.

My particular Intermediate happened to be empty till I reached Nasirabad, when a big black-browed gentleman in shirt-sleeves entered, and, following the custom of Intermediates, passed the time of day. He was a wanderer and a vagabond like myself, but with an educated taste for whiskey. He told tales of things he had seen and done, of out-of-the-way corners of the Empire into which he had penetrated, and of adventures in which he risked his life for a few days food.

'If India was filled with men like you and me, not knowing more than the crows where they'd get their next day's rations, it isn't seventy millions of revenue the land would be paying—it's seven hundred millions,' said he ; and as I looked at his mouth and chin I was disposed to agree with him.

We talked politics — the politics of Loaferdom that sees things from the underside where the lath and plaster is not smoothed off — and we talked postal arrangements because my friend wanted to send a telegram back from the next station to Ajmir, the turning-off place from the Bombay to the Mhow line as you travel westward. My friend had no money beyond eight annas which he wanted for dinner, and I had no money at all, owing to the hitch in the Budget before mentioned. Further, I was going into a wilderness where, though I should resume touch with the Treasury, there were no telegraph offices. I was, therefore, unable to help him in any way.

'We might threaten a Station-master, and make him send a wire on tick,' said my friend, 'but that'd mean

enquiries for you and for me, and *I*'ve got my hands
full these days. Did you say you were travelling back
along this line within any days?'

'Within ten,' I said.

'Can't you make it eight?' said he. 'Mine is rather
urgent business.'

'I can send your telegram within ten days if that will
serve you,' I said.

'I couldn't trust the wire to fetch him now I think
of it. It's this way. He leaves Delhi on the 23rd for
Bombay. That means he'll be running through Ajmir
about the night of the 23rd.'

'But I'm going into the Indian Desert,' I explained.

'Well *and* good,' said he. 'You'll be changing at
Marwar Junction to get into Jodhpore territory — you
must do that — and he'll be coming through Marwar
Junction in the early morning of the 24th by the
Bombay Mail. Can you be at Marwar Junction on
that time? 'Twon't be inconveniencing you because I
know that there's precious few pickings to be got out
of these Central India States — even though you pretend to be correspondent of the *Backwoodsman*.'

'Have you ever tried that trick?' I asked.

'Again and again, but the Residents find you out,
and then you get escorted to the Border before you've
time to get your knife into them. But about my friend
here. I *must* give him a word o' mouth to tell him
what's come to me or else he won't know where to go.
I would take it more than kind of you if you was to
come out of Central India in time to catch him at Marwar Junction, and say to him: "He has gone South for
the week." He'll know what that means. He's a big
man with a red beard, and a great swell he is. You'll

find him sleeping like a gentleman with all his luggage round him in a Second-class apartment. But don't you be afraid. Slip down the window and say: "He has gone South for the week," and he'll tumble. It's only cutting your time of stay in those parts by two days. I ask you as a stranger — going to the West,' he said with emphasis.

'Where have *you* come from?' said I.

'From the East,' said he, 'and I am hoping that you will give him the message on the Square — for the sake of my Mother as well as your own.'

Englishmen are not usually softened by appeals to the memory of their mothers; but for certain reasons, which will be fully apparent, I saw fit to agree.

'It's more than a little matter,' said he, 'and that's why I asked you to do it — and now I know that I can depend on you doing it. A Second-class carriage at Marwar Junction, and a red-haired man asleep in it. You'll be sure to remember. I get out at the next station, and I must hold on there till he comes or sends me what I want.'

'I'll give the message if I catch him,' I said, 'and for the sake of your Mother as well as mine I'll give you a word of advice. Don't try to run the Central India States just now as the correspondent of the *Backwoodsman*. There's a real one knocking about here, and it might lead to trouble.'

'Thank you,' said he simply, 'and when will the swine be gone? I can't starve because he's ruining my work. I wanted to get hold of the Degumber Rajah down here about his father's widow, and give him a jump.'

'What did he do to his father's widow, then?'

'Filled her up with red pepper and slippered her to death as she hung from a beam. I found that out myself and I'm the only man that would dare going into the State to get hush-money for it. They'll try to poison me, same as they did in Chortumna when I went on the loot there. But you'll give the man at Marwar Junction my message?'

He got out at a little roadside station, and I reflected. I had heard, more than once, of men personating correspondents of newspapers and bleeding small Native States with threats of exposure, but I had never met any of the caste before. They lead a hard life, and generally die with great suddenness. The Native States have a wholesome horror of English newspapers, which may throw light on their peculiar methods of government, and do their best to choke correspondents with champagne, or drive them out of their mind with four-in-hand barouches. They do not understand that nobody cares a straw for the internal administration of Native States so long as oppression and crime are kept within decent limits, and the ruler is not drugged, drunk, or diseased from one end of the year to the other. They are the dark places of the earth, full of unimaginable cruelty, touching the Railway and the Telegraph on one side, and, on the other, the days of Harun-al-Raschid. When I left the train I did business with divers Kings, and in eight days passed through many changes of life. Sometimes I wore dress-clothes and consorted with Princes and Politicals, drinking from crystal and eating from silver. Sometimes I lay out upon the ground and devoured what I could get, from a plate made of leaves, and drank the running water, and slept under the same rug as my servant. It was all in the day's work.

Then I headed for the Great Indian Desert upon the proper date, as I had promised, and the night Mail set me down at Marwar Junction, where a funny little, happy-go-lucky, native-managed railway runs to Jodhpore. The Bombay Mail from Delhi makes a short halt at Marwar. She arrived as I got in, and I had just time to hurry to her platform and go down the carriages. There was only one Second-class on the train. I slipped the window and looked down upon a flaming red beard, half covered by a railway rug. That was my man, fast asleep, and I dug him gently in the ribs. He woke with a grunt and I saw his face in the light of the lamps. It was a great and shining face.

'Tickets again?' said he.

'No,' said I. 'I am to tell you that he is gone South for the week. He has gone South for the week!'

The train had begun to move out. The red man rubbed his eyes. 'He has gone South for the week,' he repeated. 'Now that's just like his impidence. Did he say that I was to give you anything? 'Cause I won't.'

'He didn't,' I said and dropped away, and watched the red lights die out in the dark. It was horribly cold because the wind was blowing off the sands. I climbed into my own train — not an Intermediate carriage this time — and went to sleep.

If the man with the beard had given me a rupee I should have kept it as a memento of a rather curious affair. But the consciousness of having done my duty was my only reward.

Later on I reflected that two gentlemen like my friends could not do any good if they foregathered and personated correspondents of newspapers, and might, if they black-mailed one of the little rat-trap states of Central India or Southern Rajputana, get themselves into serious difficulties. I therefore took some trouble to describe them as accurately as I could remember to people who would be interested in deporting them : and succeeded, so I was later informed, in having them headed back from the Degumber borders.

Then I became respectable, and returned to an Office where there were no Kings and no incidents outside the daily manufacture of a newspaper. A newspaper office seems to attract every conceivable sort of person, to the prejudice of discipline. Zenana-mission ladies arrive, and beg that the Editor will instantly abandon all his duties to describe a Christian prize-giving in a back-slum of a perfectly inaccessible village ; Colonels who have been overpassed for command sit down and sketch the outline of a series of ten, twelve, or twenty-four leading articles on Seniority *versus* Selection ; missionaries wish to know why they have not been permitted to escape from their regular vehicles of abuse and swear at a brother-missionary under special patronage of the editorial We ; stranded theatrical companies troop up to explain that they cannot pay for their advertisements, but on their return from New Zealand or Tahiti will do so with interest ; inventors of patent punkah-pulling machines, carriage couplings and unbreakable swords and axle-trees call with specifications in their pockets and hours at their disposal ; tea-companies enter and elaborate their prospectuses with the office pens; secretaries of ball-committees clamour to have the glories of their last dance more fully described; strange ladies rustle in and say: 'I want a hundred lady's cards printed *at once*, please,' which is manifestly part of an Editor's duty; and every dissolute ruffian that ever tramped the Grand Trunk Road makes it his business to ask for employment as a proof-reader. And, all the time, the telephone-bell is ringing madly, and Kings are being killed on the Continent, and Empires are saying — 'You're another,' and Mister Gladstone is calling down brimstone upon the British Dominions, and the little black copy-boys are whining, '*kaa-pi chay-ha-yeh*' (copy wanted) like tired bees, and most of the paper is as blank as Modred's shield.

But that is the amusing part of the year. There are six other months when none ever come to call, and the thermometer walks inch by inch up to the top of the glass, and the office is darkened to just above reading-light, and the press-machines are red-hot of touch, and nobody writes anything but accounts of amusements in the Hill-stations or obituary notices. Then the telephone becomes a tinkling terror, because it tells you of the sudden deaths of men and women that you knew intimately, and the prickly-heat covers you with a garment, and you sit down and write: 'A slight increase of sickness is reported from the Khuda Janta Khan District. The outbreak is purely sporadic in its nature, and, thanks to the energetic efforts of the District authorities, is now almost at an end. It is, however, with deep regret we record the death,' etc.

Then the sickness really breaks out, and the less recording and reporting the better for the peace of the

subscribers.   But the Empires and the Kings continue
to divert themselves as selfishly as before, and the
Foreman thinks that a daily paper really ought to
come out once in twenty-four hours, and all the people
at the Hill-stations in the middle of their amusements
say: 'Good gracious!   Why can't the paper be spark-
ling?   I'm sure there's plenty going on up here.'

That is the dark half of the moon, and, as the advertisements say, 'must be experienced to be appreciated.'

It was in that season, and a remarkably evil season,
that the paper began running the last issue of the
week on Saturday night, which is to say Sunday morning, after the custom of a London paper.   This was a
great convenience, for immediately after the paper was
put to bed, the dawn would lower the thermometer
from 96° to almost 84° for half an hour, and in that
chill — you have no idea how cold is 84° on the grass
until you begin to pray for it — a very tired man could
get off to sleep ere the heat roused him.

One Saturday night it was my pleasant duty to put
the paper to bed alone.   A King or courtier or a
courtesan or a Community was going to die or get a
new Constitution, or do something that was important
on the other side of the world, and the paper was to be
held open till the latest possible minute in order to
catch the telegram.

It was a pitchy black night, as stifling as a June
night can be, and the *loo*, the red-hot wind from the
westward, was booming among the tinder-dry trees
and pretending that the rain was on its heels.   Now
and again a spot of almost boiling water would fall on
the dust with the flop of a frog, but all our weary
world knew that was only pretence.   It was a shade

cooler in the press-room than the office, so I sat there, while the type ticked and clicked, and the night-jars hooted at the windows, and the all but naked compositors wiped the sweat from their foreheads, and called for water. The thing that was keeping us back, whatever it was, would not come off, though the *loo* dropped and the last type was set, and the whole round earth stood still in the choking heat, with its finger on its lip, to wait the event. I drowsed, and wondered whether the telegraph was a blessing, and whether this dying man, or struggling people, might be aware of the inconvenience the delay was causing. There was no special reason beyond the heat and worry to make tension, but, as the clock-hands crept up to three o'clock and the machines spun their fly-wheels two and three times to see that all was in order, before I said the word that would set them off, I could have shrieked aloud.

Then the roar and rattle of the wheels shivered the quiet into little bits. I rose to go away, but two men in white clothes stood in front of me. The first one said: 'It's him!' The second said: 'So it is!' And they both laughed almost as loudly as the machinery roared, and mopped their foreheads. 'We seed there was a light burning across the road and we were sleeping in that ditch there for coolness, and I said to my friend here, The office is open. Let's come along and speak to him as turned us back from the Degumber State,' said the smaller of the two. He was the man I had met in the Mhow train, and his fellow was the red-bearded man of Marwar Junction. There was no mistaking the eyebrows of the one or the beard of the other.

I was not pleased, because I wished to go to sleep, not to squabble with loafers. 'What do you want?' I asked.

'Half an hour's talk with you, cool and comfortable, in the office,' said the red-bearded man. 'We'd *like* some drink — the Contrack doesn't begin yet, Peachey, so you needn't look — but what we really want is advice. We don't want money. We ask you as a favour, because we found out you did us a bad turn about Degumber State.'

I led from the press-room to the stifling office with the maps on the walls, and the red-haired man rubbed his hands. 'That's something like,' said he. 'This was the proper shop to come to. Now, Sir, let me introduce to you Brother Peachey Carnehan, that's him, and Brother Daniel Dravot, that is *me*, and the less said about our professions the better, for we have been most things in our time. Soldier, sailor, compositor, photographer, proof-reader, street-preacher, and correspondents of the *Backwoodsman* when we thought the paper wanted one. Carnehan is sober, and so am I. Look at us first, and see that's sure. It will save you cutting into my talk. We'll take one of your cigars apiece, and you shall see us light up.'

I watched the test. The men were absolutely sober, so I gave them each a tepid whiskey and soda.

'Well *and* good,' said Carnehan of the eyebrows, wiping the froth from his moustache. 'Let me talk now, Dan. We have been all over India, mostly on foot. We have been boiler-fitters, engine-drivers, petty contractors, and all that, and we have decided that India isn't big enough for such as us.'

They certainly were too big for the office. Dravot's

beard seemed to fill half the room and Carnehan's shoulders the other half, as they sat on the big table. Carnehan continued : 'The country isn't half worked out because they that governs it won't let you touch it. They spend all their blessed time in governing it, and you can't lift a spade, nor chip a rock, nor look for oil, nor anything like that without all the Government saying — "Leave it alone, and let us govern." Therefore, such *as* it is, we will let it alone, and go away to some other place where a man isn't crowded and can come to his own. We are not little men, and there is nothing that we are afraid of except Drink, and we have signed a Contrack on that. *Therefore*, we are going away to be Kings.'

'Kings in our own right,' muttered Dravot.

'Yes, of course,' I said. 'You've been tramping in the sun, and it's a very warm night, and hadn't you better sleep over the notion? Come to-morrow.'

'Neither drunk nor sunstruck,' said Dravot. 'We have slept over the notion half a year, and require to see Books and Atlases, and we have decided that there is only one place now in the world that two strong men can Sar-a-*whack*. They call it Kafiristan. By my reckoning it's the top right-hand corner of Afghanistan, not more than three hundred miles from Peshawar. They have two-and-thirty heathen idols there, and we'll be the thirty-third and fourth. It's a mountaineous country, and the women of those parts are very beautiful.'

'But that is provided against in the Contrack,' said Carnehan. 'Neither Woman nor Liqu-or, Daniel.'

'And that's all we know, except that no one has gone there, and they fight, and in any place where they fight a man who knows how to drill men can always

be a King.   We shall go to those parts and say to any
King we find — " D'you want to vanquish your foes ? "
and we will show him how to drill men; for that we
know better than anything else.   Then we will sub-
vert that King and seize his Throne and establish a
Dy-nasty.'

'You'll be cut to pieces before you're fifty miles
across the Border,' I said.   'You have to travel
through Afghanistan to get to that country.   It's one
mass of mountains and peaks and glaciers, and no
Englishman has been through it.   The people are
utter brutes, and even if you reached them you
couldn't do anything.'

'That's more like,' said Carnehan.   'If you could
think us a little more mad we would be more pleased.
We have come to you to know about this country, to
read a book about it, and to be shown maps.   We want
you to tell us that we are fools and to show us your
books.'   He turned to the book-cases.

'Are you at all in earnest?' I said.

'A little,' said Dravot sweetly.   'As big a map as
you have got, even if it's all blank where Kafiristan is,
and any books you've got.   We can read, though we
aren't very educated.'

I uncased the big thirty-two-miles-to-the-inch map
of India, and two smaller Frontier maps, hauled down
volume INF–KAN of the *Encyclopædia Britannica*, and
the men consulted them.

'See here !' said Dravot, his thumb on the map.
'Up to Jagdallak, Peachey and me know the road.
We was there with Roberts' Army.   We'll have to
turn off to the right at Jagdallak through Laghmann
territory.   Then we get among the hills — fourteen

thousand feet — fifteen thousand — it will be cold work there, but it don't look very far on the map.'

I handed him Wood on the *Sources of the Oxus.* Carnehan was deep in the *Encyclopædia.*

'They're a mixed lot,' said Dravot reflectively ; 'and it won't help us to know the names of their tribes. The more tribes the more they'll fight, and the better for us. From Jagdallak to Ashang. H'mm !'

'But all the information about the country is as sketchy and inaccurate as can be,' I protested. 'No one knows anything about it really. Here's the file of the *United Services' Institute.* Read what Bellew says.'

'Blow Bellew !' said Carnehan. 'Dan, they're a stinkin' lot of heathens, but this book here says they think they're related to us English.'

I smoked while the men pored over *Raverty*, *Wood*, the maps, and the *Encyclopædia.*

'There is no use your waiting,' said Dravot politely. 'It's about four o'clock now. We'll go before six o'clock if you want to sleep, and we won't steal any of the papers. Don't you sit up. We're two harmless lunatics, and if you come to-morrow evening down to the Serai we'll say good-bye to you.'

'You *are* two fools,' I answered. 'You'll be turned back at the Frontier or cut up the minute you set foot in Afghanistan. Do you want any money or a recommendation down-country ? I can help you to the chance of work next week.'

'Next week we shall be hard at work ourselves, thank you,' said Dravot. 'It isn't so easy being a King as it looks. When we've got our Kingdom in going order we'll let you know, and you can come up and help us to govern it.'

'Would two lunatics make a Contrack like that?' said Carnehan, with subdued pride, showing me a greasy half-sheet of notepaper on which was written the following. I copied it, then and there, as a curiosity —

This Contract between me and you persuing witnesseth in the name of God — Amen and so forth.

> *(One) That me and you will settle this matter together; i.e., to be Kings of Kafiristan.*
>
> *(Two) That you and me will not, while this matter is being settled, look at any Liquor, nor any Woman black, white, or brown, so as to get mixed up with one or the other harmful.*
>
> *(Three) That we conduct ourselves with Dignity and Discretion, and if one of us gets into trouble the other will stay by him.*
>
> *Signed by you and me this day.*
> *Peachey Taliaferro Carnehan.*
> *Daniel Dravot.*
> *Both Gentlemen at Large.*

'There was no need for the last article,' said Carnehan, blushing modestly; 'but it looks regular. Now you know the sort of men that loafers are — we *are* loafers, Dan, until we get out of India — and *do* you think that we would sign a Contrack like that unless we was in earnest? We have kept away from the two things that make life worth having.'

'You won't enjoy your lives much longer if you are going to try this idiotic adventure. Don't set the office on fire,' I said, 'and go away before nine o'clock.'

I left them still poring over the maps and making notes on the back of the 'Contrack.' 'Be sure to come down to the Serai to-morrow,' were their parting words.

The Kumharsen Serai is the great four-square sink of humanity where the strings of camels and horses from the North load and unload. All the nationalities of Central Asia may be found there, and most of the folk of India proper. Balkh and Bokhara there meet Bengal and Bombay, and try to draw eye-teeth. You can buy ponies, turquoises, Persian pussy-cats, saddle-bags, fat-tailed sheep and musk in the Kumharsen Serai, and get many strange things for nothing. In the afternoon I went down to see whether my friends intended to keep their word or were lying there drunk.

A priest attired in fragments of ribbons and rags stalked up to me, gravely twisting a child's paper whirli-gig. Behind him was his servant bending under the load of a crate of mud toys. The two were loading up two camels, and the inhabitants of the Serai watched them with shrieks of laughter.

'The priest is mad,' said a horse-dealer to me. 'He is going up to Kabul to sell toys to the Amir. He will either be raised to honour or have his head cut off. He came in here this morning and has been behaving madly ever since.'

'The witless are under the protection of God,' stammered a flat-cheeked Usbeg in broken Hindi. 'They foretell future events.'

'Would they could have foretold that my caravan would have been cut up by the Shinwaris almost within shadow of the Pass!' grunted the Eusufzai agent of a Rajputana trading-house whose goods had been diverted into the hands of other robbers just across the Border, and whose misfortunes were the laughing-stock of the bazar. 'Ohé, priest, whence come you and whither do you go?'

'From Roum have I come,' shouted the priest, waving his whirligig; 'from Roum, blown by the breath of a hundred devils across the sea! O thieves, robbers, liars, the blessing of Pir Khan on pigs, dogs, and perjurers! Who will take the Protected of God to the North to sell charms that are never still to the Amir? The camels shall not gall, the sons shall not fall sick, and the wives shall remain faithful while they are away, of the men who give me place in their caravan. Who will assist me to slipper the King of the Roos with a golden slipper with a silver heel? The protection of Pir Khan be upon his labours!' He spread out the skirts of his gaberdine and pirouetted between the lines of tethered horses.

'There starts a caravan from Peshawar to Kabul in twenty days, *Huzrut*,' said the Eusufzai trader. 'My camels go therewith. Do thou also go and bring us good-luck.'

'I will go even now!' shouted the priest. 'I will depart upon my winged camels, and be at Peshawar in a day! Ho! Hazar Mir Khan,' he yelled to his servant, 'drive out the camels, but let me first mount my own.'

He leaped on the back of his beast as it knelt, and, turning round to me, cried: 'Come thou also, Sahib, a little along the road, and I will sell thee a charm — an amulet that shall make thee King of Kafiristan.'

Then the light broke upon me, and I followed the two camels out of the Serai till we reached open road and the priest halted.

'What d'you think o' that?' said he in English.
'Carnehan can't talk their patter, so I've made him my
servant. He makes a handsome servant. 'Tisn't for
nothing that I've been knocking about the country for
fourteen years. Didn't I do that talk neat? We'll
hitch on to a caravan at Peshawar till we get to Jagdallak, and then we'll see if we can get donkeys for our
camels, and strike into Kafiristan. Whirligigs for the
Amir, O Lor! Put your hand under the camel-bags
and tell me what you feel.'

I felt the butt of a Martini, and another and another.

'Twenty of 'em,' said Dravot placidly. 'Twenty of
'em and ammunition to correspond, under the whirligigs and the mud dolls.'

'Heaven help you if you are caught with those
things!' I said. 'A Martini is worth her weight in
silver among the Pathans.'

'Fifteen hundred rupees of capital — every rupee
we could beg, borrow, or steal — are invested on these
two camels,' said Dravot. 'We won't get caught.
We're going through the Khaiber with a regular caravan. Who'd touch a poor mad priest?'

'Have you got everything you want?' I asked,
overcome with astonishment.

'Not yet, but we shall soon. Give us a memento of
your kindness, *Brother*. You did me a service, yesterday, and that time in Marwar. Half my Kingdom shall
you have, as the saying is.' I slipped a small charm compass from my watch chain and handed it up to the priest.

'Good-bye,' said Dravot, giving me hand cautiously.
'It's the last time we'll shake hands with an Englishman these many days. Shake hands with him, Carnehan,' he cried, as the second camel passed me.

Carnehan leaned down and shook hands. Then the camels passed away along the dusty road, and I was left alone to wonder. My eye could detect no failure in the disguises. The scene in the Serai proved that they were complete to the native mind. There was just the chance, therefore, that Carnehan and Dravot would be able to wander through Afghanistan without detection. But, beyond, they would find death — certain and awful death.

Ten days later a native correspondent giving me the news of the day from Peshawar, wound up his letter with : 'There has been much laughter here on account of a certain mad priest who is going in his estimation to sell petty gauds and insignificant trinkets which he ascribes as great charms to H.H. the Amir of Bokhara. He passed through Peshawar and associated himself to the Second Summer caravan that goes to Kabul. The merchants are pleased because through superstition they imagine that such mad fellows bring good-fortune.'

The two, then, were beyond the Border. I would have prayed for them, but, that night, a real King died in Europe, and demanded an obituary notice.

*   *   *   *   *   *   *   *   *

The wheel of the world swings through the same phases again and again. Summer passed and winter thereafter, and came and passed again. The daily paper continued and I with it, and upon the third summer there fell a hot night, a night-issue, and a strained waiting for something to be telegraphed from the other side of the world, exactly as had happened before. A few great men had died in the past two years, the machines worked with more clatter, and some of the trees in the Office garden were a few feet taller. But that was all the difference.

I passed over to the press-room, and went through just such a scene as I have already described. The nervous tension was stronger than it had been two years before, and I felt the heat more acutely. At three o'clock I cried, 'Print off,' and turned to go, when there crept to my chair what was left of a man. He was bent into a circle, his head was sunk between his shoulders, and he moved his feet one over the other like a bear. I could hardly see whether he walked or crawled — this rag-wrapped, whining cripple who ad-dressed me by name, crying that he was come back. 'Can you give me a drink?' he whimpered. 'For the Lord's sake, give me a drink!'

I went back to the office, the man following with groans of pain, and I turned up the lamp.

'Don't you know me?' he gasped, dropping into a chair, and he turned his drawn face, surmounted by a shock of gray hair, to the light.

I looked at him intently. Once before had I seen eyebrows that met over the nose in an inch-broad black band, but for the life of me I could not tell where.

'I don't know you,' I said, handing him the whiskey. 'What can I do for you?'

He took a gulp of the spirit raw, and shivered in spite of the suffocating heat.

'I've come back,' he repeated; 'and I was the King of Kafiristan — me and Dravot — crowned Kings we was! In this office we settled it — you setting there and giving us the books. I am Peachey — Peachey Taliaferro Carnehan, and you've been setting here ever since — O Lord!'

I was more than a little astonished, and expressed my feelings accordingly.

'It's true,' said Carnehan, with a dry cackle, nursing his feet, which were wrapped in rags. 'True as gospel. Kings we were, with crowns upon our heads — me and Dravot — poor Dan — oh, poor, poor Dan, that would never take advice, not though I begged of him!'

'Take the whiskey,' I said, 'and take your own time. Tell me all you can recollect of everything from beginning to end. You got across the border on your camels, Dravot dressed as a mad priest and you his servant. Do you remember that?'

'I ain't mad — yet, but I shall be that way soon. Of course I remember. Keep looking at me, or maybe my words will go all to pieces. Keep looking at me in my eyes and don't say anything.'

I leaned forward and looked into his face as steadily as I could. He dropped one hand upon the table and I grasped it by the wrist. It was twisted like a bird's claw, and upon the back was a ragged, red, diamond-shaped scar.

'No, don't look there. Look at *me*,' said Carnehan. 'That comes afterwards, but for the Lord's sake don't distrack me. We left with that caravan, me and Dravot playing all sorts of antics to amuse the people we were with. Dravot used to make us laugh in the evenings when all the people was cooking their dinners — cooking their dinners, and . . . what did they do then? They lit little fires with sparks that went into Dravot's beard, and we all laughed — fit to die. Little red fires they was, going into Dravot's big red beard — so funny.' His eyes left mine and he smiled foolishly.

'You went as far as Jagdallak with that caravan,' I

said at a venture, 'after you had lit those fires. To
Jagdallak, where you turned off to try to get into
Kafiristan.'

'No, we didn't neither. What are you talking about?
We turned off before Jagdallak, because we heard the
roads was good. But they wasn't good enough for our
two camels — mine and Dravot's. When we left the
caravan, Dravot took off all his clothes and mine too,
and said we would be heathen, because the Kafirs didn't
allow Mohammedans to talk to them. So we dressed
betwixt and between, and such a sight as Daniel Dravot
I never saw yet nor expect to see again. He burned
half his beard, and slung a sheep-skin over his shoulder,
and shaved his head into patterns. He shaved mine,
too, and made me wear outrageous things to look like
a heathen. That was in a most mountaineous country,
and our camels couldn't go along any more because of
the mountains. They were tall and black, and coming
home I saw them fight like wild goats — there are lots
of goats in Kafiristan. And these mountains, they
never keep still, no more than the goats. Always
fighting they are, and don't let you sleep at night.'

'Take some more whiskey,' I said very slowly.
'What did you and Daniel Dravot do when the camels
could go no further because of the rough roads that led
into Kafiristan?'

'What did which do? There was a party called
Peachey Taliaferro Carnehan that was with Dravot.
Shall I tell you about him? He died out there in the
cold. Slap from the bridge fell old Peachey, turning
and twisting in the air like a penny whirligig that you
can sell to the Amir. — No; they was two for three
ha'pence, those whirligigs, or I am much mistaken and

woeful sore. . . . And then these camels were no use, and Peachey said to Dravot — "For the Lord's sake let's get out of this before our heads are chopped off," and with that they killed the camels all among the mountains, not having anything in particular to eat, but first they took off the boxes with the guns and the ammunition, till two men came along driving four mules. Dravot up and dances in front of them, singing — "Sell me four mules." Says the first man — "If you are rich enough to buy, you are rich enough to rob;" but before ever he could put his hand to his knife, Dravot breaks his neck over his knee, and the other party runs away. So Carnehan loaded the mules with the rifles that was taken off the camels, and together we starts forward into those bitter cold mountaineous parts, and never a road broader than the back of your hand.'

He paused for a moment, while I asked him if he could remember the nature of the country through which he had journeyed.

'I am telling you as straight as I can, but my head isn't as good as it might be. They drove nails through it to make me hear better how Dravot died. The country was mountaineous and the mules were most contrary, and the inhabitants was dispersed and solitary. They went up and up, and down and down, and that other party, Carnehan, was imploring of Dravot not to sing and whistle so loud, for fear of bringing down the tremenjus avalanches. But Dravot says that if a King couldn't sing it wasn't worth being King, and whacked the mules over the rump, and never took no heed for ten cold days. We came to a big level valley all among the mountains, and the mules were near dead, so we killed them, not having anything in special for them or us to eat. We sat upon the boxes, and played odd and even with the cartridges that was jolted out.

'Then ten men with bows and arrows ran down that valley, chasing twenty men with bows and arrows, and the row was tremenjus. They was fair men — fairer than you or me — with yellow hair and remarkable well built. Says Dravot, unpacking the guns — "This is the beginning of the business. We'll fight for the ten men," and with that he fires two rifles at the twenty men, and drops one of them at two hundred yards from the rock where he was sitting. The other men began to run, but Carnehan and Dravot sits on the boxes picking them off at all ranges, up and down the valley. Then we goes up to the ten men that had run across the snow too, and they fires a footy little arrow at us. Dravot he shoots above their heads and they all falls down flat. Then he walks over them and kicks them, and then he lifts them up and shakes hands all round to make them friendly like. He calls them and gives them the boxes to carry, and waves his hand for all the world as though he was King already. They takes the boxes and him across the valley and up the hill into a pine wood on the top, where there was half a dozen big stone idols. Dravot he goes to the biggest — a fellow they call Imbra — and lays a rifle and a cartridge at his feet, rubbing his nose respectful with his own nose, patting him on the head, and saluting in front of it. He turns round to the men and nods his head, and says — "That's all right. I'm in the know too, and all these old jim-jams are my friends." Then he opens his mouth and points down

it, and when the first man brings him food, he says—
" No ; " and when the second man brings him food he
says — " No ; " but when one of the old priests and the
boss of the village brings him food, he says — " Yes ; "
very haughty, and eats it slow. That was how he
came to our first village, without any trouble, just as
though we had tumbled from the skies. But we
tumbled from one of those damned rope-bridges, you
see and — you couldn't expect a man to laugh much
after that?'

'Take some more whiskey and go on,' I said. 'That
was the first village you came into. How did you get
to be King?'

'I wasn't King,' said Carnehan. 'Dravot he was the
King, and a handsome man he looked with the gold
crown on his head and all. Him and the other party
stayed in that village, and every morning Dravot sat
by the side of old Imbra, and the people came and worshipped. That was Dravot's order. Then a lot of men
came into the valley, and Carnehan Dravot picks them
off with the rifles before they knew where they was,
and runs down into the valley and up again the other
side and finds another village, came as the first one,
and the people all falls down flat on their faces, and
Dravot says — " Now what is the trouble between you
two villages? " and the people points to a woman, as
fair as you or me, that was carried off, and Dravot
takes her back to the first village and counts up the
dead — eight there was. For each dead man Dravot
pours a little milk on the ground and waves his arms
like a whirligig and " That's all right," says he. Then
he and Carnehan takes the big boss of each village by
the arm and walks them down into the valley, and

shows them how to scratch a line with a spear right
down the valley, and gives each a sod of turf from
both sides of the line. Then all the people comes
down and shouts like the devil and all, and Dravot
says — " Go and dig the land, and be fruitful and mul-
tiply," which they did, though they didn't understand.
Then we asks the names of things in their lingo —
bread and water and fire and idols and such, and
Dravot leads the priest of each village up to the idol,
and says he must sit there and judge the people, and if
anything goes wrong he is to be shot.

'Next week they was all turning up the land in the
valley as quiet as bees and much prettier, and the
priests heard all the complaints and told Dravot in
dumb show what it was about. "That's just the
beginning," says Dravot. "They think we're Gods."
He and Carnehan picks out twenty good men and
shows them how to click off a rifle, and form fours,
and advance in line, and they was very pleased to do
so, and clever to see the hang of it. Then he takes out
his pipe and his baccy-pouch and leaves one at one
village, and one at the other, and off we two goes to
see what was to be done in the next valley. That was
all rock, and there was a little village there, and Carnehan says — " Send 'em to the old valley to plant," and
takes 'em there and gives 'em some land that wasn't
took before. They were a poor lot, and we blooded
'em with a kid before letting 'em into the new Kingdom. That was to impress the people, and then they
settled down quiet, and Carnehan went back to Dravot
who had got into another valley, all snow and ice and
most mountaineous. There was no people there and
the Army got afraid, so Dravot shoots one of them,

and goes on till he finds some people in a village, and the Army explains that unless the people wants to be killed they had better not shoot their little match-locks; for they had matchlocks. We makes friends with the priest and I stays there alone with two of the Army, teaching the men how to drill, and a thundering big Chief comes across the snow with kettle-drums and horns twanging, because he heard there was a new God kicking about. Carnehan sights for the brown of the men half a mile across the snow and wings one of them. Then he sends a message to the Chief that, unless he wished to be killed, he must come and shake hands with me and leave his arms behind. The Chief comes alone first, and Carnehan shakes hands with him and whirls his arms about, same as Dravot used, and very much surprised that Chief was, and strokes my eyebrows. Then Carnehan goes alone to the Chief, and asks him in dumb show if he had an enemy he hated. " I have," says the Chief. So Carnehan weeds out the pick of his men, and sets the two of the Army to show them drill and at the end of two weeks the men can manœuvre about as well as Volunteers. So he marches with the Chief to a great big plain on the top of a mountain, and the Chief's men rushes into a village and takes it; we three Martinis firing into the brown of the enemy. So we took that village too, and I gives the Chief a rag from my coat and says, " Occupy till I come ; " which was scriptural. By way of a reminder, when me and the Army was eighteen hundred yards away, I drops a bullet near him stand-ing on the snow, and all the people falls flat on their faces. Then I sends a letter to Dravot wherever he be by land or by sea.'

At the risk of throwing the creature out of train I interrupted — 'How could you write a letter up yonder ? '

'The letter ? — Oh ! — The letter ! Keep looking at me between the eyes, please. It was a string-talk letter, that we'd learned the way of it from a blind beggar in the Punjab.'

I remember that there had once come to the office a blind man with a knotted twig and a piece of string which he wound round the twig according to some cipher of his own. He could, after the lapse of days or hours, repeat the sentence which he had reeled up. He had reduced the alphabet to eleven primitive sounds; and tried to teach me his method, but I could not understand.

'I sent that letter to Dravot,' said Carnehan ; 'and told him to come back because this Kingdom was growing too big for me to handle, and then I struck for the first valley, to see how the priests were working. They called the village we took along with the Chief, Bashkai, and the first village we took, Er-Heb. The priests at Er-Heb was doing all right, but they had a lot of pending cases about land to show me, and some men from another village had been firing arrows at night. I went out and looked for that village, and fired four rounds at it from a thousand yards. That used all the cartridges I cared to spend, and I waited for Dravot, who had been away two or three months, and I kept my people quiet.

'One morning I heard the devil's own noise of drums and horns, and Dan Dravot marches down the hill with his Army and a tail of hundreds of men, and, which was the most amazing, a great gold crown on his head. "My Gord, Carnehan," says Daniel, "this is a tremenjus business, and we've got the whole country as far as it's worth having. I am the son of Alexander by Queen Semiramis, and you're my younger brother and a God too! It's the biggest thing we've ever seen. I've been marching and fighting for six weeks with the Army, and every footy little village for fifty miles has come in rejoiceful; and more than that, I've got the key of the whole show, as you'll see, and I've got a crown for you! I told 'em to make two of 'em at a place called Shu, where the gold lies in the rock like suet in mutton. Gold I've seen, and turquoise I've kicked out of the cliffs, and there's garnets in the sands of the river, and here's a chunk of amber that a man brought me. Call up all the priests and, here, take your crown."

'One of the men opens a black hair bag, and I slips the crown on. It was too small and too heavy, but I wore it for the glory. Hammered gold it was — five pound weight, like a hoop of a barrel.

'"Peachey," says Dravot, "we don't want to fight no more. The Craft's the trick so help me!" and he brings forward that same Chief that I left at Bashkai — Billy Fish we called him afterwards, because he was so like Billy Fish that drove the big tank-engine at Mach on the Bolan in the old days. "Shake hands with him," says Dravot, and I shook hands and nearly dropped, for Billy Fish gave me the Grip. I said nothing, but tried him with the Fellow Craft Grip. He answers, all right, and I tried the Master's Grip, but that was a slip. "A Fellow Craft he is!" I says to Dan. "Does he know the word?"—"He does," says Dan, "and all the priests know. It's a miracle!

The Chiefs and the priests can work a Fellow Craft
Lodge in a way that's very like ours, and they've cut
the marks on the rocks, but they don't know the Third
Degree, and they've come to find out. It's Gord's
Truth. I've known these long years that the Afghans
knew up to the Fellow Craft Degree, but this is a
miracle. A God and a Grand-Master of the Craft am
I, and a Lodge in the Third Degree I will open, and
we'll raise the head priests and the Chiefs of the villages."

' " It's against all the law," I says, "holding a Lodge
without warrant from any one; and you know we never
held office in any Lodge."

' " It's a master-stroke o' policy," says Dravot. " It
means running the country as easy as a four-wheeled
bogie on a down grade. We can't stop to enquire now,
or they'll turn against us. I've forty Chiefs at my
heel, and passed and raised according to their merit
they shall be. Billet these men on the villages, and
see that we run up a Lodge of some kind. The temple
of Imbra will do for the Lodge-room. The women
must make aprons as you show them. I'll hold a levee
of Chiefs to-night and Lodge to-morrow."

' I was fair run off my legs, but I wasn't such a fool
as not to see what a pull this Craft business gave us. I
showed the priests' families how to make aprons of the
degrees, but for Dravot's apron the blue border and
marks was made of turquoise lumps on white hide, not
cloth. We took a great square stone in the temple for
the Master's chair, and little stones for the officers'
chairs, and painted the black pavement with white
squares, and did what we could to make things
regular.

'At the levee which was held that night on the hillside with big bonfires, Dravot gives out that him and
me were Gods and sons of Alexander, and Past Grand-
Masters in the Craft, and was come to make Kafiristan
a country where every man should eat in peace and
drink in quiet, and specially obey us.   Then the Chiefs
come round to shake hands, and they were so hairy and
white and fair it was just shaking hands with old
friends.   We gave them names according as they was
like men we had known in India — Billy Fish, Holly
Dilworth, Pikky Kergan, that was Bazar-master when
I was at Mhow, and so on, and so on.

' *The* most amazing miracles was at Lodge next night.
One of the old priests was watching us continuous, and
I felt uneasy, for I knew we'd have to fudge the Ritual,
and I didn't know what the men knew.   The old priest
was a stranger come in from beyond the village of
Bashkai.   The minute Dravot puts on the Master's
apron that the girls had made for him, the priest
fetches a whoop and a howl, and tries to overturn
the stone that Dravot was sitting on.   "It's all up
now," I says.   "That comes of meddling with the
Craft without warrant!"   Dravot never winked an
eye, not when ten priests took and tilted over the
Grand-Master's chair — which was to say the stone of
Imbra.   The priest begins rubbing the bottom end of
it to clear away the black dirt, and presently he shows
all the other priests the Master's Mark, same as was on
Dravot's apron, cut into the stone.   Not even the priests
of the temple of Imbra knew it was there.   The old chap
falls flat on his face at Dravot's feet and kisses 'em.
"Luck again," says Dravot, across the Lodge to me.
"they say it's the missing Mark that no one could

understand the why of. We're more than safe now."
Then he bangs the butt of his gun for a gavel and
says : " By virtue of the authority vested in me by
my own right hand and the help of Peachey, I declare
myself Grand-Master of all Freemasonry in Kafiristan
in this the Mother Lodge o' the country, and King of
Kafiristan equally with Peachey ! " At that he puts
on his crown and I puts on mine — I was doing Senior
Warden — and we opens the Lodge in most ample form.
It was a amazing miracle! The priests moved in Lodge
through the first two degrees almost without telling, as
if the memory was coming back to them. After that,
Peachey and Dravot raised such as was worthy — high
priests and Chiefs of far-off villages. Billy Fish was
the first, and I can tell you we scared the soul out of
him. It was not in any way according to Ritual, but
it served our turn. We didn't raise more than ten of
the biggest men, because we didn't want to make the
Degree common. And they was clamouring to be
raised.

' " In another six months," says Dravot, " we'll hold
another Communication, and see how you are working." Then he asks them about their villages, and
learns that they was fighting one against the other,
and were sick and tired of it. And when they wasn't
doing that they was fighting with the Mohammedans.
" You can fight those when they come into our country," says Dravot. " Tell off every tenth man of your
tribes for a Frontier guard, and send two hundred at
a time to this valley to be drilled. Nobody is going
to be shot or speared any more so long as he does well,
and I know that you won't cheat me, because you're
white people — sons of Alexander — and not like com-

mon, black Mohammedans.   You are *my* people, and by
God," says he, running off into English at the end —
"I'll make a damned fine Nation of you, or I'll die in
the making !"

'I can't tell all we did for the next six months, because Dravot did a lot I couldn't see the hang of, and
he learned their lingo in a way I never could.   My
work was to help the people plough, and now and
again go out with some of the Army and see what the
other villages were doing, and make 'em throw rope-
bridges across the ravines which cut up the country
horrid.   Dravot was very kind to me, but when he
walked up and down in the pine wood pulling that
bloody red beard of his with both fists I knew he was
thinking plans I could not advise about, and I just
waited for orders.

'But Dravot never showed me disrespect before
the people.   They were afraid of me and the Army,
but they loved Dan.   He was the best of friends with
the priests and the Chiefs; but any one could come
across the hills with a complaint, and Dravot would
hear him out fair, and call four priests together and
say what was to be done.   He used to call in Billy
Fish from Bashkai, and Pikky Kergan from Shu, and
an old Chief we called Kafuzelum — it was like enough
to his real name — and hold councils with 'em when there
was any fighting to be done in small villages.   That
was his Council of War, and the four priests of Bashkai, Shu, Khawak, and Madora was his Privy Council.
Between the lot of 'em they sent me, with forty men
and twenty rifles, and sixty men carrying turquoises,
into the Ghorband country to buy those hand-made
Martini rifles, that come out of the Amir's workshops

at Kabul, from one of the Amir's Herati regiments that would have sold the very teeth out of their mouths for turquoises.

'I stayed in Ghorband a month, and gave the Governor there the pick of my baskets for hush-money, and bribed the Colonel of the regiment some more, and, between the two and the tribes-people, we got more than a hundred hand-made Martinis, a hundred good Kohat Jezails that'll throw to six hundred yards, and forty man-loads of very bad ammunition for the rifles. I came back with what I had, and distributed 'em among the men that the Chiefs sent in to me to drill. Dravot was too busy to attend to those things, but the old Army that we first made helped me, and we turned out five hundred men that could drill, and two hundred that knew how to hold arms pretty straight. Even those cork-screwed, hand-made guns was a miracle to them. Dravot talked big about powder-shops and factories, walking up and down in the pine wood when the winter was coming on.

' "I won't make a Nation," says he. "I'll make an Empire! These men aren't niggers; they're English! Look at their eyes — look at their mouths. Look at the way they stand up. They sit on chairs in their own houses. They're the Lost Tribes, or something like it, and they've grown to be English. I'll take a census in the spring if the priests don't get frightened. There must be a fair two million of 'em in these hills. The villages are full o' little children. Two million people — two hundred and fifty thousand fighting men — and all English! They only want the rifles and a little drilling. Two hundred and fifty thousand men, ready to cut in on Russia's right flank when she tries for

India! Peachey, man," he says, chewing his beard in great hunks, "we shall be Emperors — Emperors of the Earth! Rajah Brooke will be a suckling to us. I'll treat with the Viceroy on equal terms. I'll ask him to send me twelve picked English — twelve that I know of — to help us govern a bit. There's Mackray, Sergeant-pensioner at Segowli — many's the good dinner he's given me, and his wife a pair of trousers. There's Donkin, the Warder of Tounghoo Jail; there's hundreds that I could lay my hand on if I was in India. The Viceroy shall do it for me, I'll send a man through in the spring for those men, and I'll write for a dispensation from the Grand Lodge for what I've done as Grand-Master. That — and all the Sniders that'll be thrown out when the native troops in India take up the Martini. They'll be worn smooth, but they'll do for fighting in these hills. Twelve English, a hundred thousand Sniders run through the Amir's country in driblets — I'd be content with twenty thousand in one year — and we'd be an Empire. When everything was shipshape, I'd hand over the crown — this crown I'm wearing now — to Queen Victoria on my knees, and she'd say: 'Rise up, Sir Daniel Dravot.' Oh, it's big! It's big, I tell you! But there's so much to be done in every place — Bashkai, Khawak, Shu, and everywhere else."

'"What is it?" I says. "There are no more men coming in to be drilled this autumn. Look at those, fat, black clouds. They're bringing the snow."

'"It isn't that," says Daniel, putting his hand very hard on my shoulder; "and I don't wish to say anything that's against you, for no other living man would have followed me and made me what I am as you have done.   You're a first-class Commander-in-Chief, and the people know you; but — it's a big country, and somehow you can't help me, Peachey, in the way I want to be helped."

'"Go to your blasted priests, then!" I said, and I was sorry when I made that remark, but it did hurt me sore to find Daniel talking so superior when I'd drilled all the men, and done all he told me.

'"Don't let's quarrel, Peachey," says Daniel without cursing. "You're a King too, and the half of this Kingdom is yours; but can't you see, Peachey, we want cleverer men than us now — three or four of 'em, that we can scatter about for our Deputies. It's a hugeous great State, and I can't always tell the right thing to do, and I haven't time for all I want to do, and here's the winter coming on and all." He put half his beard into his mouth, all red like the gold of his crown.

'"I'm sorry, Daniel," says I.   "I've done all I could. I've drilled the men and shown the people how to stack their oats better; and I've brought in those tin-ware rifles from Ghorband — but I know what you're driving at.   I take it Kings always feel oppressed that way."

'"There's another thing too," says Dravot, walking up and down.   "The winter's coming and these people won't be giving much trouble, and if they do we can't move about.   I want a wife."

'"For Gord's sake leave the women alone!" I says. "We've both got all the work we can, though I *am* a fool.   Remember the Contrack, and keep clear o' women."

'"The Contrack only lasted till such time as we was Kings; and Kings we have been these months past," says Dravot, weighing his crown in his hand. "You go get a wife too, Peachey — a nice, strappin', plump girl that'll keep you warm in the winter. They're prettier than English girls, and we can take the pick of 'em. Boil 'em once or twice in hot water, and they'll come out like chicken and ham."

'"Don't tempt me!" I says. "I will not have any dealings with a woman not till we are a dam' side more settled than we are now. I've been doing the work o' two men, and you've been doing the work o' three. Let's lie off a bit, and see if we can get some better tobacco from Afghan country and run in some good liquor; but no women."

'"Who's talking o' *women*?" says Dravot. "I said *wife* — a Queen to breed a King's son for the King. A Queen out of the strongest tribe, that'll make them your blood-brothers, and that'll lie by your side and tell you all the people thinks about you and their own affairs. That's what I want."

'"Do you remember that Bengali woman I kept at Mogul Serai when I was a plate-layer?" says I. "A fat lot o' good she was to me. She taught me the lingo and one or two other things; but what happened? She ran away with the Station Master's servant and half my month's pay. Then she turned up at Dadur Junction in tow of a half-caste, and had the impidence to say I was her husband — all among the drivers in the running-shed too!"

'"We've done with that," says Dravot, "these women are whiter than you or me, and a Queen I will have for the winter months."

'"For the last time o' asking, Dan, do *not*," I says. "It'll only bring us harm. The Bible says that Kings

Q

ain't to waste their strength on women, 'specially when they've got a new raw Kingdom to work over.''

'"For the last time of answering I will," said Dravot, and he went away through the pine-trees looking like a big red devil, the sun being on his crown and beard and all.

'But getting a wife was not as easy as Dan thought. He put it before the Council, and there was no answer till Billy Fish said that he'd better ask the girls. Dravot damned them all round. "What's wrong with me?" he shouts, standing by the idol Imbra. "Am I a dog or am I not enough of a man for your wenches? Haven't I put the shadow of my hand over this country? Who stopped the last Afghan raid?" It was me really, but Dravot was too angry to remember. "Who bought your guns? Who repaired the bridges? Who's the Grand-Master of the sign cut in the stone?" says he, and he thumped his hand on the block that he used to sit on in Lodge, and at Council, which opened like Lodge always. Billy Fish said nothing and no more did the others. "Keep your hair on, Dan," said I; "and ask the girls. That's how it's done at Home, and these people are quite English."

'"The marriage of the King is a matter of State," says Dan, in a white-hot rage, for he could feel, I hope, that he was going against his better mind. He walked out of the Council-room, and the others sat still, looking at the ground.

'"Billy Fish," says I to the Chief of Bashkai, "what's the difficulty here? A straight answer to a true friend."

'"You know," says Billy Fish. "How should a man tell you who knows everything? How can daughters of men marry Gods or Devils? It's not proper."

'I remembered something like that in the Bible; but if, after seeing us as long as they had, they still believed we were Gods, it wasn't for me to undeceive them.

'"A God can do anything," says I. "If the King is fond of a girl he'll not let her die." — "She'll have to," said Billy Fish. "There are all sorts of Gods and Devils in these mountains, and now and again a girl marries one of them and isn't seen any more. Besides, you two know the Mark cut in the stone. Only the Gods know that. We thought you were men till you showed the sign of the Master."

'I wished then that we had explained about the loss of the genuine secrets of a Master-Mason at the first go-off; but I said nothing. All that night there was a blowing of horns in a little dark temple half-way down the hill, and I heard a girl crying fit to die. One of the priests told us that she was being prepared to marry the King.

'"I'll have no nonsense of that kind," says Dan. "I don't want to interfere with your customs, but I'll take my own wife." — "The girl's a little bit afraid," says the priest. "She thinks she's going to die, and they are a-heartening of her up down in the temple."

'"Hearten her very tender, then," says Dravot, "or I'll hearten you with the butt of a gun so you'll never want to be heartened again." He licked his lips, did Dan, and stayed up walking about more than half the night, thinking of the wife that he was going to get in the morning. I wasn't any means comfortable, for I knew that dealings with a woman in foreign parts, though you was a crowned King twenty times over, could not but be risky. I got up very early in the morning while Dravot was asleep, and I saw the priests talking together in whispers, and the Chiefs talking together too, and they looked at me out of the corners of their eyes.

' "What is up, Fish?" I say to the Bashkai man, who was wrapped up in his furs and looking splendid to behold.

' "I can't rightly say," says he ; "but if you can make the King drop all this nonsense about marriage, you'll be doing him and me and yourself a great service."

' "That I do believe," says I. " But sure, you know, Billy, as well as me, having fought against and for us, that the King and me are nothing more than two of the finest men that God Almighty ever made. Nothing more, I do assure you."

' "That may be," says Billy Fish, "and yet I should be sorry if it was." He sinks his head upon his great fur cloak for a minute and thinks. " King," says he, "be you man or God or Devil, I'll stick by you to-day. I have twenty of my men with me, and they will follow me. We'll go to Bashkai until the storm blows over."

' A little snow had fallen in the night, and everything was white except the greasy fat clouds that blew down and down from the north. Dravot came out with his crown on his head, swinging his arms and stamping his feet, and looking more pleased than Punch.

' "For the last time. drop it. Dan." says I in a whisper, "Billy Fish here says that there will be a row.'

'"A row among my people!" says Dravot. "Not much. Peachey, you're a fool not to get a wife too. Where's the girl?" says he with a voice as loud as the braying of a jackass. "Call up all the Chiefs and priests, and let the Emperor see if his wife suits him."

'There was no need to call any one. They were all there leaning on their guns and spears round the clearing in the centre of the pine wood. A lot of priests went down to the little temple to bring up the girl, and the horns blew fit to wake the dead. Billy Fish saunters round and gets as close to Daniel as he could, and behind him stood his twenty men with matchlocks. Not a man of them under six feet. I was next to Dravot, and behind me was twenty men of the regular Army. Up comes the girl, and a strapping wench she was, covered with silver and turquoises but white as death, and looking back every minute at the priests.

'"She'll do," said Dan, looking her over. "What's to be afraid of, lass? Come and kiss me." He puts his arm round her. She shuts her eyes, gives a bit of a squeak, and down goes her face in the side of Dan's flaming red beard.

'"The slut's bitten me!" says he, clapping his hand to his neck, and, sure enough, his hand was red with blood. Billy Fish and two of his matchlock-men catches hold of Dan by the shoulders and drags him into the Bashkai lot, while the priests howls in their lingo,— "Neither God nor Devil but a man!" I was all taken aback, for a priest cut at me in front, and the Army behind began firing into the Bashkai men.

'"God A'mighty!" says Dan. "What is the meaning o' this?"

'"Come back! Come away!" says Billy Fish.

"Ruin and Mutiny is the matter. We'll break for Bashkai if we can."

'I tried to give some sort of orders to my men — the men o' the regular Army — but it was no use, so I fired into the brown of 'em with an English Martini and drilled three beggars in a line. The valley was full of shouting, howling creatures, and every soul was shrieking, "Not a God nor a Devil but only a man!" The Bashkai troops stuck to Billy Fish all they were worth, but their matchlocks wasn't half as good as the Kabul breech-loaders, and four of them dropped. Dan was bellowing like a bull, for he was very wrathy; and Billy Fish had a hard job to prevent him running out at the crowd.

'"We can't stand," says Billy Fish. "Make a run for it down the valley! The whole place is against us." The matchlock-men ran, and we went down the valley in spite of Dravot. He was swearing horrible and crying out he was a King. The priests rolled great stones on us, and the regular Army fired hard, and there wasn't more than six men, not counting Dan, Billy Fish, and Me, that came down to the bottom of the valley alive.

'Then they stopped firing and the horns in the temple blew again. "Come away — for Gord's sake come away!" says Billy Fish. "They'll send runners out to all the villages before ever we get to Bashkai. I can protect you there, but I can't do anything now."

'My own notion is that Dan began to go mad in his head from that hour. He stared up and down like a stuck pig. Then he was all for walking back alone and killing the priests with his bare hands; which he could have done. "An Emperor am I," says Daniel, "and next year I shall be a Knight of the Queen."

' "All right, Dan," says I; "but come along now while there's time."

' "It's your fault," says he, "for not looking after your Army better. There was mutiny in the midst, and you didn't know — you damned engine-driving, plate-laying, missionary's-pass-hunting hound!" He sat upon a rock and called me every foul name he could lay tongue to. I was too heart-sick to care, though it was all his foolishness that brought the smash.

' "I'm sorry, Dan," says I, "but there's no accounting for natives. This business is our Fifty-Seven. Maybe we'll make something out of it yet, when we've got to Bashkai."

' "Let's get to Bashkai, then," says Dan, "and, by God, when I come back here again I'll sweep the valley so there isn't a bug in a blanket left!"

' We walked all that day, and all that night Dan was stumping up and down on the snow, chewing his beard and muttering to himself.

' "There's no hope o' getting clear," said Billy Fish. "The priests will have sent runners to the villages to say that you are only men. Why didn't you stick on as Gods till things was more settled? I'm a dead man," says Billy Fish, and he throws himself down on the snow and begins to pray to his Gods.

' Next morning we was in a cruel bad country — all up and down, no level ground at all, and no food either. The six Bashkai men looked at Billy Fish hungry-way as if they wanted to ask something, but they said never a word. At noon we came to the top of a flat mountain all covered with snow, and when we climbed up into it, behold, there was an Army in position waiting in the middle!

'"The runners have been very quick," says Billy Fish, with a little bit of a laugh. "They are waiting for us."

'Three or four men began to fire from the enemy's side, and a chance shot took Daniel in the calf of the leg. That brought him to his senses. He looks across the snow at the Army, and sees the rifles that we had brought into the country.

'"We're done for," says he. "They are Englishmen, these people, — and it's my blasted nonsense that has brought you to this. Get back, Billy Fish, and take your men away; you've done what you could, and now cut for it. Carnehan," says he, "shake hands with me and go along with Billy. Maybe they won't kill you. I'll go and meet 'em alone. It's me that did it. Me, the King!"

'"Go!" says I. "Go to Hell, Dan. I'm with you here. Billy Fish, you clear out, and we two will meet those folk."

'"I'm a Chief," says Billy Fish, quite quiet. "I stay with you. My men can go."

'The Bashkai fellows didn't wait for a second word but ran off, and Dan and Me and Billy Fish walked across to where the drums were drumming and the horns were horning. It was cold — awful cold. I've got that cold in the back of my head now. There's a lump of it there.'

The punkah-coolies had gone to sleep. Two kerosene lamps were blazing in the office, and the perspiration poured down my face and splashed on the blotter as I leaned forward. Carnehan was shivering, and I feared that his mind might go. I wiped my face, took a fresh grip of the piteously mangled hands, and said : ' What happened after that ? '

The momentary shift of my eyes had broken the clear current.

' What was you pleased to say ? ' whined Carnehan. ' They took them without any sound. Not a little whisper all along the snow, not though the King knocked down the first man that set hand on him — not though old Peachey fired his last cartridge into the brown of 'em. Not a single solitary sound did those swines make. They just closed up tight, and I tell you their furs stunk. There was a man called Billy Fish, a good friend of us all, and they cut his throat, Sir, then and there, like a pig ; and the King kicks up the bloody snow and says : " We've had a dashed fine run for our money. What's coming next ? " But Peachey, Peachey Taliaferro, I tell you, Sir, in confidence as betwixt two friends, he lost his head, Sir. No, he didn't neither. The King lost his head, so he did, all along o' one of those cunning rope-bridges. Kindly let me have the paper-cutter, Sir. It tilted this way. They marched him a mile across that snow to a rope-bridge over a ravine with a river at the bottom. You may have seen such. They prodded him behind like an ox. " Damn your eyes ! " says the King. " D'you suppose I can't die like a gentleman ? " He turns to Peachey — Peachey that was crying like a child. " I've brought you to this, Peachey," says he. " Brought you out of your happy life to be killed in Kafiristan, where you was late Commander-in-Chief of the Emperor's forces. Say you forgive me, Peachey." — " I do," says Peachey. " Fully and freely do I forgive

you, Dan." — " Shake hands, Peachey," says he.   " I'm
going now."   Out he goes, looking neither right nor
left, and when he was plumb in the middle of those
dizzy dancing ropes, — " Cut, you beggars," he shouts ,
and they cut, and old Dan fell, turning round and round
and round, twenty thousand miles, for he took half an
hour to fall till he struck the water, and I could see his
body caught on a rock with the gold crown close beside.

'But do you know what they did to Peachey between
two pine-trees? They crucified him, Sir, as Peachey's
hand will show. They used wooden pegs for his
hands and his feet; and he didn't die. He hung
there and screamed, and they took him down next
day, and said it was a miracle that he wasn't dead.
They took him down — poor old Peachey that hadn't
done them any harm — that hadn't done them any——'

He rocked to and fro and wept bitterly, wiping his
eyes with the back of his scarred hands and moaning
like a child for some ten minutes.

'They was cruel enough to feed him up in the
temple, because they said he was more of a God than
old Daniel that was a man. Then they turned him out
on the snow, and told him to go home, and. Peachey
came home in about a year, begging along the roads
quite safe; for Daniel Dravot he walked before and
said: " Come along, Peachey. It's a big thing we're
doing."   The mountains they danced at night, and
the mountains they tried to fall on Peachey's head,
but Dan he held up his hand, and Peachey came along
bent double. He never let go of Dan's hand, and he
never let go of Dan's head. They gave it to him as a
present in the temple, to remind him not to come again,
and though the crown was pure gold, and Peachey was

starving, never would Peachey sell the same. You knew Dravot, Sir! You knew Right Worshipful Brother Dravot! Look at him now!'

He fumbled in the mass of rags round his bent waist; brought out a black horsehair bag embroidered with silver thread; and shook therefrom on to my table — the dried, withered head of Daniel Dravot! The morning sun that had long been paling the lamps struck the red beard and blind sunken eyes; struck, too, a heavy circlet of gold studded with raw turquoises, that Carnehan placed tenderly on the battered temples.

'You be'old now,' said Carnehan, 'the Emperor in his 'abit as he lived — the King of Kafiristan with his crown upon his head. Poor old Daniel that was a monarch once!'

I shuddered, for, in spite of defacements manifold, I recognised the head of the man of Marwar Junction. Carnehan rose to go. I attempted to stop him. He was not fit to walk abroad. 'Let me take away the whiskey, and give me a little money,' he gasped. 'I was a King once. I'll go to the Deputy Commissioner and ask to set in the Poorhouse till I get my health. No, thank you, I can't wait till you get a carriage for me. I've urgent private affairs — in the south — at Marwar.'

He shambled out of the office and departed in the direction of the Deputy Commissioner's house. That day at noon I had occasion to go down the blinding hot Mall, and I saw a crooked man crawling along the white dust of the roadside, his hat in his hand, quavering dolorously after the fashion of street-singers at Home. There was not a soul in sight, and he was

out of all possible earshot of the houses.   And he
sang through his nose, turning his head from right to
left : —

> 'The Son of Man goes forth to war,
>   A golden crown to gain ;
> His blood-red banner streams afar —
>   Who follows in his train?'

I waited to hear no more, but put the poor wretch
into my carriage and drov him off to the nearest missionary for eventual transfer to the Asylum.   He repeated the hymn twice while he was with me whom he
did not in the least recognise, and I left him singing it
to the missionary.

Two days later I enquired after his welfare of the
Superintendent of the Asylum.

'He was admitted suffering from sun-stroke.   He
died early yesterday morning,' said the Superintendent.   'Is it true that he was half an hour bare-
headed in the sun at midday ? '

'Yes,' said I, 'but do you happen to know if he
had anything upon him by any chance when he died ? '

'Not to my knowledge,' said the Superintendent.

And there the matter rests.

WEE WILLIE WINKIE

'An officer and a gentleman.'

HIS full name was Percival William Williams, but
he picked up the other name in a nursery-book, and
that was the end of the christened titles.   His mother's
ayah called him Willie-*Baba*, but as he never paid the
faintest attention to anything that the *ayah* said, her
wisdom did not help matters.

His father was the Colonel of the 195th, and as soon
as Wee Willie Winkie was old enough to understand
what Military Discipline meant, Colonel Williams put
him under it.   There was no other way of managing
the child.   When he was good for a week, he drew
good-conduct pay; and when he was bad, he was deprived of his good-conduct stripe.   Generally he was
bad, for India offers many chances of going wrong to
little six-year-olds.

Children resent familiarity from strangers, and Wee
Willie Winkie was a very particular child.   Once he
accepted an acquaintance, he was graciously pleased to
thaw.   He accepted Brandis, a subaltern of the 195th,
on sight.   Brandis was having tea at the Colonel's,
and Wee Willie Winkie entered strong in the possession of a good-conduct badge won for not chasing the
hens round the compound.   He regarded Brandis with
gravity for at least ten minutes, and then delivered
himself of his opinion.

237

'I like you,' said he slowly, getting off his chair and coming over to Brandis. 'I like you. I shall call you Coppy, because of your hair. Do you *mind* being called Coppy? It is because of ve hair, you know.'

Here was one of the most embarrassing of Wee Willie Winkie's peculiarities. He would look at a stranger for some time, and then, without warning or explanation, would give him a name. And the name stuck. No regimental penalties could break Wee Willie Winkie of this habit. He lost his good-conduct badge for christening the Commissioner's wife 'Pobs'; but nothing that the Colonel could do made the Station forego the nickname, and Mrs. Collen remained 'Pobs' till the end of her stay. So Brandis was christened 'Coppy,' and rose, therefore, in the estimation of the regiment.

If Wee Willie Winkie took an interest in any one, the fortunate man was envied alike by the mess and the rank and file. And in their envy lay no suspicion of self-interest. 'The Colonel's son' was idolised on his own merits entirely. Yet Wee Willie Winkie was not lovely. His face was permanently freckled, as his legs were permanently scratched, and in spite of his mother's almost tearful remonstrances he had insisted upon having his long yellow locks cut short in the military fashion. 'I want my hair like Sergeant Tummil's,' said Wee Willie Winkie, and, his father abetting, the sacrifice was accomplished.

Three weeks after the bestowal of his youthful affections on Lieutenant Brandis — henceforward to be called 'Coppy' for the sake of brevity — Wee Willie Winkie was destined to behold strange things and far beyond his comprehension.

Coppy returned his liking with interest. Coppy had

let him wear for five rapturous minutes his own big sword — just as tall as Wee Willie Winkie. Coppy had promised him a terrier puppy; and Coppy had permitted him to witness the miraculous operation of shaving. Nay, more — Coppy had said that even he, Wee Willie Winkie, would rise in time to the ownership of a box of shiny knives, a silver soap-box and a silver-handled 'sputter-brush,' as Wee Willie Winkie called it. Decidedly, there was no one except his father, who could give or take away good-conduct badges at pleasure, half so wise, strong, and valiant as Coppy with the Afghan and Egyptian medals on his breast. Why, then, should Coppy be guilty of the unmanly weakness of kissing — vehemently kissing — a 'big girl,' Miss Allardyce to wit? In the course of a morning ride, Wee Willie Winkie had seen Coppy so doing, and, like the gentleman he was, had promptly wheeled round and cantered back to his groom, lest the groom should also see.

Under ordinary circumstances he would have spoken to his father, but he felt instinctively that this was a matter on which Coppy ought first to be consulted.

'Coppy,' shouted Wee Willie Winkie, reining up outside that subaltern's bungalow early one morning —'I want to see you, Coppy!'

'Come in, young 'un,' returned Coppy, who was at early breakfast in the midst of his dogs. 'What mischief have you been getting into now?'

Wee Willie Winkie had done nothing notoriously bad for three days, and so stood on a pinnacle of virtue.

'I've been doing nothing bad,' said he, curling himself into a long chair with a studious affectation of the

Colonel's languor after a hot parade. He buried his freckled nose in a tea-cup and, with eyes staring roundly over the rim, asked: 'I say, Coppy, is it pwoper to kiss big girls?'

'By Jove! You're beginning early. Who do you want to kiss?'

'No one. My muvver's always kissing me if I don't stop her. If it isn't pwoper, how was you kissing Major Allardyce's big girl last morning, by ve canal?'

Coppy's brow wrinkled. He and Miss Allardyce had with great craft managed to keep their engagement secret for a fortnight. There were urgent and imperative reasons why Major Allardyce should not know how matters stood for at least another month, and this small marplot had discovered a great deal too much.

'I saw you,' said Wee Willie Winkie calmly. 'But ve *sais* didn't see. I said, "*Hut jao!*"'

'Oh, you had that much sense, you young Rip,' groaned poor Coppy, half amused and half angry. 'And how many people may you have told about it?'

'Only me myself. You didn't tell when I twied to wide ve buffalo ven my pony was lame; and I fought you wouldn't like.'

'Winkie,' said Coppy enthusiastically, shaking the small hand, 'you're the best of good fellows. Look here, you can't understand all these things. One of these days — hang it, how can I make you see it! — I'm going to marry Miss Allardyce, and then she'll be Mrs. Coppy, as you say. If your young mind is so scandalised at the idea of kissing big girls, go and tell your father.'

'What will happen?' said Wee Willie Winkie, who firmly believed that his father was omnipotent.

'I shall get into trouble,' said Coppy, playing his trump card with an appealing look at the holder of the ace.

'Ven I won't,' said Wee Willie Winkie briefly. 'But my faver says it's un-man-ly to be always kissing, and I didn't fink *you'd* do vat, Coppy.'

'I'm not always kissing, old chap. It's only now and then, and when you're bigger you'll do it too. Your father meant it's not good for little boys.'

'Ah!' said Wee Willie Winkie, now fully enlightened. 'It's like ve sputter-brush?'

'Exactly,' said Coppy gravely.

'But I don't fink I'll ever want to kiss big girls, nor no one, 'cept my muvver. And I *must* vat, you know.'

There was a long pause, broken by Wee Willie Winkie.

'Are you fond of vis big girl, Coppy?'

'Awfully!' said Coppy.

'Fonder van you are of Bell or ve Butcha — or me?'

'It's in a different way,' said Coppy. 'You see, one of these days Miss Allardyce will belong to me, but you'll grow up and command the Regiment and — all sorts of things. It's quite different, you see.'

'Very well,' said Wee Willie Winkie, rising. 'If you're fond of ve big girl, I won't tell any one. I must go now.'

Coppy rose and escorted his small guest to the door, adding — 'You're the best of little fellows, Winkie. I tell you what. In thirty days from now you can tell if you like — tell any one you like.'

Thus the secret of the Brandis-Allardyce engagement was dependent on a little child's word. Coppy, who knew Wee Willie Winkie's idea of truth, was at ease, for he felt that he would not break promises. Wee Willie Winkie betrayed a special and unusual interest in Miss Allardyce, and, slowly revolving round that embarrassed young lady, was used to regard her gravely with unwinking eye. He was trying to discover why Coppy should have kissed her. She was not half so nice as his own mother. On the other hand, she was Coppy's property, and would in time belong to him. Therefore it behooved him to treat her with as much respect as Coppy's big sword or shiny pistol.

The idea that he shared a great secret in common with Coppy kept Wee Willie Winkie unusually virtuous for three weeks. Then the Old Adam broke out, and he made what he called a 'camp-fire' at the bottom of the garden. How could he have foreseen that the flying sparks would have lighted the Colonel's little hay-rick and consumed a week's store for the horses? Sudden and swift was the punishment — deprivation of the good-conduct badge and, most sorrowful of all, two days' confinement to barracks — the house and veranda — coupled with the withdrawal of the light of his father's countenance.

He took the sentence like the man he strove to be, drew himself up with a quivering under-lip, saluted, and, once clear of the room, ran to weep bitterly in his nursery — called by him 'my quarters.' Coppy came in the afternoon and attempted to console the culprit.

'I'm under awwest,' said Wee Willie Winkie mournfully, 'and I didn't ought to speak to you.'

Very early the next morning he climbed on to the

roof of the house — that was not forbidden — and beheld Miss Allardyce going for a ride.

'Where are you going?' cried Wee Willie Winkie.

'Across the river,' she answered, and trotted forward.

Now the cantonment in which the 195th lay was bounded on the north by a river — dry in the winter. From his earliest years, Wee Willie Winkie had been forbidden to go across the river, and had noted that even Coppy — the almost almighty Coppy — had never set foot beyond it. Wee Willie Winkie had once been read to, out of a big blue book, the history of the Princess and the Goblins — a most wonderful tale of a land where the Goblins were always warring with the children of men until they were defeated by one Curdie. Ever since that date it seemed to him that the bare black and purple hills across the river were inhabited by Goblins, and, in truth, every one had said that there lived the Bad Men. Even in his own house the lower halves of the windows were covered with green paper on account of the Bad Men who might, if allowed clear view, fire into peaceful drawing-rooms and comfortable bedrooms. Certainly, beyond the river, which was the end of all the Earth, lived the Bad Men. And here was Major Allardyce's big girl, Coppy's property, preparing to venture into their borders! What would Coppy say if anything happened to her? If the Goblins ran off with her as they did with Curdie's Princess? She must at all hazards be turned back.

The house was still. Wee Willie Winkie reflected for a moment on the very terrible wrath of his father; and then — broke his arrest! It was a crime unspeakable. The low sun threw his shadow, very large and very black, on the trim garden-paths, as he went down to the stables and ordered his pony. It seemed to him in the hush of the dawn that all the big world had been bidden to stand still and look at Wee Willie Winkie guilty of mutiny. The drowsy *sais* gave him his mount, and, since the one great sin made all others insignificant, Wee Willie Winkie said that he was going to ride over to Coppy Sahib, and went out at a foot-pace, stepping on the soft mould of the flower-borders.

The devastating track of the pony's feet was the last misdeed that cut him off from all sympathy of Humanity. He turned into the road, leaned forward, and rode as fast as the pony could put foot to the ground in the direction of the river.

But the liveliest of twelve-two ponies can do little against the long canter of a Waler. Miss Allardyce was far ahead, had passed through the crops, beyond the Police-posts, when all the guards were asleep, and her mount was scattering the pebbles of the river-bed as Wee Willie Winkie left the cantonment and British India behind him. Bowed forward and still flogging, Wee Willie Winkie shot into Afghan territory, and could just see Miss Allardyce a black speck, flickering across the stony plain. The reason of her wandering was simple enough. Coppy, in a tone of too-hastily-assumed authority, had told her over night that she must not ride out by the river. And she had gone to prove her own spirit and teach Coppy a lesson.

Almost at the foot of the inhospitable hills, Wee Willie Winkie saw the Waler blunder and come down heavily. Miss Allardyce struggled clear, but her ankle had been severely twisted, and she could not stand. Having fully shown her spirit, she wept, and was surprised by the apparition of a white, wide-eyed child in khaki, on a nearly spent pony.

'Are you badly, badly hurted?' shouted Wee Willie Winkie, as soon as he was within range. 'You didn't ought to be here.'

'I don't know,' said Miss Allardyce ruefully, ignoring the reproof. 'Good gracious, child, what are *you* doing here?'

'You said you was going acwoss ve wiver,' panted Wee Willie Winkie, throwing himself off his pony. 'And nobody — not even Coppy — must go acwoss ve wiver, and I came after you ever so hard, but you wouldn't stop, and now you've hurted yourself, and Coppy will be angwy wiv me, and — I've bwoken my awwest! I've bwoken my awwest!'

The future Colonel of the 195th sat down and sobbed. In spite of the pain in her ankle the girl was moved.

'Have you ridden all the way from cantonments, little man? What for?'

'You belonged to Coppy. Coppy told me so!' wailed Wee Willie Winkie disconsolately. 'I saw him kissing you, and he said he was fonder of you van Bell or ve Butcha or me. And so I came. You must get up and come back. You didn't ought to be here. Vis is a bad place, and I've bwoken my awwest.'

'I can't move, Winkie,' said Miss Allardyce, with a groan. 'I've hurt my foot. What shall I do?'

She showed a readiness to weep anew, which steadied Wee Willie Winkie, who had been brought up to believe that tears were the depth of unmanliness. Still, when one is as great a sinner as Wee Willie Winkie, even a man may be permitted to break down.

'Winkie,' said Miss Allardyce, 'when you've rested a little, ride back and tell them to send out something to carry me back in. It hurts fearfully.'

The child sat still for a little time and Miss Allardyce closed her eyes; the pain was nearly making her faint. She was roused by Wee Willie Winkie tying up the reins on his pony's neck and setting it free with a vicious cut of his whip that made it whicker. The little animal headed towards the cantonments.

'Oh, Winkie! What are you doing?'

'Hush!' said Wee Willie Winkie. 'Vere's a man coming — one of ve Bad Men. I must stay wiv you. My faver says a man must *always* look after a girl. Jack will go home, and ven vey'll come and look for us. Vat's why I let him go.'

Not one man but two or three had appeared from behind the rocks of the hills, and the heart of Wee Willie Winkie sank within him, for just in this manner were the Goblins wont to steal out and vex Curdie's soul. Thus had they played in Curdie's garden, he had seen the picture, and thus had they frightened the Princess's nurse. He heard them talking to each other, and recognised with joy the bastard Pushto that he had picked up from one of his father's grooms lately dismissed. People who spoke that tongue could not be the Bad Men. They were only natives after all.

They came up to the bowlders on which Miss Allardyce's horse had blundered.

Then rose from the rock Wee Willie Winkie, child of the Dominant Race, aged six and three-quarters, and said briefly and emphatically '*Jao!*' The pony had crossed the river-bed.

The men laughed, and laughter from natives was the one thing Wee Willie Winkie could not tolerate. He asked them what they wanted and why they did not depart. Other men with most evil faces and crooked-stocked guns crept out of the shadows of the hills, till, soon, Wee Willie Winkie was face to face with an audience some twenty strong. Miss Allardyce screamed.

'Who are you?' said one of the men.

'I am the Colonel Sahib's son, and my order is that you go at once. You black men are frightening the Miss Sahib. One of you must run into cantonments and take the news that the Miss Sahib has hurt herself, and that the Colonel's son is here with her.'

'Put our feet into the trap?' was the laughing reply. 'Hear this boy's speech!'

'Say that I sent you — I, the Colonel's son. They will give you money.'

'What is the use of this talk? Take up the child and the girl, and we can at least ask for the ransom. Ours are the villages on the heights,' said a voice in the background.

These *were* the Bad Men — worse than Goblins — and it needed all Wee Willie Winkie's training to prevent him from bursting into tears. But he felt that to cry before a native, excepting only his mother's *ayah*, would be an infamy greater than any mutiny. Moreover, he, as future Colonel of the 195th, had that grim regiment at his back.

'Are you going to carry us away?' said Wee Willie Winkie, very blanched and uncomfortable.

'Yes, my little *Sahib Bahadur*,' said the tallest of the men, 'and eat you afterwards.'

'That is child's talk,' said Wee Willie Winkie. 'Men do not eat men.'

A yell of laughter interrupted him, but he went on firmly — 'And if you do carry us away, I tell you that all my regiment will come up in a day and kill you all without leaving one. Who will take my message to the Colonel Sahib?'

Speech in any vernacular — and Wee Willie Winkie had a colloquial acquaintance with three — was easy to the boy who could not yet manage his 'r's' and 'th's' aright.

Another man joined the conference, crying: 'O foolish men! What this babe says is true. He is the heart's heart of those white troops. For the sake of peace let them go both, for if he be taken, the regiment will break loose and gut the valley. *Our* villages are in the valley, and we shall not escape. That regiment are devils. They broke Khoda Yar's breastbone with kicks when he tried to take the rifles; and if we touch this child they will fire and rape and plunder for a month, till nothing remains. Better to send a man back to take the message and get a reward. I say that this child is their God, and that they will spare none of us, nor our women, if we harm him.'

It was Din Mahommed, the dismissed groom of the Colonel, who made the diversion, and an angry and heated discussion followed. Wee Willie Winkie, standing over Miss Allardyce, waited the upshot. Surely his 'wegiment,' his own 'wegiment,' would not desert him if they knew of his extremity.

    *   *   *   *   *   *   *   *   *

The riderless pony brought the news to the 195th, though there had been consternation in the Colonel's household for an hour before. The little beast came in through the parade-ground in front of the main barracks, where the men were settling down to play Spoil-five till the afternoon. Devlin, the Colour-Sergeant of E Company, glanced at the empty saddle and tumbled through the barrack-rooms, kicking up each Room Corporal as he passed. 'Up, ye beggars! There's something happened to the Colonel's son,' he shouted.

'He couldn't fall off! S'elp me, 'e *couldn't* fall off,' blubbered a drummer-boy. 'Go an' hunt acrost the river. He's over there if he's anywhere, an' maybe those Pathans have got 'im. For the love o' Gawd don't look for 'im in the nullahs! Let's go over the river.'

'There's sense in Mott yet,' said Devlin. 'E Company, double out to the river — sharp!'

So E Company, in its shirt-sleeves mainly, doubled for the dear life, and in the rear toiled the perspiring Sergeant, adjuring it to double yet faster. The cantonment was alive with the men of the 195th hunting for Wee Willie Winkie, and the Colonel finally overtook E Company, far too exhausted to swear, struggling in the pebbles of the river-bed.

Up the hill under which Wee Willie Winkie's Bad Men were discussing the wisdom of carrying off the child and the girl, a look-out fired two shots.

'What have I said?' shouted Din Mahommed. 'There is the warning! The *pulton* are out already and are coming across the plain! Get away! Let us not be seen with the boy!'

The men waited for an instant, and then, as another

shot was fired, withdrew into the hills, silently as they
had appeared.

'The wegiment is coming,' said Wee Willie Winkie
confidently to Miss Allardyce, 'and it's all wight.
Don't cwy!'

He needed the advice himself, for ten minutes later,
when his father came up, he was weeping bitterly with
his head in Miss Allardyce's lap.

And the men of the 195th carried him home with
shouts and rejoicings; and Coppy, who had ridden a
horse into a lather, met him, and, to his intense disgust, kissed him openly in the presence of the men.

But there was balm for his dignity. His father
assured him that not only would the breaking of arrest
be condoned, but that the good-conduct badge would
be restored as soon as his mother could sew it on his
blouse-sleeve. Miss Allardyce had told the Colonel
a story that made him proud of his son.

'She belonged to you, Coppy,' said Wee Willie
Winkie, indicating Miss Allardyce with a grimy fore-
finger. 'I *knew* she didn't ought to go acwoss ve
wiver, and I knew ve wegiment would come to me if
I sent Jack home.'

'You're a hero, Winkie,' said Coppy — 'a *pukka*
hero!'

'I don't know what vat means,' said Wee Willie
Winkie, 'but you mustn't call me Winkie any no more.
I'm Percival Will'am Will'ams.'

And in this manner did Wee Willie Winkie enter
into his manhood.

BAA BAA, BLACK SHEEP

Baa Baa, Black Sheep,
Have you any wool?
Yes, Sir, yes, Sir, three bags full.
One for the Master, one for the Dame —
None for the Little Boy that cries down the lane.

Nursery Rhyme.

THE FIRST BAG

When I was in my father's house, I was in a better place.

THEY were putting Punch to bed — the *ayah* and the *hamal* and Meeta, the big *Surti* boy, with the red and gold turban. Judy, already tucked inside her mosquito-curtains, was nearly asleep. Punch had been allowed to stay up for dinner. Many privileges had been accorded to Punch within the last ten days, and a greater kindness from the people of his world had encompassed his ways and works, which were mostly obstreperous. He sat on the edge of his bed and swung his bare legs defiantly.

'Punch-*baba* going to bye-lo?' said the *ayah* suggestively.

'No,' said Punch. 'Punch-*baba* wants the story about the Ranee that was turned into a tiger. Meeta must tell it, and the *hamal* shall hide behind the door and make tiger-noises at the proper time.'

'But Judy-*baba* will wake up,' said the *ayah*.

'Judy-*baba* is waked,' piped a small voice from the

251

mosquito-curtains. 'There was a Ranee that lived at Delhi. Go on, Meeta,' and she fell fast asleep again while Meeta began the story.

Never had Punch secured the telling of that tale with so little opposition. He reflected for a long time. The *hamal* made the tiger-noises in twenty different keys.

''Top!' said Punch authoritatively. 'Why doesn't Papa come in and say he is going to give me *put-put?*'

'Punch-*baba* is going away,' said the *ayah*. 'In another week there will be no Punch-*baba* to pull my hair any more.' She sighed softly, for the boy of the household was very dear to her heart.

'Up the Ghauts in a train?' said Punch, standing on his bed. 'All the way to Nassick where the Ranee-Tiger lives?'

'Not to Nassick this year, little Sahib,' said Meeta, lifting him on his shoulder. 'Down to the sea where the cocoanuts are thrown, and across the sea in a big ship. Will you take Meeta with you to *Belait?*'

'You shall all come,' said Punch, from the height of Meeta's strong arms. 'Meeta and the *ayah* and the *hamal* and Bhini-in-the-Garden, and the salaam-Captain-Sahib-snake-man.'

There was no mockery in Meeta's voice when he replied — 'Great is the Sahib's favour,' and laid the little man down in the bed, while the *ayah*, sitting in the moonlight at the doorway, lulled him to sleep with an interminable canticle such as they sing in the Roman Catholic Church at Parel. Punch curled himself into a ball and slept.

Next morning Judy shouted that there was a rat in the nursery, and thus he forgot to tell her the wonderderful news. It did not much matter, for Judy was only three and she would not have understood. But Punch was five; and he knew that going to England would be much nicer than a trip to Nassick.

* * * * * * * * *

Papa and Mamma sold the brougham and the piano, and stripped the house, and curtailed the allowance of crockery for the daily meals, and took long council together over a bundle of letters bearing the Rockling-ton postmark.

'The worst of it is that one can't be certain of any-thing,' said Papa, pulling his moustache. 'The letters in themselves are excellent, and the terms are moderate enough.'

'The worst of it is that the children will grow up away from me,' thought Mamma: but she did not say it aloud.

'We are only one case among hundreds,' said Papa bitterly. 'You shall go Home again in five years, dear.'

'Punch will be ten then — and Judy eight. Oh, how long and long and long the time will be! And we have to leave them among strangers.'

'Punch is a cheery little chap. He's sure to make friends wherever he goes.'

'And who could help loving my Ju?'

They were standing over the cots in the nursery late at night, and I think that Mamma was crying softly. After Papa had gone away, she knelt down by the side of Judy's cot. The *ayah* saw her and put up a prayer that the *memsahib* might never find the love of her chil-dren taken away from her and given to a stranger.

Mamma's own prayer was a slightly illogical one.

Summarised it ran: 'Let strangers love my children and be as good to them as I should be, but let *me* preserve their love and their confidence for ever and ever. Amen.' Punch scratched himself in his sleep, and Judy moaned a little.

Next day, they all went down to the sea, and there was a scene at the Apollo Bunder when Punch discovered that Meeta could not come too, and Judy learned that the *ayah* must be left behind. But Punch found a thousand fascinating things in the rope, block, and steam-pipe line on the big P. and O. Steamer long before Meeta and the *ayah* had dried their tears.

'Come back, Punch-*baba*,' said the *ayah*.

'Come back,' said Meeta, 'and be a *Burra-Sahib*' (a big man).

'Yes,' said Punch, lifted up in his father's arms to wave good-bye. 'Yes, I will come back, and I will be a *Burra Sahib Bahadur!*' (a very big man indeed).

At the end of the first day Punch demanded to be set down in England, which he was certain must be close at hand. Next day there was a merry breeze, and Punch was very sick. 'When I come back to Bombay,' said Punch on his recovery, 'I will come by the road—in a broom *gharri*. This is a very naughty ship.'

The Swedish boatswain consoled him, and he modified his opinions as the voyage went on. There was so much to see and to handle and ask questions about that Punch nearly forgot the *ayah* and Meeta and the *hamal*, and with difficulty remembered a few words of the Hindustani, once his second-speech.

But Judy was much worse. The day before the steamer reached Southampton, Mamma asked her if she would not like to see the *ayah* again.   Judy's blue eyes turned to the stretch of sea that had swallowed all her tiny past, and said: '*Ayah!*   What *ayah?*'

Mamma cried over her and Punch marvelled.   It was then that he heard for the first time Mamma's passionate appeal to him never to let Judy forget Mamma. Seeing that Judy was young, ridiculously young, and that Mamma, every evening for four weeks past, had come into the cabin to sing her and Punch to sleep with a mysterious rune that he called 'Sonny, my soul,' Punch could not understand what Mamma meant.   But he strove to do his duty; for, the moment Mamma left the cabin, he said to Judy: 'Ju, you bemember Mamma?'

''Torse I do,' said Judy.

'Then *always* bemember Mamma, 'r else I won't give you the paper ducks that the red-haired Captain Sahib cut out for me.'

So Judy promised always to 'bemember Mamma.'

Many and many a time was Mamma's command laid upon Punch, and Papa would say the same thing with an insistence that awed the child.

'You must make haste and learn to write, Punch,' said Papa, 'and then you'll be able to write letters to us in Bombay.'

'I'll come into your room,' said Punch, and Papa choked.

Papa and Mamma were always choking in those days. If Punch took Judy to task for not 'bemembering,' they choked.   If Punch sprawled on the sofa in the Southampton lodging-house and sketched his future in purple and gold, they choked; and so they did if Judy put her mouth for a kiss.

Through many days all four were vagabonds on the

face of the earth — Punch with no one to give orders to, Judy too young for anything, and Papa and Mamma grave, distracted, and choking.

'Where,' demanded Punch, wearied of a loathsome contrivance on four wheels with a mound of luggage atop — '*where* is our broom-*gharri*? This thing talks so much that *I* can't talk. Where is our *own* broom-*gharri*? When I was at Bandstand before we comed away, I asked Inverarity Sahib why he was sitting in it, and he said it was his own. And I said, "I will *give* it you" — I like Inverarity Sahib — and I said, "Can you put your legs through the pully-wag loops by the windows?" And Inverarity Sahib said No, and laughed. *I* can put my legs through the pully-wag loops. I can put my legs through *these* pully-wag loops. Look! Oh, Mamma's crying again! I didn't know I wasn't not to do *so*.'

Punch drew his legs out of the loops of the four-wheeler: the door opened and he slid to the earth, in a cascade of parcels, at the door of an austere little villa whose gates bore the legend 'Downe Lodge.' Punch gathered himself together and eyed the house with dis favour. It stood on a sandy road, and a cold wind tickled his knickerbockered legs.

'Let us go away,' said Punch. 'This is not a pretty place.'

But Mamma and Papa and Judy had left the cab, and all the luggage was being taken into the house. At the doorstep stood a woman in black, and she smiled largely, with dry chapped lips. Behind her was a man, big, bony, gray, and lame as to one leg — behind him a boy of twelve, black-haired and oily in appearance. Punch surveyed the trio, and advanced without fear, as he had

been accustomed to do in Bombay when callers came
and he happened to be playing in the veranda.

'How do you do?' said he. 'I am Punch.' But
they were all looking at the luggage — all except the
gray man, who shook hands with Punch, and said he
was 'a smart little fellow.' There was much running
about and banging of boxes, and Punch curled himself
up on the sofa in the dining-room and considered
things.

'I don't like these people,' said Punch. 'But never
mind. We'll go away soon. We have always went
away soon from everywhere. I wish we was gone back
to Bombay *soon*.'

The wish bore no fruit. For six days Mamma wept
at intervals, and showed the woman in black all Punch's
clothes — a liberty which Punch resented. 'But p'raps
she's a new white *ayah*,' he thought. 'I'm to call her
Antirosa, but she doesn't call *me* Sahib. She says just
Punch,' he confided to Judy. 'What is Antirosa?'

Judy didn't know. Neither she nor Punch had
heard anything of an animal called an aunt. Their
world had been Papa and Mamma, who knew everything, permitted everything, and loved everybody —
even Punch when he used to go into the garden at
Bombay and fill his nails with mould after the weekly
nail-cutting, because, as he explained between two
strokes of the slipper to his sorely tried Father, his
fingers 'felt so new at the ends.'

In an undefined way Punch judged it advisable to
keep both parents between himself and the woman in
black and the boy in black hair. He did not approve
of them. He liked the gray man, who had expressed a
wish to be called 'Uncleharri.' They nodded at each

s

other when they met, and the gray man showed him a
little ship with rigging that took up and down.

'She is a model of the *Brisk* — the little *Brisk* that
was sore exposed that day at Navarino.' The gray man
hummed the last words and fell into a reverie. 'I'll
tell you about Navarino, Punch, when we go for walks
together; and you mustn't touch the ship, because she's
the *Brisk*.'

Long before that walk, the first of many, was taken,
they roused Punch and Judy in the chill dawn of a
February morning to say Good-bye; and of all people
in the wide earth to Papa and Mamma — both crying
this time. Punch was very sleepy and Judy was cross.

'Don't forget us,' pleaded Mamma. 'Oh, my little
son, don't forget us, and see that Judy remembers too.'

'I've told Judy to bemember,' said Punch, wriggling,
for his father's beard tickled his neck. 'I've told
Judy — ten — forty — 'leven thousand times. But Ju's
so young — quite a baby — isn't she?'

'Yes,' said Papa, 'quite a baby, and you must be
good to Judy, and make haste to learn to write and —
and — and ——'

Punch was back in his bed again. Judy was fast
asleep, and there was the rattle of a cab below. Papa
and Mamma had gone away. Not to Nassick; that was
across the sea. To some place much nearer, of course,
and equally of course they would return. They came
back after dinner-parties, and Papa had come back after
he had been to a place called 'The Snows,' and Mamma
with him, to Punch and Judy at Mrs. Inverarity's
house in Marine Lines. Assuredly they would come
back again. So Punch fell asleep till the true morning, when the black-haired boy met him with the in-

formation that Papa and Mamma had gone to Bombay, and that he and Judy were to stay at Downe Lodge 'for ever.' Antirosa, tearfully appealed to for a contradiction, said that Harry had spoken the truth, and that it behooved Punch to fold up his clothes neatly on going to bed. Punch went out and wept bitterly with Judy, into whose fair head he had driven some ideas of the meaning of separation.

When a matured man discovers that he has been deserted by Providence, deprived of his God, and cast, without help, comfort, or sympathy, upon a world which is new and strange to him, his despair, which may find expression in evil-living, the writing of his experiences, or the more satisfactory diversion of suicide, is generally supposed to be impressive. A child, under exactly similar circumstances as far as its knowledge goes, cannot very well curse God and die. It howls till its nose is red, its eyes are sore, and its head aches. Punch and Judy, through no fault of their own, had lost all their world. They sat in the hall and cried; the black-haired boy looking on from afar.

The model of the ship availed nothing, though the gray man assured Punch that he might pull the rigging up and down as much as he pleased; and Judy was promised free entry into the kitchen. They wanted Papa and Mamma gone to Bombay beyond the seas, and their grief while it lasted was without remedy.

When the tears ceased the house was very still. Antirosa had decided that it was better to let the children 'have their cry out,' and the boy had gone to school. Punch raised his head from the floor and sniffed mournfully. Judy was nearly asleep. Three short years had not taught her how to bear sorrow with full knowledge. There was a distant, dull boom in the air — a repeated heavy thud. Punch knew that sound in Bombay in the Monsoon. It was the sea — the sea that must be traversed before any one could get to Bombay.

'Quick, Ju!' he cried, 'we're close to the sea. I can hear it! Listen! That's where they've went. P'raps we can catch them if we was in time. They didn't mean to go without us. They've only forgot.'

'Iss,' said Judy. 'They've only forgotted. Less go to the sea.'

The hall-door was open and so was the garden-gate.

'It's very, very big, this place,' he said, looking cautiously down the road, 'and we will get lost; but *I* will find a man and order him to take me back to my house — like I did in Bombay.'

He took Judy by the hand, and the two ran hatless in the direction of the sound of the sea. Downe Villa was almost the last of a range of newly-built houses running out, through a field of brick-mounds, to a heath where gypsies occasionally camped and where the Garrison Artillery of Rocklington practised. There were few people to be seen, and the children might have been taken for those of the soldiery who ranged far. Half an hour the wearied little legs tramped across heath, potato-patch, and sand-dune.

'I'se so tired,' said Judy, 'and Mamma will be angry.'

'Mamma's *never* angry. I suppose she is waiting at the sea now while Papa gets tickets. We'll find them and go along with. Ju, you mustn't sit down. Only a little more and we'll come to the sea. Ju, if you sit down I'll *thmack* you!' said Punch.

They climbed another dune, and came upon the great

gray sea at low tide.   Hundreds of crabs were scuttling about the beach, but there was no trace of Papa and Mamma, not even of a ship upon the waters — nothing but sand and mud for miles and miles.

And 'Uncleharri' found them by chance — very muddy and very forlorn — Punch dissolved in tears, but trying to divert Judy with an 'ickle trab,' and Judy wailing to the pitiless horizon for 'Mamma, Mamma!' — and again 'Mamma!'

THE SECOND BAG

Ah, well-a-day, for we are souls bereaved!
Of all the creatures under Heaven's wide scope
We are most hopeless, who had once most hope,
And most beliefless, who had most believed.
The City of Dreadful Night.

ALL this time not a word about Black Sheep.   He came later, and Harry the black-haired boy was mainly responsible for his coming.

Judy — who could help loving little Judy? — passed, by special permit, into the kitchen and thence straight to Aunty Rosa's heart.   Harry was Aunty Rosa's one child, and Punch was the extra boy about the house. There was no special place for him or his little affairs, and he was forbidden to sprawl on sofas and explain his ideas about the manufacture of this world and his hopes for his future.   Sprawling was lazy and wore out sofas, and little boys were not expected to talk.   They were talked to, and the talking to was intended for the benefit of their morals.   As the unquestioned despot of the house at Bombay, Punch could not quite understand how he came to be of no account in this his new life.

Harry might reach across the table and take what he
wanted; Judy might point and get what she wanted.
Punch was forbidden to do either.   The gray man was
his great hope and stand-by for many months after
Mamma and Papa left, and he had forgotten to tell
Judy to 'bemember Mamma.'

This lapse was excusable, because in the interval
he had been introduced by Aunty Rosa to two very
impressive things — an abstraction called God, the inti-
mate friend and ally of Aunty Rosa, generally believed
to live behind the kitchen-range because it was hot
there — and a dirty brown book filled with unintelli-
gible dots and marks.   Punch was always anxious to
oblige everybody.   He therefore welded the story of
the Creation on to what he could recollect of his Indian
fairy tales, and scandalised Aunty Rosa by repeating
the result to Judy.   It was a sin, a grievous sin, and
Punch was talked to for a quarter of an hour.   He
could not understand where the iniquity came in, but
was careful not to repeat the offence, because Aunty
Rosa told him that God had heard every word he had
said and was very angry.   If this were true, why
didn't God come and say so, thought Punch, and dismissed the matter from his mind.   Afterwards he
learned to know the Lord as the only thing in the
world more awful than Aunty Rosa — as a Creature
that stood in the background and counted the strokes
of the cane.

But the reading was, just then, a much more serious
matter than any creed.   Aunty Rosa sat him upon a
table and told him that A B meant ab.

'Why?' said Punch.   'A is a and B is bee.   *Why*
does A B mean ab?'

'Because I tell you it does,' said Aunty Rosa, 'and you've got to say it.'

Punch said it accordingly, and for a month, hugely against his will, stumbled through the brown book, not in the least comprehending what it meant. But Uncle Harry, who walked much and generally alone, was wont to come into the nursery and suggest to Aunty Rosa that Punch should walk with him. He seldom spoke, but he showed Punch all Rocklington, from the mud-banks and the sand of the back-bay to the great har-bours where ships lay at anchor, and the dockyards where the hammers were never still, and the marine-store shops, and the shiny brass counters in the Offices where Uncle Harry went once every three months with a slip of blue paper and received sovereigns in exchange; for he held a wound-pension. Punch heard, too, from his lips the story of the battle of Navarino, where the sailors of the Fleet, for three days afterwards, were deaf as posts and could only sign to each other. 'That was because of the noise of the guns,' said Uncle Harry, 'and I have got the wadding of a bullet somewhere inside me now.'

Punch regarded him with curiosity. He had not the least idea what wadding was, and his notion of a bullet was a dockyard cannon-ball bigger than his own head. How could Uncle Harry keep a cannon-ball inside him? He was ashamed to ask, for fear Uncle Harry might be angry.

Punch had never known what anger — real anger — meant until one terrible day when Harry had taken his paint-box to paint a boat with, and Punch had pro-tested. Then Uncle Harry had appeared on the scene and, muttering something about 'strangers' children,'

had with a stick smitten the black-haired boy across
the shoulders till he wept and yelled, and Aunty Rosa
came in and abused Uncle Harry for cruelty to his own
flesh and blood, and Punch shuddered to the tips of his
shoes. 'It wasn't my fault,' he explained to the boy,
but both Harry and Aunty Rosa said that it was, and
that Punch had told tales, and for a week there were no
more walks with Uncle Harry.

But that week brought a great joy to Punch.

He had repeated till he was thrice weary the statement that 'the Cat lay on the Mat and the Rat came in.'

'Now I can truly read,' said Punch, 'and now I will
never read anything in the world.'

He put the brown book in the cupboard where his
school-books lived and accidentally tumbled out a
venerable volume, without covers, labelled *Sharpe's
Magazine*. There was the most portentous picture of a
griffin on the first page, with verses below. The griffin
carried off one sheep a day from a German village, till
a man came with a 'falchion' and split the griffin open.
Goodness only knew what a falchion was, but there was
the Griffin, and his history was an improvement upon
the eternal Cat.

'This,' said Punch, 'means things, and now I will
know all about everything in all the world.' He read
till the light failed, not understanding a tithe of the
meaning, but tantalised by glimpses of new worlds
hereafter to be revealed.

'What is a "falchion"? What is a "e-wee lamb"?
What is a "base *us*surper"? What is a "verdant
me-ad"?' he demanded with flushed cheeks, at bedtime, of the astonished Aunty Rosa.

'Say your prayers and go to sleep,' she replied, and

that was all the help Punch then or afterwards found at her hands in the new and delightful exercise of reading.

'Aunty Rosa only knows about God and things like that,' argued Punch. 'Uncle Harry will tell me.'

The next walk proved that Uncle Harry could not help either; but he allowed Punch to talk, and even sat down on a bench to hear about the Griffin. Other walks brought other stories as Punch ranged further afield, for the house held large store of old books that no one ever opened — from *Frank Fairlegh* in serial numbers, and the earlier poems of Tennyson, contributed anonymously to *Sharpe's Magazine*, to '62 Exhibition Catalogues, gay with colours and delightfully incomprehensible, and odd leaves of *Gulliver's Travels*.

As soon as Punch could string a few pot-hooks together, he wrote to Bombay, demanding by return of post 'all the books in all the world.' Papa could not comply with this modest indent, but sent *Grimm's Fairy Tales* and a Hans Andersen. That was enough. If he were only left alone Punch could pass, at any hour he chose, into a land of his own, beyond reach of Aunty Rosa and her God, Harry and his teasements, and Judy's claims to be played with.

'Don't disturve me, I'm reading. Go and play in the kitchen,' grunted Punch. 'Aunty Rosa lets *you* go there.' Judy was cutting her second teeth and was fretful. She appealed to Aunty Rosa, who descended on Punch.

'I was reading,' he explained, 'reading a book. I *want* to read.'

'You're only doing that to show off,' said Aunty

Rosa. 'But we'll see. Play with Judy now, and don't open a book for a week.'

Judy did not pass a very enjoyable playtime with Punch, who was consumed with indignation. There was a pettiness at the bottom of the prohibition which puzzled him.

'It's what I like to do,' he said, 'and she's found out that and stopped me. Don't cry, Ju — it wasn't your fault — *please* don't cry, or she'll say I made you.'

Ju loyally mopped up her tears, and the two played in their nursery, a room in the basement and half underground, to which they were regularly sent after the midday dinner while Aunty Rosa slept. She drank wine — that is to say, something from a bottle in the cellaret — for her stomach's sake, but if she did not fall asleep she would sometimes come into the nursery to see that the children were really playing. Now bricks, wooden hoops, ninepins, and chinaware cannot amuse for ever, especially when all Fairyland is to be won by the mere opening of a book, and, as often as not, Punch would be discovered reading to Judy or telling her interminable tales. That was an offence in the eyes of the law, and Judy would be whisked off by Aunty Rosa, while Punch was left to play alone, 'and be sure that I hear you doing it.'

It was not a cheering employ, for he had to make a playful noise. At last, with infinite craft, he devised an arrangement whereby the table could be supported as to three legs on toy bricks, leaving the fourth clear to bring down on the floor. He could work the table with one hand and hold a book with the other. This he did till an evil day when Aunty Rosa pounced upon him unawares and told him that he was 'acting a lie.'

'If you're old enough to do that,' she said — her temper was always worst after dinner — 'you're old enough to be beaten.'

'But — I'm — I'm not a animal!' said Punch aghast. He remembered Uncle Harry and the stick, and turned white. Aunty Rosa had hidden a light cane behind her, and Punch was beaten then and there over the shoulders. It was a revelation to him. The room-door was shut, and he was left to weep himself into repentance and work out his own gospel of life.

Aunty Rosa, he argued, had the power to beat him with many stripes. It was unjust and cruel, and Mamma and Papa would never have allowed it. Unless perhaps, as Aunty Rosa seemed to imply, they had sent secret orders. In which case he was abandoned indeed. It would be discreet in the future to propitiate Aunty Rosa, but, then, again, even in matters in which he was innocent, he had been accused of wishing to 'show off.' He had 'shown off' before visitors when he had attacked a strange gentleman — Harry's uncle, not his own — with requests for information about the Griffin and the falchion, and the precise nature of the Tilbury in which Frank Fairlegh rode — all points of paramount interest which he was bursting to understand. Clearly it would not do to pretend to care for Aunty Rosa.

At this point Harry entered and stood afar off, eying Punch, a dishevelled heap in the corner of the room, with disgust.

'You're a liar — a young liar,' said Harry, with great unction, 'and you're to have tea down here because you're not fit to speak to us. And you're not to speak to Judy again till Mother gives you leave. You'll corrupt her.   You're only fit to associate with the servant.   Mother says so.'

Having reduced Punch to a second agony of tears, Harry departed upstairs with the news that Punch was still rebellious.

Uncle Harry sat uneasily in the dining-room.   'Damn it all, Rosa,' said he at last, 'can't you leave the child alone?   He's a good enough little chap when I meet him.'

'He puts on his best manners with you, Henry,' said Aunty Rosa, 'but I'm afraid, I'm very much afraid, that he is the Black Sheep of the family.'

Harry heard and stored up the name for future use. Judy cried till she was bidden to stop, her brother not being worth tears; and the evening concluded with the return of Punch to the upper regions and a private sitting at which all the blinding horrors of Hell were revealed to Punch with such store of imagery as Aunty Rosa's narrow mind possessed.

Most grievous of all was Judy's round-eyed reproach, and Punch went to bed in the depths of the Valley of Humiliation.   He shared his room with Harry and knew the torture in store.   For an hour and a half he had to answer that young gentleman's question as to his motives for telling a lie, and a grievous lie, the precise quantity of punishment inflicted by Aunty Rosa, and had also to profess his deep gratitude for such religious instruction as Harry thought fit to impart.

From that day began the downfall of Punch, now Black Sheep.

'Untrustworthy in one thing, untrustworthy in all,' said Aunty Rosa, and Harry felt that Black Sheep was delivered into his hands.   He would wake him up in the night to ask him why he was such a liar.

'I don't know,' Punch would reply.

'Then don't you think you ought to get up and pray to God for a new heart?'

'Y-yess.'

'Get out and pray, then!'   And Punch would get out of bed with raging hate in his heart against all the world, seen and unseen.   He was always tumbling into trouble.   Harry had a knack of cross-examining him as to his day's doings, which seldom failed to lead him, sleepy and savage, into half a dozen contradictions — all duly reported to Aunty Rosa next morning.

'But it *wasn't* a lie,' Punch would begin, charging into a laboured explanation that landed him more hopelessly in the mire.   'I said that I didn't say my prayers *twice* over in the day, and *that* was on Tuesday.   *Once* I did. I *know* I did, but Harry said I didn't,' and so forth, till the tension brought tears, and he was dismissed from the table in disgrace.

'You usen't to be as bad as this?' said Judy, awe-stricken at the catalogue of Black Sheep's crimes. 'Why are you so bad now?'

'I don't know,' Black Sheep would reply.   'I'm not, if I only wasn't bothered upside down.   I knew what I *did*, and I want to say so; but Harry always makes it out different somehow, and Aunty Rosa doesn't believe a word I say.   Oh, Ju! don't *you* say I'm bad too.'

'Aunty Rosa says you are,' said Judy.   'She told the Vicar so when he came yesterday.'

'Why does she tell all the people outside the house about me?   It isn't fair,' said Black Sheep.   'When I was in Bombay, and was bad — *doing* bad, not made-up bad like this — Mamma told Papa, and Papa told me he knew, and that was all. *Outside* people didn't know too — even Meeta didn't know.'

'I don't remember,' said Judy wistfully. 'I was all little then. Mamma was just as fond of you as she was of me, wasn't she?'

''Course she was. So was Papa. So was everybody.'

'Aunty Rosa likes me more than she does you. She says that you are a Trial and a Black Sheep, and I'm not to speak to you more than I can help.'

'Always? Not outside of the times when you mustn't speak to me at all?'

Judy nodded her head mournfully. Black Sheep turned away in despair, but Judy's arms were round his neck.

'Never mind, Punch,' she whispered. 'I *will* speak to you just the same as ever and ever. You're my own own brother though you are — though Aunty Rosa says you're Bad, and Harry says you're a little coward. He says that if I pulled your hair hard, you'd cry.'

'Pull, then,' said Punch.

Judy pulled gingerly.

'Pull harder — as hard as you can! There! I don't mind how much you pull it *now*. If you'll speak to me same as ever I'll let you pull it as much as you like — pull it out if you like. But I know if Harry came and stood by and made you do it I'd cry.'

So the two children sealed the compact with a kiss, and Black Sheep's heart was cheered within him, and by extreme caution and careful avoidance of Harry he acquired virtue, and was allowed to read undisturbed for a week. Uncle Harry took him for walks, and

consoled him with rough tenderness, never calling him
Black Sheep. 'It's good for you, I suppose, Punch,'
he used to say. 'Let us sit down. I'm getting tired.'
His steps led him now not to the beach, but to the
Cemetery of Rocklington, amid the potato-fields. For
hours the gray man would sit on a tombstone, while
Black Sheep read epitaphs, and then with a sigh would
stump home again.

'I shall lie there soon,' said he to Black Sheep, one
winter evening, when his face showed white as a worn
silver coin under the light of the lych-gate. 'You
needn't tell Aunty Rosa.'

A month later, he turned sharp round, ere half a
morning walk was completed, and stumped back to the
house. 'Put me to bed, Rosa,' he muttered. 'I've
walked my last. The wadding has found me out.'

They put him to bed, and for a fortnight the shadow
of his sickness lay upon the house, and Black Sheep
went to and fro unobserved. Papa had sent him some
new books, and he was told to keep quiet. He retired
into his own world, and was perfectly happy. Even at
night his felicity was unbroken. He could lie in bed
and string himself tales of travel and adventure while
Harry was downstairs.

'Uncle Harry's going to die,' said Judy, who now
lived almost entirely with Aunty Rosa.

'I'm very sorry,' said Black Sheep soberly. 'He
told me that a long time ago.'

Aunty Rosa heard the conversation. 'Will nothing
check your wicked tongue?' she said angrily. There
were blue circles round her eyes.

Black Sheep retreated to the nursery and read *Cometh
up as a Flower* with deep and uncomprehending in-

terest.   He had been forbidden to open it on account
of its 'sinfulness,' but the bonds of the Universe were
crumbling, and Aunty Rosa was in great grief.

'I'm glad,' said Black Sheep.   'She's unhappy now.
It wasn't a lie, though.   *I* knew.   He told me not
to tell.'

That night Black Sheep woke with a start.   Harry
was not in the room, and there was a sound of sobbing
on the next floor.   Then the voice of Uncle Harry,
singing the song of the Battle of Navarino, came
through the darkness : —

> 'Our vanship was the Asia —
> The Albion and Genoa!'

'He's getting well,' thought Black Sheep, who knew
the song through all its seventeen verses.   But the
blood froze at his little heart as he thought.   The
voice leapt an octave, and rang shrill as a boatswain's
pipe : —

> 'And next came on the lovely Rose,
> The Philomel, her fire-ship, closed,
> And the little Brisk was sore exposed
> That day at Navarino.'

'That day at Navarino, Uncle Harry!' shouted Black
Sheep, half wild with excitement and fear of he knew
not what.

A door opened, and Aunty Rosa screamed up the
staircase: 'Hush! For God's sake hush, you little
devil.   Uncle Harry is *dead!*'

THE THIRD BAG

Journeys end in lovers' meeting,
Every wise man's son doth know.

'I WONDER what will happen to me now,' thought Black Sheep, when semi-pagan rites peculiar to the burial of the Dead in middle-class houses had been accomplished, and Aunty Rosa, awful in black crape, had returned to this life. 'I don't think I've done anything bad that she knows of. I suppose I will soon. She will be very cross after Uncle Harry's dying, and Harry will be cross too. I'll keep in the nursery.'

Unfortunately for Punch's plans, it was decided that he should be sent to a day-school which Harry attended. This meant a morning walk with Harry, and perhaps an evening one; but the prospect of freedom in the interval was refreshing. 'Harry'll tell everything I do, but I won't do anything,' said Black Sheep. Fortified with this virtuous resolution, he went to school only to find that Harry's version of his character had preceded him, and that life was a burden in consequence. He took stock of his associates. Some of them were unclean, some of them talked in dialect, many dropped their h's, and there were two Jews and a negro, or some one quite as dark, in the assembly. 'That's a *hubshi*,' said Black Sheep to himself. 'Even Meeta used to laugh at a *hubshi*. I don't think this is a proper place.' He was indignant for at least an hour, till he reflected that any expostulation on his part would be by Aunty Rosa construed into 'showing off,' and that Harry would tell the boys.

T

'How do you like school?' said Aunty Rosa at the end of the day.

'I think it is a very nice place,' said Punch quietly.

'I suppose you warned the boys of Black Sheep's character?' said Aunty Rosa to Harry.

'Oh yes,' said the censor of Black Sheep's morals. 'They know all about him.'

'If I was with my father,' said Black Sheep, stung to the quick, 'I shouldn't *speak* to those boys. He wouldn't let me. They live in shops. I saw them go into shops — where their fathers live and sell things.'

'You're too good for that school, are you?' said Aunty Rosa, with a bitter smile. 'You ought to be grateful, Black Sheep, that those boys speak to you at all. It isn't every school that takes little liars.'

Harry did not fail to make much capital out of Black Sheep's ill-considered remark; with the result that several boys, including the *hubshi*, demonstrated to Black Sheep the eternal equality of the human race by smacking his head, and his consolation from Aunty Rosa was that it 'served him right for being vain.' He learned, however, to keep his opinions to himself, and by propitiating Harry in carrying books and the like to get a little peace. His existence was not too joyful. From nine till twelve he was at school, and from two to four, except on Saturdays. In the evenings he was sent down into the nursery to prepare his lessons for the next day, and every night came the dreaded cross-questionings at Harry's hand. Of Judy he saw but little. She was deeply religious — at six years of age Religion is easy to come by — and sorely divided between her natural love for Black Sheep and her love for Aunty Rosa, who could do no wrong.

The lean woman returned that love with interest, and Judy, when she dared, took advantage of this for the remission of Black Sheep's penalties. Failures in lessons at school were punished at home by a week without reading other than schoolbooks, and Harry brought the news of such a failure with glee. Further, Black Sheep was then bound to repeat his lessons at bedtime to Harry, who generally succeeded in making him break down, and consoled him by gloomiest forebodings for the morrow. Harry was at once spy, practical joker, inquisitor, and Aunty Rosa's deputy executioner. He filled his many posts to admiration. From his actions, now that Uncle Harry was dead, there was no appeal. Black Sheep had not been permitted to keep any self-respect at school: at home he was of course utterly discredited, and grateful for any pity that the servant-girls — they changed frequently at Downe Lodge because they, too, were liars — might show. 'You're just fit to row in the same boat with Black Sheep,' was a sentiment that each new Jane or Eliza might expect to hear, before a month was over, from Aunty Rosa's lips; and Black Sheep was used to ask new girls whether they had yet been compared to him. Harry was 'Master Harry' in their mouths; Judy was officially 'Miss Judy'; but Black Sheep was never anything more than Black Sheep *tout court*.

As time went on and the memory of Papa and Mamma became wholly overlaid by the unpleasant task of writing them letters, under Aunty Rosa's eye, each Sunday, Black Sheep forgot what manner of life he had led in the beginning of things. Even Judy's appeals to 'try and remember about Bombay' failed to quicken him.

'I can't remember,' he said. 'I know I used to give orders and Mamma kissed me.'

'Aunty Rosa will kiss you if you are good,' pleaded Judy.

'Ugh! I don't want to be kissed by Aunty Rosa. She'd say I was doing it to get something more to eat.'

The weeks lengthened into months, and the holidays came; but just before the holidays Black Sheep fell into deadly sin.

Among the many boys whom Harry had incited to 'punch Black Sheep's head because he daren't hit back,' was one more aggravating than the rest, who, in an unlucky moment, fell upon Black Sheep when Harry was not near. The blows stung, and Black Sheep struck back at random with all the power at his command. The boy dropped and whimpered. Black Sheep was astounded at his own act, but, feeling the unresisting body under him, shook it with both his hands in blind fury and then began to throttle his enemy; meaning honestly to slay him. There was a scuffle, and Black Sheep was torn off the body by Harry and some colleagues, and cuffed home tingling but exultant. Aunty Rosa was out: pending her arrival, Harry sent himself to lecture Black Sheep on the sin of murder — which he described as the offence of Cain.

'Why didn't you fight him fair? What did you hit him when he was down for, you little cur?'

Black Sheep looked up at Harry's throat and then at a knife on the dinner-table.

'I don't understand,' he said wearily. 'You always set him on me and told me I was a coward when I blubbed. Will you leave me alone until Aunty Rosa comes in? She'll beat me if you tell her I ought to be beaten; so it's all right.'

'It's all wrong,' said Harry magisterially. 'You nearly killed him, and I shouldn't wonder if he dies.'

'Will he die?' said Black Sheep.

'I dare say,' said Harry, 'and then you'll be hanged, and go to Hell.'

'All right,' said Black Sheep, picking up the table-knife. 'Then I'll kill *you* now. You say things and do things and — and *I* don't know how things happen, and you never leave me alone — and I don't care *what* happens!'

He ran at the boy with the knife, and Harry fled upstairs to his room, promising Black Sheep the finest thrashing in the world when Aunty Rosa returned. Black Sheep sat at the bottom of the stairs, the table-knife in his hand, and wept for that he had not killed Harry. The servant-girl came up from the kitchen, took the knife away, and consoled him. But Black Sheep was beyond consolation. He would be badly beaten by Aunty Rosa; then there would be another beating at Harry's hands; then Judy would not be allowed to speak to him; then the tale would be told at school and then ——

There was no one to help and no one to care, and the best way out of the business was by death. A knife would hurt, but Aunty Rosa had told him, a year ago, that if he sucked paint he would die. He went into the nursery, unearthed the now disused Noah's Ark, and sucked the paint off as many animals as remained. It tasted abominable, but he had licked Noah's Dove clean by the time Aunty Rosa and Judy returned. He went upstairs and greeted them with:

'Please, Aunty Rosa, I believe I've nearly killed a boy at school, and I've tried to kill Harry, and when you've done all about God and Hell, will you beat me and get it over?'

The tale of the assault as told by Harry could only be explained on the ground of possession by the Devil. Wherefore Black Sheep was not only most excellently beaten, once by Aunty Rosa and once, when thoroughly cowed down, by Harry, but he was further prayed for at family prayers, together with Jane who had stolen a cold rissole from the pantry and snuffled audibly as her sin was brought before the Throne of Grace. Black Sheep was sore and stiff but triumphant. He would die that very night and be rid of them all. No, he would ask for no forgiveness from Harry, and at bed-time would stand no questioning at Harry's hands, even though addressed as 'Young Cain.'

'I've been beaten,' said he, 'and I've done other things. I don't care what I do. If you speak to me to-night, Harry, I'll get out and try to kill you. Now you can kill me if you like.'

Harry took his bed into the spare room, and Black Sheep lay down to die.

It may be that the makers of Noah's Arks know that their animals are likely to find their way into young mouths, and paint them accordingly. Certain it is that the common, weary next morning broke through the windows and found Black Sheep quite well and a good deal ashamed of himself, but richer by the knowledge that he could, in extremity, secure himself against Harry for the future.

When he descended to breakfast on the first day of the holidays, he was greeted with the news that Harry,

Aunty Rosa, and Judy were going away to Brighton, while Black Sheep was to stay in the house with the servant. His latest outbreak suited Aunty Rosa's plans admirably. It gave her good excuse for leaving the extra boy behind. Papa in Bombay, who really seemed to know a young sinner's wants to the hour, sent, that week, a package of new books. And with these, and the society of Jane on board-wages, Black Sheep was left alone for a month.

The books lasted for ten days. They were eaten too quickly in long gulps of twelve hours at a time. Then came days of doing absolutely nothing, of dreaming dreams and marching imaginary armies up and down stairs, of counting the number of banisters, and of measuring the length and breadth of every room in handspans — fifty down the side, thirty across, and fifty back again. Jane made many friends, and, after receiving Black Sheep's assurance that he would not tell of her absences, went out daily for long hours. Black Sheep would follow the rays of the sinking sun from the kitchen to the dining-room and thence upward to his own bedroom until all was gray dark, and he ran down to the kitchen fire and read by its light. He was happy in that he was left alone and could read as much as he pleased. But, later, he grew afraid of the shadows of window-curtains and the flapping of doors and the creaking of shutters. He went out into the garden, and the rustling of the laurel-bushes frightened him.

He was glad when they all returned — Aunty Rosa, Harry, and Judy — full of news, and Judy laden with gifts. Who could help loving loyal little Judy? In return for all her merry babblement, Black Sheep confided to her that the distance from the hall-door to the top of the first landing was exactly one hundred and eighty-four handspans. He had found it out himself.

Then the old life recommenced; but with a difference, and a new sin. To his other iniquities Black Sheep had now added a phenomenal clumsiness — was as unfit to trust in action as he was in word. He himself could not account for spilling everything he touched, upsetting glasses as he put his hand out, and bumping his head against doors that were manifestly shut. There was a gray haze upon all his world, and it narrowed month by month, until at last it left Black Sheep almost alone with the flapping curtains that were so like ghosts, and the nameless terrors of broad daylight that were only coats on pegs after all.

Holidays came and holidays went and Black Sheep was taken to see many people whose faces were all exactly alike; was beaten when occasion demanded, and tortured by Harry on all possible occasions; but defended by Judy through good and evil report, though she hereby drew upon herself the wrath of Aunty Rosa.

The weeks were interminable, and Papa and Mamma were clean forgotten. Harry had left school and was a clerk in a Banking-Office. Freed from his presence, Black Sheep resolved that he should no longer be deprived of his allowance of pleasure-reading. Consequently when he failed at school he reported that all was well, and conceived a large contempt for Aunty Rosa as he saw how easy it was to deceive her. 'She says I'm a little liar when I don't tell lies, and now I do, she doesn't know,' thought Black Sheep. Aunty Rosa had credited him in the past with petty cunning and stratagem that had never entered into his head. By the light of the sordid knowledge that she

had revealed to him he paid her back full tale.   In
a household where the most innocent of his motives,
his natural yearning for a little affection, had been
interpreted into a desire for more bread and jam or
to ingratiate himself with strangers and so put Harry
into the background, his work was easy.   Aunty Rosa
could penetrate certain kinds of hypocrisy, but not all.
He set his child's wits against hers and was no more
beaten.   It grew monthly more and more of a trouble
to read the schoolbooks, and even the pages of the
open-print story-books danced and were dim.   So
Black Sheep brooded in the shadows that fell about
him and cut him off from the world, inventing horrible
punishments for 'dear Harry,' or plotting another line
of the tangled web of deception that he wrapped round
Aunty Rosa.

Then the crash came and the cobwebs were broken.
It was impossible to foresee everything.   Aunty Rosa
made personal enquiries as to Black Sheep's progress
and received information that startled her.   Step by
step, with a delight as keen as when she convicted an
underfed housemaid of the theft of cold meats, she followed the trail of Black Sheep's delinquencies.   For
weeks and weeks, in order to escape banishment from
the book-shelves, he had made a fool of Aunty Rosa, of
Harry, of God, of all the world!   Horrible, most horrible, and evidence of an utterly depraved mind.

Black Sheep counted the cost.   'It will only be one
big beating and then she'll put a card with "Liar" on
my back, same as she did before.   Harry will whack
me and pray for me, and she will pray for me at prayers
and tell me I'm a Child of the Devil and give me hymns
to learn.   But I've done all my reading and she never

knew.   She'll say she knew all along.   She's an old liar too,' said he.

For three days Black Sheep was shut in his own bed-room — to prepare his heart. 'That means two beat-ings. One at school and one here. *That* one will hurt most.' And it fell even as he thought. He was thrashed at school before the Jews and the *hubshi*, for the heinous crime of bringing home false reports of progress. He was thrashed at home by Aunty Rosa on the same count, and then the placard was produced. Aunty Rosa stitched it between his shoulders and bade him go for a walk with it upon him.

'If you make me do that,' said Black Sheep very quietly, 'I shall burn this house down, and perhaps I'll kill you.   I don't know whether I *can* kill you — you're so bony — but I'll try.'

No punishment followed this blasphemy, though Black Sheep held himself ready to work his way to Aunty Rosa's withered throat, and grip there till he was beaten off.   Perhaps Aunty Rosa was afraid, for Black Sheep, having reached the Nadir of Sin, bore himself with a new recklessness.

In the midst of all the trouble there came a visitor from over the seas to Downe Lodge, who knew Papa and Mamma, and was commissioned to see Punch and Judy. Black Sheep was sent to the drawing-room and charged into a solid tea-table laden with china.

'Gently, gently, little man,' said the visitor, turning Black Sheep's face to the light slowly. 'What's that big bird on the palings?'

'What bird?' asked Black Sheep.

The visitor looked deep down into Black Sheep's eyes

for half a minute, **and** then **said** suddenly: 'Good God, the little chap's **nearly blind!**'

It was a most business-like visitor. He gave orders, on his own responsibility, that Black Sheep was not to go to school or open a book until Mamma came home. 'She'll be here in three weeks, as you know of course,' said he, 'and I'm Inverarity Sahib. I ushered you into this wicked world, young man, and a nice use you seem to have made of your time. You must do nothing whatever. Can you do that?'

'Yes,' said Punch in a dazed way. He had known that Mamma was coming. There was a chance, then, of another beating. Thank Heaven, Papa wasn't coming too. Aunty Rosa had said of late that he ought to be beaten by a man.

For the next three weeks Black Sheep was strictly allowed to do nothing. He spent his time in the old nursery looking at the broken toys, for all of which account must be rendered to Mamma. Aunty Rosa hit him over the hands if even a wooden boat were broken. But that sin was of small importance compared to the other revelations, so darkly hinted at by Aunty Rosa.

'When your Mother comes, and hears what I have to tell her, she may appreciate you properly,' she said grimly, and mounted guard over Judy lest that small maiden should attempt to comfort her brother, to the peril of her soul.

And Mamma came — in a four-wheeler — fluttered with tender excitement. Such a Mamma! She was young, frivolously young, and beautiful, with delicately flushed cheeks, eyes that shone like stars, and a voice that needed no appeal of outstretched arms to draw little ones to her heart. Judy ran straight to her, but

Black Sheep hesitated.   Could this wonder be 'showing off'?   She would not put out her arms when she
knew of his crimes.   Meantime was it possible that
by fondling she wanted to get anything out of Black
Sheep?   Only all his love and all his confidence; but
that Black Sheep did not know.   Aunty Rosa withdrew and left Mamma, kneeling between her children,
half laughing, half crying, in the very hall where
Punch and Judy had wept five years before.

'Well, chicks, do you remember me?'

'No,' said Judy frankly, 'but I said, "God bless Papa
and Mamma," ev'vy night.'

'A little,' said Black Sheep.   'Remember I wrote to
you every week, anyhow.   That isn't to show off, but
'cause of what comes afterwards.'

'What comes after?   What should come after, my
darling boy?'   And she drew him to her again.   He
came awkwardly, with many angles.   'Not used to
petting,' said the quick Mother-soul.   'The girl is.'

'She's too little to hurt any one,' thought Black Sheep,
'and if I said I'd kill her, she'd be afraid.   I wonder
what Aunty Rosa will tell.'

There was a constrained late dinner, at the end of
which Mamma picked up Judy and put her to bed with
endearments manifold.   Faithless little Judy had shown
her defection from Aunty Rosa already.   And that
lady resented it bitterly.   Black Sheep rose to leave
the room.

'Come and say good-night,' said Aunty Rosa, offer-
ing a withered cheek.

'Huh!' said Black Sheep.   'I never kiss you, and
I'm not going to show off.   Tell that woman what I've
done, and see what she says.'

Black Sheep climbed into bed feeling that he had lost Heaven after a glimpse through the gates. In half an hour 'that woman' was bending over him. Black Sheep flung up his right arm. It wasn't fair to come and hit him in the dark. Even Aunty Rosa never tried that. But no blow followed.

'Are you showing off? I won't tell you anything more than Aunty Rosa has, and *she* doesn't know everything,' said Black Sheep as clearly as he could for the arms round his neck.

'Oh, my son—my little, little son! It was my fault —*my* fault, darling—and yet how could we help it? Forgive me, Punch.' The voice died out in a broken whisper, and two hot tears fell on Black Sheep's forehead.

'Has she been making you cry too?' he asked. 'You should see Jane cry. But you're nice, and Jane is a Born Liar—Aunty Rosa says so.'

'Hush, Punch, hush! My boy, don't talk like that. Try to love me a little bit—a little bit. You don't know how I want it. Punch-*baba*, come back to me! I am your Mother—your own Mother—and never mind the rest. I know—yes, I know, dear. It doesn't matter now. Punch, won't you care for me a little?'

It is astonishing how much petting a big boy of ten can endure when he is quite sure that there is no one to laugh at him. Black Sheep had never been made much of before, and here was this beautiful woman treating him—Black Sheep, the Child of the Devil and the inheritor of undying flame—as though he were a small God.

'I care for you a great deal, Mother dear,' he whispered at last, 'and I'm glad you've come back; but are you sure Aunty Rosa told you everything?'

'Everything. What *does* it matter? But' — the voice broke with a sob that was also laughter — 'Punch, my poor, dear, half-blind darling, don't you think it was a little foolish of you?'

'*No*. It saved a lickin'.'

Mamma shuddered and slipped away in the darkness to write a long letter to Papa. Here is an extract: —

. . . Judy is a dear, plump little prig who adores the woman, and wears with as much gravity as her religious opinions — only eight, Jack! — a venerable horse-hair atrocity which she calls her Bustle! I have just burnt it, and the child is asleep in my bed as I write. She will come to me at once. Punch I cannot quite understand. He is well nourished, but seems to have been worried into a system of small deceptions which the woman magnifies into deadly sins. Don't you recollect our own upbringing, dear, when the Fear of the Lord was so often the beginning of falsehood? I shall win Punch to me before long. I am taking the children away into the country to get them to know me, and, on the whole, I am content, or shall be when you come home, dear boy, and then, thank God, we shall be all under one roof again at last!

Three months later, Punch, no longer Black Sheep, has discovered that he is the veritable owner of a real, live, lovely Mamma, who is also a sister, comforter, and friend, and that he must protect her till the Father comes home. Deception does not suit the part of a protector, and, when one can do anything without question, where is the use of deception?

'Mother would be awfully cross if you walked through that ditch,' says Judy, continuing a conversation.

'Mother's never angry,' says Punch. 'She'd just say, "You're a little *pagal;*" and that's not nice, but I'll show.'

Punch walks through the ditch and mires himself

to the knees. 'Mother, dear,' he shouts, 'I'm just as dirty as I can pos-*sib*-ly be!'

'Then change your clothes as quickly as you pos-*sib*-ly can!' Mother's clear voice rings out from the house. 'And don't be a little *pagal!*'

'There! 'Told you so,' says Punch. 'It's all different now, and we are just as much Mother's as if she had never gone.'

Not altogether, O Punch, for when young lips have drunk deep of the bitter waters of Hate, Suspicion, and Despair, all the Love in the world will not wholly take away that knowledge; though it may turn darkened eyes for a while to the light, and teach Faith where no Faith was.

HIS MAJESTY THE KING

Where the word of a King is, there is power: And who may say
unto him — What doest thou?

'YETH! And Chimo to sleep at ve foot of ve bed,
and ve pink pikky-book, and ve bwead — 'cause I will
be hungwy in ve night — and vat's all, Miss Biddums.
And now give me one kiss and I'll go to sleep. — So!
Kite quiet. Ow! Ve pink pikky-book has slidded
under ve pillow and ve bwead is cwumbling! Miss
Biddums! Miss *Bid*-dums! I'm *so* uncomfy! Come
and tuck me up, Miss Biddums.'

His Majesty the King was going to bed; and poor,
patient Miss Biddums, who had advertised herself
humbly as a 'young person, European, accustomed to
the care of little children,' was forced to wait upon
his royal caprices. The going to bed was always a
lengthy process, because His Majesty had a convenient
knack of forgetting which of his many friends, from
the *mehter's* son to the Commissioner's daughter, he
had prayed for, and, lest the Deity should take offence,
was used to toil through his little prayers, in all rever-
ence, five times in one evening. His Majesty the
King believed in the efficacy of prayer as devoutly as
he believed in Chimo the patient spaniel, or Miss Biddums, who could reach him down his gun — 'with cur-
suffun caps — *reel* ones' — from the upper shelves of
the big nursery cupboard.

At the door of the nursery his authority stopped.
Beyond lay the empire of his father and mother — twc

very terrible people who had no time to waste upon His Majesty the King. His voice was lowered when he passed the frontier of his own dominions, his actions were fettered, and his soul was filled with awe because of the grim man who lived among a wilderness of pigeon-holes and the most fascinating pieces of red tape, and the wonderful woman who was always getting into or stepping out of the big carriage.

To the one belonged the mysteries of the '*duftar-room*,' to the other the great, reflected wilderness of the 'Memsahib's room' where the shiny, scented dresses hung on pegs, miles and miles up in the air, and the just-seen plateau of the toilet-table revealed an acreage of speckly combs, broidered 'hanafitch-bags,' and 'white-headed' brushes.

There was no room for His Majesty the King either in official reserve or worldly gorgeousness. He had discovered that, ages and ages ago — before even Chimo came to the house, or Miss Biddums had ceased grizzling over a packet of greasy letters which appeared to be her chief treasure on earth. His Majesty the King, therefore, wisely confined himself to his own territories, where only Miss Biddums, and she feebly, disputed his sway.

From Miss Biddums he had picked up his simple theology and welded it to the legends of gods and devils that he had learned in the servants' quarters.

To Miss Biddums he confided with equal trust his tattered garments and his more serious griefs. She would make everything whole. She knew exactly how the Earth had been born, and had reassured the trembling soul of His Majesty the King that terrible time in July when it rained continuously for seven days and

U

seven nights, and — there was no Ark ready and all the ravens had flown away! She was the most powerful person with whom he was brought into contact — always excepting the two remote and silent people beyond the nursery door.

How was His Majesty the King to know that, six years ago, in the summer of his birth, Mrs. Austell, turning over her husband's papers, had come upon the intemperate letter of a foolish woman who had been carried away by the silent man's strength and personal beauty? How could he tell what evil the overlooked slip of notepaper had wrought in the mind of a desperately jealous wife? How could he, despite his wisdom, guess that his mother had chosen to make of it excuse for a bar and a division between herself and her husband, that strengthened and grew harder to break with each year; that she, having unearthed this skeleton in the cupboard, had trained it into a household God which should be about their path and about their bed, and poison all their ways?

These things were beyond the province of His Majesty the King. He only knew that his father was daily absorbed in some mysterious work for a thing called the *Sirkar* and that his mother was the victim alternately of the *Nautch* and the *Burrakhana*. To these entertainments she was escorted by a Captain-Man for whom His Majesty the King had no regard.

'He *doesn't* laugh,' he argued with Miss Biddums, who would fain have taught him charity. 'He only makes faces wiv his mouf, and when he wants to o-muse me I am *not* o-mused.' And His Majesty the King shook his head as one who knew the deceitfulness of this world.

Morning and evening it was his duty to salute his father and mother — the former with a grave shake of the hand, and the latter with an equally grave kiss. Once, indeed, he had put his arms round his mother's neck, in the fashion he used towards Miss Biddums. The openwork of his sleeve-edge caught in an earring, and the last stage of His Majesty's little overture was a suppressed scream and summary dismissal to the nursery.

'It is w'ong,' thought His Majesty the King, 'to hug Memsahibs wiv fings in veir ears. I will amember.' He never repeated the experiment.

Miss Biddums, it must be confessed, spoilt him as much as his nature admitted, in some sort of recompense for what she called 'the hard ways of his Papa and Mamma.' She, like her charge, knew nothing of the trouble between man and wife — the savage contempt for a woman's stupidity on the one side, or the dull, rankling anger on the other. Miss Biddums had looked after many little children in her time, and served in many establishments. Being a discreet woman, she observed little and said less, and, when her pupils went over the sea to the Great Unknown, which she, with touching confidence in her hearers, called 'Home,' packed up her slender belongings and sought for employment afresh, lavishing all her love on each successive batch of ingrates. Only His Majesty the King had repaid her affection with interest; and in his uncomprehending ears she had told the tale of nearly all her hopes, her aspirations, the hopes that were dead, and the dazzling glories of her ancestral home in '*Cal*cutta, close to Wellington Square.'

Everything above the average was in the eyes of His

Majesty the King 'Calcutta good.' When Miss Biddums had crossed his royal will, he reversed the epithet
to vex that estimable lady, and all things evil were,
until the tears of repentance swept away spite, 'Calcutta bad.'

Now and again Miss Biddums begged for him the
rare pleasure of a day in the society of the Commissioner's child — the wilful four-year-old Patsie, who,
to the intense amazement of His Majesty the King,
was idolised by her parents. On thinking the question
out at length, by roads unknown to those who have
left childhood behind, he came to the conclusion that
Patsie was petted because she wore a big blue sash and
yellow hair.

This precious discovery he kept to himself. The
yellow hair was absolutely beyond his power, his own
tousled wig being potato-brown; but something might
be done towards the blue sash. He tied a large knot
in his mosquito-curtains in order to remember to con-
sult Patsie on their next meeting. She was the only
child he had ever spoken to, and almost the only one
that he had ever seen. The little memory and the
very large and ragged knot held good.

'Patsie, lend me your blue wiband,' said His Majesty
the King.

'You'll bewy it,' said Patsie doubtfully, mindful of
certain atrocities committed on her doll.

'No, I won't — twoofanhonour. It's for me to
wear.'

'Pooh!' said Patsie. 'Boys don't wear sa-ashes.
Zey's only for dirls.'

'I didn't know.' The face of His Majesty the King
fell.

'Who wants ribands? Are you playing horses, chick-abiddies?' said the Commissioner's wife, stepping into the veranda.

'Toby wanted my sash,' explained Patsie.

'I don't now,' said His Majesty the King hastily, feeling that with one of these terrible 'grown ups' his poor little secret would be shamelessly wrenched from him, and perhaps — most burning desecration of all — laughed at.

'I'll give you a cracker-cap,' said the Commissioner's wife. 'Come along with me, Toby, and we'll choose it.'

The cracker-cap was a stiff, three-pointed vermilion-and-tinsel splendour. His Majesty the King fitted it on his royal brow. The Commissioner's wife had a face that children instinctively trusted, and her action, as she adjusted the toppling middle spike, was tender.

'Will it do as well?' stammered His Majesty the King.

'As what, little one?'

'As ve wiban?'

'Oh, quite. Go and look at yourself in the glass.'

The words were spoken in all sincerity and to help forward any absurd 'dressing-up' amusement that the children might take into their minds. But the young savage has a keen sense of the ludicrous. His Majesty the King swung the great cheval-glass down, and saw his head crowned with the staring horror of a fool's cap — a thing which his father would rend to pieces if it ever came into his office. He plucked it off, and burst into tears.

'Toby,' said the Commissioner's wife gravely, 'you

shouldn't give way to temper. I am very sorry to see it. It's wrong.'

His Majesty the King sobbed inconsolably, and the heart of Patsie's mother was touched. She drew the child on to her knee. Clearly it was not temper alone.

'What is it, Toby? Won't you tell me? Aren't you well?'

The torrent of sobs and speech met, and fought for a time, with chokings and gulpings and gasps. Then, in a sudden rush, His Majesty the King was delivered of a few inarticulate sounds, followed by the words—'Go a—way you—dirty—little debbil!'

'Toby! What do you mean?'

'It's what he'd say. I *know* it is! He said vat when vere was only a little, little eggy mess, on my t-t-unic; and he'd say it again, and laugh, if I went in wif vat on my head.'

'Who would say that?'

'M-m-my Papa! And I fought if I had ve blue wiban, he'd let me play in ve waste-paper basket under ve table.'

'*What* blue riband, childie?'

'Ve same vat Patsie had—ve big blue wiban w-w-wound my t-ttummy!'

'What is it, Toby? There's something on your mind. Tell me all about it, and perhaps I can help.'

'Isn't anyfing,' sniffed His Majesty, mindful of his manhood, and raising his head from the motherly bosom upon which it was resting. 'I only fought vat you—you petted Patsie 'cause she had ve blue wiban, and—and if I'd had ve blue wiban too, m-my Papa w-would pet me.'

The secret was out, and His Majesty the King

sobbed bitterly in spite of the arms around him, and the murmur of comfort on his heated little forehead.

Enter Patsie tumultuously, embarrassed by several lengths of the Commissioner's pet *mahseer*-rod. 'Tum along, Toby! Zere's a *chu-chu* lizard in ze *chick*, and I've told Chimo to watch him till we tum. If we poke him wiz zis his tail will go *wiggle-wiggle* and fall off. Tum along! I can't weach.'

'I'm comin',' said His Majesty the King, climbing down from the Commissioner's wife's knee after a hasty kiss.

Two minutes later, the *chu-chu* lizard's tail was wriggling on the matting of the veranda, and the children were gravely poking it with splinters from the *chick*, to urge its exhausted vitality into 'just one wiggle more, 'cause it doesn't hurt *chu-chu*.'

The Commissioner's wife stood in the doorway and watched — 'Poor little mite! A blue sash —— and my own precious Patsie! I wonder if the best of us, or we who love them best, ever understood what goes on in their topsy-turvy little heads.'

She went indoors to devise a tea for His Majesty the King.

'Their souls aren't in their tummies at that age in this climate,' said the Commissioner's wife, 'but they are not far off. I wonder if I could make Mrs. Austell understand. Poor little fellow!'

With simple craft, the Commissioner's wife called on Mrs. Austell and spoke long and lovingly about children; inquiring specially for His Majesty the King.

'He's with his governess,' said Mrs. Austell, and the tone showed that she was not interested.

The Commissioner's wife, unskilled in the art of

war, continued her questionings. 'I don't know,' said Mrs. Austell. 'These things are left to Miss Biddums, and, of course, she does not ill-treat the child.'

The Commissioner's wife left hastily. The last sentence jarred upon her nerves. 'Doesn't *ill-treat* the child! As if that were all! I wonder what Tom would say if I only "didn't ill-treat" Patsie!'

Thenceforward, His Majesty the King was an honoured guest at the Commissioner's house, and the chosen friend of Patsie, with whom he blundered into as many scrapes as the compound and the servants' quarters afforded. Patsie's Mamma was always ready to give counsel, help, and sympathy, and, if need were and callers few, to enter into their games with an *abandon* that would have shocked the sleek-haired subalterns who squirmed painfully in their chairs when they came to call on her whom they profanely nicknamed 'Mother Bunch.'

Yet, in spite of Patsie and Patsie's Mamma, and the love that these two lavished upon him, His Majesty the King fell grievously from grace, and committed no less a sin than that of theft — unknown, it is true, but burdensome.

There came a man to the door one day, when His Majesty was playing in the hall and the bearer had gone to dinner, with a packet for His Majesty's Mamma. And he put it upon the hall-table, and said that there was no answer, and departed.

Presently, the pattern of the dado ceased to interest His Majesty, while the packet, a white, neatly wrapped one of fascinating shape, interested him very much indeed. His Mamma was out, so was Miss Biddums, and there was pink string round the packet. He greatly

desired pink string.   It would help him in many of his
little businesses — the haulage across the floor of his
small cane-chair, the torturing of Chimo, who could
never understand harness — and so forth.   If he took
the string it would be his own, and nobody would be
any the wiser.   He certainly could not pluck up sufficient courage to ask Mamma for it.   Wherefore, mount-
ing upon a chair, he carefully untied the string and,
behold, the stiff white paper spread out in four direc-
tions, and revealed a beautiful little leather box with
gold lines upon it!   He tried to replace the string, but
that was a failure.   So he opened the box to get full
satisfaction for his iniquity, and saw a most beautiful
Star that shone and winked, and was altogether lovely
and desirable.

'Vat,' said His Majesty meditatively, 'is a 'parkle
cwown, like what I will wear when I go to heaven.   I
will wear it on my head — Miss Biddums says so.   I
would like to wear it *now*.   I would like to play wiv
it.   I will take it away and play wiv it, very careful,
until Mamma asks for it.   I fink it was bought for me
to play wiv — same as my cart.'

His Majesty the King was arguing against his conscience, and he knew it, for he thought immediately
after: 'Never mind, I will keep it to play wiv until
Mamma says where it is, and then I will say — "I tookt
it and I am sorry."   I will not hurt it because it is a
'parkle cwown.   But Miss Biddums will tell me to put
it back.   I will not show it to Miss Biddums.'

If Mamma had come in at that moment all would
have gone well.   She did not, and His Majesty the
King stuffed paper, case, and jewel into the breast of
his blouse and marched to the nursery.

'When Mamma asks I will tell,' was the salve that he laid upon his conscience. But Mamma never asked, and for three whole days His Majesty the King gloated over his treasure. It was of no earthly use to him, but it was splendid, and, for aught he knew, something dropped from the heavens themselves. Still Mamma made no enquiries, and it seemed to him, in his furtive peeps, as though the shiny stones grew dim. What was the use of a 'parkle cwown if it made a little boy feel all bad in his inside? He had the pink string as well as the other treasure, but greatly he wished that he had not gone beyond the string. It was his first experience of iniquity, and it pained him after the flush of possession and secret delight in the ''parkle cwown' had died away.

Each day that he delayed rendered confession to the people beyond the nursery doors more impossible. Now and again he determined to put himself in the path of the beautifully attired lady as she was going out, and explain that he and no one else was the possessor of a ''parkle cwown,' most beautiful and quite unenquired for. But she passed hurriedly to her carriage, and the opportunity was gone before His Majesty the King could draw the deep breath which clinches noble resolve. The dread secret cut him off from Miss Biddums, Patsie, and the Commissioner's wife, and — doubly hard fate — when he brooded over it Patsie said, and told her mother, that he was cross.

The days were very long to His Majesty the King, and the nights longer still. Miss Biddums had informed him, more than once, what was the ultimate destiny of 'fieves,' and when he passed the interminable mud flanks of the Central Jail, he shook in his little strapped shoes.

But release came after an afternoon spent in playing boats by the edge of the tank at the bottom of the garden. His Majesty the King went to tea, and, for the first time in his memory, the meal revolted him. His nose was very cold, and his cheeks were burning hot. There was a weight about his feet, and he pressed his head several times to make sure that it was not swelling as he sat.

'I feel vevy funny,' said His Majesty the King, rubbing his nose. 'Vere's a buzz-buzz in my head.'

He went to bed quietly. Miss Biddums was out and the bearer undressed him.

The sin of the ''parkle cwown' was forgotten in the acuteness of the discomfort to which he roused after a leaden sleep of some hours. He was thirsty, and the bearer had forgotten to leave the drinking-water. 'Miss Biddums! Miss Biddums! I'm so kirsty!'

No answer. Miss Biddums had leave to attend the wedding of a Calcutta schoolmate. His Majesty the King had forgotten that.

'I want a dwink of water!' he cried, but his voice was dried up in his throat. 'I want a dwink! Vere is ve glass?'

He sat up in bed and looked round. There was a murmur of voices from the other side of the nursery door. It was better to face the terrible unknown than to choke in the dark. He slipped out of bed, but his feet were strangely wilful, and he reeled once or twice. Then he pushed the door open and staggered — a puffed and purple-faced little figure — into the brilliant light of the dining-room full of pretty ladies.

'I'm vevy hot! I'm vevy uncomfitivle,' moaned His Majesty the King, clinging to the portière, 'and

vere's no water in ve glass, and I'm *so* kirsty. Give
me a dwink of water.'

An apparition in black and white — His Majesty the
King could hardly see distinctly — lifted him up to the
level of the table, and felt his wrists and forehead.
The water came, and he drank deeply, his teeth chattering against the edge of the tumbler. Then every one
seemed to go away — every one except the huge man
in black and white, who carried him back to his bed;
the mother and father following. And the sin of the
"parkle cwown' rushed back and took possession of
the terrified soul.

'I'm a fief!' he gasped. 'I want to tell Miss Biddums vat I'm a fief. Vere is Miss Biddums?'

Miss Biddums had come and was bending over him.
'I'm a fief,' he whispered. 'A fief — like ve men in
the pwison. But I'll tell now. I tookt — I tookt ve
'parkle cwown when the man that came left it in ve
hall. I bwoke ve paper and ve little bwown box, and
it looked shiny, and I tookt it to play wif, and I was
afwaid. It's in ve dooly-box at ve bottom. No one
never asked for it, but I was afwaid. Oh, go an' get
ve dooly-box!'

Miss Biddums obediently stooped to the lowest shelf
of the *almirah* and unearthed the big paper box in which
His Majesty the King kept his dearest possessions.
Under the tin soldiers, and a layer of mud pellets for
a pellet-bow, winked and blazed a diamond star, wrapped
roughly in a half-sheet of notepaper whereon were a
few words.

Somebody was crying at the head of the bed, and a
man's hand touched the forehead of His Majesty the
King, who grasped the packet and spread it on the bed.

'Vat is ve 'parkle cwown,' he said, and wept bitterly; for now that he had made restitution he would fain have kept the shining splendour with him.

'It concerns you too,' said a voice at the head of the bed. 'Read the note. This is not the time to keep back anything.'

The note was curt, very much to the point, and signed by a single initial. '*If you wear this to-morrow night I shall know what to expect.*' The date was three weeks old.

A whisper followed, and the deeper voice returned: 'And you drifted as far apart as *that!* I think it makes us quits now, doesn't it? Oh, can't we drop this folly once and for all? Is it worth it, darling?'

'Kiss me too,' said His Majesty the King dreamily. 'You isn't *vevy* angwy, is you?'

The fever burned itself out, and His Majesty the King slept.

When he waked, it was in a new world — peopled by his father and mother as well as Miss Biddums: and there was much love in that world and no morsel of fear, and more petting than was good for several little boys. His Majesty the King was too young to moralise on the uncertainty of things human, or he would have been impressed with the singular advantages of crime — ay, black sin. Behold, he had stolen the ''parkle cwown,' and his reward was Love, and the right to play in the waste-paper basket under the table 'for always.'

*   *   *   *   *   *   *   *   *

He trotted over to spend an afternoon with Patsie, and the Commissioner's wife would have kissed him. 'No, not vere,' said His Majesty the King, with superb insolence, fencing one corner of his mouth with his hand. 'Vat's my Mamma's place — vere *she* kisses me.'

'Oh!' said the Commissioner's wife briefly. Then to herself: 'Well, I suppose I ought to be glad for his sake. Children are selfish little grubs and — I've got my Patsie.'

THE DRUMS OF THE FORE AND AFT

In the Army List they still stand as 'The Fore and Fit Princess Hohenzollern-Sigmaringen-Anspach's Mer-ther-Tydfilshire Own Royal Loyal Light Infantry, Regimental District 329A,' but the Army through all its barracks and canteens knows them now as the 'Fore and Aft.' They may in time do something that shall make their new title honourable, but at present they are bitterly ashamed, and the man who calls them 'Fore and Aft' does so at the risk of the head which is on his shoulders.

Two words breathed into the stables of a certain Cavalry Regiment will bring the men out into the streets with belts and mops and bad language; but a whisper of 'Fore and Aft' will bring out this regiment with rifles.

Their one excuse is that they came again and did their best to finish the job in style. But for a time all their world knows that they were openly beaten, whipped, dumb-cowed, shaking and afraid. The men know it; their officers know it; the Horse Guards know it, and when the next war comes the enemy will know it also. There are two or three regiments of the Line that have a black mark against their names which they will then wipe out; and it will be excessively inconvenient for the troops upon whom they do their wiping.

The courage of the British soldier is officially sup-

posed to be above proof, and, as a general rule, it is so.
The exceptions are decently shovelled out of sight, only
to be referred to in the freshest of unguarded talk that
occasionally swamps a Mess-table at midnight. Then
one hears strange and horrible stories of men not following their officers, of orders being given by those who
had no right to give them, and of disgrace that, but for
the standing luck of the British Army, might have ended
in brilliant disaster. These are unpleasant stories to
listen to, and the Messes tell them under their breath,
sitting by the big wood fires, and the young officer bows
his head and thinks to himself, please God, his men shall
never behave unhandily.

The British soldier is not altogether to be blamed
for occasional lapses; but this verdict he should not know.
A moderately intelligent General will waste six months
in mastering the craft of the particular war that he
may be waging; a Colonel may utterly misunderstand
the capacity of his regiment for three months after it
has taken the field, and even a Company Commander
may err and be deceived as to the temper and temperament of his own handful: wherefore the soldier, and
the soldier of to-day more particularly, should not be
blamed for falling back. He should be shot or hanged
afterwards — to encourage the others; but he should
not be vilified in newspapers, for that is want of tact
and waste of space.

He has, let us say, been in the service of the Empress
for, perhaps, four years. He will leave in another two
years. He has no inherited morals, and four years are
not sufficient to drive toughness into his fibre, or to
teach him how holy a thing is his Regiment. He wants
to drink, he wants to enjoy himself — in India he wants

to save money — and he does not in the least like getting hurt.   He has received just sufficient education to make him understand half the purport of the orders he receives, and to speculate on the nature of clean, incised, and shattering wounds.   Thus, if he is told to deploy under fire preparatory to an attack, he knows that he runs a very great risk of being killed while he is deploying, and suspects that he is being thrown away to gain ten minutes' time.   He may either deploy with desperate swiftness, or he may shuffle, or bunch, or break, according to the discipline under which he has lain for four years.

Armed with imperfect knowledge, cursed with the rudiments of an imagination, hampered by the intense selfishness of the lower classes, and unsupported by any regimental associations, this young man is suddenly introduced to an enemy who in eastern lands is always ugly, generally tall and hairy, and frequently noisy. If he looks to the right and the left and sees old soldiers — men of twelve years' service, who, he knows, know what they are about — taking a charge, rush, or demonstration without embarrassment, he is consoled and applies his shoulder to the butt of his rifle with a stout heart.   His peace is the greater if he hears a senior, who has taught him his soldiering and broken his head on occasion, whispering : 'They'll shout and carry on like this for five minutes.   Then they'll rush in, and then we've got 'em by the short hairs!'

But, on the other hand, if he sees only men of his own term of service, turning white and playing with their triggers and saying : 'What the Hell's up now?' while the Company Commanders are sweating into their sword-hilts and shouting : 'Front-rank, fix bayonets

x

Steady there — steady! Sight for three hundred — no, for five! Lie down, all! Steady! Front-rank kneel! and so forth, he becomes unhappy; and grows acutely miserable when he hears a comrade turn over with the rattle of fire-irons falling into the fender, and the grunt of a pole-axed ox. If he can be moved about a little and allowed to watch the effect of his own fire on the enemy he feels merrier, and may be then worked up to the blind passion of fighting, which is, contrary to general belief, controlled by a chilly Devil and shakes men like ague. If he is not moved about, and begins to feel cold at the pit of the stomach, and in that crisis is badly mauled and hears orders that were never given, he will break, and he will break badly; and of all things under the light of the Sun there is nothing more terrible than a broken British regiment. When the worst comes to the worst and the panic is really epidemic, the men must be e'en let go, and the Company Commanders had better escape to the enemy and stay there for safety's sake. If they can be made to come again they are not pleasant men to meet; because they will not break twice.

About thirty years from this date, when we have succeeded in half-educating everything that wears trousers, our Army will be a beautifully unreliable machine. It will know too much and it will do too little. Later still, when all men are at the mental level of the officer of to-day, it will sweep the earth. Speaking roughly, you must employ either blackguards or gentlemen, or, best of all, blackguards commanded by gentlemen, to do butcher's work with efficiency and despatch. The ideal soldier should, of course, think for himself — the *Pocket-book* says so. Unfortunately,

to attain this virtue, he has to pass through the phase
of thinking of himself, and that is misdirected genius.
A blackguard may be slow to think for himself, but he
is genuinely anxious to kill, and a little punishment
teaches him how to guard his own skin and perforate
another's A powerfully prayerful Highland Regiment, officered by rank Presbyterians, is, perhaps, one
degree more terrible in action than a hard-bitten thousand of irresponsible Irish ruffians led by most improper
young unbelievers. But these things prove the rule —
which is that the midway men are not to be trusted
alone. They have ideas about the value of life and an
upbringing that has not taught them to go on and take
the chances. They are carefully unprovided with a
backing of comrades who have been shot over, and until
that backing is re-introduced, as a great many Regimental Commanders intend it shall be, they are more
liable to disgrace themselves than the size of the Empire
or the dignity of the Army allows. Their officers are
as good as good can be, because their training begins
early, and God has arranged that a clean-run youth of
the British middle classes shall, in the matter of back-
bone, brains, and bowels, surpass all other youths. For
this reason a child of eighteen will stand up, doing
nothing, with a tin sword in his hand and joy in his
heart until he is dropped. If he dies, he dies like a
gentleman If he lives, he writes Home that he has
been 'potted,' 'sniped,' 'chipped,' or 'cut over,' and
sits down to besiege Government for a wound-gratuity
until the next little war breaks out, when he perjures
himself before a Medical Board, blarneys his Colonel,
burns incense round his Adjutant, and is allowed to go
to the Front once more.

Which homily brings me directly to a brace of the most finished little fiends that ever banged drum or tootled fife in the Band of a British Regiment. They ended their sinful career by open and flagrant mutiny and were shot for it. Their names were Jakin and Lew — Piggy Lew — and they were bold, bad drummer-boys, both of them frequently birched by the Drum-Major of the Fore and Aft.

Jakin was a stunted child of fourteen, and Lew was about the same age. When not looked after, they smoked and drank. They swore habitually after the manner of the Barrack-room, which is cold-swearing and comes from between clinched teeth, and they fought religiously once a week. Jakin had sprung from some London gutter and may or may not have passed through Dr. Barnardo's hands ere he arrived at the dignity of drummer-boy. Lew could remember nothing except the Regiment and the delight of listening to the Band from his earliest years. He hid somewhere in his grimy little soul a genuine love for music, and was most mistakenly furnished with the head of a cherub: insomuch that beautiful ladies who watched the Regiment in church were wont to speak of him as a 'darling.' They never heard his vitriolic comments on their manners and morals, as he walked back to barracks with the Band and matured fresh causes of offence against Jakin.

The other drummer-boys hated both lads on account of their illogical conduct. Jakin might be pounding Lew, or Lew might be rubbing Jakin's head in the dirt, but any attempt at aggression on the part of an outsider was met by the combined forces of Lew and Jakin; and the consequences were painful. The boys were the Ishmaels of the corps, but wealthy Ishmaels, for they sold battles in alternate weeks for the sport of the barracks when they were not pitted against other boys; and thus amassed money.

On this particular day there was dissension in the camp. They had just been convicted afresh of smoking, which is bad for little boys who use plug-tobacco, and Lew's contention was that Jakin had 'stunk so 'orrid bad from keepin' the pipe in pocket,' that he and he alone was responsible for the birching they were both tingling under.

'I tell you I 'id the pipe back o' barracks,' said Jakin pacifically.

'You're a bloomin' liar,' said Lew without heat.

'You're a bloomin' little barstard,' said Jakin, strong in the knowledge that his own ancestry was unknown.

Now there is one word in the extended vocabulary of barrack-room abuse that cannot pass without comment. You may call a man a thief and risk nothing. You may even call him a coward without finding more than a boot whiz past your ear, but you must not call a man a bastard unless you are prepared to prove it on his front teeth.

'You might ha' kep' that till I wasn't so sore,' said Lew sorrowfully, dodging round Jakin's guard.

'I'll make you sorer,' said Jakin genially, and got home on Lew's alabaster forehead. All would have gone well and this story, as the books say, would never have been written, had not his evil fate prompted the Bazar-Sergeant's son, a long, employless man of five-and-twenty, to put in an appearance after the first round. He was eternally in need of money, and knew that the boys had silver.

'Fighting again,' said he. 'I'll report you to my father, and he'll report you to the Colour-Sergeant.'

'What's that to you?' said Jakin with an unpleasant dilation of the nostrils.

'Oh! nothing to *me*. You'll get into trouble, and you've been up too often to afford that.'

'What the Hell do you know about what we've done?' asked Lew the Seraph. '*You* aren't in the Army, you lousy, cadging civilian.'

He closed in on the man's left flank.

'Jes' 'cause you find two gentlemen settlin' their diff'rences with their fistes you stick in your ugly nose where you aren't wanted. Run 'ome to your 'arf-caste slut of a Ma — or we'll give you what-for,' said Jakin.

The man attempted reprisals by knocking the boys' heads together. The scheme would have succeeded had not Jakin punched him vehemently in the stomach, or had Lew refrained from kicking his shins. They fought together, bleeding and breathless, for half an hour, and, after heavy punishment, triumphantly pulled down their opponent as terriers pull down a jackal.

'Now,' gasped Jakin, 'I'll give you what-for.' He proceeded to pound the man's features while Lew stamped on the outlying portions of his anatomy. Chivalry is not a strong point in the composition of the average drummer-boy. He fights, as do his betters, to make his mark.

Ghastly was the ruin that escaped, and awful was the wrath of the Bazar-Sergeant. Awful too was the scene in Orderly-room when the two reprobates appeared to answer the charge of half-murdering a 'civilian.' The Bazar-Sergeant thirsted for a criminal action, and his son lied. The boys stood to attention while the black clouds of evidence accumulated.

'You little devils are more trouble than the rest of the Regiment put together,' said the Colonel angrily. 'One might as well admonish thistledown, and I can't well put you in ceils or under stoppages. You must be birched again.'

'Beg y' pardon, Sir. Can't we say nothin' in our own defence, Sir?' shrilled Jakin.

'Hey! What? Are you going to argue with *me?*' said the Colonel.

'No, Sir,' said Lew. 'But if a man come to you, Sir, and said he was going to report you, Sir, for 'aving a bit of a turn-up with a friend, Sir, an' wanted to get money out o' *you*, Sir——'

The Orderly-room exploded in a roar of laughter. 'Well?' said the Colonel.

'That was what that measly *jarnwar* there did, Sir, and 'e'd 'a' *done* it, Sir, if we 'adn't prevented 'im. We didn't 'it 'im much, Sir. 'E 'adn't no manner o' right to interfere with us, Sir. I don't mind bein' birched by the Drum-Major, Sir, nor yet reported by *any* Corp'ral, but I'm — but I don't think it's fair, Sir, for a civilian to come an' talk over a man in the Army.'

A second shout of laughter shook the Orderly-room, but the Colonel was grave.

'What sort of characters have these boys?' he asked of the Regimental Sergeant-Major.

'Accordin' to the Bandmaster, Sir,' returned that revered official — the only soul in the Regiment whom the boys feared — 'they do everything *but* lie, Sir.'

'Is it like we'd go for that man for fun, Sir?' said Lew, pointing to the plaintiff.

'Oh, admonished, — admonished!' said the Colonel testily, and when the boys had gone he read the Bazar-Sergeant's son a lecture on the sin of unprofitable meddling, and gave orders that the Bandmaster should keep the Drums in better discipline.

'If either of you come to practice again with so much as a scratch on your two ugly little faces,' thundered the Bandmaster, 'I'll tell the Drum-Major to take the skin off your backs. Understand that, you young devils.'

Then he repented of his speech for just the length of time that Lew, looking like a seraph in red worsted embellishments, took the place of one of the trumpets — in hospital — and rendered the echo of a battle-piece. Lew certainly was a musician, and had often in his more exalted moments expressed a yearning to master every instrument of the Band.

'There's nothing to prevent your becoming a Band-master, Lew,' said the Bandmaster, who had composed waltzes of his own, and worked day and night in the interests of the Band.

'What did he say?' demanded Jakin after practice.

''Said I might be a bloomin' Bandmaster, an' be asked in to 'ave a glass o' sherry-wine on Mess-nights.'

'Ho! 'Said you might be a bloomin' non-combatant, did 'e! That's just about wot 'e would say. When I've put in my boy's service — it's a bloomin' shame that doesn't count for pension — I'll take on as a privit. Then I'll be a Lance in a year — knowin' what I know about the ins an' outs o' things. In three years I'll be a bloomin' Sergeant. I won't marry then, not I! I'll 'old on and learn the orf'cers' ways an' apply for exchange into a reg'ment that doesn't know all about me. Then I'll be a bloomin' orf'cer. Then I'll ask you to 'ave a glass o' sherry-wine, *Mister* Lew, an' you'll bloomin' well 'ave to stay in the hanty-room while the Mess-Sergeant brings it to your dirty 'ands.'

''S'pose I'm going to be a Bandmaster? Not I, quite. I'll be a orf'cer too. There's nothin' like takin' to a thing an' stickin' to it, the Schoolmaster says. The Reg'ment don't go 'ome for another seven years. I'll be a Lance then or near to.'

Thus the boys discussed their futures, and conducted themselves piously for a week. That is to say, Lew started a flirtation with the Colour-Sergeant's daughter, aged thirteen — 'not,' as he explained to Jakin, 'with any intention o' matrimony, but by way o' keepin' my 'and in.' And the black-haired Cris Delighan enjoyed that flirtation more than previous ones, and the other drummer-boys raged furiously together, and Jakin preached sermons on the dangers of 'bein' tangled along o' petticoats.'

But neither love nor virtue would have held Lew long in the paths of propriety had not the rumour gone abroad that the Regiment was to be sent on active service, to take part in a war which, for the sake of brevity, we will call 'The War of the Lost Tribes.'

The barracks had the rumour almost before the Mess-room, and of all the nine hundred men in barracks, not ten had seen a shot fired in anger. The Colonel had, twenty years ago, assisted at a Frontier expedition; one of the Majors had seen service at the Cape; a confirmed deserter in E Company had helped to clear streets in Ireland; but that was all. The Regiment had been put by for many years. The over-whelming mass of its rank and file had from three to

four years' service; the non-commissioned officers were
under thirty years old; and men and sergeants alike
had forgotten to speak of the stories written in brief
upon the Colours — the New Colours that had been
formally blessed by an Archbishop in England ere the
Regiment came away.

They wanted to go to the Front — they were enthusiastically anxious to go — but they had no knowledge
of what war meant, and there was none to tell them.
They were an educated regiment, the percentage of
school-certificates in their ranks was high, and most of
the men could do more than read and write. They
had been recruited in loyal observance of the territorial
idea; but they themselves had no notion of that idea.
They were made up of drafts from an over-populated
manufacturing district. The system had put flesh and
muscle upon their small bones, but it could not put
heart into the sons of those who for generations had
done overmuch work for overscanty pay, had sweated
in drying-rooms, stooped over looms, coughed among
white-lead, and shivered on lime-barges. The men had
found food and rest in the Army, and now they were
going to fight 'niggers' — people who ran away
if you shook a stick at them. Wherefore they
cheered lustily when the rumour ran, and the shrewd,
clerkly non-commissioned officers speculated on the
chances of batta and of saving their pay. At Headquarters, men said: 'The Fore and Fit have never
been under fire within the last generation. Let us,
therefore, break them in easily by setting them to
guard lines of communication.' And this would have
been done but for the fact that British Regiments were
wanted — badly wanted — at the Front, and there

THE DRUMS OF THE FORE AND AFT

were doubtful Native Regiments that could fill the minor duties. 'Brigade 'em with two strong Regiments,' said Headquarters. 'They may be knocked about a bit, but they'll learn their business before they come through. Nothing like a night-alarm and a little cutting-up of stragglers to make a Regiment smart in the field. Wait till they've had half a dozen sentries' throats cut.'

The Colonel wrote with delight that the temper of his men was excellent, that the Regiment was all that could be wished, and as sound as a bell. The Majors smiled with a sober joy, and the subalterns waltzed in pairs down the Mess-room after dinner, and nearly shot themselves at revolver-practice. But there was consternation in the hearts of Jakin and Lew. What was to be done with the Drums? Would the Band go to the Front? How many of the Drums would accompany the Regiment?

They took council together, sitting in a tree and smoking.

'It's more than a bloomin' toss-up they'll leave us be'ind at the Depôt with the women. You'll like that,' said Jakin sarcastically.

''Cause o' Cris, y' mean? Wot's a woman, or a 'ole bloomin' depôt o' women, 'longside o' the chanst o' field-service? You know I'm as keen on goin' as you,' said Lew.

''Wish I was a bloomin' bugler,' said Jakin sadly. 'They'll take Tom Kidd along, that I can plaster a wall with, an' like as not they won't take us.'

'Then let's go an' make Tom Kidd so bloomin' sick 'e can't bugle no more. You 'old 'is 'ands an' I'll kick him,' said Lew, wriggling on the branch.

'That ain't no good neither. We ain't the sort o' characters to presoon on our rep'tations — they're bad. If they have the Band at the Depôt we don't go, and no error *there*. If they take the Band we may get cast for medical unfitness. Are you medical fit, Piggy?' said Jakin, digging Lew in the ribs with force.

'Yus,' said Lew with an oath. 'The Doctor says your 'eart's weak through smokin' on an empty stummick. Throw a chest an' I'll try yer.'

Jakin threw out his chest, which Lew smote with all his might. Jakin turned very pale, gasped, crowed, screwed up his eyes and said — 'That's all right.'

'You'll do,' said Lew. 'I've 'eard o' men dying when you 'it 'em fair on the breastbone.'

'Don't bring us no nearer goin', though,' said Jakin. 'Do you know where we're ordered?'

'Gawd knows, an' 'E won't split on a pal. Somewheres up to the Front to kill Paythans — hairy big beggars that turn you inside out if they get 'old 'o you. They say their women are good-looking, too.'

'Any loot?' asked the abandoned Jakin.

'Not a bloomin' anna, they say, unless you dig up the ground an' see what the niggers 'ave 'id. They're a poor lot.' Jakin stood upright on the branch and gazed across the plain.

'Lew,' said he, 'there's the Colonel coming. 'Colonel's a good old beggar. Let's go an' talk to 'im.'

Lew nearly fell out of the tree at the audacity of the suggestion. Like Jakin he feared not God, neither regarded he Man, but there are limits even to the audacity of a drummer-boy, and to speak to a Colonel was ——

But Jakin had slid down the trunk and doubled in

the direction of the Colonel.   That officer was walking wrapped in thought and visions of a C.B. — yes, even a K.C.B., for had he not at command one of the best Regiments of the Line — the Fore and Fit?   And he was aware of two small boys charging down upon him. Once before it had been solemnly reported to him that 'the Drums were in a state of mutiny,' Jakin and Lew being the ringleaders.   This looked like an organised conspiracy.

The boys halted at twenty yards, walked to the regulation four paces, and saluted together, each as well set-up as a ramrod and little taller.

The Colonel was in a genial mood; the boys appeared very forlorn and unprotected on the desolate plain, and one of them was handsome.

'Well!' said the Colonel, recognising them.   'Are you going to pull me down in the open?   I'm sure I never interfere with you, even though' — he sniffed suspiciously — 'you have been smoking.'

It was time to strike while the iron was hot.   Their hearts beat tumultuously.

'Beg y' pardon, Sir,' began Jakin.   'The Reg'ment's ordered on active service, Sir?'

'So I believe,' said the Colonel courteously.

'Is the Band goin', Sir?' said both together.   Then, without pause, 'We're goin', Sir, ain't we?'

'You!' said the Colonel, stepping back the more fully to take in the two small figures.   'You!   You'd die in the first march.'

'No, we wouldn't, Sir.   We can march with the Reg'ment anywheres — p'rade an' anywhere else,' said Jakin.

'If Tom Kidd goes 'e'll shut up like a clasp-knife,'

said Lew. 'Tom 'as very-close veins in both 'is legs, Sir.'

'Very how much?'

'Very-close veins, Sir. That's why they swells after long p'rade, Sir. If 'e can go, we can go, Sir.'

Again the Colonel looked at them long and intently.

'Yes, the Band is going,' he said as gravely as though he had been addressing a brother officer. 'Have you any parents, either of you two?'

'No, Sir,' rejoicingly from Lew and Jakin. 'We're both orphans, Sir. There's no one to be considered of on our account, Sir.'

'You poor little sprats, and you want to go up to the Front with the Regiment, do you? Why?'

'I've wore the Queen's Uniform for two years,' said Jakin. 'It's very 'ard, Sir, that a man don't get no recompense for doin' of 'is dooty, Sir.'

'An' — an' if I don't go, Sir,' interrupted Lew, 'the Bandmaster 'e says 'e'll catch an' make a bloo — a blessed musician o' me, Sir. Before I've seen any service, Sir.'

The Colonel made no answer for a long time. Then he said quietly: 'If you're passed by the Doctor I dare say you can go. I shouldn't smoke if I were you.'

The boys saluted and disappeared. The Colonel walked home and told the story to his wife, who nearly cried over it. The Colonel was well pleased. If that was the temper of the children, what would not the men do?

Jakin and Lew entered the boys' barrack-room with great stateliness, and refused to hold any conversation with their comrades for at least ten minutes. Then, bursting with pride, Jakin drawled: 'I've bin intervooin' the Colonel. Good old beggar is the Colonel. Says I to 'im "Colonel," says I, "let me go to the Front, along o' the Reg'ment." — "To the Front you shall go," says 'e, "an' I only wish there was more like you among the dirty little devils that bang the bloomin' drums." Kidd, if you throw your 'courtrements at me for tellin' you the truth to your own advantage, your legs'll swell.'

None the less there was a Battle-Royal in the barrack-room, for the boys were consumed with envy and hate, and neither Jakin nor Lew behaved in conciliatory wise.

'I'm goin' out to say adoo to my girl,' said Lew, to cap the climax. 'Don't none o' you touch my kit because it's wanted for active service; me bein' specially invited to go by the Colonel.'

He strolled forth and whistled in the clump of trees at the back of the Married Quarters till Cris came to him, and, the preliminary kisses being given and taken, Lew began to explain the situation.

'I'm goin' to the Front with the Reg'ment,' he said valiantly.

'Piggy, you're a little liar,' said Cris, but her heart misgave her, for Lew was not in the habit of lying.

'Liar yourself, Cris,' said Lew, slipping an arm round her. 'I'm goin'. When the Reg'ment marches out you'll see me with 'em, all galliant and gay. Give us another kiss, Cris, on the strength of it.'

'If you'd on'y a-stayed at the Depôt — where you *ought* to ha' bin — you could get as many of 'em as — as you dam please,' whimpered Cris, putting up her mouth.

'It's 'ard, Cris. I grant you it's 'ard. But what's a man to do? If I'd a-stayed at the Depôt, you wouldn't think anything of me.'

'Like as not, but I'd 'ave you with me, Piggy.   An' all the thinkin' in the world isn't like kissin'.'

'An' all the kissin' in the world isn't like 'avin' a medal to wear on the front o' your coat.'

'*You* won't get no medal.'

'Oh yus, I shall though.   Me an' Jakin are the only acting-drummers that'll be took along.   All the rest is full men, an' we'll get our medals with them.'

'They might ha' taken anybody but you, Piggy. You'll get killed — you're so venturesome.   Stay with me, Piggy, darlin', down at the Depôt, an' I'll love you true, for ever.'

'Ain't you goin' to do that *now*, Cris?   You said you was.'

'O' course I am, but th' other's more comfortable. Wait till you've growed a bit, Piggy.   You aren't no taller than me now.'

'I've bin in the Army for two years an' I'm not goin' to get out of a chanst o' seein' service an' don't you try to make me do so.   I'll come back, Cris, an' when I take on as a man I'll marry you — marry you when I'm a Lance.'

'Promise, Piggy?'

Lew reflected on the future as arranged by Jakin a short time previously, but Cris's mouth was very near to his own.

'I promise, s'elp me, Gawd!' said he.

Cris slid an arm round his neck.

'I won't 'old you back no more, Piggy.   Go away an' get your medal, an' I'll make you a new button-bag as nice as I know how,' she whispered.

'Put some o' your 'air into it, Cris, an' I'll keep it in my pocket so long's I'm alive.'

Then Cris wept anew, and the interview ended. Public feeling among the drummer-boys rose to fever pitch and the lives of Jakin and Lew became unenviable. Not only had they been permitted to enlist two years before the regulation boy's age — fourteen — but, by virtue, it seemed, of their extreme youth, they were allowed to go to the Front — which thing had not happened to acting-drummers within the knowledge of boy. The Band which was to accompany the Regiment had been cut down to the regulation twenty men, the surplus returning to the ranks. Jakin and Lew were attached to the Band as supernumeraries, though they would much have preferred being company buglers.

''Don't matter much,' said Jakin after the medical inspection. 'Be thankful that we're 'lowed to go at all. The Doctor 'e said that if we could stand what we took from the Bazar-Sergeant's son we'd stand pretty nigh anything.'

'Which we will,' said Lew, looking tenderly at the ragged and ill-made housewife that Cris had given him, with a lock of her hair worked into a sprawling 'L' upon the cover.

'It was the best I could,' she sobbed. 'I wouldn't let mother nor the Sergeant's tailor 'elp me. Keep it always, Piggy, an' remember I love you true.'

They marched to the railway station, nine hundred and sixty strong, and every soul in cantonments turned out to see them go. The drummers gnashed their teeth at Jakin and Lew marching with the Band, the married women wept upon the platform, and the Regiment cheered its noble self black in the face.

'A nice level lot,' said the Colonel to the Second-in-

Command as they watched the first four companies entraining.

'Fit to do anything,' said the Second-in-Command enthusiastically. 'But it seems to me they're a thought too young and tender for the work in hand. It's bitter cold up at the Front now.'

'They're sound enough,' said the Colonel. 'We must take our chance of sick casualties.'

So they went northward, ever northward, past droves and droves of camels, armies of camp-followers, and legions of laden mules, the throng thickening day by day, till with a shriek the train pulled up at a hopelessly congested junction where six lines of temporary track accommodated six forty-waggon trains; where whistles blew, Babus sweated and Commissariat officers swore from dawn till far into the night amid the wind-driven chaff of the fodder-bales and the lowing of a thousand steers.

'Hurry up — you're badly wanted at the Front,' was the message that greeted the Fore and Aft, and the occupants of the Red Cross carriages told the same tale.

'''Tisn't so much the bloomin' fightin','' gasped a headbound trooper of Hussars to a knot of admiring Fore and Afts. ''Tisn't so much the bloomin' fightin', though there's enough o' that. It's the bloomin' food an' the bloomin' climate. Frost all night 'cept when it hails, and biling sun all day, and the water stinks fit to knock you down. I got my 'ead chipped like a egg; I've got pneumonia too, an' my guts is all out o' order. 'Tain't no bloomin' picnic in those parts, I can tell you.'

'Wot are the niggers like?' demanded a private.

'There's some prisoners in that train yonder. Go an' look at 'em. They're the aristocracy o' the country.

The common folk are a dashed sight uglier. If you want to know what they fight with, reach under my seat an' pull out the long knife that's there.'

They dragged out and beheld for the first time the grim, bone-handled, triangular Afghan knife. It was almost as long as Lew.

'That's the thing to jint ye,' said the trooper feebly. 'It can take off a man's arm at the shoulder as easy as slicing butter. I halved the beggar that used that 'un, but there's more of his likes up above. They don't understand thrustin', but they're devils to slice.'

The men strolled across the tracks to inspect the Afghan prisoners. They were unlike any ' niggers ' that the Fore and Aft had ever met — these huge, black-haired, scowling sons of the Beni-Israel. As the men stared the Afghans spat freely and muttered one to another with lowered eyes.

'My eyes! Wot awful swine!' said Jakin, who was in the rear of the procession. 'Say, old man, how you got *puckrowed*, eh? *Kiswasti* you wasn't hanged for your ugly face, hey?'

The tallest of the company turned, his leg-irons clanking at the movement, and stared at the boy. 'See!' he cried to his fellows in Pushto. 'They send children against us. What a people, and what fools!'

'*Hya!*' said Jakin, nodding his head cheerily. 'You go down-country. *Khana* get, *peenikapanee* get — live like a bloomin' Raja *ke marfik*. That's a better *bandobust* than baynit get it in your innards. Good-bye, ole man. Take care o' your beautiful figure-'ed, an' try to look *kushy*.'

The men laughed and fell in for their first march when they began to realise that a soldier's life was not

all beer and skittles.   They were much impressed with
the size and bestial ferocity of the niggers whom they
had now learned to call 'Paythans,' and more with
the exceeding discomfort of their own surroundings.
Twenty old soldiers in the corps would have taught
them how to make themselves moderately snug at night,
but they had no old soldiers, and, as the troops on the
line of march said, 'they lived like pigs.'   They learned
the heart-breaking cussedness of camp-kitchens and
camels and the depravity of an E.P. tent and a wither-
wrung mule.   They studied animalculæ in water, and
developed a few cases of dysentery in their study.

At the end of their third march they were disagreea-
bly surprised by the arrival in their camp of a hammered
iron slug which, fired from a steady rest at seven hundred yards, flicked out the brains of a private seated by
the fire.   This robbed them of their peace for a night,
and was the beginning of a long-range fire carefully
calculated to that end.   In the daytime they saw nothing except an unpleasant puff of smoke from a crag
above the line of march.   At night there were distant
spurts of flame and occasional casualties, which set the
whole camp blazing into the gloom and, occasionally,
into opposite tents.   Then they swore vehemently and
vowed that this was magnificent but not war.

Indeed it was not.   The Regiment could not halt for
reprisals against the sharpshooters of the country-side.
Its duty was to go forward and make connection with
the Scotch and Gurkha troops with which it was bri-
gaded.   The Afghans knew this, and knew too, after
their first tentative shots, that they were dealing with a
raw regiment.   Thereafter they devoted themselves to
the task of keeping the Fore and Aft on the strain.

Not for anything would they have taken equal liberties with a seasoned corps — with the wicked little Gurkhas, whose delight it was to lie out in the open on a dark night and stalk their stalkers — with the terrible, big men dressed in women's clothes, who could be heard praying to their God in the night-watches, and whose peace of mind no amount of 'sniping' could shake — or with those vile Sikhs, who marched so ostentatiously unprepared and who dealt out such grim reward to those who tried to profit by that unpreparedness. This white regiment was different — quite different. It slept like a hog, and, like a hog, charged in every direction when it was roused. Its sentries walked with a footfall that could be heard for a quarter of a mile; would fire at anything that moved — even a driven donkey — and when they had once fired, could be scientifically 'rushed' and laid out a horror and an offence against the morning sun. Then there were camp-followers who straggled and could be cut up without fear. Their shrieks would disturb the white boys, and the loss of their services would inconvenience them sorely.

Thus, at every march, the hidden enemy became bolder and the regiment writhed and twisted under attacks it could not avenge. The crowning triumph was a sudden night-rush ending in the cutting of many tent-ropes, the collapse of the sodden canvas and a glorious knifing of the men who struggled and kicked below. It was a great deed, neatly carried out, and it shook the already shaken nerves of the Fore and Aft. All the courage that they had been required to exercise up to this point was the 'two o'clock in the morning courage'; and, so far, they had only succeeded in shooting their comrades and losing their sleep.

Sullen, discontented, cold, savage, sick, with their uniforms dulled and unclean, the Fore and Aft joined their Brigade.

'I hear you had a tough time of it coming up,' said the Brigadier. But when he saw the hospital-sheets his face fell.

'This is bad,' said he to himself. 'They're as rotten as sheep.' And aloud to the Colonel — 'I'm afraid we can't spare you just yet. We want all we have, else I should have given you ten days to recover in.'

The Colonel winced. 'On my honour, Sir,' he returned, 'there is not the least necessity to think of sparing us. My men have been rather mauled and upset without a fair return. They only want to go in somewhere where they can see what's before them.'

'Can't say I think much of the Fore and Fit,' said the Brigadier in confidence to his Brigade-Major. 'They've lost all their soldiering, and, by the trim of them, might have marched through the country from the other side. A more fagged-out set of men I never put eyes on.'

'Oh, they'll improve as the work goes on. The parade gloss has been rubbed off a little, but they'll put on field polish before long,' said the Brigade-Major. 'They've been mauled, and they quite don't understand it.'

They did not. All the hitting was on one side, and it was cruelly hard hitting with accessories that made them sick. There was also the real sickness that laid hold of a strong man and dragged him howling to the grave. Worst of all, their officers knew just as little of the country as the men themselves, and looked as if they did. The Fore and Aft were in a thoroughly unsatisfactory condition, but they believed that all would be well if they could once get a fair go-in at the enemy. Pot-shots up and down the valleys were unsatisfactory, and the bayonet never seemed to get a chance. Perhaps it was as well, for a long-limbed Afghan with a knife had a reach of eight feet, and could carry away lead that would disable three Englishmen.

The Fore and Aft would like some rifle-practice at the enemy — all seven hundred rifles blazing together. That wish showed the mood of the men.

The Gurkhas walked into their camp, and in broken, barrack-room English strove to fraternise with them; offered them pipes of tobacco and stood them treat at the canteen. But the Fore and Aft, not knowing much of the nature of the Gurkhas, treated them as they would treat any other 'niggers,' and the little men in green trotted back to their firm friends the Highlanders, and with many grins confided to them: 'That dam white regiment no dam use. Sulky — ugh! Dirty — ugh! Hya, any tot for Johnny?' Whereat the Highlanders smote the Gurkhas as to the head, and told them not to vilify a British Regiment, and the Gurkhas grinned cavernously, for the Highlanders were their elder brothers and entitled to the privileges of kinship. The common soldier who touches a Gurkha is more than likely to have his head sliced open.

Three days later the Brigadier arranged a battle according to the rules of war and the peculiarity of the Afghan temperament. The enemy were massing in inconvenient strength among the hills, and the moving of many green standards warned him that the tribes were 'up' in aid of the Afghan regular troops. A Squadron and a half of Bengal Lancers represented the available Cavalry, and two screw-guns borrowed from a column thirty miles away, the Artillery at the General's disposal.

'If they stand, as I've a very strong notion that they will, I fancy we shall see an infantry fight that will be worth watching,' said the Brigadier. 'We'll do it in style. Each regiment shall be played into action by its Band, and we'll hold the Cavalry in reserve.'

'For *all* the reserve?' somebody asked.

'For all the reserve; because we're going to crumple them up,' said the Brigadier, who was an extraordinary Brigadier, and did not believe in the value of a reserve when dealing with Asiatics. Indeed, when you come to think of it, had the British Army consistently waited for reserves in all its little affairs, the boundaries of Our Empire would have stopped at Brighton beach.

That battle was to be a glorious battle.

The three regiments debouching from three separate gorges, after duly crowning the heights above, were to converge from the centre, left, and right upon what we will call the Afghan army, then stationed towards the lower extremity of a flat-bottomed valley. Thus it will be seen that three sides of the valley practically belonged to the English, while the fourth was strictly Afghan property. In the event of defeat the Afghans had the rocky hills to fly to, where the fire from the guerilla tribes in aid would cover their retreat. In the event of victory these same tribes would rush down and lend their weight to the rout of the British.

The screw-guns were to shell the head of each Afghan rush that was made in close formation, and the Cavalry, held in reserve in the right valley, were to gently stimulate the break-up which would follow on the combined attack. The Brigadier, sitting upon a rock overlooking the valley, would watch the battle unrolled at his feet. The Fore and Aft would debouch from the central gorge, the Gurkhas from the left, and the Highlanders from the right, for the reason that the left flank of the enemy seemed as though it required the most hammering. It was not every day that an Afghan force would take ground in the open, and the Brigadier was resolved to make the most of it.

'If we only had a few more men,' he said plaintively, 'we could surround the creatures and crumple 'em up thoroughly. As it is, I'm afraid we can only cut them up as they run. It's a great pity.'

The Fore and Aft had enjoyed unbroken peace for five days, and were beginning, in spite of dysentery, to recover their nerve. But they were not happy, for they did not know the work in hand, and had they known, would not have known how to do it. Throughout those five days in which old soldiers might have taught them the craft of the game, they discussed together their misadventures in the past — how such an one was alive at dawn and dead ere the dusk, and with what shrieks and struggles such another had given up his soul under the Afghan knife. Death was a new and horrible thing to the sons of mechanics who were used to die decently of zymotic disease; and their careful conservation in barracks had done nothing to make them look upon it with less dread.

Very early in the dawn the bugles began to blow, and the Fore and Aft, filled with a misguided enthusiasm, turned out without waiting for a cup of coffee and a biscuit; and were rewarded by being kept under arms in the cold while the other regiments leisurely prepared for the fray. All the world knows that it is ill taking the breeks off a Highlander. It is much iller to try to make him stir unless he is convinced of the necessity for haste.

The Fore and Aft waited, leaning upon their rifles and listening to the protests of their empty stomachs. The Colonel did his best to remedy the default of lining as soon as it was borne in upon him that the affair would not begin at once, and so well did he succeed that the coffee was just ready when — the men moved off, their Band leading. Even then there had been a mistake in time, and the Fore and Aft came out into the valley ten minutes before the proper hour. Their Band wheeled to the right after reaching the open, and retired behind a little rocky knoll still playing while the Regiment went past.

It was not a pleasant sight that opened on the uninstructed view, for the lower end of the valley appeared to be filled by an army in position — real and actual regiments attired in red coats, and — of this there was no doubt — firing Martini-Henri bullets which cut up the ground a hundred yards in front of the leading company. Over that pock-marked ground the Regiment had to pass, and it opened the ball with a general and profound courtesy to the piping pickets; ducking in perfect time, as though it had been brazed on a rod. Being half-capable of thinking for itself, it fired a volley by the simple process of pitching its rifle into its shoulder and pulling the trigger. The bullets may have accounted for some of the watchers on the hillside, but they certainly did not affect the mass of enemy in front, while the noise of the rifles drowned any orders that might have been given.

'Good God!' said the Brigadier, sitting on the rock high above all. 'That regiment has spoilt the whole show. Hurry up the others, and let the screw-guns get off.'

But the screw-guns, in working round the heights, had stumbled upon a wasp's nest of a small mud fort which they incontinently shelled at eight hundred yards, to the huge discomfort of the occupants, who were unaccustomed to weapons of such devilish precision.

The Fore and Aft continued to go forward but with shortened stride. Where were the other regiments, and why did these niggers use Martinis? They took open order instinctively, lying down and firing at random, rushing a few paces forward and lying down again, according to the regulations. Once in this formation, each man felt himself desperately alone, and edged in towards his fellow for comfort's sake.

Then the crack of his neighbour's rifle at his ear led him to fire as rapidly as he could — again for the sake of the comfort of the noise. The reward was not long delayed. Five volleys plunged the files in banked smoke impenetrable to the eye, and the bullets began to take ground twenty or thirty yards in front of the firers, as the weight of the bayonet dragged down and to the right arms wearied with holding the kick of the leaping Martini. The Company Commanders peered helplessly through the smoke, the more nervous mechanically trying to fan it away with their helmets.

'High and to the left!' bawled a Captain till he was hoarse. 'No good! Cease firing, and let it drift away a bit.'

Three and four times the bugles shrieked the order,

and when it was obeyed the Fore and Aft looked that
their foe should be lying before them in mown swaths
of men. A light wind drove the smoke to leeward,
and showed the enemy still in position and apparently
unaffected. A quarter of a ton of lead had been buried
a furlong in front of them, as the ragged earth attested.

That was not demoralising to the Afghans, who have
not European nerves. They were waiting for the mad
riot to die down, and were firing quietly into the heart
of the smoke. A private of the Fore and Aft spun up
his company shrieking with agony, another was kicking the earth and gasping, and a third, ripped through
the lower intestines by a jagged bullet, was calling
aloud on his comrades to put him out of his pain.
These were the casualties, and they were not soothing
to hear or see. The smoke cleared to a dull haze.

Then the foe began to shout with a great shouting
and a mass — a black mass — detached itself from the
main body, and rolled over the ground at horrid speed.
It was composed of, perhaps, three hundred men, who
would shout and fire and slash if the rush of their fifty
comrades who were determined to die carried home.
The fifty were Ghazis, half-maddened with drugs and
wholly mad with religious fanaticism. When they
rushed the British fire ceased, and in the lull the order
was given to close ranks and meet them with the
bayonet.

Any one who knew the business could have told the
Fore and Aft that the only way of dealing with a Ghazi
rush is by volleys at long ranges; because a man who
means to die, who desires to die, who will gain heaven
by dying, must, in nine cases out of ten, kill a man
who has a lingering prejudice in favour of life. Where

they should have closed and gone forward, the Fore and Aft opened out and skirmished, and where they should have opened out and fired, they closed and waited.

A man dragged from his blankets half awake and unfed is never in a pleasant frame of mind. Nor does his happiness increase when he watches the whites of the eyes of three hundred six-foot fiends upon whose beards the foam is lying, upon whose tongues is a roar of wrath, and in whose hands are yard-long knives.

The Fore and Aft heard the Gurkha bugles bringing that regiment forward at the double, while the neighing of the Highland pipes came from the left. They strove to stay where they were, though the bayonets wavered down the line like the oars of a ragged boat. Then they felt body to body the amazing physical strength of their foes; a shriek of pain ended the rush, and the knives fell amid scenes not to be told. The men clubbed together and smote blindly — as often as not at their own fellows. Their front crumpled like paper, and the fifty Ghazis passed on; their backers, now drunk with success, fighting as madly as they.

Then the rear-ranks were bidden to close up, and the subalterns dashed into the stew — alone. For the rear-ranks had heard the clamour in front, the yells and the howls of pain, and had seen the dark stale blood that makes afraid. They were not going to stay. It was the rushing of the camps over again. Let their officers go to Hell, if they chose; they would get away from the knives.

'Come on!' shrieked the subalterns, and their men, cursing them, drew back, each closing into his neighbour and wheeling round.

Charteris and Devlin, subalterns of the last company, faced their death alone in the belief that their men would follow.

'You've killed me, you cowards,' sobbed Devlin and dropped, cut from the shoulder-strap to the centre of the chest, and a fresh detachment of his men retreating, always retreating, trampled him under foot as they made for the pass whence they had emerged.

> I kissed her in the kitchen and I kissed her in the hall.
> Child'un, child'un, follow me !
> Oh Golly, said the cook, is he gwine to kiss us all ?
> Halla — Halla — Halla — Hallelujah !

The Gurkhas were pouring through the left gorge and over the heights at the double to the invitation of their Regimental Quick-step. The black rocks were crowned with dark green spiders as the bugles gave tongue jubilantly : —

> In the morning ! In the morning *by* the bright light !
> When Gabriel blows his trumpet in the morning !

The Gurkha rear-companies tripped and blundered over loose stones. The front-files halted for a moment to take stock of the valley and to settle stray boot-laces. Then a happy little sigh of contentment soughed down the ranks, and it was as though the land smiled, for behold there below was the enemy, and it was to meet them that the Gurkhas had doubled so hastily. There was much enemy. There would be amusement. The little men hitched their *kukris* well to hand, and gaped expectantly at their officers as terriers grin ere the stone is cast for them to fetch. The Gurkhas' ground sloped downward to the valley, and they enjoyed a fair view of the proceedings. They sat upon the bowlders to watch, for their officers were not going to waste their wind in assisting to repulse a Ghazi rush more than half a mile away. Let the white men look to their own front.

'Hi! yi!' said the Subadar-Major, who was sweating profusely. 'Dam fools yonder, stand close-order! This is no time for close order, it is the time for volleys. Ugh!'

Horrified, amused, and indignant, the Gurkhas beheld the retirement of the Fore and Aft with a running chorus of oaths and commentaries.

'They run! The white men run! Colonel Sahib, may *we* also do a little running?' murmured Runbir Thappa, the Senior Jemadar.

But the Colonel would have none of it. 'Let the beggars be cut up a little,' said he wrathfully. ''Serves 'em right. They'll be prodded into facing round in a minute.' He looked through his field-glasses, and caught the glint of an officer's sword.

'Beating 'em with the flat — damned conscripts! How the Ghazis are walking into them!' said he.

The Fore and Aft, heading back, bore with them their officers. The narrowness of the pass forced the mob into solid formation, and the rear-ranks delivered some sort of a wavering volley. The Ghazis drew off, for they did not know what reserve the gorge might hide. Moreover, it was never wise to chase white men too far. They returned as wolves return to cover, satisfied with the slaughter that they had done, and only stopping to slash at the wounded on the ground. A quarter of a mile had the Fore and Aft retreated, and now, jammed in the pass, was quivering with pain, shaken and demoralised with fear, while the officers, maddened beyond control, smote the men with the hilts and the flats of their swords.

'Get back! Get back, you cowards — you women! Right about face — column of companies, form — you hounds!' shouted the Colonel, and the subalterns swore aloud. But the Regiment wanted to go — to go anywhere out of the range of those merciless knives. It swayed to and fro irresolutely with shouts and outcries, while from the right the Gurkhas dropped volley after volley of cripple-stopper Snider bullets at long range into the mob of the Ghazis returning to their own troops.

The Fore and Aft Band, though protected from direct fire by the rocky knoll under which it had sat down, fled at the first rush. Jakin and Lew would have fled also, but their short legs left them fifty yards in the rear, and by the time the Band had mixed with the Regiment, they were painfully aware that they would have to close in alone and unsupported.

'Get back to that rock,' gasped Jakin. 'They won't see us there.'

And they returned to the scattered instruments of the Band; their hearts nearly bursting their ribs.

'Here's a nice show for *us*,' said Jakin, throwing himself full length on the ground. 'A bloomin' fine show for British Infantry! Oh, the devils! They've gone an' left us alone here! Wot'll we do?'

Lew took possession of a cast-off water bottle, which naturally was full of canteen rum, and drank till he coughed again.

'Drink,' said he shortly. 'They'll come back in a minute or two — you see.'

Jakin drank, but there was no sign of the Regiment's return. They could hear a dull clamour from the head of the valley of retreat, and saw the Ghazis slink back, quickening their pace as the Gurkhas fired at them.

'We're all that's left of the Band, an' we'll be cut up as sure as death,' said Jakin.

'I'll die game, then,' said Lew thickly, fumbling with his tiny drummer's sword. The drink was working on his brain as it was on Jakin's.

''Old on! I know something better than fightin',' said Jakin, stung by the splendour of a sudden thought due chiefly to rum. 'Tip our bloomin' cowards yonder the word to come back. The Paythan beggars are well away. Come on, Lew! We won't get hurt. Take the fife an' give me the drum. The Old Step for all your bloomin' guts are worth! There's a few of our men coming back now. Stand up, ye drunken little defaulter. By your right — quick march!'

He slipped the drum-sling over his shoulder, thrust the fife into Lew's hand, and the two boys marched out of the cover of the rock into the open, making a hideous hash of the first bars of the 'British Grenadiers.'

As Lew had said, a few of the Fore and Aft were coming back sullenly and shamefacedly under the stimulus of blows and abuse; their red coats shone at the head of the valley, and behind them were wavering bayonets. But between this shattered line and the enemy, who with Afghan suspicion feared that the hasty retreat meant an ambush, and had not moved therefore, lay half a mile of a level ground dotted only by the wounded.

The tune settled into full swing and the boys kept shoulder to shoulder, Jakin banging the drum as one possessed. The one fife made a thin and pitiful squeaking, but the tune carried far, even to the Gurkhas.

'Come on, you dogs!' muttered Jakin to himself. 'Are we to play forhever?' Lew was staring straight in front of him and marching more stiffly than ever he had done on parade.

And in bitter mockery of the distant mob, the old tune of the Old Line shrilled and rattled: —

> Some talk of Alexander,
>   And some of Hercules;
> Of Hector and Lysander,
>   And such great names as these!

There was a far-off clapping of hands from the Gurkhas, and a roar from the Highlanders in the distance, but never a shot was fired by British or Afghan. The two little red dots moved forward in the open parallel to the enemy's front.

> But of all the world's great heroes
>   There's none that can compare,
> With a tow-row-row-row-row-row,
>   To the British Grenadier!

The men of the Fore and Aft were gathering thick at the entrance into the plain. The Brigadier on the heights far above was speechless with rage. Still no movement from the enemy. The day stayed to watch the children.

Jakin halted and beat the long roll of the Assembly, while the fife squealed despairingly.

'Right about face! Hold up, Lew, you're drunk,' said Jakin. They wheeled and marched back: —

> Those heroes of antiquity
>   Ne'er saw a cannon-ball,
> Nor knew the force o' powder,

'Here they come!' said Jakin. 'Go on, Lew': —

> To scare their foes withal!

The Fore and Aft were pouring out of the valley.

What officers had said to men in that time of shame and humiliation will never be known; for neither officers nor men speak of it now.

'They are coming anew!' shouted a priest among the Afghans. 'Do not kill the boys! Take them alive, and they shall be of our faith.'

But the first volley had been fired, and Lew dropped on his face. Jakin stood for a minute, spun round and collapsed, as the Fore and Aft came forward, the curses of their officers in their ears, and in their hearts the shame of open shame.

Half the men had seen the drummers die, and they made no sign. They did not even shout. They doubled out straight across the plain in open order, and they did not fire.

'This,' said the Colonel of Gurkhas, softly, 'is the real attack, as it should have been delivered. Come on, my children.'

'Ulu-lu-lu-lu!' squealed the Gurkhas, and came down with a joyful clicking of *kukris* — those vicious Gurkha knives.

On the right there was no rush. The Highlanders, cannily commending their souls to God (for it matters as much to a dead man whether he has been shot in a Border scuffle or at Waterloo), opened out and fired according to their custom, that is to say without heat and without intervals, while the screw-guns, having disposed of the impertinent mud fort aforementioned, dropped shell after shell into the clusters round the flickering green standards on the heights.

'Charrging is an unfortunate necessity,' murmured the Colour-Sergeant of the right company of the Highlanders. 'It makes the men sweer so, but I am thinkin''

that it will come to a charrge if these black devils stand
much longer. Stewarrt, man, you're firing into the eye
of the sun, and he'll not take any harm for Government
ammuneetion. A foot lower and a great deal slower!
What are the English doing? They're very quiet there
in the centre. Running again?'

The English were not running. They were hacking
and hewing and stabbing, for though one white man is
seldom physically a match for an Afghan in a sheepskin
or wadded coat, yet, through the pressure of many white
men behind, and a certain thirst for revenge in his
heart, he becomes capable of doing much with both ends
of his rifle. The Fore and Aft held their fire till one
bullet could drive through five or six men, and the front
of the Afghan force gave on the volley. They then
selected their men, and slew them with deep gasps and
short hacking coughs, and groanings of leather belts
against strained bodies, and realised for the first time
that an Afghan attacked is far less formidable than an
Afghan attacking; which fact old soldiers might have
told them.

But they had no old soldiers in their ranks.

The Gurkhas' stall at the bazar was the noisiest, for
the men were engaged — to a nasty noise as of beef
being cut on the block — with the *kukri*, which they preferred to the bayonet; well knowing how the Afghan
hates the half-moon blade.

As the Afghans wavered, the green standards on the
mountain moved down to assist them in a last rally.
This was unwise. The Lancers chafing in the right
gorge had thrice despatched their only subaltern as gal-
loper to report on the progress of affairs. On the third
occasion he returned, with a bullet-graze on his knee,

swearing strange oaths in Hindustani, and saying that all things were ready. So that Squadron swung round the right of the Highlanders with a wicked whistling of wind in the pennons of its lances, and fell upon the remnant just when, according to all the rules of war, it should have waited for the foe to show more signs of wavering.

But it was a dainty charge, deftly delivered, and it ended by the Cavalry finding itself at the head of the pass by which the Afghans intended to retreat; and down the track that the lances had made streamed two companies of the Highlanders, which was never intended by the Brigadier. The new development was successful. It detached the enemy from his base as a sponge is torn from a rock, and left him ringed about with fire in that pitiless plain. And as a sponge is chased round the bath-tub by the hand of the bather, so were the Afghans chased till they broke into little detachments much more difficult to dispose of than large masses.

'See!' quoth the Brigadier. 'Everything has come as I arranged. We've cut their base, and now we'll bucket 'em to pieces.'

A direct hammering was all that the Brigadier had dared to hope for, considering the size of the force at his disposal; but men who stand or fall by the errors of their opponents may be forgiven for turning Chance into Design. The bucketing went forward merrily. The Afghan forces were upon the run — the run of wearied wolves who snarl and bite over their shoulders. The red lances dipped by twos and threes, and, with a shriek, uprose the lance-butt, like a spar on a stormy sea, as the trooper cantering forward cleared his point.

The Lancers kept between their prey and the steep hills, for all who could were trying to escape from the valley of death. The Highlanders gave the fugitives two hundred yards' law, and then brought them down, gasping and choking ere they could reach the protection of the bowlders above. The Gurkhas followed suit; but the Fore and Aft were killing on their own account, for they had penned a mass of men between their bayonets and a wall of rock, and the flash of the rifles was lighting the wadded coats.

'We cannot hold them, Captain Sahib!' panted a Ressaidar of Lancers. 'Let us try the carbine. The lance is good, but it wastes time.'

They tried the carbine, and still the enemy melted away — fled up the hills by hundreds when there were only twenty bullets to stop them. On the heights the screw-guns ceased firing — they had run out of ammunition — and the Brigadier groaned, for the musketry fire could not sufficiently smash the retreat. Long before the last volleys were fired, the doolies were out in force looking for the wounded. The battle was over, and, but for want of fresh troops, the Afghans would have been wiped off the earth. As it was they counted their dead by hundreds, and nowhere were the dead thicker than in the track of the Fore and Aft.

But the Regiment did not cheer with the Highlanders, nor did they dance uncouth dances with the Gurkhas among the dead. They looked under their brows at the Colonel as they leaned upon their rifles and panted.

'Get back to camp, you. Haven't you disgraced yourself enough for one day! Go and look to the wounded. It's all you're fit for,' said the Colonel. Yet for the past hour the Fore and Aft had been doing all that mortal commander could expect.   They had lost heavily because they did not know how to set about their business with proper skill, but they had borne themselves gallantly, and this was their reward.

A young and sprightly Colour-Sergeant, who had begun to imagine himself a hero, offered his water bottle to a Highlander, whose tongue was black with thirst.   'I drink with no cowards,' answered the youngster huskily, and, turning to a Gurkha, said, 'Hya, Johnny!   Drink water got it?'   The Gurkha grinned and passed his bottle.   The Fore and Aft said no word.

They went back to camp when the field of strife had been a little mopped up and made presentable, and the Brigadier, who saw himself a Knight in three months, was the only soul who was complimentary to them. The Colonel was heart-broken, and the officers were savage and sullen.

'Well,' said the Brigadier, 'they are young troops of course, and it was not unnatural that they should retire in disorder for a bit.'

'Oh, my only Aunt Maria!' murmured a junior Staff Officer.   'Retire in disorder!   It was a bally run!'

'But they came again as we all know,' cooed the Brigadier, the Colonel's ashy-white face before him, 'and they behaved as well as could possibly be expected. Behaved beautifully, indeed.   I was watching them. It's not a matter to take to heart, Colonel.   As some German General said of his men, they wanted to be shooted over a little, that was all.'   To himself he said —'Now they're blooded I can give 'em responsible work.   It's as well that they got what they did.   'Teach 'em more than half a dozen rifle flirtations, that will — later — run alone and bite.   Poor old Colonel, though.'

All that afternoon the heliograph winked and flickered on the hills, striving to tell the good news to a mountain forty miles away. And in the evening there arrived, dusty, sweating, and sore, a misguided Correspondent who had gone out to assist at a trumpery village-burning, and who had read off the message from afar, cursing his luck the while.

'Let's have the details somehow — as full as ever you can, please. It's the first time I've ever been left this campaign,' said the Correspondent to the Brigadier, and the Brigadier, nothing loth, told him how an Army of Communication had been crumpled up, destroyed, and all but annihilated by the craft, strategy, wisdom, and foresight of the Brigadier.

But some say, and among these be the Gurkhas who watched on the hillside, that that battle was won by Jakin and Lew, whose little bodies were borne up just in time to fit two gaps at the head of the big ditch-grave for the dead under the heights of Jagai.

THE END

The Country Life Press
Garden City, N. Y.